Chris, on yo

The dedication in a few pages sums this novel up (check it out), but it's about more than just a love of films. Underneath, it's about the nature of creativity and its relationship to personal development, with the 16 to 17-year-old period an especially potent time: going out, discovering music, trying to fit in.

Happy reading,

[signature]

May 2023

Also by Jonathan Last and
available from Amazon

Teaching with Chopsticks

TEFL from the Frontline

How hard could it be?

Looking to 'do something totally random and out of character', recent graduate Jonathan Last took his lack of classroom experience and wariness about children onto a plane heading for Sanbon, South Korea and into a job teaching English as a foreign language (TEFL).

His year turned out to be a fascinating, honest insight into a diverse worldwide industry of countless personalities and cultures. His sometimes fun, sometimes painful, frequently hilarious journey required him to think on his feet and learn fast – not least about himself.

Also by Jonathan Last and
available from Amazon

The Great Football Conspiracy

Football fans always think that there is a conspiracy against their club... so what if they were right?

On the first day of the new football season, disgraced ex-coach Frank Tuttle stumbles upon a global plot to corrupt the game and the ancient quest that he must take to stop it.

Frank solves clues around London's stadia, delving deeper into a scandal that involves players, managers, FA employees and PR agencies, leading to a dark secret deep within Wembley.

Can Frank defend his reputation, tackle his failing marriage, and save football – all before 3pm?

Contact the author

Email jonathanlastauthor@gmail.com

Website jonathanlastauthor.com

© Copyright 2022 Jonathan Last
The right of Jonathan Last to be identified as author of this work has been asserted by him/her in accordance with the Copyright, Designs and Patents Act 1988
All Rights Reserved

Diary of a Young Filmmaker

This book is for Simps, Jake, Gabe, Matt, and anyone else who is never happier than when in a darkened room facing a bright screen.

'The point lies in you, not in time. Become a sun and everyone will see you. The sun must be the sun first of all.'
– Fyodor Dostoevsky, *Crime and Punishment*

'What am I working on? Uh... I'm working on something that will change the world and human life as we know it.'
– Jeff Goldblum, *The Fly*

'It is an act of courage to make a film, a courage for which you are not prepared by the rest of your life.'
– John Carpenter

AUTUMN

September 1995

Friday 1st September

Big decision to make about tomorrow night. The whole year will be there at Vicky Motson's party (except the Sads, of course) so I need to choose carefully. Do I give them something different or stick with what worked last time? *Slaughter 2* went down well at the GCSE results party, but my audience might be clamouring for something new.

Saturday 2nd September

Went with *Slaughter 2* again but dug out *Respiratory Failure* and *Gutless* to make a triple-bill.

Vicky Moston may have a huge widescreen TV with surround-sound, but I still refuse to watch my own stuff and turned away as soon as 'Four Amigos Productions' presents came up on the screen. Instead, I studied people's reactions to what they were watching. During the surgery sequence in *Failure* they recoiled at Gavin's internal organs slipping out, and they cracked up at Barry's over-the-top scream when Clive's homemade fake blood hits him in the eye. They were having such a good time that they were laughing at parts that weren't actually supposed to be funny.

Even the Hards were full of praise. There I was on the patio, alone in the crowd, studying Ruth down the other end of the garden. She was surrounded by friends as usual and looking gorgeous in a white tank top and denim mini-skirt combo. I was trying to get my confidence up to approach her and was concentrating so hard that I didn't see the punch on the arm coming.

'Oi, Ricketts!'

When they come up to you in a gang it still feels like they're going to start on you, even if we're all too old for that stuff now. Apparently, at least.

Harris had me fixed with his beady eyes and bared his B&H-yellowed teeth. Harris kind of resembles a cigarette, in fact: tall and thin, with ash-black hair and grey skin, ready to burn you if you're not careful. He always stinks of fags, too, though that's more to do with his mum and stepdad being chain-smokers. It's been a while, but from what I remember his house is full of overflowing ashtrays.

Harris said, 'Them films are proper quality.' His knuckle-dragging entourage backed him up.

I said, 'Thanks, Dean.' I could see the other Amigos through the patio window, safely encamped in a corner of the kitchen.

'You going Sixth Form, ain't you?'

'Yeah, A Levels.'

Not just GNVQs like him, although of course I would never dare point that out.

Harris said, 'He's a proper chancer, this one. Spent as much time in Irving's office last year as me but they're letting both of us stay on. Mugs!'

Just as I was starting to wonder if this is what peer acceptance must feel like, Sean Birrell contributed to the conversation. He's known as Birrell the Squirrel, owing to his enormous front teeth and general rodent-like appearance.

Birrell said, 'Yeah.' He swigged from a bottle of Smirnoff Mule. 'Except, thing is, right, difference is, Ricketts here only got into Sixth

Form 'cause he let Old Man Irving bend him over the desk when *he* was in with him on detention!'

'Yeah, that's right! Always knew you were a poof, Ricketts!'

Away from Harris and the others, Birrell is about as intimidating as one of his bushy-tailed brothers. Makes you wonder about some of these so-called hard lads, whether they just lucked out by palling up with someone like Harris and in another life could easily be targets themselves.

I only had to stand there and take a bit more of this before Vicky came round asking if everyone was having a good time and whether they had enough to drink, and once Harris started flirting with her (yuck) I was able to scurry back inside to the kitchen.

It was several drinks later when the setting sun hit my eye through the patio window that I knew my time was running out, and that I would have to venture back outside again now if I was going to complete my carefully devised pulling plan.

Phase one had gone fine: I necked bottle after bottle of Foster's Ice until I lost count. Phase two was less successful. It started out promisingly: with a push from Gavin and a *go for it* from Barry, I lurched towards Ruth and her gang. But walking in a straight line proved to be a challenge and I swerved towards the pond. Luckily, I didn't fall in, like some '80s teen movie. Instead, I keeled over and threw up into the water. I lifted my head to see Vicky, fixing me with her best hands-on-hips Head Girl glare. I could definitely pick out Ruth's voice among the laughter.

Body after body passed behind me while I sat there by the pond and I received slaps on the back and the odd *nice one, Ricketts!* By the time I had wiped my face clean with my *Big Trouble in Little China* T-shirt and gathered myself together, the garden was empty.

Not completely empty, of course.

I looked up at my fellow Amigos. 'Where'd they all go?'

Gavin said, 'One of those cool Bromley pubs.'

Barry said, 'Someone mentioned The Bell.'

Clive said, 'My dad will be here in a minute.' He looked at his watch.

So, there we stood. Clive with his thick peado glasses and greasy French crop, Gav, whose bright ginger hair and pale skin earn him the nickname Strawberry Split, and Bazza, AKA Try Hard with A Vengeance, in tight white jeans and a pink sleeveless shirt.

Quite the wild bunch.

Clive's dad drove the four of us home.

Pubs. I finally find a way of getting into the parties and now there's a new thing. Typical.

Sunday 3rd September

Dad had a go at me for coming in noisily last night. Martin used to get the same treatment when he was still living at home, then he got into uni against all odds and could suddenly do no wrong.

Mum was shocked to learn that I still don't have a suit for my first day of Sixth Form on Wednesday. I need two, for some reason. What a hassle.

So I jumped on a 138 to Bromley and went straight for the charity shops. The smallest suit jackets were in Oxfam and I found some 30-inch waist trousers in British Heart Foundation that nearly match. They had a bucket of slightly soiled ties, too.

I spent barely anything, leaving the rest for *Slaughter 3* or whatever the next film ends up being. Good fake blood costs, you know, and butchers' off cuts aren't free.

When I got home, I grabbed an old M&S bag and stuffed my purchases into it.

Mum was sceptical. 'Where are the tags?'

'Took them off already.'

'And the receipt? Do I get any change?'

'Sorry, lost the receipt and spent all the money.'

Having raised two *difficult* boys while looking after other people's kids for a living, my mum's got no energy left these days to argue.

Saw the Amigos down The Harvester, AKA The Harvey, or The Keitel if we're feeling a bit rhyming-slangy. It's one of these barbeque-restaurant places, the type where they serve everything on a skewer and have a big salad bar in the middle. The restaurant is upstairs, but the downstairs, where you come in, is this kind of glorified waiting area with a bar. People don't go there to drink, or maybe they'll have one if they're a bit early and then go up to have their meal. If the staff think you're here to eat, they're a lot less bothered about you drinking underage, and so we can usually get two or even three lagers in before we start to look suspicious. Then we'll walk around toward the stairs as if we're going up, but instead we sneak out the back exit. The only times we ever come in are Sunday or Monday nights, when it's usually so dead that no one pays us much any attention, and it's been months now with still no challenges for ID. It's just down the road from our school, too, which makes it about as far from a cool pub as you can get and so the last place we're going to bump into anyone. Anyway, the idea is that the practice of being in a pub (or at least pub-like) environment will help us with getting into the cool places, when we can finally summon the bottle up to actually try. I for one can't rely on my appearance alone.

Clive said something odd when I was standing with him and Barry at the bar. He said, 'I can't believe we got away with it.'

I said, 'With what?' glancing at the barman and hoping he didn't think Clive meant our underage-ness. We may never have been ID'd there but there's a first time for everything.

'Getting invited to those summer parties.'

Bazza said, 'That's the end of that, now that everyone's going to pubs instead.'

Clive said, 'Good. That lot are so shallow. They only wanted a bit of cheap entertainment from the comedies.'

'Maybe, but did I tell you that at Vicky's do I saw up this girl's skirt while she was throwing up in the bushes?'

'What, her actual knickers?'

'Wait, Clive,' I said, 'what did you mean, "the comedies"?'

'The films. Everyone thinks they're hilarious.'

'But we don't make comedies.'

Clive shrugged. 'People laugh at them, so they're comedies. What does it matter?'

Barry said, 'I don't mind the piss-taking.' He paid the barman with a handful of change. 'It's not really me who gets it anyway.'

Then they took their pints and joined Gavin at the fruit machine, leaving me alone at the bar.

Piss-taking?

Tuesday 5th September

Finally, some decent weather. On the last bloody day of the holidays. Wanted to read *Film Fanatic* in the garden but guess who was out there talking to my mum? Only bloody David Nolan. His little brother is joining her day care and apparently David will be picking the boy up from time to time.

He's grown out his hair all messy like the singer in an indie band, as opposed to mine, which is shapeless-greasy-mop messy. His clothes have logos all over them. Even his acne scars just prove that for him that war is over. Oh, if we were all so lucky.

If David's going to be popping over here sometimes, I'm gonna have to watch my step. There's no way I'm getting stuck in a conversation with him. That ship has sailed.

Later I was getting a Kit-Kat from the fridge and passed Mum, sitting by the kitchen window to get some light for the latest masterpiece she's working on.

She peered up from the canvas. 'David's such a nice boy. It's a shame you don't hang out together anymore.'

Shudder.

I immediately ran upstairs and watched *The Terminator* and *Terminator 2* back-to-back.

Wednesday 6th September

It never gets any easier. Year in, year out, holidays end and back we go to wonderful school, one step closer to some dull office job with even longer hours and even less time off.

But never for me. Not on your life.

As the new Lower Sixth, we wear suits instead of uniforms and share the common room with the year above plus have some lessons in the posher classrooms. And in today's welcome assembly Mrs Rebus, Head of Sixth Form, was droning on about how we're now in an honoured position as the top level of the school and have a responsibility and blah-blah-blah.

They don't fool me. We're still this side of the desk, they're on the other, and all that's changed is we've ditched the crusty old blazer. Doesn't matter if we have our own little play pen, with tables and chairs strewn about, a couple of threadbare sofas, a wall-mounted TV, a hi-fi and a vending machine, and that we are allowed out during free periods. It's still prison, only now with day-release.

The biggest change is the girls. I've seen them on own-clothes day and at the parties but now they look all mature, with their tight skirts and blouses that pop open between buttons to show some bra. When Ruth leaned forward during Rebus's speech, I glimpsed a mole that I'd somehow missed before. How will I ever concentrate on my precious education? Lots of the girls shouted out *nice suit!* as I walked past, so maybe I'm in with a chance now that they're mature enough to appreciate me.

The only class I had was Psychology with baldy Bryant, who is probably the most miserable and intense teacher in the whole school. Confusingly, last year he was my PE teacher. Don't know how that works. I reckon at the start of the year teachers pick subjects at random from a big machine, like the National Lottery.

So, Bryant goes to me, 'What are you doing in my class, Ricketts?'

'Because I chose it, sir?'

'I thought English was more your game.'

Yeah, right. I may have got an A* in GCSE English, but I've got to think about my future here. Reading a bunch of boring old books is hardly going to help me develop my films. But I figure that in Psychology we're going to study famous criminals who I'll be able to use as the basis for villains.

Thursday 7th September

Philosophy today. Can tell it's going to be a complete doss: it's all a matter of opinion, which means that there are no wrong answers. And it's full of girls.

Felt compelled to show off in front of Ruth about how my films explore philosophical ideas. As I leaned over her desk, rambling on, she stared right at me. Those glossy lips, a shimmer in her green eyes, the afternoon sun in her hair... for two glorious minutes I had her attention.

Cue that smartarse Vicky Motson.

'Oh, give us a break, Stephen.'

I reluctantly glanced in her direction. Vicky's got this sharp-featured face, a witch's face, nose and chin pointing right at you.

'I've seen more philosophy in an episode of *Play Bus*.'

So cocky. Just because she let people round her house on Saturday to raid her parents' drinks cabinet and get off with each other in the bathroom.

Shamed as usual, I turned back to my own desk.

But Vicky wasn't done. When the laughter had died down, she piped up again.

'Sorry Steve. It's just that everyone thinks your movies are a total joke. Didn't you know?'

Barely suppressed sniggers all round.

'Oh, and by the way, you owe my parents three new koi carp.'

Ruth and the rest fell about in hysterics.

Friday 8th September

The big one: Media Studies.

All I have to do is sleepwalk through the assignments while borrowing all their equipment for my real work. Actual editing, instead of tape-to-tape with its wavy streaks of doom. Sound booms, proper lights. All the treasures that I was denied while in regular school but that they are letting us play with now we're in Sixth Form.

The teacher is new and she's called Ms Harper. She looks like a reject from some hippy commune, thirty years and four stone later. She asked the class whether anyone had any filmmaking experience, and all heads turned to me and my fellow Amigos.

I studied my classmates' faces. I'm used to their looks, but I'd never paid much attention to *how* they look at me. Today instead of launching into an answer I hesitated, and clocked that they were straining to contain their giggles, waiting eagerly for me to go off on one.

So this time I kept my trap shut.

So then this Ms Harper said, 'From what I hear, we have our very own Steven Spielberg.'

Well, I couldn't hold my peace at that.

'No way. I hate being compared to Spielberg. It gets on my nerves how he's the only director people have heard of. For me, it's all about the three Cs: John Carpenter, David Cronenberg and James Cameron.'

Then she started quizzing me on all this technical stuff, like not crossing the 180 axis and how I get my T-light readings. I looked to Clive, Gaz and Bazza to see if they had a clue what she was going on about, but they were all looking sheepish.

Someone yelled from the back, 'He just makes it up as he goes along, Miss.'

When the laughter had died down, Ms Harper turned to me, this all-serious expression on her ruddy face, and said, 'You're going to have to step up if you want to get anywhere in my class, Stephen Ricketts. Playtime is over.'

Patronising cow.

Spent the rest of the day all riled up. This Harper woman hasn't even *seen* my films, so who is she to judge? I've managed to pull off some class moves over the years: recreating *Lethal Weapon*'s handcuffed suicide jump for *Deadly Pursuit,* London crews facing off in *Gang Wars* like the ones from New York in *The Warriors,* and the *Slaughter* movies have disgusted viewers as much as anything in *Braindead* or *Cannibal Holocaust.*

People love my movies.

She can piss off.

Saturday 9th September

My movies are shit.

No wonder I've always stopped myself from watching them back until now: they're cheap, random, stupid, and pointless. Just Clive, Barry, Gavin and whoever else we could get hold of (siblings, cousins, neighbours) mugging away with some gore thrown in, often literally, and it's clearly just ketchup, corn syrup and animal innards. Bazza is even more in love with the camera than he is with himself... Gav, our six-foot-three human special effect, has all the screen presence of a lamppost... and Clive's acting range doesn't extend any further than keeping on or taking off his glasses.

Why do I never do more than one take? Why have I never written a script? Why don't I edit out the blunders?

What a waste of time. Full-on humiliation.

Moped around the house trying to get some sympathy. Fat chance. Dad thinks I should be out playing football, or at the very least watching *Grandstand.* Mum suggested that I visit my brother. I did phone his flat but there was no answer, so he was probably laying around with a hangover.

In the end I watched a triple-bill of *Assault on Precinct 13*, *The Fog* and *Escape from New York* in bed to cheer myself up. At least Carpenter had Debra Hill to encourage him in those early days.

Sunday 10th September

Uncle Eamon came round for Sunday lunch with Aunt Sheila in tow. He'd brought some new releases for me to borrow: *Bad Boys*, *Outbreak*, *Clerks*, and *Congo*.

I waited until we were alone and asked Eamon what he thinks about my short films. He said that they were 'grand' and 'fine for what they are'. But he definitely hesitated before he answered.

Then Eamon quickly changed the subject and asked me how many shifts I can do in the shop now that summer holidays are over. I said not as many because of school, but there's still the evenings and I get free periods now as well.

He said, 'Don't be falling behind at school, though. Education is important, lad.'

Eamon is obviously pretty cool, owning a video shop. But he does have some funny ideas.

No sleep. Can't get the idea that I'm a crap director out of my head. My own waking nightmare.

Monday 11th September

Had my first General Studies class, the only subject they force you to take, and it's even more wishy-washy than I imagined.

There is one plus: the teacher, Miss Yates. She can't be older than twenty-one and looks like the sister you wish your mate had. Absolutely stunning, with long dark curly hair, these incredible brown eyes and a body that wouldn't look out of place in *FHM* magazine. She was wearing this black skirt with a high slit so that when she sat down and crossed her legs you could see plenty of thigh. And she had on this blouse that was cream coloured with silhouettes of cats all over it and that showed her dark bra underneath.

She's only gone and given us an assignment after one bloody lesson. We have to research a *big issue* and give a ten-minute presentation. This
will never do.

Wednesday 13th September

Bumped into Mr Irving today on my way to the common room. He congratulated me on my GCSE A* from his Media Studies class and wasn't I proud of myself and blah-blah-blah. (Irving pulled double duty last year as my Media Studies teacher as well as Head of Year 11.)

I did what you're supposed to do in these situations and reeled off the standard stuff about studying hard and doing my best.

Old Irving said, 'So, will you finally be joining the Audio/Visual Club this year?' The hairs in his nostrils were reaching out and trying to pull me in.

I said, 'I'd love to, sir, but I'll be too busy with my A Level studies for those kinds of extra-curricular commitments.'

Irving was disappointed and it's a shame as I like the bloke, but I don't want to be part of any crappy after school club and waste my time helping *them*.

Friday 15th September

Delivered my General Studies speech today.

'*The Big Issue* is a magazine sold by homeless people. A man sells it outside the train station. His name is Alvin. It says so on his name badge, which identifies him as an official *The Big Issue* seller. I'd never paid much attention to Alvin before, let alone the publication he sells. But on the way to school this morning I bought this: *The Big Issue*, October 1995 edition. And let me tell you, one look inside confirms that it is definitely a big issue. Well, not in terms of size, as you can see, but more the actual issues covered. Those to which you can undoubtedly apply the adjective *big*. So, in conclusion, although this issue of *The Big Issue* is not especially big, I defy anyone to find issues bigger than the ones explored within... *The Big Issue*. Thank you.'

Not quite ten minutes, but I'm a busy man. Miss Yates was unimpressed and gave me a D, which she said was generous. The view when she leaned forward to give me a telling off was pretty generous, too.

We've got some new joiners to the Sixth Form who have come from other schools. This one bloke, Nigel Green, has been ignoring the established pecking order by spending break times alternately sitting with both the Sads and the Four Amigos. The Sads, bless 'em, are down to only two members now, the rest having joined Orpington College or something, leaving Peter and Kevin as the sole social outcasts, hunched over a table in the corner silently painting *Games Workshop* figures, avoiding eye contact, virtually invisible. I swear, it's like they're competing in a Bromley's Biggest Glasses competition, with runner-up prize going to the one with the most acne.

Today in the common room this Nigel (who looks like a saddo himself with his big Fozzie Bear barnet and podgy mole-like face) was lurking while we Amigos were having our usual sophisticated film chat. Barry was debating whether to go full-frontal in *Slaughter 3*. He suggested we use a sausage then cut it off in close-up as part of Ken Slaughter's zombified girlfriend's revenge.

Clive said, 'I could inject fake blood into a frankfurter with a syringe.'

Barry said, 'A saveloy, more like!'

Gavin said, 'You mean a chipolata!'

I cut through their rapier-sharp wit to point out that I don't think my ears can handle another screeching performance from Bazza's mate Terry from taekwondo in a bad wig as Ken Slaughter's girlfriend.

That was when this Nigel said, 'Oh, so *you're* the Tarantino wannabe.'

I turned to him slowly. At least he'd bypassed Spielberg and only compared me to the general public's *second* best-known director (with Martin Scorsese coming in at number three).

I said, 'Yeah, something like that.'

'I was just going to lend Gavin this.' He handed Gav a VHS copy of *Leon*.

Not bad. But I stayed silent.

Barry said, 'Isn't that the paedo one?'

Nigel said, 'Maybe in the subtext. But you should see the action scenes.'

I rolled my eyes. *Subtext*. Another dull academic, and yet my pals seem to be warming to him.

I'm going to have to keep my eye on Mr Nigel Green.

Despite my best intentions today, I got home from school at the same time as David Nolan was picking up his brother Freddy. I'd managed to avoid him up to now.

Small talk was pretty stilted. I said, 'How's life in your posh school?' and he said, 'Things have got a lot more intense in Key Stage 5,' and I told him I agreed. David is doing A Levels in subjects like Drama and Art, where you prance about reciting Shakespeare and flicking paint at the wall. What's so intense about that?

Sunday 17th September

Met the lads at the pool club this evening. Along with The Harvey it's the other place we can get served, since we all lied about our dates of birth for our membership cards. Martin started to bring me when I was a kid (which I've always suspected was Dad's idea, one of his attempts to get me into sport) and he signed me up as a seventeen-year-old when I was only fourteen. No pubs will take the pool club card on the door, unfortunately.

I need to sort myself a proper fake ID. All people talk about on Fridays since school's been back is where they're headed at the weekend: Bromley or Croydon. I haven't had the guts to try either yet. Naturally the girls never have any issues, they can just flirt their way in. I doubt there are many gay bouncers on the doors of southeast London's trendy pubs and bars, and any that are won't be interested in pasty five-foot-six rake-thin virgins who only shave once a week.

So anyway, the pool club is just like one of those places you see in movies like *The Color of Money*: dingy, smoky, a bit of a rank smell, possibly full of people hustling each other and then getting into fights outside. I mean, I've never seen anything like that but I wouldn't rule it out. We don't really mix with the other regulars, who are exclusively male and mostly old geezers who hang around watching the horses (the only thing they ever have on the TVs, either live or highlights) while drinking pints of ale with a copy of the *Racing Post* stuffed into their back pockets. The staff are much the same and since we keep ourselves to ourselves no one ever bothers us. So we pop along when we want a change from The Harvey, taking our drinks from the small bar over to our table to have while we play. It's not exactly somewhere we're going to meet any girls or be able to show off about back at school, but it's ours. Went there on my sixteenth birthday a few weeks ago, just the four of us as usual, and let's just say it wasn't the kind of wild night people write into lads' mags like *FHM* bragging about.

I *still* haven't actually ever snogged anyone. Barry reckons he got off with this French girl on a family holiday in Calais, and Gavin claims that he *has experience* but never goes into any detail. Clive is my best mate, at least these days, and even then only by default, but he never wants to talk about that kind of thing. Which does mean that the long phone chats we used to have are getting a lot shorter these days, since it's all I ever think about. That and movies, of course.

Tonight, conversation between frames with my fellow Amigos turns again to our next filmmaking project.

I tell them, 'I dunno, boys. Maybe we need to give it a rest.'

Gav thinks about this for a moment while he chalks his cue. 'Well, things *are* different now. A Levels. Proper business.'

I scoff.

Barry pots his last stripe. 'And aren't you a bit sick of getting laughed at, Steve?'

'I don't care what people think.'

Barry glances up at Gavin and Clive, then focusses down his cue and pots the black.

As Clive racks up the balls for his game with Bazza, I realise something.

I usually come up with loads of new film ideas while playing pool. For some reason, my mind wanders while I'm playing and things just pop into my head.

But tonight, nothing.

Wednesday 20th September

Was standing behind Ruth in the canteen queue and overheard her tell one of her friends the she's applying for a job at Asda in Bromley. I've been thinking that I need some part-time work myself, could use the money to help break into the cool pub scene. Plus, if we're working at the same place, I'll get loads of chances to talk to Ruth.

Having grabbed a supermarket application form on the way home from school, I sat in my room filling it out. And it occurred to me that for the first time I'm thinking about spending money on something other than making films. Instead of coming up with ways to conclude the *Slaughter* trilogy, I'm imagining being in pubs and clubs and getting off with girls and getting off with Ruth.

Maybe it's a sign. The fact is, every time I think about picking up my camcorder, I get flashes of my classmates laughing in my face. Or worse, all the girls just sitting there in grim silence, their legs clamped shut in a joint statement of anti-arousal.

Thursday 21st September

Ended the day with a free period so went to see *Braveheart*. Not usually a fan of your epic, olden-days, battle-type movies but this one was pretty good. Rousing score by James Horner and Gibson keeps the pace going despite the bum-numbing run time. And talk about taking the old cliché of the English being the bad guys and running with it!

The experience was almost ruined, however, by Barry being late to meet me in the foyer. We nearly missed the trailers. I gave him a good earful about that.

Popped into the video shop afterwards to give Eamon a hand and told him about my filmmaking funk.

He said, 'Well, you're still only young.'

'I don't *feel* young, Uncle Eamon.'

Then he asked me why it is I make films in the first place.

I thought that was obvious: I want them to move me up to being a proper director so that people take me seriously and I never have to work a boring, shitty job like some loser.

Eamon smiled at this. 'So, you think that will just happen, if you keep pointing your camcorder at things enough times?'

I said, 'Look, Uncle. I *want* to be a film director. It's *all* I want. And you can't want something that badly and not get it, right?'

Friday 22nd September

Finished my Asda application during a free. Fucking thing is massive.

They wanted a list of my strengths, so I put 'taking orders, not thinking independently, dealing with awkward people, being polite and respectful'.

Then I handed it to some jobsworth on the fag counter on my way to Eamon's to return some videotapes.

Monday 25th September

Mr Bryant is a miserable old bastard. Must be bitter that he drew Psychology from the subjects' lottery machine for this year: he has to spend time in a classroom instead of chasing young boys in shorts around a playing field.

Bryant was banging on to any wannabe Dr Frauds in his midst about how it takes years of study and hard work to get a PhD, and even then, you're under constant pressure to be published if you want to stay in a job. So we should basically just give up now and go wash cars for a living.

Then he gave me the eye and I knew what was coming next: how any creative aspirations that we are naive enough to harbour will inevitably get shot down upon entering The Big Bad World.

I really don't think this is what they have in mind on those adverts when they say, 'Become a teacher and inspire young people!'

Tuesday 26th September

Came home from school to a message from Asda, inviting me for an interview at the supermarket on Saturday. That was quick. Seems I successfully presented myself as another willing servant with no mind of my own. Wonder if there will be any good-looking birds there. Apart from Ruth, obviously.

Bashed one out in bed thinking about getting cornered in a stockroom by Ruth, Sharon Stone and Sandra Bullock, that one from *Speed*. All were wearing sexed-up Asda uniforms, but Ruth was my equal and the other two were like our supervisors, telling us exactly what to do and giving us a thorough induction into the business.

Need to start keeping an extra box of man-sized Kleenex under my bed.

Friday 29th September

Finally tried to get into some cool pubs tonight. 'Tried' being the optimal word.

Feeding off the usual common room buzz of people planning their Friday nights out in Bromley, the Four Amigos hatched our own plan, led by Gavin.

Gav said, 'Some people like to meet in The Tiger's Head, on Mason's Hill.' The rest of us were huddled around him conspiracy-style, like he was Donald Sutherland on the park bench in *JFK*. 'It's a pub just off from the town centre. No bouncers.'

Barry said, 'No bouncers...' He stared off wistfully.

Gaz continued. 'So, we get in and then once other people turn up, we sort of merge into them and carry on wherever they go.'

I said, 'Sounds good.'

Clive was silent. Poor bloke, he really needs to accept that this is the future. We have to start going to cool pubs if we're ever going to *be* cool.

Barry said, 'We should invite Nigel.'

I said, 'Good plan, Baz, but with just one drawback. How are you gonna manage to get through the pub door with your nose stuck up Nigel's arse?'

So the four of us turned up outside The Tiger's Head at 7 p.m., and guess what? There *were* bouncers. Two huge blokes in black bomber jackets, just starting their shift. We ducked behind the bus stop before we were seen.

Clive said, 'Now what?' He passed me the bottle of vodka that Barry had brought along, stolen from his parents' liquor cabinet. We'd been taking courage-sips, despite it tasting horrible. I don't know how they're always drinking straight spirits in the movies.

We'd come all this way, so we had to at least give it a go. We decided to pair off to attract less attention. My obvious choice was Gav, he's a giant and has proper facial hair. Clive is tall too but baby-faced and the thick specs make him look gormless. Barry works out in his room with his weights, but is still more chubby than well-built and resembles one of those Cabbage Patch Kids.

I said, 'Me and Gav first.'

Would being next to Gavin make it seem like I was older like him or younger compared to him?

Gavin was fine, he got: 'You, in.'

I got: 'You, ID.'

Out of the other two Barry got in but Clive was denied.

Clive and I only had to hang around outside wondering what to do next for a couple of minutes before Gavin and Barry re-appeared. They'd been ID'd at the bar, the dreaded second hurdle.

So we ended up having a fun-filled night on a bench in Churchill Park, choking down the rest of the vodka.

Clive said, 'Could be working on a film right now.'

Worst thing was that we could see gangs of blokes and girls on the high street going past the park's entrance, all off to have a cracking boozy night with their tongues down each other's throats in a shower of lager and Bacardi Breezers.

Saturday 30th September

Aced my Asda interview.

The questions were the standard will-you-do-what-we-say and are-you-going-to-behave stuff I've nodded my way through during countless detentions. They asked me about my hobbies and interests, and I mentioned my films as a reflex, prompting one of the suits to quip, 'So, what, do you want your name badge to say *Steven Spielberg* instead of *Stephen Ricketts?*'

Met Clive and Barry at the Odeon afterwards to see *Apollo 13*. Both were late and then they talked during the slower bits. Next time I am going to the movies by myself.

Film was good. I've always enjoyed it when you have a group of characters dealing with a crisis in a single location. When things started to go really pear-shaped, I half expected Bill Paxton to break down and start shouting 'game over, man!'

On the bus home we saw a load of people from school who were on their way to clubbing in Croydon: Harris and the rest of the Hards, Adrian Smith and his gang of Sports, loads of girls. Everyone pretended not to recognise us.

When I got in, I went straight to bed and put on *Aliens: The Director's Cut*.

October 1995

Monday 2nd October

Sounded like the whole bloody Sixth Form was in Croydon's Blue Orchid nightclub on Saturday night, the amount people were banging on about it in the common room. No one bothered to ask us lot whether we were there.

My fellow Amigos are now actively trying to get us to merge with Nigel and the Sads. Forget it, my social position is dodgy enough as it is. I know I've never reached the highest branches of the popularity tree, but I got us into our first ever parties at the tail end of the summer. What have Nigel and his new cronies ever done? They even manage to make playing cards uncool with this *Magic: The Gathering* game they seem to be obsessed with.

With no film project on the go my mind is on other things. I want to find out where I really stand in the social pecking order. And I know one person who will give it to me straight.

Tuesday 3rd October

I caught Harris while he was having a fag behind B Block.

He said, 'You're a clown, intcha?'

I asked him what he meant.

'It's like... what is it. King had one. Geezer in a hat with bells.'

'A jester.'

'Yeah, jester. Why you think I got you into those parties?'

'So I'm... the court jester.'

'Thing is, bruv, it's all right round someone's house. But people don't want all that jester bollocks outside, you get me?'

He flicked his B&H away and exited the frame.

So, there you have it. Failed filmmaker and now failed object of amusement.

Up in my room later I tried to console myself by cracking one off about Ruth in her tight green V-neck jumper, but I couldn't focus and after struggling for a few minutes I admitted defeat.

I pulled my trousers back up and wandered downstairs. There was a letter addressed to me on the mat.

So it turns out I will be working in Asda's in-store bakery. I can see a new career path opening up: entertaining the punters by juggling baguettes while balancing a custard tart on my nose.

Wednesday 4th October

General Studies continues to be the biggest waste of time school has ever offered up, and that's saying something.

Today we were talking about the concept of freedom. Before, I might have been tempted to shout the word out like at the end of *Braveheart*, or to quote bits of Morgan Freeman's voiceover from *The Shawshank Redemption*. But instead, I just kept my peace and admired Miss Yates's white trouser and red blouse combo. She also had on this head scarf with kittens all over it (woman seems to love cats) that somehow rocketed her sexiness through the roof.

Model student that I am, I did her new homework assignment as soon as I got home: 1,000 words on what freedom means to you. My essay starts 'Freederm is a brand of face wash. To me, it means an end to troublesome skin conditions…'

Friday 6th October

I was doing group work in Philosophy, amusing myself by mispronouncing Socrates like they do in *Bill and Ted's Excellent Adventure*, when I overheard someone ask Ruth where she was getting on it tonight.

'Bromley,' she said. Then she looked right at me and added in this funny voice, 'What about *you*, Steve, where are *you* going tonight?'

I shrugged cautiously.

Then she grinned and said, 'Oh, because I heard that the benches at Churchill Park with a bottle of vodka is *so* the in-scene these days.'

I am destined to be a shelf-stacking outcast, sunk into a tatty armchair watching movies on repeat while my camcorder gathers dust, forgotten in the corner next to a box of expired condoms.

Saturday 7th October

Induction day at Asda. This woman in one of their uniforms collected a group of us newbies from the entrance and took us through the main store, which is pretty much the biggest supermarket in Bromley, and then through this staff-only door and up some stairs. We went through a canteen and ended up in this big meeting room place.

We had to talk about when we'd had a good shopping experience and brainstorm what makes good customer service, that kind of crap. Seems like this job will be money for nothing and there was a free lunch, too.

After her performance yesterday, I did my best to avoid Ruth. Luckily, we weren't the only people there from school. Early on I spied a familiar mop of thick blonde hair: sporty Adrian Smith. He ended up in my group for these role-plays they made us do to practice customer interactions and he cracked us all up by pretending to be an old woman. Adrian only cares about his football and his cricket and whatever else he plays, so wasn't taking any of it seriously. And who could? What the hell is the point in rehearsing? You just have to turn up and get on with it on the day, like with making a film.

When we broke for lunch, Ruth asked if she could sit next to me. She apologised about what happened in Philosophy, saying that she was *just having a laugh*. Then she asked when the next movie will be ready and I told her that I wasn't sure, that I'm not feeling too confident about all that right now.

She said, 'Oh no, you can't stop making your films. They're too good.'

'You mean funny.'

'No, not just funny, I actually think they're really impressive. Don't listen to people taking the piss, it doesn't mean anything. They're probably jealous that you've actually gone out and done something.'

I swear, you could see right between the top two buttons of her new Asda blouse. That cheeky mole was staring right at me.

Ruth said, 'You must know so much about filmmaking. I bet you've read loads of books about it.'

'Er, right.'

She gave my arm a reassuring squeeze.

Sod it. What do those idiots at school know about how good my films are? I was holding a video camera before my voice broke. Maybe all I need is to brush up on a little theory.

After they turfed us out of the induction, I bowled straight into Bromley Library.

Sunday 8th October

Spent half an hour to reading *The Filmmaker's Bible*, which claims to tell you about everything a director needs. But I've made twenty-something shorts and I've never had a shot list, or a cinematographer, or a production assistant. Then there's all this rubbish about movies being a joint effort. Sure, lots of people work on a film, but it's the director who yells *cut!* and *action!* and gets the *a film by* credit.

The book was beginning to sound like Ms Media Studies Harper harping on. I put it down and decided not to bother with the others I borrowed from the library. They're going straight back on Monday. What a waste of time.

Martin came round for a Sunday roast. He looked like he'd had a late one, all bleary-eyed and yawning. He told me away from Mum and Dad that he'd only gone to bed at 9 a.m. this morning.

I said, 'How did you stay out so late when clubs close at three?'

'Not all clubs, mate. This one went on 'til six and then I had to wait at London Bridge for the first train.' He hardly ate any lunch, complaining that his stomach was *still the size of a walnut*.

I hope he's looking after himself over there in Penge.

Martin brought a video of *Species* over to watch with me, that sci-fi horror where the sexy woman is really an alien who seduces men and then kills them. I'd wanted to see it in the cinema, but I couldn't get in because it's an 18.

When it was finished, my brother turned to me and said, 'You could do much better than that, mate.'

Tuesday 10th October

You read about directors who got their shorts into film festivals and won awards right from when they started out as kids. Robert Rodriguez, for one, always goes on about opening his mailbox and having a waterfall of acceptances pour out every day. Well, I might not feel like starting a new project at the moment, but I do have this backlog of short films just sitting about in my room, so maybe I should do something useful with them.

I popped out during lunch to check out Bromley Library's reference section. There was a back catalogue of *Film Fanatic*, alongside a bunch of posher movie mags, titles like *Vision and Audio* and *The Accomplished Film Viewer*. Some of them had details of how to enter film festivals. And bloody hell! The festival applications are longer than that fucking Asda one! Apparently, they ask you for a list of crew. Well, no one really has a set job on my films, except me as director. And they want to know all about your *themes* and *intentions*. God, I'm already doing a Psychology A Level, I'm not about to start self-examining *myself*!

Pretentious wankers.

Another grand scheme bites the dust.

Arseholes.

Total Recall was on ITV when I went to bed. But as soon as I realised it was the edited-for-TV version I switched off in disgust.

Wednesday 11th October

I just can't figure Ruth out.

Had my first shift on Asda's bakery tonight, the lone man left to restock the shelves, serve cakes, slice leftover bread, throw away unsold confectionery, and close up. It's pretty easy stuff, and the best part comes at the end of the shift. Anything with today's date on gets reduced to a lower and lower price across the evening and then you're allowed to take to a till and buy what hasn't sold after you close up. So as soon as I found the reduction gun, I put 5p stickers on a chocolate ring donut and a custard slice and stashed them in the fridge round the back.

So anyway, Ruth. Half-way through my four-hour shift I was putting some freshly cut loaves out on the shelves, feeling pleased with myself for not slicing off my fingers in the machine and daydreaming about using my first paycheque to raid the new film releases section of Virgin Megastore, when I heard a familiar voice.

The object of my obsession was passing by the bakery on the shop floor, chatting to a colleague.

I said, 'Hey, Ruth.'

I should have read the warning signs when she looked embarrassed and glanced at the old dear she was with before replying with only an *mmm*.

But like an idiot, I pressed on. 'So I've been thinking about maybe making another film,' I blathered. 'Not sure what about, or anything, but—'

Then Ruth's colleague, this blue-rinsed trout with a puckered Dot Cotton mouth, piped up.

She said, 'Like filming things, do ya, eh? Filming through a hole in the girls' bogs, is that your game?'

Then she launched into this huge cackle. And instead of defending me Ruth joined in. And off they went.

Thursday 12th October

I was still riled up by yesterday's incident when I got to school. How can Ruth be so nice on her own but such a bitch when she's around other people? Why is she so two-faced?

I was in such a bad mood that instead of keeping myself to myself in Media as I have been so far this term, I picked a fight with Ms Harper.

We were studying suspense in film (ironically one of the more tedious topics they make us do for this class) and my learned educator was cracking out the predictable titles for us to examine.

Ms Harper opened the first cassette box.

I said, 'Oh no, anything but *Psycho*. It's *so* boring.'

She said, '*Psycho* is boring?'

'Yes! Take out the shower scene and it's like a TV movie. That's forty-five good seconds in a two-hour film. *Psycho II* is miles better.'

'You must be joking, surely Stephen?'

'It's got a tighter plot, cleverly toys with your sympathies, has the more suspenseful set pieces...'

By now the rest of the class were watching us, but I didn't care.

Ms Harper popped the tape into the machine. 'Stephen, *Psycho* is a known classic by the master of suspense. *Psycho II* is a twenty-years-later cash-in.'

'So, what, it's crap because it was made in the '80s? Why can't a sequel improve on the original? Your problem, Miss, is that you *say* you want us to think for ourselves, but all *you* do is roll out the same old tired stuff the school tells you to.'

Her look could have stripped paint, but she kept her voice even. 'We'll talk about this after class.'

I shrugged. She pressed play.

When everyone else had gone out to break, the two of us sat facing each other across her desk.

'What's the matter, Stephen?'

So I told her about how I've started to doubt my abilities as a director.

She said, 'An artist can only judge himself on the passion he puts into his work.'

'*Artist.*' I rolled my eyes.

'That's what you are, like it or not. How you use your gift is your choice. It would be nice if you chose to apply it to your class work.'

That'll be the day. I've been muddling through her bullshit assignments, picking up Bs as I go.

Then she asked if I had ever shown my films to anyone beyond my peers. I said no, unless you count Uncle Eamon and my brother Martin.

She nodded slowly. 'And what about the future, have you thought about what you'll be doing after A Levels?'

'I'd always thought that I'd go to uni to do film.'

'And now?'

'I don't know anymore.'

Ms Harper narrowed her eyes a little, then a smile started to spread across her face. She got up and opened a cupboard and returned to me with a couple of glossy pamphlets.

I opened one up. 'What are these?'

'Universities with a film specialism.'

I started to leaf through. Wow! These places have studios on site as well as state-of-the art kit, editing facilities, and they even give you a budget. Blokes just a couple of years older than me were pushing cameras on dollies, looking through one of those viewfinder things... lots of birds among them, too. In one photo this blonde in a top that shows loads of cleavage is staring admiringly at the young director while he consults his script. She seems to be part of the crew, too, not just some groupie hanging around.

It all became clear to me then. It doesn't matter how good I am *now*, it's about how good I can be *there*, finally in a place where I'm taken seriously.

'Film is a pretty broad subject,' Miss was saying as I salivated over the pictures. 'Have you got your eye on any aspect in particular? Pure filmmaking or with an academic focus?'

'Oh no. When I'm done with school, that'll be the *last* time I do anything academic. Pure-as-the-driven-snow film, definitely.'

'And what do your parents think?'

Ugh. I'd always just assumed that old ma and pa know I don't care about anything other than films and so had accepted that I'll study directing. But thinking about it, they're both very big on the whole academic thing. It's what they pushed Martin into, and as soon as he went down that road, they got off his case about all the drinking and partying. Although it sounds to me like he just spent three years at Leeds uni doing more of the same.

Ms Harper was staring at me intensely.

'I think you need to have a serious talk with your mum and dad.'

Again: ugh.

Friday 13th October

I resisted the urge to stay in and watch *Friday the 13th* movies in tribute to today's date (part six is the best, closely followed by four, in case you're wondering) and instead decided to give the Bromley pub scene another go with the boys.

This time I was press-ganged into letting Nigel come along. Fine. Mercifully, he didn't bring the two Sads, Peter and Kevin. They at least know their place.

The five of us (definitely *not* the Five Amigos) entered The Tiger's Head at 6:30 p.m., before the bouncers had started. On Barry's suggestion we wore our Sixth Form suits and acted like we'd come straight from work, chatting loudly about our hard week in the office and throwing expressions around like *balancing the returns sheet* and *maintaining the equity flow*. It was my first time in a legitimate pub without my parents or for a birthday lunch or something like that and I was bricking it the whole time. Despite this, there was a thrill as well. Okay, it wasn't a *cool* pub, but it was still a *pub*. To be honest with you, I don't really know how to tell that somewhere actually *is* cool. I've only got people mentioning the names in the common room to go on. But even I could see that this place was a bog-standard old man's pub, or a place for office drones to drown their sorrows about their wasted lives.

Our businessman patter was fine in The Tiger's Head and no one got ID'd at the bar, either. But when we tried to move on to The Bell the bouncers refused us all point blank.

I said, 'But we've come straight from work. Look at our suits!'

He said, 'Call that a suit, mate?'

Trudging back down the high street, Clive tried to lighten the mood by mentioning how he was watching the *Pride and Prejudice* adaptation on BBC One last Sunday with his mum, and she pointed out that The Bell is referenced in the source novel.

Nigel said, 'Yeah, we were watching that too. But I didn't hear anyone order a pint of Stella or ask for change for the fag machine.'

And everyone duly cracked up.

Oh, he's a funny one, our Nigel.

Gavin suggested we try the next closest name venue, this cocktail bar called Henry's. The other three were up for that, but I decided to head home.

On the way, I picked up a copy of *FHM* magazine from the off licence. Cindy Crawford is on the cover and her photo shoot inside came in handy when I got the mag upstairs to in my room.

But what I really bought it for were the ads in the back. Something that will put an end to my troubles getting into pubs.

Saturday 14th October

Waited all day for Clive to call me to report back about how last night carried on after I left. When the phone still hadn't rung at 3 p.m., I had to resort to contacting him.

'It was okay.'

That was the extent of his analysis.

'Come on mate, where did you end up?'

'Managed to get into Henry's. Nigel persuaded the bouncers.'

I bit my tongue.

'... And?'

'It was good. Look, I've got to go, my dad's calling me to come and help him in his workshop.'

Then Clive hung up on me.

My own dad was down Selhurst Park football stadium at the time. He's long since given up inviting me to join him.

Sunday 15th October

Usually I've got more important things to do than watch Sunday night TV with Mum and Dad, but this particular evening I needed to talk to them. I had to sit through crap like *The Clothes Show*, *Keeping Up Appearances* and *Last of the Summer Wine* before finally gathering the courage to speak up during an ad break in *Heartbeat*.

'So… I've been thinking about my future. My education.'

'First time for everything,' Dad said without looking up from his *Sunday Times*.

'How… would you feel about me… possibly… doing a film degree?'

Mum said, 'Oh no. You know what they say about eggs and baskets, Stevie. You don't want to tie yourself down.'

'Your mother's right,' the old man added. 'Give yourself as broad a range of options as possible. Like Business Studies. You do want to get a job, don't you? Well, *business* is another word for *job*.'

'But film is what I'm interested in. You know that.'

Mum said, 'It's not a very marketable skill though, is it Stephen? It's very competitive.'

Dad said, 'And *you're* not very competitive, are you?'

I ignored him and turned to Mum.

'Just because *you* gave up on your creative dream doesn't mean I will.'

'Don't talk to your mother that way!'

I stormed off.

'Don't forget who pays for your education!' Dad called after me.

Bloody typical. Him a wage slave spending all hours up town working in insurance, and her looking after other people's kids all day and managing to flick some paint around when she has enough energy left. Of course they don't understand ambition. Well, James Cameron flunked out of college and he hasn't done too badly for himself, even if

True Lies was a bit of a let-down (but then how *do* you follow up *Terminator 2?*)

Monday 16th October

Locked myself in my room all evening after school, not wanting to speak to *them*.

I refused dinner, but later Mum came upstairs with some chicken casserole.

'Thanks,' I said.

We sat on my bed and had a little chat.

She said, 'There's nothing wrong with having a hobby and not relying on it for your livelihood.'

'You mean, like you?'

'Well, yes, but what I meant was, I was talking to David Nolan's mum the other day—'

'Oh God...'

'And she was saying that David's dialled down his acting ambitions to focus on his A Levels.'

'Good for him.'

Martin did a degree in Journalism and has moved onto a master's at UCL. In a way, I envy him for fitting in with a straight path.

But in another way, I feel really sorry for him.

Tuesday 17th October

I told Ms Harper that I discussed doing a film degree with the folks and that they are all for it.

Then she informed me that I need to get my parents' signatures on any university applications.

And that to get a place on one of their courses, I need to wow the unis not only with my grades but with examples of my own movies.

Bollocks. So what I've done so far *does* matter.

Wednesday 18th October

Gritted my teeth and re-watched all of my shorts again today, one after the other.

They are definitely shit.

What was I thinking? Filming people acting out pretend situations then editing tape-to-tape will loosely result in a narrative film. Fine. But that doesn't mean it will be a *good* film, or even a competent one. Half of them aren't even finished, they just stop when we got bored or were called in for dinner.

And another blow: the uni application forms are even more detailed than those for the festivals and for Asda *combined*. And the students' testimonials that are supposed to help us with what to put down sound like a bloody thesaurus. *Mise en scene* this and *composition* that and all this stuff about 8mm vs 16mm and blowing up to 35mm. It was like a foreign language. And they go on about Bergman and Antonioni and Godard and Melville. Who the fuck are these people?

Ms Harper said, 'You know Ingmar Bergman.'

'I do?'

'Playing chess with Death in *Bill and Ted?*'

'That's in the sequel, *Bogus Journey.*'

'It's spoofing *The Seventh Seal*. I don't have any Bergman here. But hold on...'

She opened her cupboard of VHS tapes and dug three out for me.

I read the titles aloud, or at least gave it my best shot. '*L'Avvventura, A Bout de Souffle, Le Samourai*. Are these subtitled?'

'You *have* watched foreign films before, haven't you Stephen?'

Everyone's a smart-arse.

As I was walking out, she said, 'Don't you think it's ironic that you complain about people being ignorant about directors beyond Spielberg when you yourself don't know the old masters?'

I don't think that it's at all ironic.

Popped into Eamon's shop after work and showed him Ms Harper's videos.

He chuckled while he examined them. 'Wee bit different for you, lad. Good that you're looking into a bit of film history, so it is.' Then he rummaged about behind the counter. 'Here, if you struggle with them ones, these might be a bit more up your street.'

And he gave me yet more tapes with weird foreign titles and black and white photos on the boxes.

Thursday 19th October

Have watched all three of Ms Harper's so-called classics.

The box for *L'Avvventura* claims that *Antonioni's masterpiece created a new cinematic language.* Sod me if I know what that means, but I do know that watching it was one of the most boring, pointless, tedious experiences of my life. This *new language* seems to have forgotten to include words like *story*, *incident*, and *entertainment*.

A Bout de Souffle is just amateurish. A lot of running around Paris and meandering off on tangents. This director Jean-Luc Godard was blatantly making it up as he went along. It never feels like an actual movie, just a bunch of mates messing around. The only things I liked were the jumpy edits, which at least gave it some energy, and the good-looking French women.

Finally, *Le Samourai*. This one sounded quite cool, about a hitman and apparently an influence on *Leon* and John Woo's *The Killer*. Well, give me the modern films any day. This one substituted shoot-outs, explosions and stylish slow-mo for a bloke with no facial expression wandering around Paris (again) having quiet conversations with people for two hours.

I am bang in trouble if this is the stuff I'm supposed to be into. Couldn't face looking at Eamon's films after that, so I just flung them into the back of my wardrobe.

Friday 20th October

Media again today, so after the lesson I gave Ms Harper my verdict on the *classics* she lent me.

'I've seen it all done before, and much better, in more modern films,' I explained. 'Today's directors loved all that old stuff growing up, when there weren't any alternatives, but now they've taken what was around then and improved it for my generation by making their own films. So now that I've got *those* films to enjoy, that are actually being made *today*, why on Earth should I bother going back to the boring old ones?'

Ms Harper frowned, her thick eyebrows joining together in conference. 'You can't just ignore that Godard and Melville were part of the French New Wave, one of the most important cinematic movements of this century.'

'Okay, but what's that got to do with me right now? Although, all right, I will admit that I liked Godard's jump-cuts.'

'You know, he only did that because he needed to make the film shorter for the distributor. So instead of removing scenes he just made little cuts here and there.'

'Wait, the best thing about the film is something that he just did to make sure it would get released? And because he couldn't be arsed to choose which scenes to cut out?'

That lazy bastard!

Ms Harper rummaged about in her cupboard again. 'I've got some others... here, you'll be able to relate to this one: Fellini's *8 ½*.'

'No, you're all right.'

As well as returning her films I lent Miss a video with five of my least awful shorts on it. She said she'd watch them with a glass of wine over the weekend.

Saw David Nolan coming towards me on the way home from school and I crossed the road to avoid bumping into him. Pretty sure he didn't see me.

Saturday 21st October

Have been falling behind with my schoolwork. What's new, sure, but it's looking like my standard last-minute power-blag approach is going to be harder to pull off with A Levels. Not impossible, just more of an ordeal. I'll have to cut my film-watching down a tad, cinema visits especially.

It would be easier if I was one of the Sads, who actually like school. But that means liking somewhere they tell you what to do, where to be, when to be there, how to dress… and worst of all, they expect you to be grateful, with all this be-proud-of-your-school bollocks. I'd rather blow the place up, like Christian Slater in *Heathers*.

The fake ID I ordered from an ad in the back of *FHM* came in the post today. It looks okay… I think, anyway. I used a photo where there's a shadow across my mouth that makes it look like I have stubble. At a glance, from a distance. Now I just need to work up the courage to use it.

Monday 23rd October

Time goes a lot faster at Asda when you've got someone to chat to. Tonight, Adrian Smith was stacking shelves near the bakery. We've always got on, despite him being one of the Sports. And I never realised that he's into films. He was trying to persuade me that *Die Hard 2* is better than *Die Hard*. Ridiculous, of course, but I appreciate that he at least has an opinion.

Wednesday 25th October

Ms Harper avoided eye contact with me all through Media today. I asked her a question during group work and she let that arrogant Vicky Motson butt in and answer, a childish attempt by our Head Girl to get one up on me.

When class ended, Ms Harper was unusually keen to get to the staff room.

I followed her as she hurried down the corridor.

'Miss?'

I caught up with her, but she still wouldn't face me.

'I'm sorry Stephen,' she said finally. 'Your films showed promise, but...'

'... But?'

She was torn. 'I was hoping to see that you'd put your heart into them, used some of your passion. I get that you think that school is just pushing you through a meat-grinder. But your own projects, your own art...'

'What?'

'It's just so... half-arsed.'

I could hardly argue with that.

'So, nothing that will wow these uni people?'

'I'm so sorry.'

Thursday 26th October

Today was Sixth Form Careers Day. Going in, I thought it would be a forgettable little dossy replacement for regular classes. As it turned out, it may have changed my life. Although not because of any of their lame advice, you understand.

So there I am, shuffling into the sports hall with everyone else. They have these tables set up with company logos plastered all over them (Barclay's Bank, Churchill Insurance, Debenhams, and loads more I don't recognise) and people wearing suits and name badges are standing behind, smiling and enticing us to come and talk to them. A lot of them are trying to bribe us to sell our souls with pots full of stuff like branded pens and chocolates and mini-calculators. I recoil from the whole thing, of course, and just wander around ignoring everyone until I can pass successfully out the other end, although not before taking a couple of chocolates from one of the stands that's occupied by this pair of stunning women.

Anyway, after getting through all that unscathed, I've got my one-on-one chat with the careers counsellor. It's either that or return to class early, so I plonk myself outside the office and read my *Film Fanatic* until I'm called to go in.

The counsellor turns out to be this old dear in her seventies, who I at first mistake for a lost dinner lady. I'm supposed to be guided by someone who was born before the advent of sound in film?

So, okay, there I am in the office with her, and this old crone asks me what job I see myself doing.

'Film director.'

'Ha!'

Yes, she actually laughs in my face.

'Sorry,' she non-apologises, 'but after years of doing this, the really silly answers still take me by surprise.'

'What's so silly about it?'

'I suppose you could train to be a cameraman, work on a soap opera...'

'No, not a cameraman, a director. Not TV, film.'

'So you've been to the pictures a few times and now you want to be Cecil B DeMille?'

I assume that's some name from the pre-who-gives-a-shit era.

She sighs. 'Look,' she consults her notes, 'Stephen. It's easy to bounce back from disappointment at your age, you don't have anything at stake. But as you get older, you'll have less and less time to reverse a bad decision. Don't waste your life on childish dreams. There are plenty of exciting careers you could choose from. Here, I've got some pamphlets.'

And with that, the careers adviser advises me to give up on my dream career.

I walk out wondering what the fuck I have to do to get people to believe that I *am* going to be a film director.

And as I'm dumping her stupid bits of paper in the bin, I'm thinking that it's going to take something really crazy... something no one could ever see coming from a sixteen-year-old.

Something like making a full-length feature film.

Friday 27th October

No sleep last night after the thought had burrowed its way into my head.

Could I make a feature? At 3 a.m. I wrote down the obstacles and how to overcome them.

It will cost too much money.

I'll earn it. Asda is in the bag, and I'm sure I can figure out other ways of bringing in some cash.

I don't have the time.

All I need to do is use the months I would have spent making multiple shorts for single project, and pace it so I have enough time along the way to keep my grades above getting-chucked-out level.

I can't handle a longer project

I just have to make sure I have enough material so I don't run out of things to film. Again, it's just like making a short, only longer. And there are plenty of tricks to pad it out: shoot longer scenes, throw in some dream sequences, flashbacks... maybe even flash*forwards!* And loads of slow-mo, of course.

I don't have enough experience.

The combined running time of my shorts easily adds up to a full-length film. So, in a sense, I've already made a feature.

Nothing is impossible.
Babbled my idea to Ms Harper in my sleep-deprived state. I explained that if these snooty unis want samples and my shorts aren't up to it, then I'll wow them with a feature. None of the posh twats in the photos ever tried *that* at sixteen.

She raised an eyebrow and said, 'Yes, but Orson Welles at least waited until he was twenty-six to make *Citizen Kane*, and *that* was considered young.'

She nevertheless advised me to watch my own films back (again!) and note things that I could improve on.

I said, 'I don't tend to do that. When they're done, I'm done with them.'

'Try using the analytical techniques you've learned in class. You don't want to keep repeating the same mistakes. Then apply those processes to other people's films that inspire you so you can learn from those, too.'

It all sounded a bit too much like hard work, so I changed the subject.

'Making a feature will also prove to my parents that I deserve to do a film degree.'

'I thought they were already behind the idea?'

'Oh, they are. But I want them to really *understand* it, too.'

'Well, making a feature film is pretty ambitious,' she said. But I could see that, beneath her professional exterior, she was excited for me. 'Just don't let your schoolwork suffer.'

As if I would...

Leaving the classroom, I saw that my old pal Vicky Motson was hanging around, pretending to drink from the water fountain. I walked past her but she followed me while I tried to lose her in the corridors.

'Hey, Stephen.'

'I don't want to be late for my next class, Victoria.'

'Like you care... look, what do you keep staying behind to speak to Ms Harper about?'

'That's part of student-teacher confidentiality, I'm afraid.'

'Come off it. Is it one of your stupid short movies? You're not trying to borrow school equipment for your own use, are you?'

'If you must know, I was asking Ms Harper about feminism in cinema. It's a subject I care about deeply. Now if you'll excuse me,' (I stopped outside the gents) 'I have some business to attend to.'

Vicky probably fancies me. Shudder.

Saturday 28th October

Down the pool club, I told the boys about my advancement to feature filmmaking. We were having a break from play and sitting around the bar, which is even more pathetic and run down than the one at The Harvester.

They weren't quite as excited as I'd hoped but seemed willing to go along with it. Gav said that we might as well, Bazza reiterated his offer to go full-frontal and Clive said he would need a greatly increased budget for his practical effects.

So, this is it. I've heard my calling and I'm going to answer it. It's half-term holiday now so I've got the chance to figure everything out while still dutifully ploughing through my coursework.

Sunday 29th October

Had another film chat with Adrian Smith at work, although I don't feel confident enough yet to tell him about the feature. I was on cookie duty and any that come out of the oven not perfectly round can't be sold. Well, wouldn't you know it, the ones I baked somehow came out practically rectangular, and so Adrian and I were forced to eat them round the back.

While we polished off the misshaped cookies, Adrian started chatting to the other bakery lads about football and I struggled to keep up. I made the odd comment but I could tell that Ade knew I was blagging, but to be fair to him he didn't try to catch me out.

Later on, Adrian told me that there's going to be a kickabout over on Baston playing fields on Thursday. Him and the other Sports are always up there playing at the goals, and he said that they want to have a proper match against *the rest of you lot*. He said there will be rolling subs and that his team will start with a minus goal-difference to give us normals a fighting chance.

I got so carried away that I said that I'd be there.

When I got home, I put on *El Mariachi* for an example of a self-funded feature debut. It does look like someone's home movie, where

Rodriguez has only used the actors, sets and props that were available to him. But things like the stunts and the quick editing and the guns make it so engrossing that you don't care.

Robert Rodriguez famously did *Mariachi* for $7,000. I'll be lucky to scrape together £700.

Monday 30th October

Watched *The Evil Dead* today. A low-budget debut that really delivers. Sam Raimi (who was nineteen at the time!) used inventive-but-cheap methods and Bruce Campbell's comedic and physical performance is a special effect in itself. Barry is the equivalent in my films. He can't act, he's not *interested* in being a real actor, but he is a good clown.

Making your own feature *can* be done, with a little dedication and planning! And here's another example I just thought of: *Clerks*, which I watched a couple of weeks ago. Kevin Smith filmed that on credit cards at the shop where he worked after hours, when it was closed.

Now I just need an idea. And some money (too young for credit cards, annoyingly). And a script, I guess.

Walking past my dad's study, I realised that I have a whole information superhighway at my fingertips to help me. Pity Dad was on the PC tonight doing his spreadsheets, with that Godawful classical music playing on the radio. Never mind, you can never do too much research, so I stayed up all night revisiting Cronenberg's first three features: *Shivers*, *Rabid* and *The Brood*.

Tuesday 31st October

I'm going to have to cut down on trips to the movies even more now that I'm saving money for this feature. But *The Net* was still showing at Bromley Odeon and I do need help with using the World Wide Web. That it stars Sandra Bullock didn't hurt, either.

I didn't want to risk my mates being late again, so I went on my own, which is a big social no-no. Once the lights went down and I was confident that I hadn't been recognised, I enjoyed the experience. Had a free seat next to me for my coat and popcorn, and I could concentrate without anyone constantly asking questions.

Film was watchable enough, although the only thing I learned about the Internet was that if I'm not careful I'll have my identity erased and get chased around the country by government agents.

Then, after the credits were rolling: disaster. I found myself face to face with Ruth and her gang in the foyer.

'Hi Steve,' purred the infuriating goddess herself. She had her hair up and was wearing this figure-hugging coat. 'What have you just seen?'

'*The Net*. Don't bother, it's rubbish.'

'We're going to see *Clueless*, it's meant to be hilarious,' one of her gaggle blurted between loud gum-chewing. 'You here on your own, or what?'

'No, I'm with Clive Marrow. He's in the bogs, I'm waiting for him.'

The girls just giggled, as girls do.

Then Ruth got an idea.

'Hey, I'm having a Bonfire Night party Saturday. Free house. You should totally come.'

Nurse, we have an increased pulse here.

'And make sure you bring along some of your films.' She smiled and touched my arm, just like she did at the Asda induction.

I staggered away, my Clive cover story forgotten.

But when I got outside, I felt a chill go right through me, and it wasn't the autumn weather. As I walked to the bus stop, I started to question exactly why Ruth would be so keen for me to come to her party.

Inspired by today's date, I grabbed a copy of *Halloween: The Curse of Michael Myers* from Eamon's shop on the way home. Wow, they really do make some crap these days. Oh, for the glory days of film, those dozen wonderful years between 1982 and 1994. I guess it's up to pioneers like me to usher in a new golden era.

November 1995

Wednesday 1st November

Took the plunge and looked for advice about making a feature film in some online chat rooms. But it turns out most of these Internet message boards are nothing but people slagging each other off. I couldn't find anything useful so shut the PC down.

I was just heading outside to get some fresh air when I bumped into David, popping round to pick up little Freddy. For Christ's sake.

'Still making the short movies, Steve?' He was doing up the kid's trainers when he asked this, so I couldn't see his face, but I detected the old smug tone.

Nevertheless, I found myself blurting out, 'Actually, I've moved on to features now.'

He looked up at me. 'Is that so?'

'Yeah, I'm in the middle of pre-production. In fact, if you'll excuse me, I'm just off out to scout some locations.'

I had to wait around the corner for a full fifteen minutes before it was safe to come home again without bumping into him.

Thursday 2nd November

Today marks the last time I ever take part in a team activity.

Managed to get Barry and Gavin to turn up for this football match. (Clive claimed he was ill.) I met the two of them at the bus stop and we tentatively made our way down this country lane and around the corner to Baston playing fields, where there are something like ten football pitches next to each other that back off onto some woods. We heard the noise before we saw anyone: cheering, laughing, some shrieking. Quite intimidating, as if the whole thing wasn't out of our comfort zone enough already.

The first humiliation came before we'd even kicked a ball. Adrian hadn't said what to wear, so I had advised the boys to come in plain white T-shirts and shorts. To quote Arnie in *Last Action Hero*: big mistake. All of the other lads were wearing replica football shirts. On seeing us someone yelled out *what you think this is, PE?*

And the other players were also all wearing football boots. I do have a pair, left over from when we did have to do PE. They're stuck together with mud somewhere in the garage, but I just didn't think. My mates and I were slipping and sliding all over the place in our trainers and our shorts soon looked like we'd soiled ourselves.

Girls were scattered around the edges supporting their boyfriends and having a good laugh, mostly at yours truly. Yes, Ruth was there and no, she didn't speak to me.

I was put on the edge of the defence by our captain, my old mate Dean Harris, and for a while I got away with doing nothing: Harris's crony Sean Birrell was headering everything away.

But then one of the opposition's kicks sent the ball bouncing over Birrell towards me. It was going to cross the line next to our goal and go off the pitch, so I swung out a leg to stop it. I ended up hitting it with my heel and it flew past our goalie and into the net. I'd scored a home goal and Harris substituted me straight away. Despite these so-called rolling subs, I never got back on. But I still had to sit there and pretend to care about whether we won or lost.

'Thanks, Steve,' Gavin said over his shoulder when the ordeal was over, and we were trudging back across the water-logged field.

I said, 'Come on lads, why don't we go catch a flick?'

Barry said, 'Well, I think *The Net*'s still showing.'

'Nah, I've already seen it,' I said without thinking.

They gave each other this look.

Gav said, 'Let's give Nigel a ring.'

A bus was pulling up at the stop and they jumped on without looking back.

So, five minutes later, I'm walking down Baston Road towards home, and this car pulls up.

'Oi, Ricketts!'

It's Adrian Smith.

I turn warily, expecting abuse following the match, but he's smiling. So I get in and he gives me a lift home.

On the way he apologises about the game and says that he thought I had played a little before.

'Never mind, mate. At least you got involved and took part.'

The truth is, I hate getting involved and I hate taking part. He sounds like my dad, if Dad ever took an interest in anything I did anymore. Actually, he would if it was football.

Adrian goes to me, 'How come you never tried playing for any teams at school?'

Because I don't like having some wanker shout orders at me while I run around freezing my bollocks off?

I go, 'Dunno.'

'Well,' he pauses to check his hair at a red light, 'it's probably too late for you now, anyway.'

Adrian has already formed a gang of mates at Asda, and when he dropped me off, he invited me to their pay-day piss-up in Bromley tomorrow night.

Fake ID don't fail me now.

Friday 3rd November

Helped out all day at Eamon's video shop. He wasn't there and the store was instead managed by Auntie Sheila. She's all right, but she's not into films like Eamon. I think it's just a business for her. At a family do a few months back they had this huge row, during which she accused Eamon of caring more about plastic VHS tapes than her.

Imagine not wanting to own a video shop! Eamon has the best job in the world. Next to actually making movies, of course.

When I'm in the shop, I basically run it. Not to the extent that I order everyone else around, I just mean that, as family, I'm in charge of the most important thing: what's showing on the TV screens.

The shop isn't massive like a Blockbusters, but it's not your bog-standard local outlet, either. It's quite narrow, but also quite long. You come in and there are shelves all along on both walls and making two aisles in the middle. Towards the back, there are a few steps down to a little kind of alcove bit, which is where the new releases sit. Older stuff is separated into genre: action, horror, sci-fi, family, drama, historical, thriller, western, fantasy, comedy and foreign. Then you've got the till at the top of the stairs, with tempting snacks (popcorn, big boxes of Maltesers, those massive American-style bags of crisps), and any bit of space not occupied with tapes to rent has film posters or those stand-up cardboard cut-outs of images from the posters, like Stallone hanging upside down off a mountain in *Cliffhanger* or Steven Seagal climbing along a train in *Under Siege 2: Dark Territory*. I know the layout by heart and always get first dibs on new cassettes when they come in. I've spent whole afternoons just browsing through the rows of titles, and I will have watched ever single tape in the place by the time I turn eighteen.

TV-wise, there are four, spread around the store, so you can always see a screen when you glance up. It's crucial that the punters are exposed to something half-decent when they come in, otherwise our reputation would be right down the pan. I'm not allowed to put on any 15s or 18s because of kids coming into the shop and that, but I do my best within the limitations. Today I chose some family-friendly favourites: *Ghostbusters 2* (an underrated sequel), *Planes, Trains and Automobiles* (the last great John Hughes film), and *The Goonies* (which has a surprising amount of fruity language, but films shown on the shop TVs are muted).

As usual I chatted to customers all day. I turned a guy onto *Hard Target*, creating a new John Woo fan, I gave *When Harry Met Sally* to another who was looking for a tolerable romantic film, and I reassured someone else that *On Her Majesty's Secret Service* is a top-tier Bond, despite starring the bloke whose name no one can ever remember and who only played the part once.

When I got home, Mum told me that David was asking about me when he came to pick his brother up today. As if I don't have enough on my mind already to start worrying about *him*.

Come the evening, come the pay-day piss-up. A chance to finally see the inside of Bromley's famous cool pubs. I wondered whether Ruth would be there, but it turns out she's not part of Adrian's boozy Asda gang.

Adrian invited me round his place for some pre-drinks, this proper nice house in Keston. His bedroom is the size of our garden, and he's got posters of girls from lads' mags and footballers all over his walls.

Ade produced a six-pack of Stella Artois and asked me which Bromley pubs I liked. For some reason, I decided to tell the truth.

'I haven't really been in any, apart from The Tiger's Head just once.'

'Fair enough. Lots of people struggle to get into the big ones. How many times have you tried?'

I admitted that it's been just the once, that time at The Bell.

'You can't give up that easily, mate.'

'But don't you only get one chance with the bouncers and then you're blacklisted?'

Adrian swallowed a big swig of lager. 'Nah. They don't remember from one week to the next. And don't forget that they were once the underage ones trying to get in. They *respect* persistence.'

Interesting. I'd never considered it from the bouncers' point of view.

'The truth is,' Ade continued, 'they *want* to let you in. Not as much as they want to let girls in, but they do need *some* blokes in there, otherwise the girls would have no reason to come.'

Then he asked me if I had a fake ID. I sheepishly got the little plastic card out.

'Back of *Maxim?*'

'*FHM.*'

He nodded. 'Not bad, but the real trick is not even needing to show it. Using the confidence you get from just having it on you.'

We got to the scene of the crime, Jane Austen's old boozer The Bell, at 7 p.m. and marched up the steps together. We made eye-contact with the bouncers and reached for our wallets without being asked. They watched this action... and nodded us in!

We never even broke stride.

The Bell (actually The Royal Bell Hotel, it turns out) is definitely old school. The entrance looks like one of those really ancient gaffs they used to drag us around on school trips, or where you might get taken to by your parents on a break up North, when they decide you've been in the arcades long enough and now need some culture. High ceilings, a big chandelier at the top of the staircase. Old paintings sticking out from peeling wallpaper, dark wooden mantlepieces with matching tables and chairs. But despite all this it's no ancient manor or whatnot. Not with the big sound system and DJ booth, the strong smell of cigarette smoke and hair gel and cologne, the chart dance music pumping out of speakers, the TVs stuck on either MTV or Sky Sports News. You could tell from the crowd that this was definitely one of the mythical *cool* venues: all lads in shirts and shoes and girls tarted up in tight dresses or braless tops over white trousers. Adrian told me that The Bell pulls them in from all over the southeastern boroughs, places like Downham, Mottingham, even Catford. And you could tell that there were some real, proper Londoners in there. Not just from the accents, or the smart clothes, but from the way some of the blokes, the *geezers*, looked at you. Not the kind of people you would want to mess with and I avoided eye-contact. I noticed that a lot of people were drinking this purple stuff, which turned out to be snakebite black: half lager, half cider, topped up with blackcurrant cordial. I had myself a couple of pints of it with Adrian's Asda gang and it went down pretty smoothly, easier to drink than just lager or cider on their own. By the time we had moved onto pitchers of JD and Coke, I was a bit more relaxed. By which, of course, I mean I was started to get properly pissed.

We finished the night in Town House, this bar up Bromley North. It seemed quite small from the outside but actually stretched far back and most of it was taken up by a huge dance floor. I soon realised that I was in what Martin would call a *meat market*.

'Everyone here is on the pull,' Adrian confirmed as we waited at the bar.

And he wasn't wrong. I spent most of my time in Town House up on the balcony overlooking the dance floor, watching the show down below. I observed how the blokes all hung around on the edges, looking for an opening to make a move. At the start of the night, they tended to move slightly further in, hesitate, and then carry on dancing with their mates, glancing back at the girls over their shoulders. Gaining a bit of ground but not making any manoeuvres. Then I saw how as the night wore on, and the dance floor got busier, the lads got bolder. They were more confident (and drunker) and bit by bit blokes started trying to dance with the girls. Many had multiple attempts, the number of bodies making it easy to gloss over a knock back, or even to pretend that it was an accident, I wasn't trying to dance with you at all, love. When closing time came, the people snogging outnumbered the ones who weren't.

A lot of blokes left Town House disappointed, but at least they had been in the game and given it a try. And as for the girls, most of the time they brushed off any unwanted advances and just enjoyed the music with their mates. Me, I was too tense to have a good time. There were too many questions swirling around my drunken head. Should I try to pull a girl? Do I have the guts? What if I try and fail: could I handle the rejection? Would Adrian and his mates respect me for giving it a try and failing, or just laugh in my face?

Still, feature filmmaker and cool pub-goer. Can't deny things are looking up.

Saturday 4th November

Decided to skip Ruth's fireworks party. My little hat with the bells on won't be coming out anymore. I've hung it up for good.

Am starting to get a little nervous about this feature endeavour. It's going to be quite the undertaking and I haven't even decided what to make the movie about yet.

Tuesday 7th November

Made a list of ways to generate money for the feature film:

> Asda (extra shifts?)
> More shifts at Video Nation (doubles as research).
> Dog-walking.
> A paper round.
> Washing cars.
> Going round people's houses and doing their ironing.
> Money I get for Christmas.
> Selling my possessions.
> Selling my body (joke).

Wish I could rent out my room and live in the shed.

Friday 10th November

Pissed it down all day today. And it's getting so that it's nearly dark when you get home from school, too. Grim times.

I asked Ms Harper for advice on how I go about making a feature film. Instead of giving me practical tips, she wanted me to get all self-analytical.

'Stephen, have you ever considered what your films are actually about?'

'Well, they're about different things. *Watch This Space* is about a mission to Saturn that goes horribly—'

'No, not the... plots. What is the film trying to *say?*'

'What do you mean?'

'Beneath all the dismemberings and blood spurts and sheep intestines falling on the floor, isn't there ever anything else going on? You got an A* in English, so you must know about exploring a text for its meanings.'

I said, 'Oh no. I don't make preachy, arty, sentimental crap. Stuff with a *meaning*. And I got that grade just by working out what the examiner wanted and giving it to them over three sides of A4.'

'But you must agree that the best movies aren't just knocked out to sell tickets, but have an artistic voice behind them?'

'My heroes, John Carpenter, David Cronenberg and James Cameron, they make pure entertainment and nothing else.'

'Well, I'm not sure about that. There's an anti-authoritarian strand to Carpenter's films, most notably *They Live*. Cronenberg is obsessed with the melding of the body with science, and don't tell me you missed the anti-technology subtext to Cameron's *Terminator* films?'

I was impressed. I'd thought she was all just Godard and Fellini and those boring old guys.

'Okay, point taken. Maybe they do have things to say. Underneath though, not banging you over the head with it.'

She smiled. 'That's the best way.'

'But I just want to make movies. I don't *have* anything to say.'

'I think you need to spend some time thinking about how true that actually is.'

It's nice that she's taking an interest. But... no.

Monday 13th November

Got in trouble in General Studies. Bad this time. Miss Yates must have just broken up with her boyfriend or something as she wasn't putting up with any of my crap today.

Citizenship was circled on the board and Miss asked us to come up in turn and write a related word. I was first, so I bowled over, changed the last letter to a *t* and sat back down again.

That little stunt landed me a trip to the senior teachers' office, which I'm more than familiar with by now. The place is a classic example of why I can't stand this school: the hypocrisy. Outside it, they've got all this prestige stuff plastered over the walls and in glass cabinets. Ancient-looking trophies, black and white group photos of sports teams from years gone by, all of that. Then you go into the outer office and it's all framed pieces of Year 7 coursework on the history of the local area or whatever, or testimonies about how wonderful the school is from some of the ex-students who went on to be famous (a couple of random footballers and other athletes). But when you go off down the corridor to the actual senior teachers' offices, you're presented only with bare, grim walls. No more accolades, no more cuddly and nostalgic images. See, by this point, the student who's been sent to see one of our overlords is supposed to be all intimidated, they want us to be cowering in our boots. So, it's outside: respectability and status, inside: Nazi torture chamber. Pathetic.

Now that I've moved up from Year 11, I'm no longer under soft old Mr Irving's jurisdiction, and the Head of Sixth Form, Mrs Rebus, is a different proposition entirely. She reminds me of our old prime minister, Margaret Thatcher: tight, high hairdo, reptilian eyes, small but power-suited frame. I strode down the corridor of doom and rapped my knuckles on the door that had her name on it.

'Come!' I opened the door and walked in. 'Mr Ricketts,' she said as I closed it behind me without waiting to be asked. I know the drill by now. 'Tell me one thing, if you would be so kind. Why is it that you treat your education with such contempt?'

A rhetorical question? I kept my mouth shut.

'Approaching manhood and still you darken this establishment's faculty doorways with your odious presence.'

I apologised profusely and promised to do the same to Miss Yates.

'It would be prudent for you to apprehend that your flippancy and supercilious countenance won't be without ramifications.'

Wow. Getting in trouble really helps build your vocabulary.

Wednesday 15th November

Was given a note for my parents in tutor time today declaring that I'm *under concern* in Gen Studies and that if my behaviour doesn't drastically improve then I'm in danger of suspension.

'When I saw how good Stephen's grades were last year,' (Miss Yates had added in pen at the bottom) 'I was confident that he was going to be one of the better-behaved members of my class.'

Talk about naive.

The note didn't demand a parental reaction, so I binned it.

Still, I don't want this to escalate. Have to keep things ticking over. Getting kicked out of school means no uni, which means no access to all that lovely equipment and free money and girls on the crew leaning over me to point out on the monitor how perfect my framing is, their sweet perfume filling my nostrils and their soft hair brushing my cheek.

Saturday 18th November

Straight from Asda to Uncle Eamon's fiftieth birthday party round his house. I used to find family dos really hard going, what with all the questions about how I'm getting on at school and whether I have a girlfriend yet. But now that I'm older, I've really started to appreciate them: as sources of free booze.

Tried to speak to Eamon about feature filmmaking, but by the time I had managed to get him on his own for a chat he was too pissed to speak coherently. He must be pushing the boat out having been let off the leash by Auntie Sheila, who I heard is staying with some friends right now. Weird that she would miss his birthday.

Martin turned up late, then annoyed Mum and Dad by only staying for half an hour before heading off to one of his London mega-clubs. I followed him to the front door and told him about my intention to make a feature, and he promised that he'll help me with anything I need.

Right. Just like when he said I could have his hi-fi after he moved out.

Monday 20th November

There have been notices in the common room for weeks about an event that's coming up this Friday night. Nigel has hired out part of Henry's, that cocktail bar in Bromley, for his seventeenth birthday. He will have told them that it's his eighteenth or, if he's really smart, his nineteenth. I'll be staying away to save for the film's budget, but today my fellow Amigos announced that they are going. Well, it's their hero Nigel, so of course they are.

As I say, my focus is elsewhere. Have been racking my brain trying to think of a story for the feature. How in God's name am I supposed to stretch one of my usual ideas to an hour and a half? I've never gone over fifteen minutes before.

I think the problem is that I'm too distracted by trivial day-to-day matters. Still need to get Miss Yates back onside. Pathetically, the only female in my life I can ask for advice is my mum.

I found her in her bedroom folding laundry.

She said, 'Come to help?' and threw a sock at me.

I sat on the bed and picked up a T-shirt.

'What's up?'

'Mum... what should you do if you've upset a... girl, and you want to apologise?'

Thankfully, she gauged my mood and rather than asking a bunch of awkward questions gave me some good pointers.

Tuesday 21st November

Came home from school to a bit of a shock.

David was helping Freddy put his coat on, nothing new there. But he clearly had something on his mind, and he stopped me as I was trying to make my usual swift getaway upstairs.

'You never returned my call,' he said in that monotone he uses when he's pissed off but doesn't want to give you the satisfaction of knowing it.

I shrugged. 'Yeah, I've been... busy.'

'Planning your feature?'

'That's right.'

He nodded slowly. I turned away, the conversation over as far as I was concerned.

But then he said, 'I want in.'

'You what?'

'I want to star and co-produce.'

I was dumbfounded. I nearly burst out laughing, but didn't dare as he had this dead serious look on his face.

'From what I heard, you've cut down on your acting to focus on school.'

'Have I bollocks. Look, I need more footage for my show-reel and being in a feature will sound prestigious. Even if it's a...' (he struggled for the right word) 'a debut.'

'I'll think about it,' I said.

He nodded. 'Come on, Freddy.' The little chap followed his brother toward the front door.

'Oh,' David said over his shoulder, 'and you might want to check out this week's *News Shopper*. First page of the ads.'

So yeah, like I say, quite a shocking development.

What the fuck is a show-reel?

Wednesday 22nd November

The corner shop didn't have any leftover copies of the *News Shopper* and neither did the off licence. I did manage to buy something for Miss Yates, though, and then I crossed the road and popped into Paws For Thought.

Thursday 23rd November

Had to rummage in our bin to recover the old newspaper. I found what David must have been talking about: an advert for The Kent Summer 1996 Film Festival. (Bromley is somehow both a southeast London borough and in the county of Kent.)

Now, this is not some young persons' event, where Billy and Sally proudly hand in their rejected *You've Been Framed* clips. It's competing against actual adults who are actually filmmakers with actual experience.

Is David mad?

It's probably a big joke, a chance for him to laugh in my face.

Miss Yates liked her Cadbury's Milk Tray, which I gave her after class having said that we needed a chat.

'I'll share these in the staff room,' she smiled. 'I'm watching my figure.'

She isn't the only one.

And she straight-up *loved* the mini-film I made her that we watched together on the classroom video player. Was quite pleased with what I managed to knock together from quickly taken shots of kittens in the pet shop cage, spliced in with comical sound effects, slow-mo, and quick dissolves. All in less than twenty-four hours, editing over lunchtime on the school's gear.

Tried to fantasise about Miss Yates before I went to sleep but couldn't focus. Maybe I'm turning gay. Ah, probably just another teenage phase.

Friday 24th November

Told Ms Harper about the film festival and she said that to even be short-listed would get the film unis chomping at the bit.

Then she announced that she's been speaking to the Head of Sixth Form about me. I feared the worst, but apparently Mrs Rebus has said she will allow me to submit parts of my film as my A Level coursework, alongside the usual bullshit write-ups, and she'll even grant me flexible deadlines to match my production schedule.

Must have been the box of chocolates in the staff room.

'I have to explain to you what this means, Stephen,' Ms H said, getting all serious. 'You'll need to satisfy the exam board's requirements with both your footage and your write-ups. If you don't, or if you don't manage to get the project off the ground at all...'

'Then I'm putting myself at risk of failing my Media Studies A Level and not having good enough grades to get into uni.'

She nodded.

But the other side of the coin is that by completing a feature I a) ace my schoolwork, b) get shown at a film festival, c) get into uni, and d) prove to everyone that I'm the real deal. I'm sure that somewhere along the way it will help me get laid, too.

Then Ms Harper added that my parents need to sign off on the arrangement.

Shit.

When I left the classroom after our chat, Vicky was again hanging around.

'Fancy running into you,' I said, not breaking stride.

Vicky kept up with me down C Block corridor. 'I know what's going on, I sit next to your mate Gavin Morrison in Biology.'

'Don't know what you're talking about.'

'If you're making a feature film then I want a piece of it.'

I stopped. She stopped.

'Okay, so if it *were* true, what makes you think I'd want *you* involved?'

'Um, hello? Top GCSE Media Studies student in the school last year?'

'Yeah, I've seen your work.' I gave her my best unimpressed grimace.

'I would strongly advise you to include me,' she said through gritted teeth. 'I want to act, Stephen, and I could be very useful to the project.'

'Oh yeah? Like how?'

'I can... get you some brilliant locations.'

I resumed grimacing.

'Look, I'm going to be late for my student council meeting. But we're going to speak about this again.'

And off she went.

Her advising *me*. And since when have I needed advice from anyone? I'm the director, for fuck's sake.

Still, on the other hand, I could do with some girls in my film to give it a bit of legitimacy and she does technically qualify as female.

In the evening, instead of going with my so-called mates to Nigel's party at the cocktail bar, I stayed at home and made a list of people who are potentially on my feature:

> David: producing, acting (leading man).
> Vicky: acting, locations, possessing two X chromosomes.
> Barry: acting (will go nude).
> Gavin: acting (provides menace due to height).
> Clive: practical effects, acting (if we need a nerdy scientist-type).
> Terry, Barry's mate from taekwondo: acting and stunts.

A bit thin on the ground, especially behind the camera. But David says that some of his posh Drama class are interested in getting involved and they have enough know-how to fill in wherever needed, plus they all have their own show-reels to fill.

My new drinking buddy, sporty Adrian Smith, is a maybe. Well, I still haven't asked him, but I reckon he'd be up for it. Not sure what he brings to the table exactly, but he has a car, which can't hurt, plus he's from the most popular group at school.

All right then. I guess we're doing this.

I rang David and we arranged to meet up tomorrow round my house, just the two of us, for our first production meeting.

Just the two of us. Here we go again, I guess.

Saturday 25th November

This is a list of what David and I (well, mostly David) think we should ideally have for the film:

> A writer/director (me).
> Producers (me and David).
> Some decent locations.
> A cast of at least ten (including some girls).
> Someone I trust to be a first assistant director, or first AD, on set (basically to make sure people are doing what they're supposed to do and being where they're supposed to be).
> Someone who knows about sound.
> Someone who knows about lighting.
> Equipment for sound and lighting (David and I can pinch from our schools).

Someone with a car.

Someone to be a runner (a general dogsbody).

Someone who knows about music to do the score.

Make-up, costume and set dresser (could be two or even one person).

Three sixty-minute hi-8 tapes from Dixons, enough to get plenty of footage and for re-takes.

An actual budget.

On that last point, I made it clear that if David's a producer like me, then he needs to put in some money like me.

He laughed at this. 'You're starting to sound like a serious businessman.'

'Well, they don't call it show*friendship*.'

'Good one, Steve.'

He assured me that he'd provide 'some' of the funding. So I left it at that.

It was getting dark and I was dreading the awkward moment when my mum would call upstairs to ask if David was staying for dinner. Luckily, he said that he had to be going before it got to that.

He did stop on his way out the front door, though.

I said, 'What?'

'You need to knock out a script, my man. That will answer a lot of these questions about what we need. And I'm no writer.'

A script... I'd forgotten about that.

After he shut the front door, I saw that my mum had been watching us from the kitchen, sporting this huge grin.

'We're working on a film project together, that's all.'

'I didn't say anything.' But she couldn't suppress that stupid smile.

I retreated to my room. I was tempted to call Clive to ask how Nigel's party last night went. But I decided to watch some Stallone films instead, getting all of the way to the end of *Tango and Cash* but falling asleep halfway through *Demolition Man*.

Monday 27th November

Monday night drinks at The Harvey with the usual suspects and conversation was a bit strained. My fellow Amigos wanted to talk among themselves about how brilliant the party on Friday was, but didn't want to make a big deal out of it in front of me. When they mentioned how Nigel Green has turned out to be some kind of a ladies' man and had girls fawning over him all night, I knew they had to be bullshitting.

Unable to stomach their Nigel love-in any longer, I steered the subject onto more important matters. I told them about David being on board with the feature and got a lot of confused looks back.

Clive said, 'David Nolan? Thought you two weren't mates anymore.'

I said, 'We're not.'

Barry said, 'You said he was a posh twat.'

'He is... but he's well-organised and we know that he has filmmaking experience, plus he has other people he can bring in. Says he'll stump up some cash, too.'

Gavin said, 'Okay.'

Clive said, 'Fine.'

A bit more enthusiasm wouldn't have gone amiss.

Barry was the most engaged of the three, keen as ever to show his (home) gym-toned physique on camera. I couldn't face telling him that David will be playing the lead role this time. But frankly this is one part of getting David involved that will definitely improve the project. The less of Bazza gurning and falling over and winking at the camera, the better.

Hmm. Maybe I can swing it so David is the one to break the news to Barry.

One thing that perked all of the Amigos up was when I revealed that we'll be working with at least one girl. Honestly, they may be my mates, but they reek of desperation.

Thursday 30th November

Went to visit Eamon in his shop at lunch time. I've been putting off telling him about the feature. I was worried that if he didn't think I could do it, I'd lose my confidence. Or maybe I was worried that he would tell me that I *can* do it, and then I'd really have no excuses left for putting off figuring out what the fucking thing is going to be about and how the hell I'm going to pull this madness off.

Eamon looked pretty rough, like he hadn't been getting much sleep. Grey stubble covered his face and he smelled like Aisle 20 of Asda last week after a bottle of Glenfiddich shattered all over the floor.

'A feature film?' He said it a bit too loudly, making a woman and her kids cower away deeper into the family movies section. 'Of course you should, lad. You've got a dream, don't let anyone stop you.' He looked right at me with bloodshot eyes and added that I should hang around at the end of my shift this Sunday because he had 'something that might come in handy' to give me.

Good old Eamon, I knew he would understand. He had his own dream: to open up a video shop, and he achieved it. It's inspiring, really.

Back at school, Ms Harper gave me the letter from the Head of Sixth Form, old Thatcher herself, about using my out-of-school activity for my A Level coursework. It includes a sentence pointing out that I'm only being given this special treatment to help me on my path to studying film production at university.

Now I have to figure out how to con my dear parents into signing off on something that they will never agree to in a million years.

December 1995

Friday 1st December

Made sure I happened to be around for when David picked up Freddy today and casually asked him if he'd like to help out in Eamon's shop with me on Sunday.

'Bring some videos to put on if you want,' I said, all offhand. 'Have to be PGs or Us, though.'

'Sure, I'll bring some tapes.'

Now I'll find out what he's *really* made of these days.

Martin came round in the evening and ended up staying the night in his old room. He told me he needed a break after burning the candle at both ends for too long.

For dinner, the two of us jumped in his car and headed out to grab some fish and chips. He had this dance music blaring out.

'Good tune,' I said, or rather shouted. Some bloke kept yelling *I got the poison!*

'The Prodigy.'

'I think I've heard it in the common room.'

'Here, get a load of this.'

He changed CDs.

This moody track started up that then went into this guy talking about having a tough time sleeping.

'What's this?'

'Faithless, "Insomnia". *Huge* tune, mate. Wait for the drop.'

When it came, I was blown away.

Martin said, 'Full club version is the bollocks.'

I read the back of the CD case. '*Eight minutes?*'

He skipped to the track and put it on repeat and we cruised around with it blaring out until the food got cold.

Saturday 2nd December

In the canteen at work I came flat out and asked Adrian if he wanted to help with my feature film.

He said, 'Me? What can *I* do?'

I hadn't thought that far ahead. I didn't want to say, 'You're good-looking and popular and you've got a car, do whatever you like.'

Instead, I went with, 'You'd be a natural on camera.'

I think he blushed.

'We want to do it in the Easter holidays.'

'Oh yeah? Why the wait?'

I explained that we need to film outside of term time, but Christmas is too close and there are various school trips going on during February half-term, so I don't know who's going to be around then. Easter holiday is our next opportunity.

Adrian said, 'Hold on a sec. My parents will be away during Easter. Why don't you film it at my house?'

'Really?'

'Yeah, why not? Something to do, innit? I'll only be bored otherwise, can't play football *every* day.'

Adrian then invited me to tonight's pay-day piss-up. I didn't really want to go but I agreed immediately.

It was the same whirlwind night of Bromley pubs and bars, finishing off in Town House again. But there was a lot more drama this time.

I got ID'd. Twice. First at the bar in The Tiger's Head, so I had to leave early and wait for the others outside, and then later at The Bell I didn't even get in. Worse still, the bouncer, who was the same one who *did* let me in last time, confiscated my ID. I had to hang around the streets again waiting for the rest of the Asda gang to move on. When they did, they took a detour this time to Henry's, which I luckily did get into, but my evening was already tainted, both with embarrassment (no one else in the group was carded) and the worry that hung over me about getting ID'd again. Henry's was pretty rubbish, too: full of wankers in suits and snooty-looking women, and I didn't even have any cocktails since they cost about the same as three pints of lager.

To my immense relief, we eventually left and then I managed to get into Town House. But that was where the real trouble started.

Pints in hand, Adrian and I had a cosy little chat on a sofa, watching the girls moving on the dance floor and the blokes standing around on the fringes, sipping their drinks and sizing up their chances.

Adrian said, 'You ever pulled?' He had to shout over the music.

'Er...'

'It sticks out a mile, mate.'

'It does?'

Adrian nodded. He went back to his pint and I thought that the conversation was over.

But then he leaned over to me again and said, 'You need to do something about that, mate.'

'Tell me about it.'

'I'm serious. Look, one in ten people are gay, right? That means in an average class at school there are going to be three homos, right? And who do you think they're most likely to be: the ones who are out there pulling girls, or the ones who aren't? If you're not careful, you'll get people talking. And once you get that reputation, then the girls aren't going to bother with you at all, are they?'

I sat there absorbing this.

While I was still mulling everything over, Adrian finished his drink, put the glass down loudly, and marched over to the dance floor. He slid up to this girl and whispered something in her ear, which made her laugh and turn around. They stared at each other and in a matter of seconds something was communicated between them. I'm attractive, you're attractive. Let's get on with it. A secret language, completely foreign to the likes of me. They started to dance together and by the time the next track was mixing in, they were sucking each other's faces off.

Ade took his girl to a different sofa without giving me another look. The rest of his Asda gang were all off either pulling random people or each other.

So I just got more and more pissed by myself. Town House do all these flavoured vodka shots, where they soak various things in the bottles to give all these weird flavours: gummy bears, Cadbury's Creme Eggs, chilli peppers. They all tasted disgusting, but definitely helped me with the old Dutch courage. The more shots I knocked back, the blurrier the shapes gyrating around under the flashing lights became, the more the music seemed to be one long repetitive song, and the antsier I got to not just be sitting there but to get up and try something and do *something*.

Eventually I stumbled into the fray. I tried to pretend that I was having a good time just dancing (there were even a couple of songs I liked) but I always had one eye over my shoulder, seeing if there was a way to move into some space near someone. I didn't care who the girl was or what she looked like, anyone missing a Y chromosome would do for me. I had no idea what I was doing, with only Adrian's example and my observations from up on the balcony last time to go on. I tried brushing up against girls, but always felt them recoil and then shuffle away. I tried making eye contact and smiling but that yielded no results. It was all quite stressful and I needed regular breaks, either to go to the gents or buy yet another drink, or sometimes just to sit down for a breather.

Finally, I decided that I needed to be more aggressive. There was only half an hour left 'til closing and I'd seen other blokes have success by grinding up against a girl and then the girl turning around and dancing with him and eventually them getting off with each other. So, from my position at the bar, I fixed my sights on a target, did my Mint Aero shot, took a deep breath, and marched over to her.

I thought at first that things were going well. I approached the girl from behind and put my hands on her thighs and just kind of moved around with her to the song, some R&B number. Then, just as I thought I might be getting somewhere—

'Oi, what the fuck you doing!'

This enormous arm was pushing me away then pointing a finger at me.

'Get your fucking hands off my bird!'

'Shit, sorry, sorry mate...' I backed away with my hands up.

The bloke/geezer was bearing down on me, all snarling rottweiler features right in my face. A space was clearing up around us and I kept backing into it. His fists were clenched. His mates were joining him. I was nearly out of dance floor and would soon be pinned against the fag machine.

Fortunately for me, the bouncers waded in to pull me and the guy apart, as if there was an equal chance of either one of us swinging a punch.

It was soon obvious that I posed zero threat to anyone, and the bouncer let me go as soon as he'd got me over to the far corner of the bar. I didn't want to be noticed again by the guy I'd pissed off, but I stole a glance and saw him back at his table downing a pint, apparently over the whole thing.

But I wasn't taking any chances. I didn't bother trying to find Adrian or his mates and left on my own, just in time to catch the last 138 home.

Sunday 3rd December

Cracking day at Video Nation, despite the hangover.

David was a natural with the customers. This group of girls came in and they were all over him as he dug out the latest rom-coms and found them some Julia Roberts garbage.

After the girls had gone, I said, 'Do *you* like those kinds of films?'

'Nah,' he said, rearranging the shelves. 'But useful to know a thing or two.' He showed me the back of his hand, where one of the girls had written her phone number.

I was shocked that the films David brought to put on in the shop were all Spielbergs. Not even any of the obscure ones, like *The Sugarland Express* or *1941* or *Empire of the Sun*. Not that there's anything wrong with *Raiders of the Lost Ark* and *Jurassic Park* and *Close Encounters of the Third Kind*... but I'd been hoping for a bit more imagination from him.

Then, as we were closing up, he gave me this sly look and said, 'Hope you liked my choice of films. You see, I thought you could do with broadening your horizons a bit.'

Cheeky bastard! He knows all about my Spielberg hang-up.

After we'd locked up, Eamon said, 'Come into my office, lads.'

Eamon cleared away crates of ex-rental tapes and dusted off a cardboard box. He pulled out some packing paper, and underneath was something magnificent.

'It's a Panavision Panaflex 35mm.'

We were speechless. Eamon carefully picked it up.

I said, 'It looks like a real camera that they make real movies with.'

David said, 'Wow.'

Eamon was grinning as he handed the camera to me. I took it like my first-born child.

'Eamon, why did you never tell me about this before?'

'Can't have a wee lad running around with this beauty. But I think you're ready for it now. Taking an interest in film history, progressing onto features. Manual's in there, and there's some tins of film. A tripod, too.'

Eamon told me to come back tomorrow so he can go through how to use it.

Not sure how I'll sleep tonight with the anticipation.

Monday 4th December

Eamon showed me the basics with the camera: loading film, powering up, attaching to the tripod.

He said, 'You know about getting light readings and all the stuff you need for sound, right?'

I said. 'Er... right, right.'

The bloody thing weighs a ton. The manual is nearly as heavy as the camera, so I tried to leave it behind. But Eamon wouldn't let me.

Later, as he helped me carry everything to the bus stop, I said, 'Eamon, how come you have this in the first place?'

'Well, you know that I used to do a bit of camera work back home, for RTE?'

'Yeah.' TV, what a waste. Not sure what he was playing at. Ireland definitely has a film industry, things like *The Commitments* and *The Crying Game*.

'Well, this was kind of a… retirement present.'

I asked no more.

Then the 119 came and we had to lift the camera and the other bits onto the bus.

I've always resisted getting Eamon's help with my films. I'm grateful for the camera now, but I still want to make them on my own. Nothing has changed.

Tuesday 5th December

Tried out the camera alone in my room after school, just taking some random shots of my bed, TV, out the window. I can't actually watch the footage back without a 35mm projector, but it looks pretty good through the viewfinder. Camcorder efforts on hi-8 tapes bought from Dixons always look like exactly what they are: cheap home movies. Not *real* films. When you're channel surfing and something comes on that looks like a film, you *know* that it's a film. And with this camera it won't matter what we shoot, it's going to look the dog's bollocks. No one will be able to tell me that it's not a film.

Thursday 7th December

Today we got the parents' permission form for the Philosophy trip to Germany. It's during the February half-term holiday, so it was definitely a good idea to not schedule the feature shoot for that week.

When I got it home, I took the form upstairs and used my Dad's staple remover to detach the parents' signatures page from the back. Then I did the same from my A Level release letter, and then stapled the signature part for the coursework release to the Germany letter.

Then I waited until after dinner, when Princess Diana was giving this warts-and-all interview to the BBC that they've been building up for weeks. My mum was so engrossed in what Lady Di was sobbing on about that she signed it sight-unseen. My dad flicked the page back and raised an eyebrow before scrawling his own name.

Then I took it upstairs, removed the staple again, and re-stapled the A Level release page back onto its actual letter. *Voila*, a signed release form for Ms Harper. I'll wait a couple of days, then get another form for the Germany trip from school and ask my parents again to sign it, telling them that I lost the first one before I got the chance to hand it in.

David called me up to make a point about the camera: where are we going to edit 35mm film? Doing it on hi-8 is as easy as hooking up two VCRs and giving it a bit of tape-to-tape. But if we are going to film this movie properly, we're going to have to edit it properly. That means finding an editing studio that will let us use their equipment, or rather hire it, at a no-doubt big expense. David said he'd look into it.

So, we've got a proper movie camera and I've committed fraud with my legal guardians and educational establishment. There's no turning back now.

WINTER

Sunday 10th December

Today I did a thorough analysis of my film collection. I pulled out every one of my videos and made a note of its genre. Turns out I have 34% action, 31% horror, 23% science fiction, 10% comedy and 2% drama.

So clearly action is what I'm the most interested in and so that's going to be the genre for my feature debut. You can't argue with statistics.

Monday 11th December

In assembly today, Mrs Rebus encouraged more of us to get involved with the end-of-term play. I was jolted out of my apathy when she said they still need someone to film it, so they have footage to show at the next open day.

So, I thought, if David's got an acting show-reel, then I need a directing one. Plus, it will give me a chance to experiment with some tricks to use on my feature.

So, at the end of assembly, I bowled straight up to Rebus and said that I wanted to be the one to film the play. She shook my hand and started going on about how pleased Mr Irving will be.

Rebus said, 'He's been directing our plays for years. Perhaps you can learn something from him.'

I managed to stifle a laugh.

Hopefully Old Man Irving doesn't hold my snubbing of his Audio/Visual Club against me. One thing's for sure: he's not going to be directing what *I'm* doing.

The production is *Hamlet: The Musical*, written (if you can call it that) by none other than Nigel Green. He's taken the old play, updated the dialogue for modern times and thrown in a bunch of pop songs at key scenes. Copying someone else's work? Really creative, Nige.

Wednesday 13th December

Have been thinking about the implications of making an action movie. Clive has been wanting to do some proper explosions for ages and the money we might have spent on a camera and film can now go towards blowing stuff up. Plus, it means I don't have to worry about the writing so much. What is an action movie other than a bunch of scenes put in to pad the violence up to feature length? It'll mostly be a lot of fast camerawork and running around with fake guns and we'll simulate car chases by hanging out of Adrian's Vauxhall Nova.

With a feature-length running time to play with I'll be able to pay tribute to pretty much every one of my favourite films, but I know that I can't possibly cram them all in. I'm used to just making quick references to scenes or parodying whole films in a shortened form. I'm getting out of my comfort zone here.

Watched *The Killer* and *Hard Boiled* before bed. Went to sleep dreaming of sliding down banisters while firing two guns.

Thursday 14th December

Gave Ms Harper my not-at-all-forged release form. She asked whether my parents fully grasp the implications of this decision, if they had read all the small print, and whether they are satisfied without needing to have a meeting with her to discuss the arrangement.

I just stood there nodding, wondering when she would just take the bloody thing.

I told her that I'm going to be making an action feature. She just said, 'If that's truly the way that you're compelled to express yourself artistically.'

Whatever.

Vicky Motson is now officially part of the project, although she rolled her eyes at my mention of an action film.

I said, 'No one's forcing you to help.'

She said, 'I think a steady female hand is going to be essential if you don't want to make another chauvinistic train wreck.'

Vicky is into talky movies, from people like Woody Allen and Cameron Crowe and even some women directors. She also likes those old screwball-comedies where everyone bangs on at each other in machine-gun banter. We watched one in GCSE Media Studies, *The Girl Friday* or something. It was exhausting, like listening to my mum talk a mile a minute on the phone to Auntie Sheila.

But I do need some girls for this project. No one ever made a feature film with absolutely no female involvement. Apart from maybe *Das Boot*.

Had a meeting in the assembly hall about the end-of-term play. Mr Irving droned on to these actors about their characters and motivations and other such pointlessness. He didn't consult me once, despite having a far more experienced director in his midst.

Nigel was at the meeting, too. Three months at our school and all the teachers already love him, resurrection of William Shakespeare that he is.

Nigel caught up to me as I hurried out at the end.

He said, 'Glad we'll be working together.'

I grunted.

'We've been rehearsing for ages so the play's locked in, but I'd still appreciate you looking over the script and telling me what you think, as a fellow writer.'

'That's okay, mate. I'm sure it's perfect just the way it is.'

And I left him in my dust.

What a suck-up.

Friday 15th December

If I'm going to make a feature-length action movie, I'm going to have to spend even more money than I had originally feared.

As well as bigger explosions, we're going to need more guns. No cap guns, replicas are what we need, ones that take blank bullets and make a really loud noise and a flash when you fire them and have the shell casings eject out. I'm getting excited here just thinking about it.

Gavin solved our problem with something he brought into school that he pinched from his brother. It was a catalogue for this shop that hires out replica guns, no questions asked. The shop's in Catford, in Lewisham, which is a proper London borough (compass-point postcode and everything) and is supposed to be a really dodgy area.

We flicked through the catalogue, drooling. Barry picked out a Beretta, like Mel Gibson in *Lethal Weapon*, and they also have James Bond's Walther PPK, Glocks, Smith & Wessons... everything. The Catford shop only does pistols, but between us we've got toy shotguns and machine guns from our younger days, so if I paint over the orange tips and give them glossy finishes they'll look real enough. I can probably add the shooting sound and flash in post-production. We also need to sort out breakable glass, bullet holes, and people taking bullets hits with fake blood flying everywhere. Clive's going to have to pull out all the stops with his practical effects wizardry.

Meanwhile, I'm going to step up my extra earning tactics. Will start by asking for as much overtime as possible at the supermarket.

Saturday 16th December

Turns out overtime is granted to full-time losers only. Looks like I can't rely on Asda to fund my film.

After work, I finally tried writing the screenplay but had problems getting started. So I watched Jean-Claude Van Damme in *Timecop* and Steven Seagal in *Marked for Death* (for research).

When I sat down afterwards to try writing again the magic still wasn't flowing, but I probably just didn't wait long enough for the inspiration to brew. So I turned off the computer and went to bed.

Sunday 17th December

Met with everyone involved with the film in the pool club after work, armed with a box of pilfered donuts. They don't serve food and so don't care if we bring it in, and their tiny bar won't have seen such a young group since... well, probably ever.

There were the usual suspects, with the additions of Adrian and Vicky. And David, but he's part of the furniture again now, it would seem.

I confirmed to all present that we're making an action film during the Easter holiday: one week to shoot and one to edit. Plenty of time.

Clive asked what the film is actually going to be about.

I said, 'I'm working on the script now.'

Gavin said, 'Yeah, but what's the story?'

Barry said, '... Morning glory!'

Vicky said, 'Do you at least have a title?'

I glanced to David for support but he was giving me the same expectant look.

So I switched to making-it-up-on-the-spot-blagging mode.

'It's about this rogue cop—'

Bazza said, 'That'll be me.'

'This rouge cop, who is also working on the side as a drug dealer to the very villains he is tracking. He has a... partner, who suspects him and who has to bring him down. The cop's wife has left him but the villain (who is an ex-cop, in fact he's our hero's former partner) kidnaps her, and it's through saving her that our hero not only defeats the baddie but also saves his marriage.'

Everyone looked at each other.

David said, 'And what's it called?'

'*Deadly... Deception.*'

Barry said, 'Sounds awesome. Let's set it in LA so I can have my shirt off.'

He flexed his arms in Vicky's direction. She rolled her eyes.

'Of course. All good cop movies are set in LA,' I said, well aware that I didn't correct Barry when he assumed he was playing the lead. I'm sure David will want words about that later.

Adrian said, 'Either LA or New York.'

'Right. So anyway, I hope you lot are good with American accents and—'

Adrian wasn't done yet. 'And I was thinking, we should have a bit where they have some blank firing guns and some that fire real bullets and they mix them up. Like in *Die Hard 2.*'

'Yeah, could do. Anyway—'

'And also do that bit in *Die Hard 2* where the bad guy pulls the trigger on his henchman and it just clicks, and he goes, "Next time, the chamber won't be empty!"'

Barry said, 'Oh yeah, I love that bit.'

Blimey. This is why you don't make movies by committee.

Vicky said, 'So, the wife, has she divorced him, or is it just a trial separation?'

'Er, the second one. Trying a separation.'

She nodded slowly. 'She needs to have a good action scene of her own.'

'Sure, why not.'

David said, 'So we're going to film all of that story at Adrian's house?'

Adrian said, 'It's a very big house.'

I said, 'Vicky will be taking care of other locations.'

She said, 'Yep.'

On our way out, Vicky announced that the pool club is 'full of old men and smells like piss'. She suggested that we have these meetings from now on at each other's houses. Fine by me, I don't want the regulars at the club to think that she's my girlfriend or anything.

On the bus back, David asked when he could see 'some pages'. I said that I'd written loads, but that I'd need to take them to school on a floppy disc since my dad's printer was out of paper.

Felt too tired to do any writing when I got home, though. But I am quite excited about this idea that I just made up on the spot. If I can come up with gold like that out of nowhere, then the actual writing, when no one else is around and putting pressure on me, is going to be a cinch.

Monday 18th December

Okay, I was wrong. Writing is actually *harder* than making something up on the spot. There's not the stress of having all eyes on you, but there is the pressure of knowing that people are waiting for you and that they're going to read what you produce. I'll be all right, because I know pretty much this whole film in my head, but I do still have to get it out of there and onto the page.

I haven't written a single word.

Everything is a distraction. Whenever I do something designed to help me write, it turns into something that keeps me *from* writing. I tried surfing the Internet for inspiration. I wasn't sure what I was looking for, I guess anything that might get my creative juices flowing. But all I found were fan Websites for films that I don't even like. Which I ended up reading anyway. And when you go to one Website, you can click on some of the words and they take you to *other* Websites. Before I knew it, I'd been surfing the information superhighway for hours.

David rang me up and told me he was popping over to pick up 'those pages'. I said I didn't get a chance to print anything out at school today, but definitely would tomorrow.

Tuesday 19th December

Finally found something helpful on one of these Internet film Websites. Apparently, when it comes to writing, the important thing is to just get in and plough through the first draft, and then you can refine it with editing.

Hold on. I not only have to write the thing, I have to write it *again?*

After yet more unsuccessful attempts at putting words onto the page, I realised something: I will never be able to write a screenplay using Microsoft Word. You have to keep doing things like pushing the text along with the *tab* key so that it looks like a proper script. I need a specialist program if I'm going to get anywhere.

Took the initiative and rang David up to say that there was no point giving him 'the pages' when they're not laid out properly, so it will take me a few days to put them into a new screenwriting programme.

He said, 'Fair enough.'

Wednesday 20th December

Some other advice I got from the Internet is that the best way to *write* a script is to *read* scripts.

Bromley Library's selection of screenplays is piss-poor. *Chinatown, Annie Hall, The Apartment...* I want to make a film that people who are alive *now* will want to see. Everything in Virgin Megastore has been moved around for Christmas, but I did manage to find a Tarantino screenplay boxset of *Pulp Fiction, Reservoir Dogs, Natural Born Killers* and *True Romance*. Then I went to the computer section to look at the screenwriting programs. No way, too expensive. I'll stick to my *tab* key, thanks very much.

After school we had the dress rehearsal for this *Hamlet* musical. Mr Irving is still paying no attention to how the production will be filmed. That is to say, he's ignoring me. So I've just been standing there pointing an imaginary camcorder at the actors with a smile on my face. But when the play is actually on it will be my time to shine, you mark my words.

Turns out all Nigel's songs that he's crowbarred in are from Genesis, that old band that have been around since the '70s or even earlier, with that slaphead singer Phil Collins. Talk about lame. Now a dance music musical, with tracks from The Prodigy, Faithless, The Chemical Brothers... *that* would be worth watching.

David rang (again!) during dinner, but I told Mum to take a message.

Resisted the urge to watch movies in bed and instead flicked through the Tarantino screenplays.

Thursday 21st December

Realised that I can't fob David off any longer, so I got up early today and did some writing before school. A screenplay is ninety pages and I got eight done, then saved the Word doc onto a floppy disk and left to catch the bus.

At school I worked on it in the library during my free. Ten more pages. Then in Psychology, when we were supposed to be researching online about the symptoms of depression, I did another six.

Twenty-four pages in one day. Not bad.

It was so simple. All I had to do was keep writing and writing and not worry about it. Just think of words and put them on the page. How hard is that?

Films are really made in the edit, anyway.

Hammered out yet more pages long into the night. Didn't turn in 'til gone 3 a.m.

Friday 22nd December

Philosophy was another end-of-term computer room lesson, so I was able to finish the script, print it out, pop it in an envelope, and drop it through David's letter box on my way home. No spending the Christmas holidays writing for me, not when you're this efficient. Then I had to go back to school again for the opening night of *Hamlet: The Musical.*

I had a wicked time. For the bit where Hamlet sees his dad's ghost (while the choir sang Genesis' 'No Son of Mine'), I used the famous dolly zoom, where you move the camera backwards and zoom in at the same time. Later, when Hamlet goes on to his girlfriend about turfing her off to a nunnery (to 'In Too Deep'), I used a low-angle Dutch tilt. Then when he catches his mum and his uncle conspiring ('Mama') I tracked around them a full 360 degrees. (Please understand that I did have to check the play's programme to find out the song titles. I don't listen to crusty old lame-o music.)

Mr Irving wasn't best pleased with my hi-jinks, gesturing at me from stage-right or whatever you call it. I just repeatedly gave him the thumbs-up. He's always wanted me to get involved with after school film activities. Well, this is me getting involved.

Following the play, students and teachers alike went to The Harvester. Yes, teachers in *our* pub, or semi-pub anyway, and so that's the end of going there for the Four Amigos. We youngsters had to stick to soft drinks while our educators guzzled down beer and wine.

'Stephen,' old Irving blustered over his tankard of ale, 'what were you thinking? Coming onto the stage like that? You were putting the actors off their cues!'

I shrugged. 'I just wanted to best capture the performance, sir.'

I thought Ms Harper would be pleased at my innovation, but she backed up her Media Studies colleague. 'We won't be able to use *that* footage for the open day,' she told me. 'Oh Stephen, all you had to do was point a camera at the stage, there was no need to go through the playbook of gimmicks.'

Philistines.

Weirdly, the only one who stood up for me was Vicky, who had been playing Hamlet's girlfriend. 'Nice moves,' she told me at the bar.

'Oh... cheers.'

'What Ms Harper and Mr Irving were saying... they haven't put you off doing the feature film, have they?'

'Fuck no.'

She looked relieved. 'Good. Listen, backstage I was telling the cast about the project and some of them want to talk to you.'

'What, they want to be in my feature?'

'Yeah, I mean, I was thinking—'

'No way. Look, present company accepted, I'm not having anyone who sucks up to the school on *my* project. This is an independent film. No studio interference.'

She gawped at me. 'Christ, Steve. You really are something else.'

I watched her storm off, deciding to take that as a compliment.

Then there was Nigel. I'd thought he might be pissed off, too. Maybe I was *hoping* he would be. We didn't really talk much in the pub, because every time I saw him, he was across the room chatting to girls who were in the play (including Vicky) and making them laugh with some witticism. But towards the end of the evening he found me and started asking me all these questions. Why I did I choose certain angles? Why did I follow Hamlet over his shoulder in one scene? How did I stay in focus?

I just sipped enigmatically from my drink, giving occasional one-word responses: *instinct, experience, talent.*

Since he was sucking up to me so much, I couldn't help myself and ended up promising that he could be part of pre-production for the feature.

But I stopped short of saying anything about him being allowed on my set when we start rolling.

Saturday 23rd December

Lots of fun at work today with no one giving a toss since the Christmas party was in the evening. After a few over the road at The Bell, me, Ruth, Adrian, and a load of the others jumped on a coach that Asda had hired which took us to the Blue Orchid nightclub in Croydon.

I'd never been to Croydon in the evening before, only to the shops during the day. I'd read it once described in my dad's *Sunday Times* as London's Manhattan. Well, if that's the case, I never want to go to New York. Ugly, grim concrete jungle is more like it. While I was still taking in my surroundings, we were marched into the club (bypassing the queue and the bouncers) and once inside I realised that I was in my first actual nightclub. I don't know how it compares to these ones Martin goes to up town in London proper, but it was huge. Every corridor led to a bar, there were two floors (three if you count the balcony around the main room, which had its own bars as well) and the loudest music I've ever heard. Asda had hired out the smallest of the rooms but we could go around the whole club as well.

It was brilliant. The drinks were expensive but I didn't give a monkey's. I recognised a number of tunes from the mix tapes my brother's been making me, like 'Let Me Be Your Fantasy', and this 'Ebenezer Goode' song that Martin thinks is hilarious for some reason. The best part was when they played 'Set U Free' and we all put our arms around each other's shoulders and jumped about together. I didn't worry about pulling girls or being seen to be trying to, I just drank and danced. Must have been the Christmas vibe that took the pressure off. I wish normal nights out could have that kind of fun and carefree atmosphere, with no need to try to get off with people or look cool.

It didn't even bother me when Adrian pulled Ruth during 'Do They Know It's Christmas'. It's not like he realises that I've fancied her forever. I don't think he does, anyway.

Sunday 24th December

A hungover Christmas Eve for me. Considered watching action movies for research but didn't think my stomach was up to it. So I went for a walk instead, stepping around a pile of vomit next to the front gate that I think I was responsible for.

Round the corner I bumped into Harris walking his pit bull.

He said, 'Nice one at The Orchid last night.' He had to restrain the growling beast by its leash.

'What d'you mean?' I couldn't even remember seeing him at the club.

'Bruv, you were on cracking form. Going round making everyone laugh. It was like the old Ricketts.'

I didn't like the sound of this.

'What was I doing?'

'You were saying that Spielberg could just go and fucking do one, and how you were gonna take a big shit on him and Tarantino and Martin Swayze because you're making a proper movie now and it's gonna be the bollocks.'

'Oh.'

'Then you invited everyone to this film festival and said they already told you how you've got in.'

He carried on walking his animal, but not before delivering an ominous parting shot.

'Me and you'll be having a word about this movie you're making, don't you worry about that, sunshine.'

Monday 25th December

Ho-ho-ho, Merry Christmas.

No surprises among my presents, just envelopes and cash: funding for the film. Although I did get Martin's old hi-fi, two years late, but at least I can start listening to music in my room now, plus having tunes on in the background is supposed to help with writing. Martin also threw in some dance CDs and a pack of Calvin Klein boxer shorts. I thought that giving underwear to your brother was a bit weird, but Martin assured me that *the ladies love 'em* and snapped up the waistband of his own pair.

Then my dear sibling pushed my hair out from my eyes and added, 'It's about time we gave you a makeover, mate.'

I batted his hand away. 'I'm not Ally Sheedy in *The Breakfast Club*.'

Mum said, 'I always thought they ruined her looks in that film.'

'A few snips here and there and we'll have Steve ruining *girls*.'

Dad said, 'Martin!'

'Look at this mop! You look like the bloody missing link, mate!'

He grabbed a handful and tugged.

'Fu— stop it, Martin!'

'Ugh, I'm gonna go wash my hands now.'

'All right, that's enough, Martin,' Mum said.

From me, everyone got a personalised video tape compilation of their scenes from our old home movies, with added music and creative editing. I clocked some disappointed looks during the unwrapping. Hey, it's the thought that counts, and I thought that the money would be better spent on bringing my creative vision to the world.

After eating too much turkey we all vegged out in front of the BBC One Christmas premiere, *Hook*. Verdict: typical Spielbergian schmaltz.

Tuesday 26th December

David came round to give me his verdict on the script.

'This is a joke, right?'

'What is?'

He handed me back the pages.

'I thought it was a Christmas prank at first, except I couldn't find the humour in it. Steve, I didn't agree to help with this project to be a laughing stock.'

'Look, if it's about the lead role, I've been meaning to tell Barry—'

'It's not about that. I actually think the partner is the more interesting part. *If* you can write it, and not just copy whatever movie you've got on in the background at the time.'

I decided that it would be pointless to clarify that no films were playing at any point during the writing process.

'Besides, I don't mind having less screen time so I can help a bit more behind the camera. But we are not making this film without a completed screenplay, Steve. You told me you've read a bunch of books about making films. Why don't you try opening one up about screenwriting?'

Wednesday 27th December

Went round Clive's to talk about his practical effects.

Clive is lucky that his parents appreciate his passion. His dad used to do special effects for *Doctor Who,* that old show that the BBC used to make, and long ago converted his garage into a workshop that the two of them share.

Clive showed me some new blood packs he's designed. He took off his T-shirt and taped one to his chest, with a wire coming out the back with a squeezy thing on the end of it. I simulated firing a gun and Clive squeezed, making it explode in a shower of red.

I said, 'That was wicked.'

'You're going to need a lot of clothes that people don't mind ruining.'

Charity shop to the rescue.

'I've been refining my explosions, too. Watch.'

He threw a combination of bangers, wires and some weird clay stuff into a flowerpot where it blew up. It looked ace and the flowerpot stayed intact.

'My dad says he can pinch some more of that sugar glass from work. Looked great in *Detonator Man*, didn't it?'

Man, this film is going to rule.

Clive said, 'Steve, this one is going to be a proper film, isn't it? Shown at that festival and everything?'

'Oh yeah. We're moving into the big time.'

'So, you'll have proper credits, including me as *practical effects by?*'

'Absolutely.'

'Good.'

Got home intending to do some re-writing, but when I sat down, I started stewing about my chat with David yesterday. Who does he think he is, criticising my script? He said it himself, he's no writer, so what does he know? I put the words on the page, that makes me a writer and therefore I know what I'm doing. Suggesting I read up on how to write a screenplay just proves how clueless he is. Writing is an art, and you can't be taught how to be an artist. Oh yeah, you can do an Art A Level and go on to become an associate professor of artistic expertise, but that doesn't make you an artist.

I knew I made a mistake letting that wanker back into my life.

Saturday 30th December

Bit calmer today.

Reading over the script David threw back in my face, I have to admit that it is a bit all over the shop. Although it pains me, I don't think I'm going to be able to salvage anything from it. I'm just going to have to start again from scratch.

The mistake I made last time was just putting in cool scene after cool scene. What I need to do is list all the cool scenes that the film has to have, then write the script thinking about how my main character, Detective Jack McRiggs, is going to get from one exciting part to the next by way of boring story bits. The only problem is that action doesn't take up as much room on the page as dialogue does, since with the speaking bits you press *enter* for each new person and so the pages fly by. The solution I've come up with is to use lots of long describing words to lengthen the action paragraphs to several pages each.

Starting to feel like I could do this writing thing for a living!

I'd just finished a marathon, finger-aching typing session when I got a phone call from David.

'What are you doing tomorrow night?'

For a second, my mind was blank.

Then I realised what he was talking about. I've been so busy with pre-production that I forgot to speak to the Amigos about our New Year's Eve tradition of watching movies round Gavin's... although no one's brought it up to me, either.

I said, 'I have no plans.'

He said, 'You do now.'

So apparently, I am going to my first New Year's Eve party tomorrow night. If you don't include family ones, which I don't. I considered asking David if I could bring the other three along, but then I thought, maybe *they're* the real reason I'm yet to pull a girl.

Sunday 31st December

As it turns out, I may have been right on the money about what's been preventing me from pulling.

The New Year's Eve party was in this big posh house in Petts Wood. We're talking gate with a code on the outside, big path up to the gaff with grounds (not a front garden, *grounds*), and the place itself looked like one of those huge American houses everyone seems to have in the movies, with pillars either side of the door, balconies around the top floor and no sign of any neighbours.

I was definitely intimidated, and once we got inside it hit me that I didn't know anyone else at the party. But charisma-magnet David was on top form, introducing me around as *a really talented filmmaker*. It certainly helped my confidence and all the free booze played its part, too.

So, there were these two Goth-looking girls who stood out among all the Ralph Lauren shirt-wearing poshos. I got talking to one, Stella, who told me that she wants to be a make-up artist.

I said, 'Like on films?'

'Yeah, maybe.'

'Like people having huge facial injuries with blood spurting out all over themselves?'

(Bear in mind I was already several drinks in when we started chatting.)

But she laughed. 'A bit more subtle than that.'

We were having a wicked time. Turned out Stella knows her business film-wise, with Tim Burton a big favourite, especially *Beetlejuice* and *Batman Returns*. Not really my cup of tea, but I can get on board with it. We were blathering away for ages, but when midnight came, we got separated in the rush to see Big Ben on the TV. I wasn't near her when everyone held hands and sang that 'Old Long Sign' song, and then couldn't find her when the *Happy New Year!* kisses were being exchanged.

But not long after, I was rooting in the fridge for a Blue WKD and felt someone sneak up behind me.

'What happened to my kiss, then?'

I nearly bumped into her when I turned around. And I nearly dropped my drink when she pushed me against the kitchen cabinet and shoved her tongue in my mouth.

So, the next thing I know, she's dragging me into a bedroom and onto this big pile of coats. She's got me pinned down and her tongue is so far down my throat that I can't breathe and her knee is digging into my stomach and her hair is all over my face. Then I'm grabbing hold of her back flesh with one hand and pushing her hair out of my nose with the other. She's heavy, and when I get a chance to pull back and breathe, I see that she has this intense look on her face, enhanced by all the black make-up and piercings. I'm a little bit scared, to be frank.

'Hold on, hold on...'

Then she goes, 'Do you want to feel my tits?'

Well, I take that as my bloody starter for ten and waste no time giving them a good squeeze over her black T-shirt, and then she takes my hands and forces them under her top and *inside her bra*. And man, they are big and they feel like they're overflowing between my fingers. There's something on her left nipple. The nipple is pierced.

Then she rolls off me and goes, with this mischievous look on her face, 'Hey, what kind of girl do you think I am?'

Then before I knew it, we were back in the party, and I spent the rest of the night snogging her on the sofa and at the top of the staircase and against the kitchen door, getting black-out drunk during the breaks for air. I don't remember much about getting home, but I do know that my final thought in the swirling nausea of my dark bedroom, before I leaned over to throw up into the bin and pass out next to it, was that I'd had the best night of my life.

January 1996

Monday 1st January

Worst hangover of my short drinking career. But the pain is offset by wonderful memories of getting off with Stella. Tongue doesn't ache as much as I'd expected.

Picked up the phone, itching to tell someone, which would usually be Clive... but was unsure how he or the other Amigos would react, seeing that I didn't even invite them to the party.

I wonder what movies they watched last night.

Called David instead to see how he was holding up.

'I feel like something crawled into my mouth and died.'

I had expected him to take the piss, since Stella is not only a Goth but quite overweight and you would struggle to describe her as pretty. But all he said was, 'I'm glad you had a good time.'

I remember Martin telling me that you need to wait three days before calling a girl. I have circled January 3rd on my calendar.

Tuesday 2nd January

She called *me!*

I was sitting in my room and heard Mum's cheerful voice come from downstairs: 'Stephen, there's a young lady on the phone for you.'

I leapt off my bed and paused my 'Insomnia' CD single.

Stella was really chilled. I had been worried about her calling me a perv or something, but she just asked how I felt the next morning and what I'd been up to since and told me again that it's so cool that I'm making a feature.

Then she said, 'So you want to meet up for a drink, then?'

I kept calm. 'Okay.'

She suggested The Swan and Mitre, a definite Goth pub. It's up the top of Bromley, where the cool pubs start to die out and become regular pubs again. So I should be safe from bumping into anyone I know. Am not going to allow myself to worry about getting ID'd.

Meanwhile, my co-producer has secured us an editing suite for the second week of Easter. Palmer's Post-Production is in Purley, right at the end of the 119 bus route, through Croydon and out the other end. David asked if I thought that a week was really enough time to edit a whole feature film. I told him that based on how long it usually takes me to edit a ten-minute short, one week will be plenty.

He said, 'But maybe we should book a bit longer, just to be on the safe side?'

I said, 'How much is it costing so far?'

When he told me, I nearly made him cut it down to only one day.

At least I got my Asda wages today. That means that tonight is another pay-day piss-up, but I won't be there, not after what happened last time, as well as how much money I ended up spunking. And anyway, if I'm going to start having actual dates with girls, I'm not gonna need to resort to drunkenly grinding up against them on dance floors in grotty bars.

Instead, having taken a few days off from writing over New Year's, I booted the PC up again. Made some decent progress on the screenplay.

Wednesday 3rd January

Still speeding through the writing, but have hit a brick wall at page forty-three, about half-way through. I know the ending (goodie and baddie face off, goodie saves wife, everything explodes), but I don't know how to get from the page I'm at *to* the ending.

Have also been sweating over locations. We do need somewhere beyond Adrian's house and garden if this film is to look like it has any production value at all.

So I rang Vicky and asked her if she can find us somewhere for an epic shoot-out climax.

She said, 'I'll look into it,' and hung up.

Thursday 4th January

Vicky got back to me already. We can use this warehouse that the school has for storing sports equipment. All we'll need to do is move some old hockey goals and piles of shin pads to one side.

She said, 'It'll be just like *Reservoir Dogs*, trust me.'

I must admit, I'm impressed with how she was able to get us the location so fast. Especially considering school doesn't start again 'til next week.

Have solved my writing dilemma. I'll put down the warehouse climax next, then go back to where I was before, page forty-three, and write the next scene to move the story forward. Then I'll return to the end of the film and write the scene just *before* the climax, and then go back again to the middle to do the next scene there, on page forty-four or whatever. Then I'll return to the end *again* and write the scene before the scene before the warehouse climax. So, by doing that, going back and forth between taking the middle forwards and the end backwards, eventually the two will meet and join together. It'll be like that footage of building the Channel Tunnel they kept showing a few years back, when we broke through a wall and the French builders were on the other side.

As well as revolutionising the writing process, I've also been focusing on how I can make some extra money. I've printed off ads for my Eazy Ironing and dog-walking services and have put them up in local shop windows. Have ruled out washing cars (too cold) and a paper round (doesn't pay enough to make it worth getting up at the crack of dawn to break my back peddling up hills.)

Friday 5th January

Barry's mate from taekwondo, Terry, confirmed that he is in for the feature. And Bazza reckons he'll bring along the whole *dojo*, so now we have a big kung-fu brawl halfway through the film. Adding that in the middle of the script takes me even closer to making my story ends meet. No need to type a blow-by-blow description of the fight, Terry will figure it out on the day.

Did more writing before bed.

Saturday 6th January

My first date since I went to see *Mrs Doubtfire* with Yvette Gunderson in Year 9.

I was so nervous tonight that I forgot to worry about the bouncers and they just waved me in. Stella was already there, sitting at a table, and she stood up and gave me a peck on the cheek. I asked if she wanted a drink and she asked for a pint of Strongbow. I got her that and a Carlsberg, the lowest strength lager, for myself, as I didn't want to get too pissed and start babbling on.

In the end, everything was cool. At first, I fought a constant battle to not look at the nipple ring poking underneath the black fabric of her top, but after a while I relaxed and actually started to pay attention to what she was saying. She talked a lot about Orpington College and her make-up GNVQ.

I said, 'Maybe you could help out on my film.'

She smiled. 'We'll see.'

We had a long snog at the bus stop. I enjoyed it even more than the other night. This time it was more sensual, with our hands all over each other inside our coats. But I was relieved to see her 352 arrive at the stop as I wasn't sure how much more I could take.

Was straight under the bed covers with the tissue box when I got home.

Sunday 7th January

Found it difficult to concentrate during my supermarket shift. Kept imagining lying around naked with Stella on a white rug in front of a roaring fire, her holding her right breast up to me and inviting me to pierce it with a long knitting needle, like that scene with James Woods and Debbie Harry's ear in *Videodrome*.

When I got home, I had to immediately launch myself into catching up with my coursework and working on the screenplay to keep my mind occupied.

It didn't help much. Have to be breaking some kind of wanking world record here.

Who knows where this will all lead? Stella's off to Italy for a few weeks now, something to do with her make-up course, so my horses will have to be held. But we said that we'd keep in touch via email while she's away.

Monday 8th January

Finished the script last night and handed David a printed copy today. Hope he won't say it needs rewriting again. I've got calluses on my two index fingers from all this typing.

Apart from the Channel Tunnel meet-in-the-middle tactic, the major breakthrough was when I realised that I was relying too much on well-known action movies for my influences. So instead, I've been steering away from the blockbusters and focusing on obscure stuff starring people who are usually villains or in supporting roles. The likes of Robert Patrick (*Zero Tolerance, Future Hunters*), Thomas Ian Griffith (*Ulterior Motive, Excessive Force*), Michael Dudikoff (*Avenging Force, River of Death*)... it makes me realise that I have wasted so much of my life locked away in my room watching whatever movies I've been reading about in *Film Fanatic*, when I could have been spending that time watching *obscure* movies. How can I expect to be original now, when my head is so full of scenes and characters and stories that millions of others have seen too? The smart thing is to be like Tarantino. No one realised he'd ripped off that Hong Kong movie for *Reservoir Dogs* until he'd already lapped up all the plaudits. And in *Pulp Fiction* he references films that no one but him has ever heard of. Smart.

David says he'll read the script during the week and then we'll meet up later this week to discuss it. He'll also use the script to set our final budget.

Tuesday 9th January

Gavin and I headed off to this inner-London replica gun shop on the 138 during our double free. Gav tried to sack it off by saying he had coursework to do but I managed to get him out of the common room and onto the bus, which goes all the way to Catford train station. I'd never dared stay on until the end of the route until now.

After managing to get out of Catford without being mugged or killed, we returned with a bag full of borrowed handguns, on long-term loan and with a discount since we got so many. Lucky for us the school doesn't have US-style metal detectors. Originally I didn't want to get any crappy revolvers, but decided to pick up one for Jack McRiggs' elderly partner. To play the partner, we'll age-up David by putting grey acrylic paint in his hair. He'll love it for that precious show-reel of his.

The replica guns took a big chunk from the budget. But they'll be worth every penny.

Wednesday 10th January

After school I had my first client for Eazy Ironing. This old lady had rung me up yesterday and said that she'd like me to come over and 'see to her bloomers'. Then she laughed manically. Must have forgotten her pills.

When I got there today, she was holding a glass of sherry and had purple stains all over her teeth.

She said, 'Come in, young man.' Her voice sounded like a squeaky door opening.

The place was like your worst nightmare of an old person's house. Wilting flowers and that pot puree stuff everywhere, pink carpet, pictures of relatives all over the walls, stale smell.

At first, she just sat there, sipping from her glass, watching me. Then, as I got to work on old woman blouses and skirts and cardigans, she kept on firing all these questions at me. First it was the usual garbage about school, but then she started asking me about whether I had a girlfriend and how I think a woman should be treated, and then she was showing me photos of her ugly granddaughters and asking me whether I would like to give them a kiss under the mistletoe (she still had her Christmas decorations up).

Man, it was hard work, both slaving over a hot iron and batting off her non-stop questions. I would go as far to say that it was one of the creepiest experiences of my life. But the hourly pay is lot better than over at Asda's.

Continued the manual graft when I got back home. I've been painting the toy guns my mates donated, covering up the bright plastic with black, silver and brown.

Halfway through my first shotgun, I remembered why I didn't do an Art A Level. Painting is so boring. It's just using a bunch of different colours, it's not proper creativity like filmmaking. How many ways are there to combine words and images and sounds? Billions. How many colours are there in the world, like, fifty?

But I can't give up now. This acrylic paint was expensive and I bought a shitload.

Stella wasn't joking about the emailing. We've been back and forth every day since she left for Italy. Mostly just what-have-you-been-up-to-

today kind of stuff, me filling her in on the challenges of planning a feature film, her going on about her make-up work at the University of Rome and the city itself, the sights she's been seeing and all that.

Thursday 11th January

Big news. We are no longer doing an action movie.

David met me at the end of my Asda shift and took the bus home with me. As we munched on my standard collection of donuts, cakes and other goodies that simply failed to sell (always seems to happen on my shift, can't imagine why), he told me that he hated the new draft even more than the first. That was bad enough, but then he presented me with the final budget estimate, quipping that we'd need to go and rob a bank to afford it. Could have been good research for the bank robbery in the screenplay, but hey-ho.

He said that the script is just action sequences with padding in between. I nodded, thinking that he was pointing out a positive. But he went on to say that the best action films have some story and characters so the viewer actually knows who is shooting at whom and why.

I asked if there was anything he reckoned we could keep. He shook his head and suggested we change genre to something less expensive.

Great, just when I thought I was done with writing, I'm going to have to start all over again. Again.

But to be honest, I'm actually relieved that we're not doing an action movie. My hands are now more paint than skin and I've only finished one shotgun, plus I haven't managed to find anyone else who will let us use their car, so our chase scene would have looked a bit one-sided.

So, no more action movie. The question now, of course, is what instead?

I suggested to David that we switch to a Tarantino-style crime movie. Mostly character bits and witty dialogue, but with the odd intense burst of violence.

He said, 'But there have been so many knock-off Tarantino movies already.'

'Yeah, but when was the last quality *British* gangster film? *The Long Good Friday*? Remember what Tarantino said when he accepted that French award for *Pulp Fiction?* He properly laid into all that costume drama stuff that we Brits are known for. So, let's show him by making the ultimate '90s British gangster epic!'

David shrugged. 'You better get on with writing it, then.'

Friday 12th January

Gave Ms Harper an update on the fast-moving world of Ricketts Productions' first feature. I told her how I've decided to abandon the action movie idea as not being ambitious enough, and that I want to bring the British film industry up to speed with the Americans by making a gangster film that kicks ass/arse.

She said, 'I'm not sure that's exactly what Tarantino meant in his *Palm d'Or* speech.'

She went on to ask me why I was following the path of another filmmaker and not forging my own.

'Miss... I don't have anything to *say* with my movies. I just want to make them.'

'Maybe, Stephen, you're a little afraid to explore these things within yourself. You think that self-analysis is a sign of weakness, when in fact it will open up your creativity and help develop you as an artist.'

Blimey.

She then gave me an actual practical suggestion: another change of genre. She might be onto something, but I'm going to have to sleep on it.

Monday 15th January

We are making a horror movie!

I can't believe I didn't think of it myself. Horrors do make up 28% of my collection, after all. As Ms Harper pointed out, loads of filmmakers got their big break in the genre and later went on to prestige: Francis Ford Coppola (*Dementia 13*), Oliver Stone (*The Hand*), Brian De Palma (*Sisters*)... yes, even Spielberg (*Duel*). You can make horror effective for little money since it's all about the suspense and fucked-up ideas. Although we'll still use Clive's gore effects and throw the guns into the mix when the characters confront the demon or whatever it turns out to be.

Saw Eamon in the shop and was moaning to him about how I'm going to have to start writing something from scratch *again*. He advised me to write a treatment, a kind of short story of what happens, and hone that with a lot of feedback before moving onto the actual screenplay.

'Nail the treatment, nail the script,' was how he put it.

On the way home, I thought about something Ms Harper said. She reckons I should make a horror film about something that scares *me*. It's a place to start, I guess.

Still keeping up the emails with Stella. We're like pen pals now or something. She told me that they visited the Trevi Fountain and people were talking about a famous scene from *La Dolce Vita*, so I had to pretend that I'd heard of the film. I think it's from one of Ms Harper's old-school European directors.

Wednesday 17th January

Film meeting round David's house after school. I hadn't been there in years, not since back when we were mates... as opposed to whatever we are now. It was the same but also different. Redecorated maybe. I had thought it would be awkward with David's mum, but she was all sweet and smiley as she tucked into my illegally discounted Asda donuts.

Everyone was stoked about making a horror. Not just my boys, with their insatiable bloodlust, but the likes of Vicky and Adrian, who started quoting at each other from their favourite horrors, *Poltergeist* and *Fright Night*. I promised everyone that I'm going to write a cracking script this time, now that I know what I'm doing. I'm definitely going to do a treatment like Eamon suggested, and I've bought a manual by this screenwriting guru named Syd Field. I've never seen the bloke actually credited as writing any films, but if they let him release a book then he must know what he's talking about.

This is my first feature film so I'm playing it by the book. Literally. I'll take some risks when I'm so famous that no one will dare to judge me.

Friday 19th January

Have finally come up with an award-worthy plot.

So, these ace filmmakers are making a new horror movie. During the shoot, a killer starts knocking them off one by one and in ways that play homage to famous onscreen deaths. The main character will be the maverick writer/producer/director, who is tormented by his deepest fear: whether he can live up to his talent and fulfil his destiny to save his country's film industry from mediocrity. He ends up making the greatest horror film of all time and saving the lives of his cast and crew to boot. Would be good if all this somehow leads to him getting his end away too, if we manage to get any girls beyond Vicky on the project.

Everyone's going to be well impressed.

David still wants to play a smaller part so that he can help out behind the camera, leaving me with Barry as my leading man again. Great.

Saturday 20th January

At a family do today, Eamon and I listed some of the famous horror deaths for my killer to imitate:

> *Psycho's* shower scene.
> Getting tossed around the room by an evil spirit like in *A Nightmare on Elm Stree*t.
> Sliced up by wires a la *Hellraiser*.
> Picking someone up while they're in a sleeping bag and bashing them to death against a tree from *Friday the 13th Part VII: The New Blood*.

Getting your intestines pulled out like in *Day of the Dead*.

Admittedly some of these are more achievable than others. But if I can come up with, say, twelve famous death scenes, and I devote around six pages/minutes of screen time to each one, then that's an hour. Then I've only got to write a couple of pages of story between each kill to pad the script out to feature length.

Eamon reckons my director should be filming his horror movie in a notorious murder house, and it's actually the old killer who comes back to carry on where he left off. And it'll need a twist too, so like he's also someone from the crew or something.

Despite being on good form coming up with ideas for my film, something is definitely not right with Uncle Eamon. He was drinking loads again and this time it was only a daytime do. And he was getting all mushy with me, thanking me for involving him with my filmmaking for once. Talk about Awkward City.

Tuesday 23rd January

Rang David as soon as I got home from school. He loves the horror pastiche idea, calling it 'self-referential and ironic' and saying that it reminded him of *Wes Craven's New Nightmare*. I was a bit put out that he compared my idea to someone else's, what with it being so blazingly original and everything. You never know, this film might lead to other people getting compared to *me!* Hitchcockian, Cronenbergian... introducing, Rickettsian!

Have to calm down.

But I'm so excited!

David and I were on the phone for over an hour, reminiscing about when we used to secretly borrow his dad's VHS tapes, like *An American Werewolf in London* or *The Shining* or *The Thing*, and watch them up in David's room in the dark, next to each other on his bed (*above* the covers).

It was a bit weird talking about that stuff. But yes, kind of nice.

Wednesday 24th January

Did my first dog-walking after school today. What a weird sub-culture. Other people with dogs wave to you and then the mutts get interested in each other, so while they're busy sniffing each other's bums you have to engage in idle chit-chat with the owner. It didn't matter how many times I said I was walking the animals for other people, these canine-obsessives still asked me loads of questions and fussed over them and also expected me to fuss over *their* dogs. Still, it all means more cash for the budget.

Meanwhile, writing a treatment has turned out to be a piece of piss. You just churn it out stream-of-consciousness style, like this book we did in GCSE English by Virginia-someone.

Thursday 25th January

How long should a treatment be? There's nothing to it: this happens, then that happens, then roll credits. Couple of sheets of A4 is enough, surely.

Well then. Bang: I'm done.

But I'm resisting the urge to hand it over to David just yet. I'm going to do a first: actively invite feedback on my work.

Saturday 27th January

Met with Nigel in The Swan and Mitre on my Asda lunch break. He was excited to take my treatment away for a read. As well he should be.

So there we are sitting with our burgers and our pints (the uniform gets you served) and at one point that 'Wonderwall' song that's been all over the radio comes on.

Nigel goes to me, 'You know, people reckon Oasis just rip off The Beatles.'

I'm no expert on guitar music so just shrug.

'The way I see it,' he continues, 'The Beatles may technically be better and the original pop band and all that, but their songs don't make me *feel* like Oasis do. Or Genesis.' He smiles all shyly from mentioning his favourite band. 'Sometimes I think the really old acts are over-hyped, romanticised by the previous generation.'

'Out of nostalgia?'

'Yeah.'

I think about that. 'So, you reckon in thirty years us lot will be doing the same about Oasis and Blur and whoever?'

'Probably!'

'What's the deal with Genesis anyway? With the school play and everything?'

Nigel takes a big sip of lager, drawing the moment out.

'Well,' he goes, 'when we moved here from Gloucester last summer, I didn't know anyone. It was the holidays, but I had no one to hang about with. So, I spent a lot of time in my room, writing and listening to music. Mostly I put the last two Genesis albums on repeat, just swapping between the cassettes.'

'But what's that got to do with Shakespeare?'

'Well, one night I had *Film 95* on in the background and Barry Norman was interviewing Kenneth Branagh about this new adaptation of *Hamlet* he's doing, and I'd actually just studied the play for GCSE English. They showed a clip of the *to be or not to be* scene just as I was listening to Genesis' "Land of Confusion" and the two seemed to complement each other. The words of the play sort of blended together with the lyrics of the song in my mind. Then I dug out my old copy of *Hamlet* and as I flicked through it, I started to see parallels to loads more Genesis tracks.'

I thought about this. 'So, two unrelated things mixed together in your head to create something new?'

'Yeah. Weird, right? It shouldn't work, but for me it does and... I dunno, maybe it doesn't, who knows. People go on about there being nothing original out there, and that's probably true, so maybe it's more about which ideas you put together, or your approach... or something like that.'

Sunday 28th January

Emailed the treatment to Eamon. With him and Nigel I now have two second opinions coming my way. If either think they're getting a co-writer credit they've got another thing coming.

Wednesday 31st January

Cannot believe the email I got back from Eamon. I'm still fuming. Here are the highlights, if you can call them that.

You haven't nailed a consistent tone, the events swing from melodrama to comedy to intense violence.

(Well yeah, Eamon, I'm attempting something no one's ever done before and I'm mashing up genres. Of course the tone is going to vary.)

Have you thought about the target audience for this film?

(Yes: anyone with the good taste to watch it.)

Are you making sure your protagonist is relatable?

(Well, he's based on me and I'm a real person, so if the audience can't relate to a real person, then that's their fault, not mine.)

I feel like it just moves from one kill to the next.

(This coming after he literally sat with me at the family do and discussed different ways to kill people off. Unbelievable.)

The twist comes out of nowhere.

(Well, if you see it coming then it's not much of a twist, is it?)

You end on a deus ex machina. One golden rule of writing is to never do this!

(I don't know what *deus ex machina* means and I'm not going to track down a Gaelic dictionary to find out.)

Feel so let down. Eamon must have been drunk, or I certainly hope he was.

See why I never asked for his help before?

February 1996

Thursday 1st February

Bit of a row with David on the phone after school.

He wanted my uncle's verdict on the treatment and I told him that Eamon called it the best thing he's ever read.

'Really?'

'Oh what, that's so hard to believe?'

In fairness, maybe *best ever* was stretching it a bit.

So I reigned things in a bit by making up some feedback.

I said, 'Eamon does think that the kills aren't gory enough. But it's because I didn't want to make the treatment too long by describing everything in detail. Oh, and he also warned me about making my first feature *too* good, otherwise I might struggle to live up to it for the rest of my career.'

David was silent for a bit. Then he said, 'And you're getting feedback from Nigel too, right?'

'Yep.'

'Is he going to email it to you like Eamon did?'

'No, we're gonna meet up.'

'Right, in that case I want to come along.'

'Um, you can't.'

'Why not?'

'Because... the best time for me is this Sunday lunchtime, and you said you're in Reading visiting your sister.'

'Okay, what about tomorrow night? You're busy then?'

'Well, Stella is back in town and so I have to keep tomorrow night free in case she wants to go out.'

'Tomorrow.'

'Yeah.'

'But you haven't arranged anything yet.'

'No, but she might be trying to call me right now.'

He sighed. 'And I suppose you're also busy on Saturday night?'

'Is that so hard to believe?'

'*Are* you?'

'Well, what if Stella wants another date?'

'Following on from your as-of-yet imaginary date the day before?'

'Yeah, and?'

'Steve, I highly doubt that is going to happen.'

'It might.'

'Yes, I'm sure your animal magnetism is such that a girl just can't stand to wait beyond twenty-four hours to see you again.'

'Oh, *that's* nice.'

'Look, Steve, just try not to be... led by the wrong organ.'

'What's that supposed to mean?'

'I just mean don't get distracted.'

'Distracted? She was saying that she'll do make-up for us. So it would technically be a business meeting. Two business meetings, potentially.'

Another sigh. 'Okay, whatever, you can meet with Nigel on your own.'

'What, I need your permission now?'

'No, but I think this project might benefit from a bit more—'

'From a bit more *what?*'

'Don't make me say something we'll both regret, Steve.'

'Oh, you want to talk about things we regret, do you?'

I'm not sure who slammed the phone down first.

Sunday 4th February

Got up early, well before I needed to leave for my shift at the supermarket, in order to walk some dogs and then do the creepy sherry-drinking old crone's ironing. Even though we are saving money by going from action to horror, I still need to top up the budget.

Met Nige in The Swan and Mitre for lunch again to discuss the treatment. We were both on our breaks from work and as we sat down with our pints, I mentioned his Early Learning Centre uniform.

He shrugged. 'Keeps me in beer money.'

I said, 'My house is a day care so I know what it's like to be surrounded by little brats.'

'On the plus side, you probably get some good-looking mums coming in to pick up their kids.'

'Not really, only David Nolan.'

'Oh, that guy from St. Olaves who's co-directing your film?'

'Wait... *co-directing?*'

'That's what Barry was saying. What's the deal with you and this David? Barry told me that his mum and your mum go back years and that the two of you used to be inseparable, but then suddenly you stopped hanging out with him and no one knows why.'

I grimaced and changed the subject.

'Never mind all that. So come on, Nige. Tell me what you thought about the treatment.'

Nigel's feedback was mostly about making sure I know what it is that each of my characters wants. Well, the killer is insane and wants to kill everyone, and everyone else wants to not be killed. Done. Nigel also said that, as it stands, you don't care about any of the victims, so their deaths have no impact. What a weird thing to say. How many people came out of *Candyman* or *Nightbreed* or *Freddy's Dead: The Final Nightmare* lamenting the death of poor... whoever? No one cares about the victims in horror movies. And Nigel is also wrong about the deaths not having any impact: we're going to push the envelope with our gore so far that people will be vomiting into their laps.

Rubbish advice notwithstanding, we had a good chat, mostly about horror films and good-looking girls from school. We were both nearly late back to work.

'Don't forget,' Nigel said as we stood up and drained our pints, 'I'm happy to help with the actual filming, anything you need, just ask.'

Nigel is obviously a smart and creative bloke, maybe even as smart and creative as me. Which is exactly why I want him well away from my set.

Monday 5th February

Film meeting round Adrian's house, and I saw a bit more of it than the night I came round before we went out boozing. The cabinets and walls and shelves and mantelpieces are choc-a-block with medals, trophies, certificates and awards. Adrian and his brothers are like my dad's dream sons.

I emailed the treatment around yesterday and assumed that cast and crew had all read it before the meeting. Same difference though, really. David seemed happy enough, probably because I actually did some rewriting for once. What I did was, I used Microsoft Word's find/replace function and swapped some words around. *Large* for *big*, *cuts* for *stabs*, *terrified* for *scared*, *shouts* for *screams*, and so on. After that, it was like a whole new film.

'Okay then,' David said, leading the meeting as we all settled down in Adrian's cavernous living room. 'From Steve's treatment, we now know the logistics of what we need. We can start to plan locations (such as this house, thank you, Adrian) practical effects (thank you, Clive) and get together our props, costumes, and equipment. And you,' he turned to me, 'you've got six weeks to draft and redraft a killer screenplay.'

'*Six weeks*? But we don't film for ten.'

'Easter is in nine weeks, actually.'

'... Right.'

'And I want us to have three weeks' rehearsal time so we'll be more efficient on set.'

Rehearsal time?

Well, I guess rehearsing means less screwing up which means fewer takes and so burning through less of the expensive 35mm film. There's no way I'm buying any on top of what we got for free from Eamon.

Tuesday 6th February

We were all given sealed white envelopes in today's tutor time. It's never anything good inside when they do that, never a birthday card or a pass for a free day off.

This time it was a reminder about parents' evening next Thursday.

I *have* been being a good boy and doing all my coursework, including Media Studies write-ups of the feature's pre-production and essays analysing its plot, not to mention pretending that it has *themes* and going on about those as well. But I've also been half-arsing it. Quarter-arsing, truth be told. Not to mention that the forgery over my Media coursework arrangement is bound to come out eventually.

Came home to a message on the answer phone from Stella. Mum had listened to it so of course asked me a million questions.

Christ. I can't wait 'til I move out and don't have to share a phone with my parents anymore.

Stella and I arranged to meet this Saturday night, somewhere quieter this time and with no bouncers: The Pickhurst, just up the road in a quiet part of West Wickham.

We ended up chatting on the phone for ages, going on about films and other less important topics.

And then it happened.

We were talking about where we live and I mentioned that The Pickhurst is just around the corner from her house.

'Yeah,' she said all flirtatiously, 'maybe when the pub chucks out, we'll pop back to mine for a bit more.'

Holy crap.

A bit more?

Surely, she can't mean...

As soon as I put down the phone, I picked it up again and rang Martin.

He said, 'This is it, mate.'

'You reckon?'

'If you play your cards right.'

Have arranged to meet up with my brother the night before I see Stella for a full strategic briefing.

Thursday 8th February

Snowed today. A welcome sight in December, but a lot of bloody good it does in February.

The atmosphere was appropriately frosty in Psychology class. Mr Cheerful himself, my old pal Bryant, handed me back my homework with a big fat *D* in the top corner. Bigger than usual, bigger than necessary, big enough for everyone else to see.

Oh, did I say 'handed'? He *slammed* the thing down on my desk.

After class, we had a cosy little chat.

'Look, Ricketts, this isn't some GCSE kiddies' play time. I don't care if you think you're George bloody Lucas, I'm not having someone pull down my class average. Especially when you're smart enough to get an A, even if you do your best to pretend otherwise.'

All the while he's prattling on (Lucas, yeah right!) I'm thinking about whether shagging Stella will impact the film. Would it be like how they say athletes shouldn't have sex before the big race? Would it affect only the shoot or could it mess up my pre-production too? Or have I got it backwards, and getting lots of sex will actually improve my directing?

Bryant started to wrap things up.

'I'm going to enjoy chatting to your mum and dad next week,' he was saying. 'And don't expect me to bend the rules for you like your pal Ms Harper. Now get out of my classroom.'

Taking A Level Psychology has turned out to be a total waste of time. We haven't studied any famous nutters or psychos and so I haven't learnt anything to inspire villains for my future movies. Pointless.

Friday 9th February

The prospect of losing my virginity is tantalisingly close and I'm terrified. Is David right about Stella being a potential distraction from the film? Or is he just jealous?

Martin and I met in his Penge local and, once he had got over the Stella Artois *wife-beater* and *one pint or two?* jokes, he let rip with the big brotherly advice.

'When you're getting down to business,' he said, 'don't rush things. But don't take it too slowly, either, or you'll look like you don't know what you're doing. Take the initiative, but let her think that she's the one in charge. And if she gets all cuddly and talkative afterwards, just ride it out, try not to snap at her or you'll never hear the end of it.'

'Okay... but Martin, what about how to *get* to getting down to business? How exactly *do* I play my cards right?'

He took a big sip of his Kronenbourg and shrugged. 'Sounds like you're in there already, mate.'

He warned me to be careful because I'm entering my prime pulling years and don't want to get tied down to one bird. Then he gave me a condom to put in my wallet, which I examined like it was an alien artefact.

Well, Stella's bound to be more experienced than me, she should know what's what. I mean, she could hardly be any *less* experienced.

Saturday 10th February

The big day. Woah boy.

Made sure that I was at the pub before Stella this time. Martin told me that it makes you look assertive. So, I got there an hour and a half early and had three pints by myself.

I was beyond tipsy by the time she arrived. She was hard to miss: big black boots with metal bits all up them, a long black coat, black top and skirt, black make-up. She had these fish-net tights on which made my chest tighten.

I'd decided that this time I *was* going to get pissed. The idea was to strike a balance between gaining confidence and not losing the ability to get it up when the time came.

We were getting along famously and soon it was 11 o'clock.

So I went for it.

'So, Stella.'

'Yeah?'

'Stella, Stella, Stella.'

I fixed her with a serious stare.

'... Yes?'

'Tell me.' I gave her a mischievous smile.

'Tell you what?' She returned my smile and my confidence rose.

'How come you wanted to meet up here, specifically, in this particular place?'

'I dunno. It's got a nice village pub feel, don't you think?'

'Near to your house, too.' I raised my eyebrows.

'Well, yeah, I walked here.'

She wasn't getting the hint. Too subtle. I had to step it up a gear. I took another wobbly sip of lager.

'Look, it's great if your parents are cool with you doing things like this, but I do need to make it clear that I can't stay the night. I'd get too many questions when I got home the next morning and—'

'Wait, *stay the night?*'

'Yeah. I don't know how long the whole thing will take. I guess that's mostly down to me, ha-ha-ha...'

'You thought I'd met up with you so you could *stay the night?*'

'You were saying... about going back to yours... once we get chucked out from here?'

'I meant to carry on drinking. And I was joking.'

'Oh.'

It was nothing dramatic. She didn't throw her drink in my face like in the movies. She just gathered her things, stood up and left the pub without another word.

I finished my pint of lager, polished off what she'd left of her cider, and then walked home in the snow.

Seems I ended up playing my cards pretty wrong in the end.

Sunday 11th February

Woke up this morning and realised that nearly a week has passed and I still haven't made a start on turning my horror treatment into a horror script.

Huh. Maybe David *was* right about Stella being a distraction.

Well, there are no distractions anymore. Except, now that I'm back to being a hopeless loser with no chance of losing my virginity, I'm too depressed to write.

There's only one solution: pop into Video Nation tonight and then skive off school tomorrow for a horror marathon in the name of research.

Monday 12th February

Watched the films I grabbed from the shop last night back-to-back all day.

I'm actually going to need to bunk off again tomorrow if I'm to finish them all. Told my mum that I was feeling 'under the weather' this morning and will do the same tomorrow. She just busies herself with her kids downstairs and leaves me to it in my room.

All this gory onscreen violence is proving to be a good distraction from the real-life horror of my non-existent love life.

Stella hasn't called. No emails, either.

Tuesday 13th February

Brain melting out of ears. Eyes bleary. Mouth dry. I feel dirty but know that a shower won't help.

In the past forty-eight hours I barely slept, didn't leave the house once, and only got up to go to the bathroom or boil the kettle for a pot noodle.

Here's what I watched: *Driller Killer*, *A Nightmare on Elm Street Part 3: The Dream Warriors*, *Hellraiser 2: Hellbound*, *From Beyond*, *The Burning*, *The Last House on the Left*, *City of the Living Dead*, *Hell Night*, *My Bloody Valentine*, *Prom Night*, *The Slumber Party Massacre*, and *Driving Miss Daisy*.

Only joking, actually finished up with *I Spit on Your Grave*.

I had intended to launch straight into writing the screenplay while still all charged up, but after that long staring at one screen I couldn't face another, so I went for a walk. I felt like dunking my head in what remains of the snow.

When I got back home, I sat down and immediately churned out twelve script pages.

And I've got a title: *The Murder House*.

Rang up David for some human interaction and he was pleased that I've been writing. Neither of us apologised for our row the other day but we are on okay terms again.

He did suggest that I change the title. And I was keen to show him that I do respond to feedback.

The film will be called *Murder House*.

Wednesday 14th February

Eamon was round ours today having A Serious Chat with my mum about something or other.

'Haven't seen you around the shop for a while,' he said when I came into the living room with David in tow.

'We must keep missing each other,' I replied coldly. I still haven't forgiven him for the unfair feedback he emailed me.

'Heard you came and grabbed some videos on Sunday. I was in my office, you should have popped in.'

'Yeah, I was in a hurry, lots of homework to do. Like you told me, education is important.'

Stick your *deus ex machina* where the sun doesn't shine, mate.

Eamon asked me if I'd found his comments on my treatment useful and since David was sitting right there, it was a bit awkward. So, I quickly changed the subject by asking Eamon if he had any tips for the production side of things. After a bit my mum went off to paint a bowl of fruit or whatever and we film folk took a round of tea into the dining room.

Eamon asked me and David what we know about lighting.

I said, 'Basically nothing.'

'You'll need a cinematographer, also known as a director of photography, or DP, who's worked with 35mm. This is a different ball game to those tapes from Dixons that you use on your video camera.'

David said, 'Absolutely.' But I think like me he only sort of understood.

My plan had been to borrow some lights from school and just set them up myself. But I guess we're going to need one of these DPs as well if we want to look professional.

David said, 'There's a guy I know, friend of my sister's, who I think would like to help. I'll set up a meeting.'

David also insisted that we not scrimp on the sound either, that we need to get someone dedicated to the audio side of things.

I said, 'Oh, I'll take care of that.'

'Really? Nice one.'

Not sure how exactly, but I didn't want David to be the only one who can bring in crew members.

After Eamon left, David wondered why I haven't asked my uncle to help out on set.

Since *stubborn pride* seemed too pathetic a reason, I told him the first thing that came into my head.

'Oh, I did ask Eamon, but he's away when we're shooting at a... video shop owners' conference, in Bradford.'

And, pre-empting his next question, I added that Nigel will be away that same week too, following Genesis on tour.

David said, 'What unfortunate coincidences.'

'Yeah, I know.'

I mean, come on. Why on Earth would I want people who don't have the capacity to appreciate my vision around when I'm trying to bring it to life?

Once David had gone, I checked the post. No Valentine's card from Stella.

You know, in case the suspense was killing you or anything.

Thursday 15th February

Just got back from parents' evening. I'm still trying to get my head round it.

So, there I was in the car on the way there, terror flowing through my body, picturing the ways all my misdeeds were finally going to catch up with me. I even toyed with throwing myself out the door when we stopped at a red light.

The walk up to the sports hall was the longest of my life. The back of my neck and all the way down was laced with sweat.

And then... nothing!

I wasn't worried about Philosophy. That's one where I've got my blagging down to a fine art, since the coursework is all speculate-this and argue-both-sides-that, and we're even fucking off to Berlin soon to absorb the lessons from the 20th century's greatest thinkers, or something like that.

But I was dreading the other subjects.

Yet despite promising to tear into me, Bryant was cheerful and complimentary. Miss Yates glossed over 'our brief wobble' in General Studies and described me as 'imaginative and one-of-a-kind'.

Then came Media Studies.

'Stephen,' Ms Harper said as we sat down. 'Stephen, Stephen, Stephen.'

'Hi, Ms Harper.'

My mum said, 'How is he doing?'

'We know he likes your class,' added my dad. 'It's the only one he talks about.'

'He's doing great. He really is.' And she was beaming from ear to ear.

It was all too surreal.

Ms Harper even went off-piste to give me all this advice, like it was just the two of us having one of our after-class chats. She wanted me to reflect on why I went so gimmicky when I filmed the school play. I asked how come stuff like that is okay for those old directors, like when we studied the long tracking shot Welles pulled off in the opening of *Touch of Evil*, or Hitchcock making it look like *Rope* was all done in one take. She said that they did it for story reasons, not to be a 'flashy, shallow, MTV director'.

'You think that studying the old masters is purely an academic exercise,' she went on. 'But you can learn real, practical lessons from them.'

'You mean rip them off.'

'I mean *absorb*. Not scavenge, not just picking off the pieces like a vulture. Rather, taking things in and being influenced.'

She didn't bring up the topic of me being allowed to do my feature film for my Media Studies coursework, so all parties remain ignorant about my forgery of the permission form.

When we got home, I was so relieved about how the night turned out that I started to bang out the *Murder House* screenplay like nobody's business.

Sunday 18th February

Another weekend over and all I've done is write. It's been nearly two months since I last went for a night out on the piss. Now that I've bollocksed things up with Stella (have given up hope that she will contact me), I guess I should really be out on the pull again. But I'm not.

Am over halfway through the script now.

Tuesday 20th February

The snow has finally all melted and we're actually getting the occasional bit of springtime sunshine, heaven forbid.

So today, David and I meet up with this director of photography guy. He's in his early-twenties, a Dutch bloke named Lukasz. He's studying at some London uni and wants to build up his show-reel (who doesn't?)

We met him in The Firkin, which was David's choice. It's in the middle of Bromley so could be called a *cool pub*, but no one ever boasts about drinking there so I'd never considered trying it before. It does seem decent, with a jukebox, pool tables and dart boards.

So anyway, we sit down with this Lukasz, David and me with our pints, him with a gin and tonic. Lukasz is skinny with glasses and a side-parting, and his untucked shirt reached the knees of his cargo pants. He seems like kind of a nerd, but it might just be the European cultural difference. First impressions are that he is a pretty straight arrow, someone who can be trusted to get on with the job with no drama. He carries this kind of quiet confidence, with no bullshit.

So the three of us are sitting there and then, with barely any pleasantries, Lukasz goes to me and David, 'Who do you like?'

He and I exchange a glance.

'Cinematographers. Who do you admire?'

'Er...'

This Lukasz leans back and strokes his bumfluff chin beard.

'You like popular movies, yes?'

'Some of them.'

'You do not know Jan De Bont, from *The Hunt for Red October* and many Paul Verhoeven films? Michael Chapman, from *The Fugitive* and early Martin Scorsese films? Robert Richardson, who works with Oliver Stone and is Scorsese's current DP?'

David and I look at him blankly.

'I need to come to your house so we can watch *Basic Instinct* together.'

Excuse me?

Thursday 22nd February

Following the love-in that was my parents' evening, I came crashing down to Earth again today in Media Studies.

Ms Harper warned me that I am slipping again in my coursework.

Blimey. Make your bloody mind up.

Then she goes and tell me that she's really gone out on a limb for me, and I need to remember the risk both she and I have taken, and that Ofsted are breathing down her neck.

Hold on, the feature-for-coursework stuff was *her* idea. Doesn't she realise that I'm under enough pressure already?

Friday 23rd February

Broke up for half-term hols, with the Philosophy trip coming up during it.

Wrote another eleven screenplay pages. Feel like I'm going to have to give this script guru bloke Syd Field co-credit at this rate. I've been following the template in his book beat by beat, which has made writing so much easier. I barely even have to think about what I'm doing now.

Looked over my Media Studies coursework again as well, to see if I could improve it. It's fine. I don't know what the hell else I'm supposed to do.

Saturday 24th February

Got another twenty script pages done in the morning.

In the afternoon, Lukasz and David came round my house, the former bringing a few films with him. I was glad that he brought his own copy of *Basic Instinct*, as mine has gone fuzzy in certain scenes. I was even gladder when he didn't want to watch those bits that everyone fast-forwards to. Instead, he showed us the part in the car after Michael Douglas has picked Sharon Stone up to take her in for questioning.

'Okay,' this Lukasz said, the three of us sitting on the edge of my bed. 'Watch the light. You see it?'

I said, 'Yes, I can see the light.'

'You see how it moves back and forth on them because they are driving, yes?'

'Right...'

'Watch when it goes onto her face.'

We watched. There it was: as Sharon delivers the line 'he falls for the wrong woman', the light hits her face and lingers there.

'You see? You see it?'

David said, 'Oh yeah.'

'You think that was an accident? You notice now because I tell you. In a cinema, you don't see it but you still know it happens. You *feel* it, and so, in the scene, you feel more.'

We nodded.

Next, he put on Ridley Scott's *The Duellists*.

'This is the last shot. Watch the man.'

'Harvey Keitel.'

'Yes. Now watch the sky.'

We watched as the light hit the camera and made this bright flash, like if you look right at the sun.

Lukasz said, 'That is a lens flare. No accident. See how it makes it look like God is reaching down and touching him, judging him.'

David and I nodded along again.

David said, 'That lens flare stuff, that happens a lot in *Die Hard*.'

'Yes. Jan De Bont. Same DP as *Basic Instinct*. A Dutch cinematographer making it in Hollywood.' And he gave us this brilliant, proud smile. 'But in that film, this effect is used to increase the intensity. It makes the action more frenetic, the frame feels more crowded and so we feel as claustrophobic as the hero, trapped in that building and fighting for his life.'

I said, 'I think I understand. You're saying that you can make lots of cool things happen with light that people might not even notice, or that they will notice but not be sure why it's there, and this'll make the film more effective.'

'Yes.'

'You're in.'

Up until now, I'd just wanted to smack the viewer in the face with things like gory effects. But this under-the-covers stuff can have even more impact. Wow.

Finished the first draft of the screenplay just before bed and sent it to David, Eamon and Nigel in the same email. If they give some positive feedback, I will of course take it on board. The trouble is, all anyone's given me so far is negativity. It's easy to be a critic, but how about trying to *encourage* a struggling artist for once?

After all that hard work writing, I deserve something for me. I've decided I need a clapper board and a director's chair. If I've got a proper cast and crew that I'm ordering around, how am I going to get them to respect me if I don't even have something to snap shut on 'action'? And what am I supposed to sit on, the floor? Maybe I can get a customised chair, like with my name on the back. That would be so fucking cool.

Sunday 25th February

David and I went round Adrian's gaff today to go over the location in full.

The house is ideal. Three floors and with a creepy-as-hell attic to boot. So many ominous corridors and corners for jump scares. Adrian has a big shower, which will be perfect for the *Psycho* tribute death, and a garage with an automatic door, so the *Omen*-style decapitation scene is going to look brilliant.

We'll film the majority in and around the (murder) house, and then we have Vicky's sports equipment warehouse that we can use for the nightmare and flashback sequences that will pad out the running time. In the script, I've left plenty of scenes blank and just written *insert creepy nightmare/flashback sequence here*.

Wednesday 28th February

Bit of respite from film concerns with the Philosophy trip to Berlin.

Our A Level class met the GNVQ rabble (who are coming along for their *cultural* unit, or something) outside the school at the crack of dawn. Never thought I would be at the place at such an ungodly hour, and I never want to be again, either. Anyway, we piled onto a coach to

Gatwick and I ended up sitting next to Dean Harris. It was like that outing to the National History Museum back in Primary School, when we spent the whole journey playing two-player link-up *Tetris* on our Game Boys.

We've barely pulled away and he's leaning into me.

'I'm gonna get my nuts off on this trip, Ricketts.'

I don't remember him saying *that* on the way to the museum.

Harris moves in even closer. The stench of fags is unbearable. 'Broke up with Chantelle, didn't I? Gotta get back in the game, ain't I?'

'Um, yeah, definitely.'

'And you're gonna help me.'

And with that, he pops his headphones on and goes back to his Snoop Doggy Dog CD.

I was hoping for a movie on the flight but no such luck. Instead, I closed my eyes and replayed a medley of *Executive Decision*, *Passenger 57* and *Alive*.

Probably should have left out *Alive*.

I don't have any mates in Philosophy, so they've got me staying with the Sads, Kevin and Peter. They started playing *Magic: The Gathering* immediately after we dumped our bags in the room. That card game does look quite interesting... but then again, I do want to have sex one day.

They've hardly got us staying in the Ritz. I didn't know what a *hostel* was (I had thought the *s* was a typo), but it turns out to be the kind of place where backpackers and people on a gap year stay. Typical cheap move by this school. We're in bunkbeds without guards on the sides, so I hope I don't roll over and fall out the bloody thing in the middle of the night.

Lying on my top bunk after lights-out, face about two inches from the ceiling, I thought about what Harris said on the coach.

How the hell can *I* help *him* get laid?

Maybe what Harris meant is that if I help him out he'll help me back in kind.

There *are* plenty of girls on this trip, but it's but impossible to think about them in the way I'd like to with those two clowns snoring only feet away. I keep thinking about David instead. A whole jumble of things, but mostly worrying about what his feedback on the script will be this time round.

Thursday 29th February

Turns out Harris wants to pull Vicky. Vicky Motson!

He dropped this bombshell over German-brand cornflakes in this big canteen, where teachers, students and backpackers alike served ourselves from this buffet of your standard breakfast fare, with the addition of about a million types of sausage.

I craned my neck. I spotted Vicky sitting a few tables away and watched her spoon Coco Pops into her mouth while simultaneously trying to blow her nose and read *The Lord of the Rings*.

I said, 'Why?'

Harris said, 'Forbidden fruit, innit? And the posh ones are always goers. What, you think I can't do it?' His tone was veering into give-me-your-lunch-money territory.

'I'm sure you can. But how do I fit in?'

'You know her, don't you?'

'Not really.'

'Ain't she doing that film with you?'

'Well, yeah...'

'There you go, then. All I need is an in. We're gonna be out drinking tonight in *das Bierhall* or whatever it's fucking called, right?

I'm an expert at pulling birds, but I ain't used to going up to no Head Girl. So, you just start banging on to her about coursework or whatever you nerds talk about, and then you go, "Oi, listen, you know that Dean Harris? He's a proper quality geezer, ain't he?"'

'Well...'

'Look, Ricketts, one back scratches the other, don't it? I can do you a favour back, can't I?'

'What favour?'

'Get me down the road to her knickers first, then we'll talk.'

Then he got up and left, leaving me and his breakfast tray behind.

Then my roommates, the two Sads, sat down and began playing their ghouls and goblins card game. The one who has slightly fewer spots, Kevin, started to deal me in.

I said, 'Christ, leave me alone!' and bolted up from the table.

So later on, we're all touring this Holocaust memorial that was like a maze of different-sized grey blocks, being told by some speccy German how Hitler burned books from philosophers like Hegel and Kant, and the whole time I'm wondering how exactly I can get Vicky to talk to Harris. She barely talks to *me*. David, Captain Charisma, tends to handle her for film matters.

The evening was a meal at this high-ceilinged schnitzel pub, sitting at benches eating sausages and drinking beer while a Godawful oompah band did their thing up on stage. They could have found somewhere that played some banging German techno, but no. At least we were able to get pissed, the teachers obviously not giving a toss that we are underage now that we're on foreign soil, and they were knocking back plenty of their own steiners of Kolsch as well. This is probably the best holiday they've had in years.

Just like at school, talk soon turned to where people were heading out to, and also just like back home, I wasn't involved in that talk. Vicky, by some miracle, gets included by the cool groups, and so I had to act quickly before she disappeared to a discothèque or whatever they have out here.

While looking for Vicky across the floor of the pub, I bumped into a very drunk Ruth.

'Hey! It's Mr Steven Sp—'

'Don't say it, Ruth, *please*.'

'What's *your* problem?'

Emboldened by tankards of high-strength German lager, I came out with it.

'Why are you so different when you're with other people? If you weren't on your own right now you wouldn't even talk to me.'

'You saying I'm two-faced?'

'You're the one who said it.'

She frowned, searching her foggy mind for a train of thought to catch.

'I really do think that your films are good,' she slurred. 'I was upset when you never came to my fireworks party.'

'Were you now.'

'You know, I could help you on this long film you're doing. It would be so much fun!'

'Sure, Ruth. Tell you what, I'll get back to you.'

She gave me a drunken thumbs-up and staggered off, straight into the arms of a German waiter.

I carried on searching for Vicky. I found her hanging around not far from where Harris happened to be, and when he noticed me, he gave me an egging-on look in her direction.

I saddled up to her and said, 'Hey, Vick.'

She offered me an uninterested smile.

'So, er, about the film... um, do you reckon we can still use that equipment warehouse as a location?'

'Yes. Why wouldn't we?'

'Oh good, that's great. Hey, so did you know, Dean Harris is really into films as well?'

Right on cue, Harris leaned in with his hand out and gave her his best reptilian grin.

It was like a switch being flicked. Vicky started fawning all over Harris, shaking his hand and giggling.

Harris said, *'Wie heisst du?'* in an *'Allo 'Allo!* German accent.

She said, *'Ich heisse Vicky.'*

It was nauseating.

Job done, I went to the gents. And when I returned, everyone had left. Familiar story.

Well, not quite everyone. There were still my roommates Peter and Kevin and some other social outcasts from the GNVQ class who I don't know and don't want to. Even the bloody teachers had buggered off somewhere.

Typical.

I downed the rest of my steiner.

Then Kevin said to Peter, 'Back to the room for some *Magic?*'

Peter nodded and they headed for the exit.

'Hey, guys,' I said chasing after them. 'Wait for me.'

The three of us picked up some little stubby bottles of beer from a German off license and then actually had a laugh back in the room. They showed me how to play their *Magic: The Gathering* game, and we slagged off school and ranked the girls on the trip and debated which *Nightmare on Elm Street* sequel is the best (*Dream Warriors*, for your information, although *The Dream Master* has its merits).

I still wouldn't be seen dead with the two of them in public, of course.

March 1996

Friday 1st March

During free time today I popped into the Berlin Museum of Kino (film). I rushed through the exhibition of old German movies (a lot of black and white images of things like weird-looking vampires with long pointy ears and teeth) and went straight for the gift shop. They had clapperboards, but all the words were in *Deutsch*, and I don't think I can pull that off without looking like *ein uber wanker*. Ditto the director's chairs.

This city is pretty creepy in places, what with its wall from the First World War still up in places. Should have brought my camcorder to shoot some random footage for *Murder House*'s nightmare sequences, like some arty low-angle shots of that Battenberg Gate. Ah well, the West Wickham war memorial will have to do.

Harris shimmied up to me during the walking tour of the city.

'That Vicky... I tell you what, mate.' He winked at me lecherously.

I said, 'No way!'

He winked again. I have to admit, I was impressed.

'No need to thank me, bruv.'

'*Me* thank *you?*'

'For acting in your film. Main role. Told you I'd do you a favour back. I'll even do it for free. Well,' he looked around to check whether Vicky was near, 'I'll be getting *something*, that's guaranteed.' And he made the fist-over-forearm *get in there!* gesture.

'And you want to play... the lead.'

'I ain't bothered with what the film's about or nothing. Though it better not be some poofy bollocks or you and me'll be having words.'

'It's a horror. *Murder House.*'

'Quality. I'll properly do some geezers in. *Bosh*, have that, ya cunt!'

Saturday 2nd March

On the plane home I mulled it over. Harris has a natural charisma. Not just with the ladies, he's all-round popular. He doesn't need to be the court jester to get invited to parties, he *is* the parties. And if anyone happens to not like him, he can just beat them up. Having him in the film, *headlining* the film, would do wonders for its profile.

And the more I think about it, the more I realise that he's just right for my main character, the Stephen Ricketts-esque genius director. Really, in terms of social standing, Harris is at the level where I should be, he's what I could have developed into. Deano, as he was known back in Primary School, was no harder than me and was even more into his Game Boys and Mega Drives than I was. He was actually a bit of a wimp. I remember one time I showed him David's dad's copy of *The Fly* and he wet himself at the end when Geena Davis slaps Brundlefly's face and it comes off. Harris simply went down one path in life and I ended up on another. So this will be like us melding together. Not unlike Jeff Goldblum and insect in the movie.

Besides, since David is only going to be in a supporting role, I need a new leading man. It can't be Barry, I *refuse* to let it be Barry. I'm so sick of his mugging, and anyway he's been barely taking any interest in the feature recently. Like the rest of my so-called Amigos, now I come to think of it. It's time I reminded people who's the boss around here. That's what Harris would do.

Sunday 3rd March

Did an Asda shift then popped round to Clive's to check on his effects work.

Clive was being... weird.

His dad didn't seem too pleased to see me, either. 'Oh,' he said bluntly when he answered my knock on the garage door. Then he turned his back on me and said, 'He's inside.'

Clive was sat in the corner of the workshop, glasses on the end of his nose, bright lamp shining on what he was working on.

I said, 'Look alive, Clive.' He jumped and dropped this little toy orc that he was painting.

'Fuck's sake, Steve.' He fumbled around on the floor for the figure.

'What you doing? Painting *Games Workshop?* Not turning Sad on me are you, mate?'

'Just doing a favour for someone.'

'Whatever. We film in a few weeks, so let's see your stuff.'

He's done a good job, as usual. But I didn't sense his usual enthusiasm, and he was showing me a lot about how to work the effects, even though that's always *his* job on set. Probably the pathetic, loser nature of the Sads rubbing off on his confidence. If he spends too much time doing favours for people like that, he'll be a virgin all the way to the nursing home.

Checked my emails in the evening and had some from my script readers (and no one else, certainly not any Goth-leaning young ladies). They actually had some positive feedback, miracle of miracles. Eamon called the screenplay 'so tasteless it's almost compelling' and said that by the end the audience will be 'drained and shaken'. Well, that's what good horror does. Nigel, meanwhile, said that he couldn't believe how far I'd gone in some places. Takes a special kind of talent, Nige my man.

I just skimmed over the rest of their comments. This is my first feature-length work. What do they want, Bill S. Shakespeare?

David hasn't got back to me with his feedback yet.

Monday 4th March

Half-term over and back to school.

Awkward chat with Barry today on the way out of Media Studies. I had to give him the news that he won't be the lead in my film. In fact, I got a bit carried away and told him that I don't want him acting in it altogether.

'So what's wrong with my acting?'

'Bazza, when the camera loves the actor, that's brilliant. When it's the other way round, that's a problem.'

'Don't you *Bazza* me... Fuck, after all the shit I've done for you...'

'It's nothing personal. Here, have a donut, I've got loads in my bag.'

'I don't want a fucking donut!'

He knocked the box to the floor. People in the corridor stopped to look.

'And what do you mean *nothing personal?* It's *completely* personal!'

Wow, I never knew he was so sensitive.

'Look, I'm sorry, mate. You could still help out, like behind the scenes? Make the tea and that?'

'Fuck off. And don't *mate* me. You dunno what the word means.'

We'd got to the doors to the playground and Barry barged through without me.

Rejection is tough. I should know. But it's part of the business. The fact is that Harris is right for the part and Barry isn't. And let's not forget that Harris will bring credibility to the project. I mean, imagine what people are gonna make of it. Hardman Dean Harris starring in *my* film, taking *my* direction!

When David came to get Freddy after school, he handed me a printed copy of my script. The thing looks like one of the murder house's victims: covered in red.

'What's all this?' I said, leafing through. 'Trying to get your pen to work?'

'It's not as bad as it looks, just a few notes. There's actually a lot I like in there, Steve. I'm pleasantly surprised.'

Talk about your back-handed compliment.

'You can knock it into shape with a bit of tweaking,' he continued. 'Sorry about the handwriting, just call me up if I've been unclear on any points. But yeah, overall, lots to work with.'

He asked me about my progress on other aspects of pre-production, like finding someone to take care of the sound and getting back in touch with Stella to see if she'll do the make-up.

I didn't want to ruin the mood, so I told him that I'm making great progress with both.

I said, 'Don't worry. Everything's going to be fine.'

Sometimes when you say that, it does actually turn out to be true.

Tuesday 5th March

Couple of free periods at the end of the day so I got the train up to Charing Cross station and then walked to Tottenham Court Road, where I bought myself a clapperboard from this film shop I'd read about in *Film Fanatic*. The director's chairs were too expensive, but maybe I can find one second hand. If there's one thing I don't want to do on this project, it's waste money.

Wednesday 6th March

Harris slid up to me in the canteen where I was eating my lunch alone, which seems to be the norm these days.

At first, I assumed he wanted a copy of the script to read but when I got one out of my bag, he shoved it away.

'Don't need that thing, bruv. Already know what I'm gonna do with me acting and all that.'

'Okay...'

'Got something to chat to you about.'

He told me that since he's doing me a favour by starring in my film, I now owe him a favour back. I tried to point out that being in the film was actually something he had wanted, and that I already did him the favour of hooking him up with Vicky. So another favour from me would, in fact, be three in a row, with none in return. But some people are so wrapped up in their own world that you just can't reason with them.

The upshot is that I've promised to do Harris's GNVQ coursework write-up of the Germany trip. Well, it won't take me long. I'm sure I can repurpose my own A Level Philosophy essay for his *See Spot Run* assignment. Then once filming starts, he'll *have* to start taking orders from his director.

Thursday 7th March

When I left work at Asda tonight, the security guards were waiting for me and asked to search my bag. Inside, they found all of the 5p donuts I'd bought myself on personal discount.

'I said, 'Reduced stock, to clear.' My heart was racing.

This heavy-set bloke, with an Eastern European accent like Luka's, examined one of the boxes.

'You usually reduce items to minimum at 6:03 p.m.?' He said, pointing at the date stamp on the sticker. 'Four hours before the store is going to be closing?'

'Well…' What could I say? That everyone does it?

'This is not the first time, we know of this.'

I said nothing.

'When you are in the next time?'

'Saturday…'

'I will speak to your manager before then.'

And he let me go.

Fucking jobsworth.

Shit.

How did they know?

Bollocks.

Saturday 9th March

So that's my main income stream cut off.

As soon as I walked through the supermarket doors at 8:55 a.m., the big European security guard zoned in on me.

'This is for you,' he said, handing me a letter. 'Please give me your discount card and locker key, and we must have your uniform back before 14 days.'

I tore the letter open. It read: 'Misuse of company property (RG11-23 reduction gun) and theft of company produce. Verdict: immediate termination.'

You're terminated, fucker! as Sarah Conner says at the end of *The Terminator*.

There was no point arguing with the man.

As they led me out, Ruth was walking in to start her shift.

She said, 'What happened?'

I said, 'Creative differences.'

I didn't stop to chat.

The company would only have thrown away the donuts if they had gone unsold, they waste tons of perfectly good food every day. But then again, if they *had* sold them, they would have made more profit than they got from my little scam.

I can't tell my beloved parents that I got fired, they'll go nuts. I'll have to carry on pretending I'm going to work. Yeah, and say that Asda now hold and launder our uniforms for us, that's why I never wear it or put it in the wash anymore.

My life is a web of lies and intrigue. Like a James Bond movie, except really dull and rubbish.

Sunday 10th March

I've done Harris's homework before. It was a major reason I never got bullied in Secondary School, or at least not too badly. I'm a bit out of practice, but all my recent focus on improving my fiction writing is coming in pretty handy.

Was watching a behind-the-scenes preview of Scorsese's new movie *Casino* on ITV while I toiled away, and noticed that they used an electronic clapperboard. It looked so cool, with the scene and take numbers on this red digital display. Much better than the crappy chalkboard version I got from up London. I chucked that embarrassment under my bed and got busy asking on the Internet chatrooms about where to find a proper one. And a used director's chair, while I was at it.

I realise that now's the time to be even more careful with money, what with my recent termination of employment. But I deserve a treat after what I've been through. It is *my* movie, after all.

Had the sudden urge to call Stella tonight, but after Barry causing a scene at school and Asda giving me the Sarah Connor treatment, I've had enough humiliation for one week, thanks.

Monday 11th March

Bit of tension between me and David at tonight's movie meeting.

We were at my house this time, spread around the living room on sofas and dining chairs brought in from the other room. Our group has nearly doubled as David brought along five of his Drama class mates, three girls and two blokes, to plug the many gaps in our cast and crew. I'd never had that many girls in my house at once and was a bit nervous around them, so I was relieved when David stood up to start the meeting. I had assumed that he was about to save me the trouble of making introductions by doing all that himself. But he had other things on his mind besides pleasantries.

'So, Steve,' he started, in a tone that was less than friendly. 'I still haven't received the second draft of the script, following the notes I gave you.'

I should have just said that I was still working on it. How would he have known?

Instead, I went with, 'I've been a bit busy with other things.'

'*Other things?* You mean, like recasting behind my back?'

'What?'

'This thug from your school.'

'Harris? All I've done is select the best actor for the role.'

'The lead role in the script that you can't be arsed to work on? You've given it to someone who didn't even bother to turn up tonight?'

'He was busy.'

'Right.'

'And *I've* been busy.'

'Do tell.'

I glanced at those assembled: Vicky, Adrian, Luka, Taekwondo Terry, Gavin, and David's Drama lot.

I composed myself. 'I've been working on the gore effects with Clive' (who was another no-show) 'and, like you say, dealing with casting issues.' (Barry, of course, also wasn't there.) 'And I've been scouting locations and getting hold of essential equipment.'

'What about finding someone to do the music and record sound on the day?'

Shit. I'd completely forgotten about promising to sort that out.

Luka put up his hand. 'I know a guy, he was at my uni and is now looking for work. He's a sound recordist and is making the music too. I should set it up that you meet him?'

'Yes, thank you Luka,' David said. He turned his probing gaze back on me. 'And what about a make-up artist?'

'Well, uh, Stella—'

Vicky said, 'Yeah, Steve, what happened with this Stella girl?'

'What do you mean, what *happened* with her?'

How the fuck does Vicky know about Stella?

'Steve,' David said, now using his impatient teacher voice, 'do we have a make-up artist on this film or not?'

'Uh, Stella has prior commitments. Sort of permanently. So, make-up will be replaced. I'm working on it.'

Like I'm ever going to prioritise that. And hey, things might still come good with Stella.

David said, 'Oh, you're *working on it*. Like you're *working* on the script?'

What's rattled *his* chain?

'Well, what have *you* been doing?' I countered.

'You mean apart from designing the call sheet and shot list templates, rounding up the extra cast and crew that we desperately need... but mostly just making sure that *you* actually do something. People are relying on you, Stephen. Don't mug them off.'

Get a load of him, with his Cockney slang. I felt like giving him a shove down the old apples and pears.

'Hey, Steve,' Adrian piped up out of nowhere, 'who do you reckon grassed you up about stealing from Asda and got you fired?'

'Oh,' Vicky said, looking at the empty biscuit tin on the coffee table, 'so *that's* why you don't bring donuts anymore.'

I was too ashamed to meet David's eyes, but I could feel them boring into me.

Tuesday 12th March

David rang me up and, in a forced attempt at compassion, asked me if I wanted to talk about what happened with Stella or with my Asda sacking.

'No, I don't.'

'Okay.' He paused. 'Look, I've got a mate who's looking to get make-up experience. Give her a call, she'd be happy to work on the film.'

He gave me a phone number.

Meanwhile, I got an email from one of the Website chatroom people, someone who is selling a director's chair. But costs way more than I was hoping to spend.

Wednesday 13th March

Met Luka's mate, Ollie the sound man, round his house in Shirley. He has what looks like a full music studio in his bedroom, with all the decks and mixers and what-have-yous, and the rest of the space is taken up by all different types of microphones and piles of CDs. Ollie is older and more grizzled than Luka, stocky and with tattoos peeking out the sleeves of his T-shirt, which had 'I'm a sound recordist, not a magician' on it above a cartoon microphone that was dressed as a wizard. It seems that he still lives at home, despite being in his twenties, but maybe that's why he can afford all this gear, and I suppose if he's determined to live the creative life and refuses to get a day job, then he isn't going to be overflowing with cash to move into his own place.

We chatted about what kind of music I want for the film. He reckons he can make us some 'high-intensity scary techno', inspired by John Carpenter's *Halloween* theme. Sounds wicked.

Then came the catch: he wants to be paid.

It was a tough decision, but with no Asda money coming in I have to prioritise. I can't see why we need a designated person on set to hold a sound boom in the air, and for post-production I'm sure I can get some GCSE Music kid to knock the soundtrack together in exchange for a couple of packets of fags.

David has sent me a blunt email saying that he wants to come over on Saturday to discuss his notes on the script. During our phone call yesterday, I gave him the impression that I would actually be writing a second draft based on those notes.

Meanwhile, I bit the bullet today and bought the director's chair, cost be damned. Will have to remember to hide it before David gets here on Saturday.

Thursday 14th March

In the corridor today Harris bowled up to me and shoved some papers in my face.

'B+? What's all that about?'

I looked at the essay. His teacher had written 'a compelling, paradoxical argument'.

'Hey, that's pretty good Dean, isn't it? Look, I couldn't have got you full marks. Would have been a bit suspicious, wouldn't it?'

He looked at me. 'What you mean?'

'Never mind.'

(The General Studies paper that I'd neglected in order to do Harris's work got 'a rush job that has undone all your recent progress' from Miss Yates and a D+.)

'Nah, just yanking yer chain,' Harris carried on. 'You did all right. What I really wanted to chat with you about is this film.'

Harris went on to inform me that his mate Sean 'the Squirrel' Birrell is going to be helping out with *Murder House*, too.

I said, 'Help out how, exactly?'

'Dunno, you figure it out. And it ain't just Birrell, neither. The other lads wanna come on board and all. You're gonna owe me big style before this thing is done, Ricketts.'

Saturday 16th March

Was supposed to have the script meeting with David tonight. And I did genuinely intend to. But things didn't quite work out that way.

David said he'd be at mine around seven. By then, Martin had turned up on one of his surprise visits. But he wasn't here to crash. He walked straight into my room and grabbed me in a headlock.

'Stop it Martin, I'm not a kid anymore!'

'Just tell me one thing, Stephanie. What are you doing tonight? What are you doing tonight? Hmm?'

'Ow—I'm—*ow stop it, Martin!*'

He let me go, and I explained that David was due round any minute.

Martin said, 'I remember old Dave Nolan. Bring him along.'

'Along where?'

As soon as I opened the front door to David, Martin pushed us both outside and into his car. Unable to be heard over the boom of house music, David and I just exchanged bewildered looks on the back seat.

We stopped at this rowdy pub on the corner of Crystal Palace high street, where Martin seemed to know everyone and bought a round of pints.

I said, 'Should you be doing that and driving?'

'That's all the drink I'm having.'

'What, we're going home?'

'Nope.'

So, after only one pint, Martin gathered up the troops and we were out the door again. About ten of us piled out into three cars. I was wedged in the back of Martin's between David and this really skinny girl with short hair dyed pink.

We drove into central London and Martin parked under a bridge somewhere. After a short walk we joined a long queue.

David said, 'Ah, so we're going to Turnmills.' I hadn't considered that we were heading to a club since everyone was dressed in T-shirts, jeans and trainers. Weekends around Bromley and Croydon you need a collar to get in, smart shoes, no blue denim.

I leaned in to David and said, 'You've been before?'

'Yeah, ended up here once. We were drinking in Holborn and moved up to Farringdon. Planned to go to Fabric, round the corner, but the queue was too long.'

I just stared at him, realising that David has this whole other life that I never bothered to ask about.

Naturally, I was nervous as hell queuing up. If I got turned away, how would I get home? I didn't know where I was or if the trains were still running. Martin would have to drive me, ruining his whole night.

But when we got to the door the bouncer didn't even look twice, he just gave me a pat-down and then Martin paid for me, him and David, saying, 'Just put me down as an executive producer on the movie.'

All my nerves exploded into excitement as we headed down some steps and I heard the pounding bass reaching up for me. Then *boom*: a room full of people dancing like mad with their hands in the air. The noise was deafening. Lasers criss-crossed and smoke billowed up from the floor. There was a DJ raised up at the back and the ravers looked like they were worshiping in his church.

Martin had already brought another round of drinks. 'Have some of this.' It was a tall and thin silver can with a picture of a bull on it. 'That'll keep you going,' he added. I took a sip and it was sickly sweet. David had one too and Martin just drank bottled water.

A couple of Martin's lot went straight into the crowd on the dance floor and started tapping people on the shoulder and whispering to them.

I said, 'Who are they looking for? Another one of your mates?'

Martin said, 'Oh yeah, he's the main geezer. He'll vibe up the place like no other man could.' He was grinning wildly.

David grabbed me by the arm. 'Come on then,' and he tugged me towards the dance floor.

I was hesitant, still getting my bearings. Everyone seemed so confident and uninhibited. Most were drenched with sweat and some of the men had their tops off. I noticed that no one was trying to get off with anyone. Instead, people had their arms around each other's shoulders, or were hugging what appeared to be complete strangers, or were swaying on the spot with their eyes closed and a huge smile on their faces.

I was still absorbing all this when I heard something familiar mixing in.

Martin was grinning at me. He nodded.

I grabbed my brother and David and we waded into the middle of the dance floor as 'Insomnia's first verse blasted out. By the time the chorus dropped, I'd forgotten all my fears and was fist-pounding the air. I totally lost myself in the music, enjoying it on my own while at the same time happy knowing that the people I was with were close by.

After dancing for something like ten club-length songs, I crashed back onto a deep sofa in the chill-out room with David.

I said, 'I'm glad you're doing the film with me.'

He turned to me slowly. He was smiling so hard it looked like it hurt and his pupils were the size of Wagon Wheels. Then he leaned over and hugged me. It was uncomfortable… and then it wasn't… and then it was again.

I broke it off, took another sip of Red Bull, and then pulled David up to get back to the music.

Sunday 17th March

Crashed at Martin's flat. We didn't get back there until about 8:00 a.m. and even then some people kept the party going. David disappeared into a bedroom with the pink-haired girl and I passed out on the sofa.

Martin drove me home in time for the family Sunday roast. It was brilliant, us both being dirty stop-outs together. Mum and Dad were oblivious, as usual.

Monday 18th March

Today I sat down and reread my *Murder House* script, all the way through from beginning to end.

You know what, I'm genuinely happy with it. I don't see any need to re-write it from David's notes. Okay, we had a *moment* in the chill-out room at Turnmills, but if he tries to change my screenplay one more time he can just go and do one.

Wednesday 20th March

David has gone and done one.

He rang me up after school to find out how the re-write was going. I told him that I'd almost started.

He said, 'Ha-ha.' David is one of those people who doesn't really laugh, he just goes *ha-ha* or tells you *that's funny*.

'Seriously, I re-read it and decided that it's actually fine just how it is.'

Silence.

'I guess you were hoping we'd discuss your script notes.'

'Did you actually read them?'

'Well...'

Silence again.

That bit in *Heat* came to mind, when De Niro goes, 'I'm talking to an empty telephone, because there's a dead man on the end of this line.'

Eventually, David said, 'Okay. Well, good luck with the film.'

Then I really was talking to an empty phone.

SPRING

Thursday 21st March

I emailed the finished script to the cast last night straight after David hung up on me.

When I saw Vicky at school today lining up outside Philosophy, she said, 'That *thing* you sent us? *That's* the shooting script? It's exactly the same as the last one! I thought you were making changes?'

'Vicky, please, I'm not in the mood.'

'I asked you to give my character more lines. And what about toning down all the misogyny...?'

Et cetera, et cetera.

Actors having opinions on the script. I ask you, whatever next?

Saturday 23rd March

Took my Asda uniform back today.

Then I had to stay out all day so that my parents would think I still have a job. Spied Adrian, Ruth and a few of my other ex-colleagues having lunch in Churchill Park and fled before they saw me.

Then I realised while wandering aimlessly around Bromley shops that I didn't have money on me for the return bus journey. In fact, I could only afford a 10p Cadbury's Chomp bar for lunch. Was knackered and starving by the time I'd walked all the way home.

Sunday 24th March

Feet hurt with blisters. Starting to feel somewhat pessimistic about the film, a perspective not eased by all the far from complimentary emails I've been getting back about the final script.

Monday 25th March

David came round to get Freddy from day care and ignored me.

In the evening I watched *Braveheart* clean up at the Oscars, while flicking through the ads in the back of *Film Fanatic* looking for electric clapperboards. Like celebrating New Year's with a bunch of movies round Gavin's, watching the Academy Awards ceremony together used to be a Four Amigos tradition. This feature film is taking over my life.

Tuesday 26th March

I keep on dialling David's number then replacing the handset before it can ring.

Got an email out of the blue from Stella: *Why haven't you got in touch with me?*

Don't know whether she wants to apologise for storming off the last time I saw her or if she just wants me to call her so she can slam the phone down on me, David-style.

I do want to speak to her... but I have to concentrate on salvaging this film first.

Thursday 28th March

I was cutting across the field on my way to Psychology today when Adrian came jogging over to me, sweaty from his lunchtime football game.

'Hey, the famous movie director!'

I smiled weakly.

'Not long to go, eh?'

'Yeah...'

'So, I was wondering, how's it gonna work with David co-directing the film?'

'Look, about David... wait, what?'

'Yeah, so will one speak to the actors while the other fiddles with the lights or what?'

'Um, I'm sure we'll figure it out.'

I walked away in a daze. This *co-directing* stuff again. What is it with people! Maybe it works for the Coen brothers but I would never sink to it. Pisses me off that people think that David was as important to this film as me. They'll soon find out the truth.

Talking of the man in question, tonight when David came to pick up his brother he had something to get off his chest.

He made Freddy wait in the other room and said, 'We need to talk.'

When we were alone, he said, 'Would you like to know *why* I'm off the film?'

'I—'

'Let's see: you aren't interested in writing a good screenplay, you spend the budget on pointless trinkets like a director's chair, you recast parts without consulting with me, you won't pay for a music score or sound recordist, you get yourself fired from Asda for stealing donuts and so put our budget in jeopardy, you piss off a potential make-up artist and don't bother to pick up the phone when I drop a perfectly good replacement right in your lap... shall I go on?'

'No, that's enough, thanks.'

'The worst thing is, you've been lying to me. I had to find a lot of this out second-hand.'

'Second-hand? From who?'

'That's not important. What *is* important is that I don't think I can trust you anymore.'

He waited for a response from me. But what was I supposed to say?

'Come on, Freddy,' he called over his shoulder, 'we're off.'

Knew I should have put that bloody director's chair out of sight last time he came round.

Friday 29th March

Gavin came up to me in the common room to tell me that he's dropped out of the film.

'You what?'

'I'm sorry, mate, but after you axed Barry and now with Clive gone—'

'Wait, Clive too?' He never told me. In fact, I haven't actually talked to him in ages.

'He said that you can use his effects and give him his credit, but he doesn't want to be on set. I think as far as you and him are concerned, you're through.'

That was why Clive made sure I actually paid attention to how his gadgets worked that last time I went round to his workshop. Am I bollocks giving him a credit.

'But Gav, come on mate, this doesn't leave me with any of the old gang left at all.'

'Seems to us, *mate*, that's just the way you want it. You're palling up with the likes of Harris and Adrian and Vicky like you don't want to be seen with us anymore. Are you so self-absorbed that you haven't noticed how we've been hanging around with Nigel and his lot?'

It's not like Gav to get so riled up. His face went a bright red, almost matching his hair.

And yeah, I realised that it was true. I have been sitting alone in the corner of the common room, making my plans. Apparently while my allies have been jumping ship.

'I thought you were just giving me some space so I could focus on pre-production,' I said. 'Not deserting me for the Sads.'

'No, Steve. And don't call them "Sads". They're sound guys. And you'd like *Magic: The Gathering* and *Games Workshop* if you gave them a chance. Kevin was saying that you even played a bit of *Magic* on your Germany trip.'

'Yeah, maybe, but come on Gav, I *do* want to—'

'Have sex one day, yeah I know the line. Nigel isn't a virgin, you know.'

'He's not?'

'Got a girlfriend at Langley Girls. Upper Sixth *and* she's got a car.'

'What?'

'Yeah, he met her at some comic-book convention.'

And on that bombshell, Gavin turned and left me in his dust.

Upper Sixth? Comic-book convention? It must be bollocks. That lot spend so much time in their made-up fantasy worlds that they can't tell what's real and what's magical fairy land anymore.

The bell went for the next lesson and I looked for people to walk out the common room with. Harris and his lot? I may write their essays but socially they wouldn't be seen dead with me. Ditto Adrian and his sporty gang. Vicky and the straight-A brigade or Ruth and her alpha females? Don't make me laugh.

So, I pretended to read over my script and waited for everyone to leave.

Then I walked out alone. Didn't feel like going to my next lesson so I kept on walking, out the gate, all the way home.

Sunday 31st March

Have been watching movies on VHS tapes all weekend. With no job, no mates, and no guarantee that my film is even happening anymore, what else is there to do?

On the plus side, I've now seen all seven entries in the *Amityville Horror* series.

April 1996

Monday 1st April

Film meeting round Luka's. I knew that it was make or break time for the feature so I snapped myself out of my stupor.

Luka lives in this student house-share in West Norwood. The living room had Bob Marley posters on the walls, ashtrays overflowing with butts from thick and thin roll-ups, and lots of empty dinner plates and takeaway packages and cans of lager.

I got to Luka's before anyone else and, naturally, he asked where David was. I told him I'd be making an announcement to the whole group. He nodded slowly, and started quizzing me on what *look* I wanted for the film. For instance, did I prefer natural or artificial light and what about the colour tone?

'Er, I thought you'd clarified all that with David?'

'No, David said that you, as the director, will decide. So, what do you want?'

I told him to just go with whatever he thinks will work.

When everyone else had arrived (minus Harris and his gang, who didn't turn up again), I swerved the brewing *where's David?* questions by holding up a sheet of A3 paper with the following on it:

> Steve: directing, working the effects, being my own first AD.
> Luka: DP/cameraman.
> Adrian: acting, location.
> Terry from taekwondo *[who still wants to be involved, despite*

Barry scarpering]: acting, holding the sound boom, fight choreographer.

Dean Harris: acting.

Sean Birrell: acting *[?]*

Harris's other mates: *acting [... presumably. I'm hoping they can play the protagonist's film crew, formerly to be portrayed by David's Drama class pals.]*

Vicky: acting and location manager.

I said, 'It may seem a little light, but we can do this, people.' I hoped my confidence didn't sound too forced.

It wasn't what I'd hoped for, but it could be worse. I explained that, in the absence of David's Drama gang, the other actors will need to take on multiple roles, depending on how many of Harris's mates turn up, and Vicky is going to have to play every female victim. We'll just shoot around it. I'm going to have to do more technical jobs on the day, but I can handle it.

I said, 'This *is* going to work. And I know you're all wondering why David has left, so I'm going to give you two words that will answer all your questions about why he's no longer on the project.'

Dramatic pause.

'Creative differences.'

Tuesday 2nd April

When David came round to pick up Freddy, I didn't want to give the immature bastard the satisfaction of ignoring me. So I made the first move, barging past so that *I* could ignore *him*.

But he wanted to speak to me. 'Steve,' he said.

I turned.

'I was thinking... maybe I was a bit harsh. You have been putting a lot of effort into the film, even if it's not always in the exact way I would like. Look, what I'm trying to say is, if you still want me, then—'

'No need, mate.'

'What?'

'Don't worry about it. The film's moving ahead fine without you.'

'... It is?'

'Had a great meeting last night and, yeah, I'm having to be a bit creative with the casting and take on more myself, but I think it's actually gonna turn out great. Even better than I thought.'

That had him flummoxed. He looked almost hurt. Then he regained his poise, grabbed Freddy's hand, and left, saying, 'Break a leg.'

Wednesday 3rd April

So since Harris's right-hand man Birrell wants to play a part in *Murder House*, it now follows that he also requires his coursework done. Harris's twisted logic has come full circle: since I'm so desperate for actors, by being in my film his gang actually *are* now doing me a big favour.

So, instead of writing call sheets and shot lists, I spent this evening typing a History essay on what the Romans did for us. Thank God for *Encarta 96*, the encyclopaedia on CD-ROM.

Call sheets and shot lists were David's bright ideas, anyway.

Thursday 4th April

Walked some dogs in the morning and ironed some clothes in the evening.

When I left to go to Sherry Lady's, I told my mum that I was heading out to my evening shift at Asda. I still haven't told the 'rents about getting fired. The first thing they'll say is that I've put a black mark on my job history. But what they will fail to appreciate is that I'm never going to need any job that isn't in film, and no one in the industry will care that I couldn't hold down a shitty part-time job at a supermarket. In fact, among the creative types, being fired from a big institution like Asda probably makes me a hero. So, if anything, this is going to *improve* my employability.

The good news is, I've scraped enough together to buy an electric clapperboard. With David gone it's an even more essential purchase, something to show them all that I do know what I'm doing. And while ironing Sherry-Face's undergarments, watching her titter on the edge of both her sofa and passing out drunk, I came up with a killer new idea for the film.

Impulsively decided to ring Stella when I got back from buying the clapperboard. She wasn't in, so I left a message with her mum.

Friday 5th April

Good Friday and the day before my first ever feature film shoot. Martin took me up town for a matinee screening of *Trainspotting* at The Prince Charles Cinema, off Leicester Square. I was nervous as I'd never got into an 18 before, but Martin bought the tickets by himself and it worked out fine.

The film was incredible. The energy, the humour, the music... *this* is what the British film industry needs.

Martin said, 'And you're gonna be part of it, mate.'

He may well be right.

Had an early night as need to be up at 6 a.m. to get round Adrian's house.

The last thing I remember thinking before I fell asleep was that I have made plenty of films without David Nolan.

Saturday 6th April

So the shoot didn't exactly have the best of starts.

Originally, I'd hoped to stay overnight at Adrian's to start setting up this morning as early as possible, but he wouldn't let me. That meant instead of taking the equipment over to his place bit by bit yesterday, I was forced to lug the huge camera and the tins of film and the tripod and the lights and the bag of guns all by myself. I used a Safeway shopping trolley I found by the side of the road and ended up looking like some kind of mental homeless dude. The twenty-minute walk took more than twice as long and I was covered with sweat by the time I got to Adrian's house, at around 7 a.m. Then when I knocked there was no answer. All I got was some neighbour leaning out a window and yelling, 'It's Saturday, you wanker!'

I roused Adrian by throwing pinecones at his bedroom window. Eventually he opened it to lean out and blearily remind me that the shoot doesn't start until 9 a.m. I calmly explained that I needed to get in to set things up and that Luka was on his way for 8 a.m.

'Come back at eight, then,' Adrian said and slammed his window shut. So I had to wait in his front garden for an hour.

Luka arrived bang on time and we were finally let into our location. While Adrian had a shower, I got a text from Vicky to say she forgot that she had an Easter family do today. I rang Harris and Taekwondo Terry to check if they were still coming. Terry said that he needed to practice for his black belt grading and Harris didn't answer.

Luka said, 'It's okay, we can shoot exteriors.'

So my DP and I filmed some establishing shots of the house and then moved inside to get footage from the killer's point of view. I was glad that Luka was operating the camera, the arsing thing weighs a ton.

We did have one actor on set, so we shot some moody shots of Adrian (playing the killer) skulking around the darkened house with all the blinds down and curtains closed. Luka was concerned that it won't really look like night, but I assured him that I'll just turn down the contrast in the edit.

Adrian was pissed off that we'd woken him 'at the crack of dawn' and then we 'didn't even do any proper filming'. He said no one will be allowed in any earlier than 9 a.m. from now on. Luka muttered something in Dutch. It dawned on me then that we should really do some night shooting, seeing as the film takes place at night. But there's no chance Adrian will be up for that.

We managed to get Adrian to agree to an 8 a.m. start time for me and my DP and 9 a.m. for everyone else.

Am having to swing by the editing place in Purley at the end of each day to drop off the tins of film, so they can be developed in time for me to come back and start editing next week. That's a daily two-hour round bus trip that I could do without.

This high-quality 35mm stuff better be worth it.

Sunday 7th April

Taekwondo Terry arrived on set this morning, shortly followed by Vicky, and then finally Harris and his gang in the afternoon.

I had been wondering how things would work between our star and leading lady and, well, basically they didn't. Vicky came straight up to me before the Hard lads had even arrived and told me that she refuses to be in the same room as Harris. The immediate problem there is that he is in multiple scenes with her character, the producer who visits the set to check up on him.

But I said, 'Sure,' reckoning that we'll just shoot around it. Somehow.

Vicky said, 'This film better be worth it...' and wandered off.

When Harris did turn up, it was with his bushy-tailed nut-munching rodent mate Sean Birrell only.

Harris said, 'The others couldn't be arsed.'

I guess my director character just likes to use an unusually small crew.

The first thing Harris and Birrell did was open Ade's fridge and ask where all the *grub* and *bevvies* were. I've been buying sandwiches and snacks from the Co-op each morning on the way in, and by the time the two latecomers turned up today, the rest of us had already eaten everything.

Birrell said, 'Where's ours, then?' His enormous front teeth were on full display through his outrage.

We don't have a runner, someone to do these kinds of dogsbody tasks. No one offered, so I ended up going to the shop myself, delaying our afternoon's shooting. Then when I got back to the house all Harris and Birrell did was complain about my sandwich choices and that I didn't buy any beer.

Vicky and Harris managed to successfully ignore each other all day. At one point, Harris moaned loudly about there being none of the 'up-for-it posh birds' here that he'd been expecting.

We spent most of the afternoon shooting Harris walking around moodily, trying to look intense and authoritative. Unfortunately, he comes across a lot less intimidating when he's putting it on, adopting this pained facial expression that makes him look constipated. Not for the first time I'm wishing I could check the rushes (or are you supposed to call them dailies?) of the day's footage, but I wasn't exactly going to fork out for a 35mm projector, so I won't be able to see anything we've shot until I start editing after we've wrapped.

I had planned on nailing some of the shootout scenes today, but Adrian took one look at the bag of guns and told me to forget it because the neighbours will go ballistic if we start making loud banging noises. To say Harris was disappointed would be an understatement. I hope that the vase he said he knocked over accidently wasn't an antique.

Towards the end of the day, I asked Terry when his taekwondo buddies were turning up for the kung-fu scenes, figuring we'd extend them to make up for the lack of gunplay.

He put down the sound boom and said, 'What taekwondo mates?' We're all multi-tasking on this shoot so Terry has been holding the boom for scenes he's not in, and for the others it's been me.

I said, 'I thought you were bringing the whole *dojo* along for some big martial arts scenes.'

'I never said that. And it's a *dojang*, anyway.'

'... Right.'

'Hey, when's Bazza gonna get here?'

'Er, not sure, to be honest.'

Try sometime after never.

To add to matters, I have forgotten to buy any batteries for my electric clapperboard, and now that the time has finally come I feel too self-conscious to use the director's chair.

Came home absolutely knackered. Message from Stella on the answer phone, saying she can't make it to the shoot but she's up for a drink once we've wrapped.

Monday 8th April

Our Lord and Saviour managed to come back from the dead on the first Easter Monday, and after today's series of calamities I'm going to need a miracle of my own to get this film back on track.

The Panavision Panaflex went and overheated. I don't know whether it was to do with the temperature in the room (the house is like a dark oven due to all the bed sheets we've put up over the windows to fake night time) or if the camera is just old. But we had to let it cool down and take an extended lunch, which put us at least five script pages behind.

Birrell quipped that it must have happened because 'the Kraut' had put up too many 'fairy lights'. Luka ignored him but gave me a look. Luka may only be a student but he's definitely the most professional person on this shoot. True enough, all the lights are making us sweat buckets, but he seems to know what he's doing. I trust him.

Matters aren't helped by how long it takes to set the lights up for each shot. I'd never realised how much hanging around there is on a film set, with the resulting boredom. I even caught Harris going through Adrian's mum's knicker drawer.

At one point I said to Luca, 'The lights definitely can't be set up any quicker, right?'

He said, 'It takes time to get the right lighting, Steve. Maybe it would be quicker if you wouldn't mind assisting me?'

'Sorry Luka, I'm too busy doing director things. Look, I mean, can we try to get it *almost* right? Like, not necessarily perfect but good enough?'

He gave me this amused smirk.

'Ah, you first-time directors.'

I just wiped my sweaty fringe out of my eyes for the hundredth time and left him to it.

Just as we were getting ready to resume shooting in the afternoon, Adrian's parents came home.

I said, 'I thought they were away all week?'

Ade said, 'No, just for the long weekend. Thought I told you that?'

'But this is the primary location for the film.'

'Don't worry, it won't be a problem. But you better all clear out for today as my mum's going to do the laundry.'

I don't need that sound bloke Ollie around to tell me that a washing machine will mess up our decimal levels, so we had no choice but to down tools at 2:30 p.m.

Bought some D-cell batteries for my electric clapperboard from the Co-op on the way home. Put them in but the fucking thing doesn't even bloody work.

Tuesday 9th April

Adrian's house has laundry hanging all over the place. I'll just have to work in that the murder house doubles as a laundrette. I'll use some voiceover to clarify.

The Smith family were all out during the day, thank God, but before she left Adrian's mum said that the upstairs is out of bounds. And at least half of our remaining scenes are supposed to take place up there.

The other major problem today was the climatic fight scene between Harris and Adrian. It's supposed to be an epic struggle, with Ade getting the upper hand before Harris smashes a clapperboard over his head and then stabs him with it. Since we'll be breaking the only working clapperboard for the sake of an ironic kill, after today I'll just have to mark the scenes by writing on bits of paper. Anyway, Harris refused to show any weakness during the fight. He said he wanted to do it 'Seagal style'. I tried to explain that showing some vulnerability will make it even more satisfying when he does beat the villain.

Harris said, 'No. I ain't looking like a poof.'

Adrian said, 'Hey Steve, how about at one point I say, "You're just the wrong guy in the wrong place at the wrong time!"'

I said, 'How about you just stick to the script, eh mate?'

Adrian's constant attempts to crowbar *Die Hard 2* references into the film are really starting to grate. Not that I can openly complain while we still need his house.

In the end, we had to shoot it Harris's way after he threatened to bugger off and take Birrell with him.

Then after dropping the cans of film off at the editing place I came home to an answer machine message from Harris, saying that he and his mate are bored now and won't be coming back tomorrow.

Wednesday 10th April

I tried to gloss over how much Harris and Birrell leaving will impact the film, though I'm sure no one believed me.

So Harris's character is now played by Taekwondo Terry. There is a four-inch height difference and Terry has longish, light-brown hair rather than Dean's short ashy-black crop, but I'll explain that away with voiceover and mess about with the contrast so that no one will ever notice. Or maybe I'll make it that the film director had a split personality that starts to manifest itself physically as the night wears on. Might have been easier to pull that off if we'd been shooting in chronological order.

As for the remaining victims... I don't like being on screen but I've been forced into a Mel Gibson-style director/actor situation. Well, old Gibbo still managed to win Best Director and Best Picture Oscars. Vicky and Ade will cover all the other parts, with Vick especially prominent since she's already playing all the other female victims who fall afoul of Adrian's killer. We raided Ade's little brother's dressing up box for costumes, so hopefully we can get away with it. I've abandoned the plan to make the deaths resemble famous ones from horror films and now just want to get them done.

With Terry in front of the camera now I'm having to hold the sound boom in every scene. Due to my sweaty hands from working in an oven, the boom keeps on slipping into frame. I'm sure I can fix it in post, and probably no one will notice anyway because they'll be so engrossed in the story.

We've only filmed half as many pages as I had hoped by now, so I'll just have to fit in as many murders as I can in the time left. The running time will probably still come up short, but I'm sure I can pad it out with slow-mo and repeat some of the footage as flashbacks.

In fact, I've come up with a cracking get-out-of-jail card: I'll splice in bits of footage from some of my old horror shorts to show the director character thinking about some of the other horror movies that *he's* made!

Sorted.

Thursday 11th April

Disaster. I couldn't get the gore effects to work. All was fine yesterday, with blood spraying on the right places and avoiding Adrian's mum's furniture. But now the equipment is kaput, and I can't exactly ring Clive up and ask for his help.

Then at barely 10 a.m., Adrian's dad burst into the living room during one of Vicky's death scenes (the fourth one, the time where she's wearing a huge black curly wig and a pink shell suit and gets impaled on an upturned table leg) and demanded that we all get out of his house. It completely ruined the take. I waited for Ade to stick up for us, but instead he said, 'Yeah, this has lost its novelty value now,' and declared himself retired from filmmaking.

So, me, Vicky, Luka and Terry were left with the rest of the day to fill. I decided that we'd shoot some footage over at the sports warehouse, but when we got there, the place looked terrible, full of deflated basketballs and dismantled netball goals. It would have taken us hours to clear everything away.

I said, 'What the fuck, Vick?'

She just shrugged. 'I was told that it would be pretty much cleared out. Why didn't you ever come and check it out yourself?'

So we went over to see Sherry Lady, my secret weapon. We aren't due there until tomorrow but I thought I'd take a chance.

I knocked on her door but she was out.

A whole day wasted.

Friday 12th April

Spent the morning round Sherry Lady's house. I never quite figured out where she fits into the story, only that she's really creepy. So, I just got Luka to light her all ominously and we shot her from a variety of angles just blathering on, glass in hand. We took it in turns to ask her questions off-screen that I will edit out later.

She soon forgot we were filming her, or maybe just never clocked in the first place, and by lunchtime she was slurring so much that it was mostly gibberish. I took that as our cue to wrap things up. As we left, she asked me, 'Scotty, why are you leaving without doing the ironing?'

Vicky chastised me on the way out for 'exploiting a mentally ill older person' and declared that she'd 'had enough of this farce'. Off she went, not before eating the lunch I'd paid for, I noticed.

So that just left me, my trusty DP, and Terry from taekwondo.

Without a location base anymore, we sat on a bench next to the West Wickham war memorial, munching our sandwiches.

Luka chomped on a BLT and said, 'How much you have left to shoot?'

I flicked through the script. 'Thirty pages.'

'Oh guys,' Terry said, standing up, 'I've got to bail now as well. See ya.'

I watched him leave, unable to decide if not bothering to come up with an excuse was rude or polite.

Luka said, 'I think we may need to rethink now what is possible still.'

So we shot the war memorial and some moody stuff (clouds, shadows moving across an empty frame, birds flying, close ups of blades of grass) and then called it a day.

I've got eight hours of footage. About two hours of that is going to be shots fluffed by actors or technical cock-ups, another two is Sherry

Lady's ramblings, and then we shot an hour's worth of random stuff today. So, from what I've got, hopefully a third of it is useable.

There's a movie in there all right. I've just got to find it in the edit.

I think I'm going to need a fucking search party.

Sunday 14th April

Slept for most of yesterday and then this afternoon took the bus for my first day at the editing studio.

Have now sat through every single minute of the footage and it's even worse than I'd feared.

The lighting is all over the place. I changed what I wanted on a whim and the light even differs from shot to shot within the same scene. Luka warned me but, pig-headed as I am, I overruled him.

The acting is horrible. Harris makes Barry look like Daniel bloody Day-Lewis.

The Sherry Lady footage is just gibberish. Two hours wasted. Don't know what I was thinking there.

The continuity is non-existent. In one scene the knife switches from Adrian's left hand to his right and back again, and fake blood stains disappear and re-appear from shot to shot. The random transforming of Harris into Terry is impossible to explain away.

It's obvious that the murder victims are played by only three people who switch clothes and wigs. The first time you see me onscreen I look like one of the comedy Scousers from *Harry Enfield and Chums*.

After we smashed our only working clapperboard for the Harris/Adrian fight, none of the takes are marked because I forgot to start using bits of paper. So, since we started to veer off-script, I have no idea where a lot of scenes are supposed to fit in.

The sound boom is in so many shots, it's like a supporting character. At one point you even see the fucking pole holding it up.

No amount of fiddling with the contrast can make our daytime footage look like it takes place at night.

Added to this, I am stuck with editing equipment that I have no idea how to use. Good work, Steve.

Monday 15th April

Took Luka with me into the editing place for a second opinion.

I met him at reception and he followed me through the winding corridors. He was very impressed, saying that he'd never been in a 35mm editing suite before, and that my ambitious choice of film stock was one of the reasons joined the project in the first place.

'I thought, you must be so serious about being a director!' he told me.

I smiled back weakly.

Once we had got to my suite and I started to show him the footage, he suddenly remembered a lecture he had to get to after sitting through about half an hour.

On the way out, walking Luka across the industrial estate to his bus stop, I apologised to him for wasting his time.

'Don't worry,' he said. 'It's still more experience for me, even if it was... very unique.'

I brought my old horror shorts with me today so I could splice them in and boost the footage up to feature length. Then I realised that they are on hi-8 tape, and I have no idea how to combine tape with 35mm film on the same project.

At least I could start to actually do some editing: they have an assistant on call who can help you with the fiddly things like loading the film and physically cutting it with scissors and so on.

On my way out, I asked at the front desk whether they're able to give me a refund on the rest of the week. The guy just laughed in my face.

Then he said, 'And it's not just during the days all this week. You've got it booked for every evening next week, as well.'

David. He must have ignored my protests and known that seven days would never be long enough to edit an entire feature film, so he paid for more time without telling me. Finding this out has made me feel a painful mixture of gratitude and guilt.

Took the replica guns back to the Catford shop today. What a monumental waste of money they were.

Tuesday 16th April

Didn't want to return to the editing place but forced myself out of bed and onto the bus.

And then, sitting on the 119 bus for that long journey, watching the grey concrete of Croydon turn into the more rural outskirts of Purley, I had an idea. I could give the film a nightmarish, David Lynch feel. Splice the footage together randomly, unsettle the audience, use dream logic.

But when I got there and watched it again, my heart sank. It's unsalvageable. It's the fucking Titanic of movie shoots. I have somehow managed to regress as a filmmaker and produce the biggest pile-of-shit waste-of-time that a seven-year-old picking up their first camcorder would be embarrassed about.

During the turmoil of the past week, I somehow found time to call Stella back to invite her for a drink. We met this evening and I told her that everything went brilliantly with the shoot.

'Honestly, it was so successful, I don't see how you being there could have improved it.'

'Thanks very much.'

'I didn't mean it like that.'

She smiled to show that she was joking, but then she did get all serious.

'I want to tell you something, Steve. I was really starting to like you back there. When I was in Rome, I used to look forward to getting your emails. I *had* thought you were different. But it turns out, just like all men, you're only after one thing.'

I wasn't sure how I could plausibly contradict that, so I just took another sip of my pint.

'You know, you could have called me,' she continued. 'I was thinking about maybe apologising, a *little* bit, for storming off that night. Instead, I get radio silence. Typical man.'

'I'm sorry about back in the pub. I guess I just thought... after New Year's...'

'What? That I was a slag?'

'No, but...'

'I was so drunk that night. *So* drunk.'

'And then when we had that one date, we did do a lot of snogging, and so...'

She stared me down.

We finished our drinks, and when we went our separate ways outside the pub I didn't get a kiss. I have no idea where this leaves us now.

But hey, at least she thinks of me as a man.

Thursday 18th April

Returned the camera to Eamon. Well, to the back room of his shop anyway, as he wasn't anywhere to be seen. Not even sure if the thing works anymore, what with all the overheating we experienced. Maybe he can sell it and the remaining film.

The back office of Video Nation was a lot emptier than usual, with most of the boxes of tapes gone. I didn't care. The last thing I feel like doing right now is watching movies.

David came to get Freddy in the afternoon. As with Stella, I pretended that everything went swimmingly.

He said, 'No hitches at all? No funny on-set stories?'

'Not really. I was amazed at how perfect it was, really.'

'I'm surprised you're not in your editing suite. Got your final cut locked already, eh?'

'Yep.'

He gave me this cryptic smile and led his little brother out of the house.

Gosh, I can't wait to get back to school on Monday so I can lie through my teeth even more.

Friday 19th April

Couldn't stand moping around the house all day so jumped on the 119 and headed back to Palmer's Post-Production. At first, I had this idea to edit the footage into a short film, but I didn't know where to start, it was all so horrific. And not in the way I'd intended.

Then I thought, why not make a trailer? A trailer for a film that doesn't exist. Trailers can be all randomly shot and incoherent, no one cares. And what's more, I can pass the Media Studies unit with a trailer, so long as I write the required bullshit about it.

I got to work.

Sunday 21st April

Finished editing the trailer. It actually looks okay, hinting at a movie that's... I wouldn't say *good* but a movie, for sure.

Leaving the editing centre for the last time, I turned to look at it. Isolated on a barren industrial estate, it seemed like a creepy house, the kind that I'd just tried to capture the horrors of in my so-called film. Not so much a house of murder, though, more an old-fashioned haunted house. And it *was* haunted, haunted with the horrific film I've spent the past week grinding through the cogs and dials of its huge machines, machines that were supposed to help me make sense of it all but which were powerless against my shortcomings. I started to think of my film sitting in that building, now part of it, like an evil spirit housed inside forever. Something that was made to be unleashed upon the world, that *wanted* to get out, but which won't now, ever. I can never let it escape.

I turned and walked away. It's been a long week.

On the bus home, it was hard to be positive. I've got no film, no coherent footage, and a trailer for a film that doesn't exist. Yes, I have something for Ms Harper's Media Studies class, but I have nothing for the Kent Film Festival and nothing that will help me get into a film uni.

When I left Palmer's Post-Production, it was for the last time. There's no point in using the extra editing evenings that David sorted.

The only word for this is *failure*.

Not sure where my career as a director goes from here.

Monday 22nd April

Barely slept last night worrying about facing the *Murder House* cast and crew at school.

In the end, no one said anything. I had classes with some of them and just kept my head down. I even spent breaks, lunch and my free period working on actual schoolwork. At one point I bumped into Ruth in the A block corridor and she asked me how all the film stuff was going. I just mumbled something about having to get to class.

Tried to watch some of my favourite movies when I got home to cheer myself up but couldn't concentrate beyond the opening credits. At dinner, Mum asked why I wasn't touching my food. I said that I wasn't hungry, and the truth is that everything tastes like cardboard now. Later, I went upstairs and tried listening to my CDs but it seemed so pointless. Even the full-length Monster Mix of 'Insomnia' did nothing for me.

Tuesday 23rd April

No sleep again. Mind keeps racing through all the bad decisions I've made.

All my teachers have been commenting on my renewed commitment to schoolwork. Mrs Harper was disappointed that I'd only produced a trailer, but she knows I've ticked the right boxes and we'll both get something out of it: a passing grade for me and a consistent class average for her. But my bigger ambitions for where the project could take me are over.

I was skulking out of class when Miss said, 'What happened?'

'Let's just say it didn't go as well as I had hoped.'

'Are you okay? You seem so down.'

'I'm fine... but I think I'm through.'

'With filmmaking?'

I nodded.

'You can't let one setback derail you, Stephen. All artists experience lows. They define the artistic experience.'

Artist this, *artist* that. The word is a stab into my phoney heart.

I wanted to tell Ms Harper everything, how I feel like I've gone backwards. Not just as a filmmaker, but in every area of my life. My friends have deserted me, I've pushed away my first chance at a girlfriend, I don't fit into any social group, I've barely developed physically... messing up my feature is just the latest disappointment and regret.

But all I said was, 'Yeah, sure, okay.'

At this rate I can see myself applying to one of those business studies degrees after all. That, or go full time at Asda... oh, wait, that's right.

Wednesday 24th April

At lunchtime in the common room today, I approached the vending machine. Harris, Birrell and the rest of their gang were sitting at a table nearby and their eyes fell on me.

'All right, Spielberg?' said Harris.

I pulled a *so-so-can't-complain* face without turning my head.

'Had quite a laugh last week, didn't we? When's the masterpiece coming out? Don't forget me in your Oscar speech.'

His mates were cackling. They reminded me of the hyenas from *The Lion King*.

'Yeah,' said Birrell the Squirrel. 'It's gonna be a right classic, innit?'

'Yep,' agreed Harris. 'Spielberg here's gone and made *Back to the Future Part 3: Back to a Shit Film*.'

Huge guffaws from the table around him.

I waited it out. It felt like the whole common room's attention was now on us.

I bent down and picked up my Mars bar.

I said, 'Actually, Spielberg didn't direct the *Back to the Future* films, he only produced them. They were directed by Robert Zemekis, who also made *Who Framed Roger Rabbit* and *Death Becomes Her* and won an Oscar last year for *Forest Gump*. And Zemekis already made a third *Back to the Future* film, the one set in the old west.'

Harris stood up. 'What you saying? You calling me a wanker?'

Only now did I look at him. As I did, I thought back to the last year of Primary School, when Harris and I first started down our different paths. I hadn't seen much of him over the summer holiday, and on the first day back in September I was looking forward to catching up at break time and finding out what new video games he'd been playing. Instead, when all the classes had spilled out onto the playground, he completely ignored me and went off to play football with the popular kids.

The Harris of today was still waiting for a reaction.

But the only one I gave him was to tear open my chocolate bar, say, 'See ya, Deano,' and walk away.

I passed the Sads' table (or whatever I should call them these days, since they now include my former Amigos, Gavin, Barry and Clive) and they all turned to look at me as I went by. But I walked straight out the exit without making eye-contact with anyone.

Later, when I got home, I called Stella.

Friday 26th April

The Philosophy and Psychology essays that I handed in earlier this week both got As and the teachers verbally assaulted me with praise. I received it with the numb acceptance that my life is heading back in a mainstream direction. On Monday we go on study leave for four weeks, during which time we have our A Level mock exams, so I suppose I'll be concentrating on those and nothing else.

I had Media Studies last thing and Ms Harper asked for one of our post-lesson chats.

'I'm worried about you, Stephen. Are you sure you're okay?'

I finally cracked. I burst into tears, in front of the bloody teacher. It all came out: how I was too cocky to take pre-production seriously, how I cast Harris just to try and make myself look popular, how I neglected the script, how I reconnected with my old best friend and then brushed him aside out of pride.

Ms Harper put an arm around me. The last time I had a hug from anyone was with David at the nightclub and realising this made me cry even more.

When I'd regained some composure, Ms Harper sat me down and asked me to go over exactly where I thought I went wrong. Then she asked me what I thought was the root of all these issues.

I said, 'Arrogance,' giving air to the word that's been spinning around my head ever since this project blew up in my face.

She said, 'I'm not so sure.'

'Oh, come on, I thought I could do things that I knew I couldn't. I thought I didn't need anyone else's help. Pretty bloody arrogant.'

She said, 'There's another word for that: naivety. You're *sixteen years old*, Steve. You're allowed to be a little naive. And you're allowed to fail.'

'Okay, so how do I *stop* being so naive?'

'It takes experience. And now you have more. Mostly bad, but that's the best kind for personal growth. But I still don't think that we've got to the root of the problem.'

She went on to say that naivety is just a symptom. The cause was an emotion.

'What emotion?'

'Fear.'

'That stuff about being afraid again?' She nodded and gave me a tissue to blow my nose with.

Ms Harper said, 'Do you feel scared a lot of the time, Stephen?'

'Well, yeah, but I'm a teenager. Isn't that normal?'

She shrugged. 'You should certainly be able to make a good horror film. I think you know a lot about being afraid. But art is about revealing part of yourself and you've been holding back. You have to overcome that hurdle, but first you have to figure something out.'

'What I'm really afraid of?'

She nodded.

I had arranged to meet up with Stella for another drink straight after, no strings attached.

'Oh my God, you look like you've been crying,' she said when she saw me approaching her table in the pub.

So I told her all about my chat with Ms Harper.

Stella said I was 'really brave' for breaking down and being so honest. She gave me a hug and even a quick kiss on the lips.

I want to see her again, even if it's just as friends. If I can still remember what it means to have one of those.

Saturday 27th April

Little Freddy left his rucksack round ours yesterday and this morning his big brother brought the boy round to get it.

David gave me a brief nod on sight and was about to leave with the kid when I said, 'Look, can we have a chat?'

He raised his eyebrows.

I walked home with them, Freddy off up ahead, jumping over cracks in the paving slabs and stopping to pick up twigs. For a while, David and I just followed in silence.

It was me who broke it. When I did, I didn't get all emotional, and I didn't start to apologise profusely, and I certainly didn't bring up the past and start going over old territory.

What I did was tell him that I was wrong to ignore his advice and not see him as an equal on the project. I admitted that I'd let my own pig-headedness ruin everything.

David exhaled noisily, then said, 'Yeah, I heard about the shoot.'

'You did?'

'From Vicky.'

'I see.' I realised then why he always knew what I'd been up to, going back to when things started to fall apart during pre-production for *Murder House*.

'And I knew that there wasn't any video shop owners' conference in Bradford,' he said. 'And Genesis weren't even touring when you said they were over Easter.'

'Huh.'

We walked on in silence again, both thinking things over.

'Thanks for booking me the extra editing tine. I definitely would have needed it, if...' I trailed off.

If he'd been on set to make sure we got enough usable footage.

David just nodded.

We caught up to Freddy and he put out his hands for me and David to swing him by the arms as we walked. The two of them were laughing and soon I was too.

We reached the Nolan house. Freddy let go of our hands and ran off up the garden path.

David stopped with me at the gate. 'Just try not to be such a prick next time, okay?' He said it with a smile.

I smiled back. 'Good to have a goal in life.'

It was only after David closed the door that I started to wonder. What did he mean by 'next time'?

Couldn't sleep with questions racing through my head all night. Maybe I'm *not* all washed-up as a filmmaker? Maybe there *will* be a next time? And, more than anything else, if David believes in me, maybe I *can* be a director?

Sunday 28th April

Went to see Eamon at Video Nation in the hope of finding some answers. In the end, I got more than I bargained for.

For once, Eamon was actually in the shop. Well, the girl on the counter told me that he was in the back, and she said it with a tone that had me fearing the worst.

I found my uncle sitting in a nearly empty storeroom on one of the only remaining boxes, his head in his hands. There was a strong smell of whiskey and a half-drunk bottle of Jameson's by his foot.

I said, 'Hi, Eamon. Um, are you okay?'

His head snapped up. 'Ah, Stephen! How are ya, so?'

'I'm... fine,' I said, moving slowly into the room. His eyes were blood-red.

I gestured around. 'Having a bit of a clear out?'

'Total, lad.'

'Eh?'

'I'm selling the shop.'

'*What?*' I stared at him, dumbfounded.

'Ah, Stephen. You're a good lad, I've always liked you.'

I didn't want to hear this. But there was nowhere to hide.

He went on, looking off wistfully. 'Yes, always watching videos, you and your brother... Stephen!' He looked right at me. 'I never wanted to be here.'

'Sorry?'

'Did you not wonder why I had a professional camera in my back office?'

'Well, I—'

'*Of course* I wanted to get into movies! But it was either feast or famine and I wanted it to be all feast and when I met your auntie Sheila...' At her name he took a long swig from the bottle.

'She made you give up your dream?'

'*She* made me?' He put the bottle down shakily. 'It was *my* choice, lad. She was a great girl, she supported me whatever. But I didn't have the bollocks. I started to look for a way out, I wanted an excuse to fail. Then, not long after we moved over here, I saw this place up for sale...'

He was lost in his memories for a moment.

Then he went on. 'I persuaded Sheila that it was a good investment, too good to pass up. But it eats you up, you know that, Stephen? Regret eats you up until you're not you anymore. In the end, no one can be with the person you've become.'

He took another swig from the bottle.

'So, Auntie Sheila's gone back to—'

'Go on, Stephen.' He waved dismissively. 'Off with you. I've got to lock up.'

'I could help—'

'No. I've embarrassed myself enough. Off with you, lad.'

So I left.

I marched back through the shop and swung the door open. As soon as my feet hit the pavement outside, I started to run. But I wasn't going home.

When I got to David's house, I banged on the front door.

The man himself opened it. 'Christ, Steve, I thought there was a fire or something.'

'David,' I spluttered, out of breath. 'Did you mean what you said yesterday, outside your house?'

'What was that, then?'

'Don't mess about, David. Do you want to make another film?'

'Now?'

'Right now. For the same festival. We still have time.'

He hesitated.

'You better come in.'

Up in his bedroom, I sat on the edge of the bed and he faced me on his desk chair.

'Steve,' he began, struggling to get something out. 'Steve, I... look, I wasn't going to tell you this, but I met up with Luka last week. I wanted to find out more about the *Murder House* shoot.'

'Okay...'

'Luka gave the whole thing a positive spin. You know how he is.'

I smiled. Good old Luka.

'He reckons you have real talent and that you and I shouldn't abandon our "blooming creative partnership".'

'*Blooming*, eh?'

'He also said that he was up for working with us again.'

David looked at me.

I looked right back at him. 'So...?'

I didn't want to say it. I wanted to hear him say it.

'So, I think... okay. Yes. Let's give it another shot.'

He looked away.

I waited until he looked back at me before I responded. When I did, it came out in a breathless ramble.

'Well, I mean, the first thing is, we definitely can't use the same script again. And the cast... and crew... you know most of them aren't going to come back.'

'Then write something else. And we'll find new people. Maybe try to bring back some who quit on us last time around.'

Gulp.

'But we'll have to start planning again from the start...'

'We have to act *fast*, Steve. No spending weeks procrastinating. We hit the ground running and we put it together in double quick time. Look, why do you think people get involved in some no-budget caper like this? Yeah, they may want the exposure or be getting something else out of it. But really, they're drawn to the creative energy, the excitement of making something new. That's what you have to find again, that urge to pick up a camera and create something that didn't exist before you pressed record.'

I went to bed happy for the first time in weeks. Still struggled to sleep, but now it was with all the adrenalin. And when I did drop off, it was the sleep of the dead.

Monday 29th April

Study leave, the first of four weeks of mock A Level exams. We don't have to be in school all day, but they still make us go to tutor time and show our faces in study rooms.

As soon as I left today, I ran over to David's house. His mum opened the door and was surprised but pleased to see me.

'David's not home from school yet,' she said as I got my breath back. 'Why don't you watch some TV while you wait for him? Help yourself to a drink, you know where everything is.'

When I heard David's key in the door, I leapt off the sofa.

I said, 'All right, all right, come on, let's get started.'

He said, 'Blimey, let me get my shoes off first.'

We sat in David's living room with glasses of orange squash and the biscuit tin. It was so much like old times that it didn't bear thinking about.

David laid out his plan. We will co-produce and it will be a *partnership*, with no more secrets or lies. David will be more on the administrative side of things, with the creative buck stopping with me, although he strongly advised me to seek out others' opinions. But the point will be to work together, not pull in different directions. David will also go back to his original plan of playing the lead role in the film, as well as being the first assistant director during the shoot: the person who has to make sure that we're on schedule, that the actors hit their marks, that kind of thing.

'If this is going to work,' David said, 'you have to realise that trust is the most important thing.'

I nodded.

'And let's still keep to just one location, if we can. That will make things a lot easier.'

'Agreed. But can I write a good enough script?'

David exhaled. 'I may have been a bit... over-the-top before. I'm not a writer, and I shouldn't be telling a writer what to do. Trust goes both ways.'

I wanted to say that I'm not exactly a writer either, but was too overwhelmed by this sort-of apology to speak.

'And anyway,' David continued, 'since time is so tight, I've actually been looking into other ways of working.'

He slid a copy of one of the posher film mags across the table. It was open at an article headlined 'Will the Dogme 95 movement change filmmaking forever?'

David said said, 'They're these Danish directors who are experimenting with a simpler approach. Loose, improvised scripts. Natural lighting. No effects.'

I picked up the magazine and said, 'Where's all this come from, David? You've been thinking about all this a lot, haven't you?'

He just smiled and prodded at the article. I scanned through it.

After a bit, I said, 'Sounds pretty amateur. I don't want people to see me as some kid running around with a camcorder.'

'But that *is* what you are. And what's wrong with that? These Danish guys, they're not worried that people won't take them seriously because they're not using five-ton cameras. We don't need a locked script, just a solid scenario, an outline. I've got loads of great improvisers in my Drama class, they'd love the chance to experiment like this. It's exciting. It's pure cinema.'

I was getting pretty excited myself. My appetite has come back, and I started badgering David to ask his mum to order Pizza Hut. They've got this new base with cheese baked into the crust that I really want to try.

While David was getting out the takeaway menu, I said, 'How long do we need to get organised?'

'We'll shoot as soon as we can. Get people all riled up and just launch into it.'

'When, David?'

'Spring half-term holiday.'

'Immediately after our mock exams?'

He nodded.

'That's in less than four weeks.'

'Yes. Look, the first-time round, I think we had *too much* time. Now, the speed we'll have to work is going to give us the creative energy that we need.'

That or heart attacks.

'And that quick turnaround will mean there's enough time for you to have a proper post-production this time, before the festival deadline.'

I leaned back on David's sofa. 'You know this means we'll probably fail our A Level mocks.'

'I'm up for it if you are. Remember *Point Break*, when Bodhi tells Johnny Utah that "it's not tragic to die doing what you love".'

'... He does die, though.'

'Yeah, but on his own terms.'

I grabbed the pizza menu. 'These are *my* terms: order me a double pepperoni and I'm in.'

May 1996

Wednesday 1st May

Part of what David's been saying about finding new ways of working is to involve other people more in shaping the film. And I'm starting to warm to the idea. Takes the pressure off me and who knows what will come out when other people's ideas come into the mix. Plus, if the actors enjoy the process, then that will surely be reflected on screen.

I have a strong urge to get my old pals, the Amigos, back on board, but I'm pretty sure I've burned my bridges there. Eye contact in the common room is rare, and they weren't talking to me in classes before we went on study leave. I don't know whether it's just for the good of the film that I want to patch things up, or out of guilt, or if I just miss them.

Another thing I feel conflicted about is going back to crappy old hi-8 film and my bog-standard video camera. But if it's all right for those Danish blokes...

After the Philosophy exam this morning, I went around school putting up posters seeking help with the film. We're actually going to audition the actors, including David's Drama mates and David himself. No one gets a free pass. I've called the film *Untitled Horror Feature Movie* on the posters and have decorated them with loads of Microsoft Word clip art, knives and people screaming and all that.

When I stuck one up in the common room, I felt eyes burning into me. Before, I would have chickened out. But now I feel different, I feel determined to do what I've got to do. It's all that matters to me now. And that's what I told Ms Harper when I asked her if we could use her classroom for the auditions. They're taking place next Thursday after school.

Thursday 2nd May

I must be feeling more like myself again as the urge to watch films has returned.

Decided to put on some of my faves last night, some of my comfort watches. And as per usual when I'm feeling happy and working on a film (and, let's face it, I'm never really happy any other time), what I was watching onscreen started to influence my thoughts about the current project.

But this time, it was different somehow.

So, I'm lying in bed watching my all-time favourite John Carpenter movie, *Prince of Darkness*, and instead of thinking of ways to recreate it on the cheap, my mind keeps drifting. Like in the bit where that one guy comes back as a zombie and approaches the remaining humans, but instead of attacking them, he starts laughing.

I've seen *Prince of Darkness* at least twenty times and this is the first time that scene has affected me. It made me think about how it feels when someone laughs at you. How it's not what you would call violent, but it's still an attack.

That's when my mind really started to spin its cogs. People laughing at you is unsettling. But why? It's so oppressive, often *more* painful than a physical attack, and that kind of pain can take a lot longer to heal. Being mocked, targeted emotionally, really sticks with you.

It's horrific. Actual, real-life horror.

Friday 3rd May

At lunch time, I went to Bromley Library and got the books on filmmaking out again that I never bothered to read all those months ago, along with some extra ones about film theory and collections of advice from famous old directors. I don't have time to pour over them cover to cover, but I've got a notepad and plan to do a lot of scanning and scribbling.

The old girl who checked out my books said, 'Oh, you must have exams on. Doing some last-minute cramming?'

I said, 'Yeah, something like that.'

I also dug out my old GCSE Media Studies and English notes, as well as the stuff I've done so far this year in Ms Harper's class.

David came round mine for a pizza takeaway (that stuffed crust is amazing) and we discussed the decision to film our feature on a bog-standard camcorder.

He said, 'As far as I see it, it's better to have a good film that looks shit than a shit film that looks good.'

'True enough. Plus, I was thinking that I want it to be a really raw film... like, emotionally?'

'Cool.'

However *raw* it might look, and indeed feel, we still need Luka back to make the lighting appropriate. We don't have to have a natural-light-only rule like those Dogme 95 directors, but we can use our lighting subtly to enhance the mood of a situation. Luka will love that.

I told my co-producer that I'm thinking of basing the film around the fear of what other people think.

David pondered this.

Then he nodded slowly and said, 'What do you reckon would be the best location? Can you think of a place where people worry about what others think a lot, and that we can use to film in?'

Saturday 4th May

Vicky rides her horses first thing at the weekends so I rang her up at about 9 a.m. after she'd got back.

I knew she would never respect me if I went into a full-blown meltdown so I was all business, David-style. I simply said that I knew I'd been wrong and I've learned from my mistakes, and that one of those mistakes was not appreciating how much she was putting into the project, and that I would love for her to help again.

'So, you definitely can't do anything with the footage you've got?'

'It's a bust.'

She sighed loudly.

'Fine. I'm back in.'

'Wicked. So, do you reckon you can get us in to film at the school during the spring half term?'

'You're going to set the film at our school now?'

'Yeah. A school is the perfect location for what it's going to be about. I'm going to do what Kevin Smith did for *Clerks*: film at the place I work while it's closed.'

'Inspired. Anyway, that's fine, I'll look into it.'

In the afternoon I met Luka for a drink. I thanked him for his confidence in me and said that we'd like him to join the new project, if he's up for it.

'Sure. You guys are crazy. It's fun.'

Have been making pages and pages of notes from these film books. Most of them agree that your film needs a theme that everything stems from. Every creative decision should be in service of it, even the ones forced by lack of budget. It is your film's spine, the thing that holds it together.

So, the fear of what others think is our theme and this will influence everything we decide going forward.

Sunday 5th May

Today, I was giving my room a much-needed tidy and found in my wardrobe the old black and white movies that Eamon gave me back in the autumn. I'd discarded them sight unseen after being unimpressed with the ones Ms Harper lent me, but now I examined the cases with curiosity. Turns out they're all European horror films from the pre-sound era.

Well, I may as well give them a shot. It's a chance to do what my Media teacher suggested at parents' evening: absorb, not scavenge. In fact I've started to do that already without realising it, like with *Prince of Darkness* the other night.

Monday 6th May

Vicky confirmed that we'll be able to film in the empty school during the week-long half-term break. In the spirit of trust that I'm trying to embrace, I'm going to take her word that everything will be fine this time with her location.

I've gone over all my notes from the film books and narrowed them down to a three-principle mission statement:

1. Stick to your theme.
2. Trust your instincts but be prepared to adapt.
3. Collaborate, collaborate, collaborate.

Tuesday 7th May

No one at school has said anything about the auditions. Not even my old gang, who were all in the same Media Studies mock exam as me today. We are seeing people the day after tomorrow, if anyone turns up.

Finished watching Eamon's horror classics and have to admit that I did get something out of each of them.

The Cabinet of Dr Caligari looks cheap, even for 1920. But it uses creepy set design to create an atmosphere. I already think that a school can be a pretty unsettling place. I don't mean just the oppression from teachers and peers, but all the corridors, winding staircases, an eerily empty canteen, abstract paintings outside the art room... I can take all that and film in a way to enhance the mood. *Dr Caligari* also gets a lot of mileage out of a completely free effect: shadows.

The Passion of Joan of Arc was pretty hard going and I wasn't sure I was going to make it to the end. The biggest thing I took away was how much you can get out of people's faces, especially in close up. I couldn't believe how intense the director (Carl Theodor Dreyer, who's Danish, like the Dogme 95 guys) made a simple shot of a woman's panicked eyes. He only seemed to use close-ups through the whole film, which added to the claustrophobic mood.

Finally, *Nosferatu*, the original vampire movie. I realise now that there had been a whole wall dedicated to it in the film museum in Berlin, with the pointy eared vampire bloke featuring front and centre. Anyway, if I compare it to Francis Ford Coppola's recent *Dracula* then I do still prefer Coppola's take. But his version wasn't really scary, and this one... I wasn't hiding behind the sofa or anything, but it did have an atmosphere. The production value is minimal, but that somehow enhances the effect, makes it more immediate and real. In fact, it looks like it was filmed on a cheap modern camcorder! They couldn't do clever effects back then because they didn't have the technology. We can't do them because we can't *afford* the technology.

Same difference, when you think about it.

Wednesday 8th May

David has dropped a bombshell. None of his Drama class mates want anything to do with the new film after the collapse last time. We are stuck with whoever turns up to Ms Harper's classroom tomorrow.

Thursday 9th May

With David's poshos as no-shows, we are, like last time, a bit thin on the ground for talent. I was pleased that Barry and Gavin came to audition. There was no tearful reconciliation, but I did apologise for being such an arsehole. I didn't bother asking them where Clive was. Vicky also came, as did Nigel Green.

The biggest surprise was Ruth.

I said, '*You* want to be in the movie?'

'Yeah. Always fancied trying acting. And I told you, I like your films.'

We moved the tables into one corner of the classroom to create an area for the auditions. I set up my camcorder as far back from the audition space as I could to stop it being too intimidating, hoping that, ideally, the person auditioning would forget it was there altogether. Zooming right in made up for the distance.

Because of the way we're doing this project, it wasn't a standard read-from-the-script type of audition. The only thing that's fixed about the characters at this point is that they are teenagers who have broken into their empty school during the summer holidays, for reasons that have yet to be established, and then an evil hidden on the premises turns against them. Or turns them against *each other?* That would be cool... anyway, they must all be motivated by the fear of what other people think about them. Other than that, the actual characters, plot, and scene-by-scene events are all still up for grabs.

Vicky said, 'So, the characters are more like archetypes that you want us to mould?'

I said, 'Um, right. Archetypes, yeah.'

David and I asked each of them to make up a monologue as their character (David too) telling us what they are most afraid of, what they want most in the world, how they see themselves and how they think other people see them. It had to be their innermost secret thoughts, things that they wouldn't dare say out loud. Then we interviewed each person (with them still in character) and this time they *were* speaking publicly. And, of course, there were a lot of differences between what they really thought and what they let people hear.

Everyone seems excited by the way we're approaching things and had a good time.

Gavin came to the audition not to be in the film, but to see if he could do something as part of the crew. He told me that he's never really liked acting and I feel a bit bad that I'd never realised before.

I said, 'How about being in charge of continuity?'

'Sure.'

'You can be the script supervisor.'

'For a film with no script. Like it.'

Gavin and Barry also brought along The (so-called) Sads, Kevin and Peter, who like Gav only want to work behind the scenes.

'You two spend ages with your paints, right? And you do Art?'

Peter said, 'Yeah.'

'Reckon you can do that stuff but on a larger scale?' I'm thinking we can give the creepiness of the school a little boost, *Dr Caligari*-style. I still have loads of acrylic paint left that I never ended up using on the toy guns.

After auditions we all went to The Firkin (which has kind of become our film pub and, luckily, doesn't have bouncers on a Thursday) where David explained the next step.

He said, 'Once we've watched back your audition tapes and decided if we can actually use everyone, we'll start to rehearse: workshopping characters and creating scenes together.'

Nigel said, 'Just like Genesis.'

I said, 'What?'

'For their last three albums they just turned up at the studio, locked themselves in for a couple of weeks, and made everything up as they went.'

'Yeah,' I smiled at him. 'We're doing this film Genesis-style.'

'Sorry to hear about Phil Collins leaving the band,' Vicky said to Nigel, who she was sitting next to. I've only just noticed that if there are any girls around, Nigel always seems to end up near them.

Nige put his head on Vicky's shoulder and let out this melodramatic sigh. 'I'm coping,' he said, sounding close to tears. 'One... one day at a time.'

This got a big laugh from everyone, me included.

After a couple of pints, David and I left the others and took the audition tapes back to his house.

We need five actors to play the five teenagers who sneak into the empty school. We have exactly that number with David himself, Vicky, Ruth, Nigel and Barry, and so if we turn anyone away, we'll have to audition again. Bazza has already confirmed that Taekwondo Terry isn't interested this time.

Most did fine (Nige and Ruth really surprised me) but we do have one problem. Barry.

David said, 'He's terrible.'

'Yep.'

I'm torn. Barry and I reconciled in the pub tonight and I'm keen to rebuild those old bridges, but if I reject him again, I could jeopardise all that. Plus, if he leaves the project, it could have a domino effect: he might take Gavin with him and then I won't get a chance to patch things up with Clive.

Then I remembered something I read in the film books. The director can actually influence how well someone performs. A great actor can be less with shoddy direction and a weak one could come to life with the right guiding hand.

I said to David, 'Do you think Barry has any potential?'

He hesitated. 'Maybe a certain presence. He is hard to take your eyes off.'

'Could be we've just got a rough diamond in our midst.'

Saturday 11th May

David and I went for a lunchtime drink with Ollie, Luka's sound guy mate, who I spoke to for *Murder House* but didn't use. We met at The Firkin, and he was wearing another T-shirt with a slogan: 'Sound Recordist' with the 'S' in 'Sound' as the *Superman* logo.

I got a bit more of an impression of Ollie this time. He has this kind of weary, been-there-done-that air to him, even though he's probably only about five years older. Seems like the kind of guy who will be reliable, but won't hesitate to tell you if he's pissed off about something. Like Luka, he's definitely more of a professional than just a kid messing about.

And the man is serious about his sound.

'You *need* a dedicated sound person on your project,' he told us. 'Both during the shoot and for doing the sound mix post-production.'

My first thought was: here we go again, more money.

I said, 'You *really* think sound is that important?'

He raised his eyebrows in a *challenge-accepted* way as he took a bit gulp of John Smiths. 'You're making a horror film,' he began. 'Think about the horror films that you love. What is essential to their scariness?'

He started to hum: *Duh-dum... duh-dum... dum-dum dum-dum, dum-dum dum-dum...*

I smiled, recognising the *Jaws* theme. 'The music.'

'Right. Same for *Halloween, A Nightmare on Elm Street, The Exorcist, The Omen...* good horrors are scarier because they have the right music and sound design. The heartbeat-like motion sensors in *Aliens*, the guy's bones cracking and stretching as he transforms *An American Werewolf in London*, Freddy Kruger's gloves down a blackboard... and have you *seen* any David Lynch movies, *Eraserhead* in particular? Sound makes any genre do its job better, but horror in particular. Fear is elemental and sound is the most elemental of the senses.'

I wasn't really sure what *elemental* meant, but he was making a good case.

'When I was a kid, I had a copy of *Predator 2* taped off the TV,' David said. 'I used to watch it over and over again, so many times that the image started to wobble, but that never used to bother me. But I had a recorded copy of *Robocop* where the sound had gone a bit wonky and I had to throw the tape away, it was unwatchable.'

Ollie was nodding. 'Dodgy visuals can be tolerated. To a degree, of course. But dodgy sound will ruin your film. It will *ruin* it.'

Ollie leaned back in his seat while we absorbed all this. He added, 'Sound tells an audience what to feel. Sound... is the door to the audience's unconscious.'

He should get *that* on a T-shirt.

I said, 'All right, you're in.'

'Cracking. I'll work on some ideas and you can come round mine again before the shoot to go over them. Trust me, your viewers are going to be scared shitless.'

Monday 13th May

Harris and I have gone back to our old pattern of moving in different circles and ignoring the fact that we used to be pals in Primary School.

More surprising is that Adrian and I are like strangers now. I thought we had become mates, yet he's been blanking me ever since the *Murder House* shoot.

So today, I decided to confront him after the General Studies exam.

I said, 'How's it going, mate?'

Adrian glanced around to see if anyone was watching us. 'Yeah, fine.'

'Could do with a hand with my new film, you know.'

'What's that got to do with me?'

I stared him down. He laughed, a nervous, uncertain laugh, and broke my gaze.

I was about to walk away, but first I had something to get off my chest.

'Let me tell you something, Adrian. I've been holding this back but now I've just got to say it.'

He frowned, waiting.

'There is no way, absolutely no way, that *Die Hard 2* is better than *Die Hard*. No way on Earth.'

Then I walked away.

Tuesday 14th May

After my Psychology exam, I sought out the group formerly known as the Sads in the common room, where the original duo and Nigel were sitting and playing their usual card game.

Nigel said, 'Steve, all right?'

'All right, guys?'

'Fancy a game of *Magic?*' Nige started to deal me in.

'Maybe later. I actually wanted to talk to Peter and Kevin.'

They looked up.

'Guys, I really appreciate you agreeing to help dress our set. It's going to be crucial for the atmosphere and I know you'll do a cracking job. But I need to ask some more favours.'

Kevin said, 'What's on your mind?'

'I need a runner. Someone to make sure the cast and crew are happy, chat to them and whatever, plus stuff like tidying up before a scene, getting the props ready...'

'So, a runner is someone who runs around helping?'

I shrugged. 'Yeah.'

'Sounds good. I've never been on a movie set, I'll make the tea if that's what you want.'

'As a matter of fact, that will probably be a big part of it. People are gonna need constant snacks and caffeine.'

Peter said, 'What about me?'

'Would you mind helping Luka, our director of photography, set up his equipment? He's really nice, Dutch bloke. If he can light the set faster, we can get through more set-ups per day.'

'No probs. You know, Steve, that was so cool a couple of weeks back with Harris, by the common room vending machine.'

'Yeah, you were like Steve McQueen.'

'Thanks, boys.'

Now came the awkward part.

'Um, so do you lot think Clive will want to help out on this project? I'm kind of *persona non grata* with him...'

'Can't be sure,' Nigel said evenly. 'I'll speak to him. But mate, we're well up for it. Making movies, it's so awesome. We were just saying that we don't know why you didn't ask for our help with the filming at Easter.'

'You dodged a bullet there, trust me. But this one really is going to be awesome.'

Wednesday 15th May

David, Ollie, Luka and I looked around the school after everyone had gone home for the day, what the film books call *doing a recce*.

We can definitely set up some nice tracking shots down the hallways, with the lockers either side creating a cool metallic, oppressive feel. Then you've got the Chemistry labs (which we can shoot to look like places where creepy experiments are performed), the winding staircases, the vast playground where an ominous figure could appear...

Ollie said that we should be fine for sound levels, so long as the school is deserted and nothing loud is going on outside.

Luka mentioned some of the practical reasons the school is a good location: access to toilets, it's familiar to most of the cast and crew, there's a kitchen, plenty of rooms to chill out in between takes, it's wide and open so shouldn't get too hot… he said that a lot of his uni projects film on their own campus for these very reasons.

Ollie said, 'Can raid your school's Drama department for props and costumes.'

Luka was also excited about all the lighting possibilities and having an assistant for the first time.

He said with a grin, 'I'll be a nice boss.'

Both were enthusiastic about our no-frills Dogme 95-influenced approach, which David and I have started to call Bromley 96.

'Steve, this film's story,' Luka said as we walked out the school, 'it sounds like *De Ontbijtclub*.'

'You what?'

'I think it's… *Breakfast Group?*'

Ollie said, '*The Breakfast Club?*'

'Yes!'

David laughed. '*The Breakfast Club* meets *The Shining*.'

Luka said, 'I would *totally* watch that.'

I did the air punch that *The Breakfast Club*'s ending is famous for and they all laughed.

This evening I met up with Stella for another drink. She greeted me with, "All right, mate?" which threw me a bit. Well, if we're friends, we're friends and as I've said, I could definitely use some these days.

Stella said she will do the make-up this time. She thinks that it'll be good for her portfolio (sounds familiar), as well as something fun to do during the holidays. I think David was right, people do get enthusiastic about a project that has creative energy. I suspect, as well, that it also makes a change from sitting around bashing buttons on a Sony Playstation and listening to the same Britpop CDs over and over again. Whether they can hack it when they realise it's going to be a lot of early mornings and hard work is another matter.

Stella, meanwhile, finished our evening together by telling me that she's looking forward to seeing me as 'Napoleon, the little emperor barking out orders'.

I think I preferred it when she saw me as a typical man, even if she meant it as an insult.

Thursday 16th May

First rehearsal, after school in the sports hall.

We only mentioned the film itself right at the end. Most of the session was David leading us through a load of activities he got from his Drama class.

A lot of these were improvisation games. One had us standing in a circle and throwing a ball to each other. The person throwing shouted out an emotion and the catcher had to then make that facial expression before they caught the ball. If you hesitated, you were out. For another, we were in pairs or threes and had to act out a conflict scenario: misunderstandings, failures to listen, not being able to see from another's perspective.

Then we did some character work, questions like *how do they feel in this moment? what are their fears and desires? what don't they want to reveal about themselves?* As well as working on their own part, the actors swapped roles with each other so that everyone got an across-the-board understanding of all the dynamics at play.

We were defining the characters and letting the story come out, but the evening was also about bonding, too. Crew as well as cast, everyone was there. We even did that trust thing where you fall backwards and let people catch you.

The teenagers trapped in a school and horror stuff happens angle gave us something to latch onto, and we now have five strong character types. *Archetypes*, to use Vicky's word. To think, I'd always thought that acting was the easy part of filmmaking, just learning a bunch of words and then repeating them.

So overall it was great fun. I'd brought in one of those big flip charts and we wrote our ideas down with marker pens as we went. We were scribbling notes up so furiously that I had to send Kevin off to get extra sheets of the huge A1 paper. We also sketched out crude drawings of what key shots will look like.

One downer: Nigel confirmed that Clive is definitely not going to be involved. I still have a lot of his gore effects left unused from *Murder House*. He hasn't asked for them back, so if I need them, I'm gonna use them.

And there is one more person who I want to get onto our crew.

Friday 17th May

'I'm flattered. But I can't do it.'

This was a surprise. I'd thought he would be thrilled.

'Why not?'

Eamon sighed over his pint of Guinness.

'This is one for you to do, lad. You don't need an old codger like me hanging around. But I'll always be available for advice.'

'Go on, then.'

'What?'

'Let's have some.'

'Ya cheeky wee... okay, let me rack the old noggin.'

So, I now have a few more pointers to remember on set:

1. Be grateful to everyone for helping you.
2. Always get a master shot. Then just keep shooting from loads of angles, getting what's known as *coverage*. You never know what will work or not in the edit.
3. As the director, you are the authority figure on set: the teacher, the parent.

I also asked Eamon how he was getting on in general and he said that he was 'just grand'. Apparently, selling the shop will make him a tidy profit, so he will have some time to figure out what he's going to do next.

It's the end of an era for me as well, that's for sure. So many hours spent trawling the rows of titles in Video Nation. Studying the artwork, with its promises of what the big black tape inside would deliver, reading the credits on the back covers to make connections, taking and returning dozens of videos each month.

Well, life goes on. I'm too busy to get all nostalgic.

Saturday 18th May

David and I decided we deserved a break from all this pre-production and so joined Martin and his raving gang again.

This time we got a train up to Victoria from Bromley South, drank in a pub in the station, then got the tube round to Farringdon. The club was Fabric, a maze of underground arches and tunnels.

I recognised a lot of the tunes: when the DJ played that track from *Trainspotting*, I went nuts chanting *lager, lager, lager!* along with everyone else. 'Insomnia' came on, too, and it's still a huge tune, but I have a new favourite, this one called 'Café del Mar' by Energy 52, which hasn't even been released yet.

I'm getting a feel now for how these tracks can go on for eight, nine, sometimes even ten minutes. It's not all full-on *thump-thump-thump*. There are peaks and troughs, melodies that carry all the way through, mini-drops, drum break-downs that build up to the climax... and suddenly you've been on the dance floor for two hours.

One track used an audio clip from *Total Recall*, the bit where the mutant leader baby thing growing out of the bloke's stomach implores Arnie to 'open your mind'.

'That was "Open Your Mind",' Martin clarified during a Red Bull break at the bar.

Later, lying together on a sofa in the chill-out room, sharing a fag (I *never* smoke), I said to David, 'You know that song with the *Total Recall* voice in it?'

He said, 'Sample.'

'What?'

'It's called a *sample*.'

'Right... it got me thinking about how a club is like a cinema. A bunch of people go in, are entertained, and when they come out it's a different time of day.'

David looked past me. A projector was playing *Akira* on the wall with no soundtrack and I gestured to the movie to underline my point.

David then leaned over and patted me slowly on the head with a clammy hand. 'You're always thinking, aren't you Steve?'

I wasn't sure how to respond, so I just gave him a *what-can-you-do* face.

David staggered to his feet. 'I need a piss... if I can manage to... and if I can find it... promise me you'll stay here, okay?'

'I'm not going anywhere.'

He looked at me all seriously. 'Not this time.'

But David was gone ages and I began to feel apprehensive lying there on my own, watching the lasers from outside hitting *Akira* and making the hoverbike chase even more frenetic.

So I got up and had a look out over the main room's dance floor. I couldn't see David or Martin or Martin's gang anywhere.

I scanned the crowd. I watched the bodies bouncing around off of each other, many with arms connected, some just standing on the spot swaying around in a world of their own, lasers cutting through and smoke engulfing them all. During my tense nights of failing to pull and worrying about getting into the right places, I never suspected that there could be an alternate going-out world, one that's like this. No aggression, no tension, just strangers enjoying the music together as one.

And yet... and yet there's something nightmarish about it, too. You're trapped away from the world until dawn, imprisoned. It's by choice, sure, but aren't a lot of our prisons self-inflicted? The disorientating mix of loud noise, lights and smoke, the lit fags and stray elbows moving around at eye-level, the psychedelic projections on the walls, the exhaustion of staying awake until the normal world starts up again. The anxiety if you lose your mates, getting trapped alone in a vast dark cavern, wandering around trying to find people but uncertain if you ever will, and if you'll ever feel safe again...

David, Martin and the rest turned out to be dancing in one of the other rooms and I joined them just as 'Higher State of Consciousness' was mixing in. I still enjoyed the night, but from that point on my mind was elsewhere, wandering by itself and trying to latch onto something.

Sunday 19th May

'If you give in to your fear of what other people think about you, you will end up alone.'

I was round David's house early-evening, having slept until late-afternoon following another *full session*, to use an expression of Martin's.

David sat on his bed, taking my statement in.

I said, 'A film needs stakes.'

'So now we have them.'

I nodded.

'By *alone*, you do mean—'

'Dead, yeah.'

'Just checking.'

Neither of us said it, but I know that, like me, he can't wait for the second rehearsal tomorrow, and for the shoot to start proper this Saturday.

Monday 20th May

Second rehearsal went even better than the first. I shared the movie's full theme just like I told David yesterday and this really helped us to map out each character's journey (or *arc*, as all the movie books call it), as well to start shaping as the overall plot and make some technical decisions around lighting, sound and how we are going to use our filming locations. But these choices are still only blueprints and I intend to remain open to changes on the day. We did a lot of blocking, practicing the movements people will make during a scene, but again we aren't married to these if a better alternative emerges when we shoot. We've also decided that everyone will use their real names in the film, so that we don't have to worry about using the wrong one during any improvised dialogue, and that each actor will bring their own costume, including one item or accessory that defines their character.

People are still really enjoying the process. At one point Luka slid up to me and said, 'Hey, Steve. I have realised something. I was reading in this month's *Film Fanatic* magazine—'

'Oh, God, I haven't even had time to open mine, been a subscriber since I was ten...'

'Well, they are reviewing *Secrets & Lies* and they interview Mike Leigh. And, you know, this process we're doing, it's a lot like how he directs his films. And he's English, like you!'

I grinned and slapped Luka on the back. 'Guess we're gonna have to call ourselves *Brom L-E-I-G-H 96* in that case, eh?'

Not everything we workshopped came off, of course. It would be impossible to use every single suggestion, but whenever someone came up with an idea that no one else thought would work, or that was just plain bonkers, we didn't say that it was *wrong* or *bad*, we just talked it through until we'd reshaped it into something that we all agreed on. Being free to express ourselves produced some gems that I never would have thought of by myself. But ultimately, I am still the director and someone has to keep order and make the final choices. And hey, I'll be editing this thing, too.

I let people know that we will be doing both day and night shooting. Vicky's got us the keys to the school, so who's going to stop us?

Tuesday 21st May

Spent the evening round Ollie's house in his studio-bedroom listening to some of the music he's come up with. I brought our A1 sheets of paper from the rehearsals and we used the ideas to tweak his work. We ended up with something creepy, ominous and electronic that's going to make people's ears bleed.

Ollie said at one point, 'What kind of music are you into?'

I said, 'Dance stuff. Trance, house, bit of techno.'

I told him about how I came up with my final film idea in Fabric and mentioned the 'Open Your Mind' song.

'Listen to this.' He put on this song that sounded just like 'Open Your Mind'.

'What's this?'

'Simple Minds' "New Gold Dream".'

'You mean—'

'Yeah, the band who did the cheesy pop song from *The Breakfast Club*. That track you heard in the club is basically a remix of one of their tracks.'

Well I never.

'So, this Simple Minds band started modern dance music?'

'Not exactly. Let me lend you some stuff, it'll be an education. Better than anything you'll learn at that school.'

As well as the Simple Minds album, he dug out a bunch of other CDs. So far, 'What Time Is Love' by The KLF (Pure Trance Original version) and Donna Summer's 'I Feel Love' have made the biggest impression on me. The latter, which Ollie says is the handiwork of this pioneering composer Giorgio Moroder, has a *thirty-minute* Disco Purrfection version! It goes on and on and on and yet never gets tiresome. But yeah, basically I've been listening to Ollie's music on repeat while I plan the film, between still obsessively playing my own favourites like 'Café del Mar' over and over again.

Thursday 23rd May

After getting home following today's third and final rehearsal, I sat on my bedroom floor with all the A1 sheets laid out and dance music blaring from my hi-fi. I worked well into the night and came up with a scriptment, James Cameron's tool of choice. More than a treatment but not quite a script, it lays out what will broadly happen scene-by-scene, so we can set up the lights and sound and dress the set, but there is still plenty of room for improvisation. For instance, the actors know what they need to communicate to keep the story moving but will come up with their actual dialogue themselves. Nigel, in turn, offered to do illustrations of the key shots to guide us on the day. We don't have time to properly storyboard the whole film, but I want to be as prepared on the technical side of things as possible.

I also finalised the call sheets and shot lists. They'll be essential for organising who needs to be on set on which days and when, and which shots we need to get that day. I emailed them around and printed a load off.

I must be getting better at this collaborating business as I've even got Mum and Dad involved, albeit only minor ways.

I asked Mum during her evening TV watching if she would be up for making some sandwiches for me to take to the set each day and leave in the canteen's fridge.

'Of course, Stephen. I don't know why you've never asked me to help out with one of your films before.'

'I dunno... I wanted to do them on my own, I guess.'

'But you can't do these things with no help at all.'

I felt A Life Lesson coming, so quickly moved the conversation on.

'I'll do something in return, don't worry.'

'You don't have to do anything for me.'

'No, come on Mum, what can I do?'

'Well... you could give me a hand with the day care during the summer holidays, when we go on outings. Just another pair of eyes.'

'No problem.'

'Thank you. But I thought you couldn't stand kids?'

'Let's just say I'm trying to be more tolerant in general.'

My dad said, 'Stephen?' He was sitting in the easy chair reading the *News Shopper*.

'Yes, Dad?'

'This film you're making.'

'Yes?'

'You're using the school as your premises?'

'Yeah.'

'You need to think about insurance. You should be covered by the school's own, as long as you've got their written consent and have provided them with a full breakdown of your planned activities.'

'Oh yes, we've definitely done that.'

'Just be careful. Don't leave wires exposed that people could trip over, or overload plug sockets. You don't want a health and safety nightmare on your hands.'

'Ha, for sure.'

Dad examined me for sarcasm and, finding none, his face morphed into something resembling interest.

'You're taking this project rather seriously, aren't you?'

'Oh yeah, no more running around with a video camera... well, we will be, but much more... organised.'

'And you're back on track with schoolwork?'

'Right on the rails, absolutely.'

He nodded slowly. 'You'll have to let me see this film when you're done. When you've locked it down or whatever the expression is.'

'Definitely.'

This is the first time that my father has ever asked to see my work.

Obviously I'm not going to get any insurance, but it was nice of him to help out in his own way.

Friday 24th May

Spent the morning with David finalising things for the start of the shoot tomorrow. Double-checking that all the cast and crew know when they need to turn up, asking about any food allergies (good idea, Mum), being sure that the camera works and that we have plenty of hi-8 tapes, and a thousand other tiny details to make sure things go as smoothly as possible.

Then David told me to take a break.

'That's an order from your partner.'

So we had an afternoon up town, wandering around the West End. We went to Sega World in the Trocadero centre where, amazingly, all the arcades are free after you pay an entrance fee. We completed *Virtua Cop* and played so many games of *Tekken* that my fingers were numb.

After a Burger King on Leicester Square we wandered up to Soho, where David knew this ace film props shop. I was admiring a poster of *Nosferatu* and considering buying it for my bedroom wall, when David handed me a large bag with the shop's logo on it.

He said, 'Pre-shoot present. So you feel like a proper director.'

Inside was a shiny brand-new clapperboard.

'You shouldn't have...'

'It's not electronic or anything...'

'It's great. Thanks.'

'And I've got something else to show you...'

He opened his coat. Bulging out of the inside pocket was an envelope full of cash.

'David! Don't get that out in the middle of the shop!'

He grinned and zipped up again.

'Where'd all that come from?'

'Refund for the second week of editing. I went to the place in Purley and managed to wrangle it. Now, if only I had someone to spend it on...'

I was literally speechless.

David grabbed my arm. 'Come on, we're going shopping.'

He took me all over the place: Fred Perry in Covent Garden, Ben Sherman on Carnaby Street, Levi's on Regent Street, where they also have a Calvin Klein shop that had a sale on underwear.

Exhausted, we rested our legs by taking in a matinee at the Empire West End. The movie was *Vampire in Brooklyn*, a real low point for Wes Craven, once a horror innovator but now churning out limp star vehicles for Eddie Murphy. And his next film, *Scream*, sounds like it's going to be another bog-standard teen horror/comedy. I feel even more spurred on in my mission to reinvigorate horror filmmaking.

David and I had one more stop, at my request.

We found a barber's just outside Charing Cross station. The bloke asked me what I wanted.

I said, 'I'm about to start an intense work project, so I don't need this mop getting in my way.'

'I got just the thing for you, mate.'

When the barber was finished, David and I took the train back home together.

Saturday 25th May

Me and David met Luka, Peter and Ollie at 7:30 a.m. outside the school gates.

While Luka and Peter began setting up the lights inside, Ollie and David helped me prop my dad's ladder against a telegraph pole so I could climb up and get some killer establishing shots of the school.

'Bloody hell, Steve,' David called up from the ground. 'Don't break your neck on the first day!'

At 9 a.m., the rest of the crew turned up (Gavin, Kevin, and Stella) as well as Ruth, the only actor other than David that we needed today, as per the call sheet. David and Ruth come into the film before anyone else and we're filming more or less chronologically. Not often done in films, but since we have only one location there's no reason not to.

I thought that it was important to say a few words, so I gathered everyone in the assembly hall (our base of production) and thanked everyone for helping out and told them all how confident I am that the movie will turn out brilliantly.

'For a change!' Gavin said. Everyone laughed, although I didn't really see the funny side.

'Anyway, let's make sure this is—'

'Yeah,' Gavin cut in again, 'I could tell you lot some stories about Steve's less-than-brilliant shoots.'

'All right Gav, come on.'

'What? Lost your sense of humour?' And he gave me this smile.

Onto our first scene. David is playing a leather jacket and sunglasses-wearing alpha male who breaks into school during the summer holidays to find a place to finally be alone with his girlfriend, played by Ruth, and prove to everyone (and himself) that he is *a real man*.

David (in his role as first assistant director) said, 'Roll sound.'

Ollie said, 'Speed.'

David said, 'Roll camera.'

Luka said, 'Rolling.'

David said, 'Mark it.'

Kevin leaned in front of the camera and snapped the clapperboard David bought me shut for the first time.

And I said, 'Action!'

I had been nervous about directing David, but it turned out to be a dream. He and Ruth have been working hard on their chemistry and seemed like a real couple. And I must be getting more professional as I didn't feel at all jealous.

David has also been superb between takes as my first AD, telling people where they have to be and reminding everyone of the schedule, leaving me free to confer with Luka or consult my shot list. (This is not the same as being my co-director, you understand. The buck still stops with me.)

The other person who really shone today was Stella. Just doing the little bits of make-up on the actors is making them look so much better on screen. There was something sexy about watching her work, too, doing things like touching up David's face, angling it to make slight adjustments.

'Stellar job, Stella,' Nigel said as he nodded at the portable 14-inch TV we have set up to watch footage back on.

Everyone has been complimentary about my number-one-all-over haircut. Stella even rubbed her hands over it, saying it was like a soft hedgehog. Nigel did point out that they told us in assembly how boys' hair has to be at least a number four in length. I honestly don't remember hearing that, but I've got bigger things to worry about right now.

Sunday 26th May

Stellar job, Stella has become a running-gag on the set. I'm glad, as it's really helping her to fit in.

This morning, we were shooting David storming off after a row with Ruth and something just wasn't working. The lighting was okay, the footsteps echoing down A Block corridor sounded fine, and David's performance was spot-on. It went exactly as planned. Yet when I watched it back, it felt wrong.

I gave Luka some instructions to change the lighting set up so we could start all over again.

'We're gonna get behind with the shot list,' David warned me when I explained what I wanted to do instead.

I said, 'It has to be right.'

So, what had been just a static medium shot became a slow dolly, achieved by Kevin pushing Luka on a Safeway's shopping trolley following David down the corridor, stopping when David is perfectly framed by the doorway and pauses to listen to a noise. By sheer luck a shadow fell over him leaving only his eyes visible, giving him this isolated, vulnerable look. The message to the viewer is that none of this is going to end well.

'I look like John Wayne at the end of *The Searchers*,' David said happily when we all watched it back.

I said, 'Never seen it, but it's on my list.'

Ruth has not been as straightforward as David to direct. She's really nervous and shows little of her real-world confidence in front of the camera.

We were filming a scene in the back office where David takes off his leather jacket and gives it to Ruth to wear. Simple stuff. She just has to take it and say thanks with the right amount of sarcasm. But she was having real problems.

'Shit!' she said after the fourth or fifth take. 'Sorry, Steve.'

I said mildly, 'Let's go again.' But inside I was getting a little impatient.

'Blimey, it's just one word,' Gavin said, watching on the outskirts. 'What's the big deal?'

That wasn't going to help matters.

I said, 'Gav, could you give Kevin a hand making the tea in the canteen?'

'I'm here for continuity, not fucking tea-making, mate.'

I glanced at David, but let it go.

And then, when we were crowded round watching a later take where Ruth did finally manage to get the line out, Gavin let out this guffaw.

He said, 'Sorry.' But he didn't sound very sorry.

Ruth said, 'I knew it, I'm horrible.' She retreated into the corner, almost in tears. I wished Stella was there, but she was chilling out in the assembly hall.

David said, 'Hey, mate, there's no need for that.'

Gavin said, 'Don't tell me what to do, Nolan.'

Then Gav stormed off, saying, 'I'll go and dunk some tea bags then if I'm not wanted here.'

He left behind an awkward atmosphere.

I'm gonna have to nip whatever this is in the bud, sharpish.

Monday 27th May

Realised when I arrived today that there are CCTV cameras all over the school. Maybe during post-production I can get hold of that footage and mix it in.

Less encouraging news is that a holiday club has started in the Primary School next door. I never even thought to check. We were trying to shoot the introduction of Vicky and Nigel's characters and all we could hear were kids running around outside screaming.

Ollie said, 'Steve...' He was looking at his handheld sound-level reader.

'I know, I know. Let's take a break, everyone.'

The woman on the Primary School's reception pointed David and me through and I was soon confronted with this battle axe, like Hattie Jacques from the *Carry On* movies.

She said, 'Are you the new holiday club volunteers?'

'No, we're student filmmakers shooting a movie in the Secondary School next door.'

'Oh, how exciting.'

'Yes... but we were wondering...' I wasn't quite sure what to say.

Luckily David turned on the charm. 'Are they always this noisy?'

'Of course, especially when we're doing outside activities. They *are* children.'

'Ha, I know, I've got a little brother.'

'Would it be all right,' I said, 'if you gave us a copy of your schedule?'

David studied it when we got back to our own school. 'This isn't too bad. We can shoot all the stuff where we're starting to lose our minds when the kids are in the playground. The background noise can reflect our descent into madness.'

Nigel said, 'Yeah, symbolising our loosening grip on reality.'

Ollie still wasn't pleased. He looked up from rolling a fag, shrugged, and said, 'I ain't promising miracles.'

So over lunch I sat with the holiday club schedule and amended the shot list.

Thank God we switch to night shoots soon.

Ruth is playing a vain and shallow girl who follows her cool, popular boyfriend (David) into the empty school. She doesn't actually like him that much but goes out with him because it makes her part of the in-crowd.

I've been thinking about how best to manage Ruth and have come up with a new rule. Only me, the actors in the scene, and the first AD are allowed to view the dailies (or should that be rushes?) back on the monitor.

Ruth said, 'Thanks, Steve. I've been feeling pretty self-conscious about my terrible performance.'

'You're not terrible Ruth, far from it.'

I felt Gavin tense up when he wasn't allowed to see the monitor anymore, but he didn't say anything so I left it.

Today when directing Ruth I went for a softly-softly approach. I took my time discussing the scene with her and was never negative when I said cut. In fact, I was worried that the word *cut* itself would be like a blow to her, so I let her decide when we should stop. If I wanted another take, I said something like "that was perfect, let's do one more for safety," or "we're ahead of schedule, so we may as well get another one".

But the real turning point was when I told her to stop over-thinking.

'Just know what your character wants in this situation and go and get it.'

We got what we needed by lunchtime and moved on.

Some sound issues in the afternoon. We were filming Ruth, Nigel and Vicky in a C Block classroom that was right across from the Primary School's playground. The kids' basketball game was causing us havoc.

Ollie was not happy. 'Going for a fag.'

I said, 'Why don't we take five minutes, everyone?'

While everyone the rest ate biscuits and drank tea and went to the loo, I sat on a desk going through my scene notes and Nigel's shot-by-shot drawings.

David sat next to me. 'We can't work around volume like *this*.'

I nodded.

David waited.

'Well...' I looked up from my papers. 'Who says we always need sound? Silence worked all right for Carl Dreyer and FW Murnau back in the '20s.'

'Who?'

'Oh, David,' I said, jumping down, 'you're so ignorant.'

So we shot the rest of the scene with no dialogue, everything done through gesture, facial expressions, camera angle and shadow. Then in post I'll put music over it.

I was worried that Ollie would be offended that I did a scene with no sound at all, but he was totally professional.

He said, 'You're the first director I've worked with who's given sound this much thought.'

Tuesday 28th May

Things finally came to a head today with Gavin.

David, Nigel and I were watching back Nigel's solo scene where he gazes at Vicky from the other side of the canteen, clearly in love with her. I could feel Gav lurking on the periphery.

I said, 'You okay, mate?'

'Just wondering why David gets to watch the takes back and I don't. Not saying he gets special treatment, *of course*.'

David turned to Gav with this amused expression. 'So, what you mean is, you *are* saying that.'

I said, 'All right, that's enough. Gavin, a word.'

I took him to the courtyard outside. We watched the holiday club in the school next door. Through a window, we could see kids painting hard-boiled eggs inside.

I said, 'What's going on with you?'

'Nothing.'

I sighed. 'Look, Gav, we've made loads of films together. You've never been like this before. Why now?'

He said, 'Dunno.'

'Maybe it would be best if you quit the project.'

He looked shocked. 'I don't want to leave.'

'Then something has to change, mate.'

I let this sink in for a moment.

'David is my assistant director, okay? He has to see what I see. It's not about me giving him special treatment.'

'But what about *me?* I'm supposed to be checking for continuity.'

I thought about this.

'You're right. I'm sorry, mate. You can watch the takes back on the monitor too.'

'Thanks.'

'But no comments, no critiquing the actors. Promise?'

'Promise.'

'And, look, I want you to know that you've been doing a great job so far.'

'Oh yeah?'

'Yeah. So, there's one other thing I'd like you to do. When we get a really good take, I've been scrawling down the number on a bit of paper. Will save time when I'm putting together the edit. But would you mind doing it for me, on your copy of the scriptment?'

'Yeah, absolutely! No problem.'

We wandered back towards the canteen. 'You know, Steve, I barely recognise you these days.'

'Oh, right,' I said, running a hand over my shaved head.

'No, it's not the hair or the clothes.'

Got through a lot of Vicky's scenes today. She is playing a tomboy outsider who manipulates the besotted Nigel into getting her into the locked school for reasons she keeps close to her chest.

I'm directing Vicky the total opposite way to Ruth. Vicky is *over-confident*, not needing any time to warm up or any pep-talks. When she messes up, she doesn't even wait for *cut*, she just soldiers on, muttering *yeah, I know, come on, let's go again.*

At first I felt undermined and wanted to exert my power as director. But I resisted the urge and have come to realise that doing it the way she does works for her, so I just go along with it. I don't say cut on her scenes, I just keep rolling, and this also means I'm accumulating lots of footage to broaden my options for the edit.

All of this non-stop shooting meant that I actually got to the end of a tape in the middle of one of Vicky's speeches. I didn't want to interrupt her so I let the rest of her performance play out un-filmed.

When it was obvious she'd run out of steam by her own accord, then and only then did I come up with a reason to halt things.

'Sorry about this, gang,' I said. 'Luka, can you quickly check the light reading on that take? I'm not sure it's matching anymore.'

I gave him a pointed look.

'Sure.' Cool as anything, my DP took the camera away into a corner. Ten minutes later, we were rolling again with a fresh tape and a refreshed actress.

Nigel, meanwhile, is playing a newcomer to town, the son of the school caretaker and a loner who is desperate to fit in. He tries to impress Vicky by stealing a spell book from his aunt (who is a witch or something like that) and breaking into the school to read it aloud. This is coincidently on the same night that David and Ruth have snuck in elsewhere on the grounds to get it on with each other. But it turns out that Vicky has her own agenda: she wants to steal the money from the canteen's lockbox to pay for a makeover that she hopes will improve her social position.

Nigel has been bringing a lot of levity to the set with his humour, both on and off camera. His character could just be your standard movie loser, but Nigel somehow makes him lovable. It would be understandable if Nige got rankled by Vicky's tetchiness, but he's been very accommodating with her, never getting impatient when I direct their scenes together totally at her pace.

Today, while Luka was putting the new tape in the camera on the sly, Nigel discussed with Vicky what he was planning to do in their next scene, which was taking place in a Chemistry lab. He told Vicky that he was going to twirl the big set of school keys around his finger. But when we started rolling, he threw them to her instead. I was zoomed in tight on Vicky's face at the time and when she stumbled to catch them, I caught a look of genuine surprise from her. Everyone laughed when I called cut but it was the good-humoured type of laughter and Vicky gave Nigel a playful punch on the arm.

He grinned as they got into place for another take. 'Don't think you can relax around me.'

She said, 'Wouldn't dream of it.'

But when it came to the scene's crucial moment, when he reads aloud from the spell book, Nigel cut out the comedy and used this tone of dread that really sold it. That was Kevin's cue to let off a perfectly timed burst of lit gas from a Bunsen burner. Can't beat a good old-fashioned jump scare.

Wednesday 29th May

Stella surprised us all by turning up at 7 a.m., the same time as the usual early birds of me, David and Luka. She held up a bulging Safeway bag.

I said, 'What's all this?'

'Good morning to you, too.' She raised the bag. 'Breakfast for a hardworking cast and crew.'

When everyone else had arrived, Stella used the school's kitchen to make an omelette, hash brown and beans feast for us all.

'Stellar job, Stella,' Barry said with a burp and a thumbs-up, catching onto the joke on his first day on set. The only person who didn't have any of Stella's breakfast was Ruth, who said, 'I'm watching my figure,' and just ate a cereal bar.

Yep, we've now got Barry in our midst, and he's given the project a real shot of energy. His presence has directly contributed to Gavin staying hassle-free, and like Nigel he helps keep the mood light. And he's taken to his character, who is different to what he's played before while still being inside his comfort zone. He's the school tough guy who is having a difficult time at home because his stepdad beats him up. So he's run away and has been living in the empty school over the summer.

Unfortunately, things aren't so good with our Bazza in front of the camera. Barry is still seriously lacking as an actor. All of the old traits were on show today: looking into camera, silly voices, sudden giggling. It was a laugh on our shorts, but it just doesn't suit the professionalism we've built
up here. Even Gavin looked embarrassed.

'Right, that was fine, moving on,' Barry announced after another fluffed take.

I said, 'Bazza, we can't move on. We haven't got what the scene needs.'

'But I thought we were doing all this improvising malarkey. So, it doesn't really matter what we do.'

David said, 'We still have to hit certain plot points.' He consulted his copy of the scriptment. 'In this scene you need to get angry at Nigel and Vicky for discovering you hiding in the school, but when they say fine, they'll leave, you don't want them to go.'

'I *did* do that.'

I said, 'Bazza, you cracked some jokes and then stuck your tongue out at the camera.'

We did eventually get some usable takes. But at this rate we won't be finished before Christmas.

At lunch, I sat on top of a canteen table munching a Mum-made sandwich and watched the morning's footage on the portable monitor.

David said, 'Shoot's going well so far.' He sat down next to me.

Luka said, 'Especially the lighting.' He planted himself next to David.

I just grunted. They were right, but I was concentrating.

Luka said, 'I like what you've been doing with all the mirrors.'

That made me look up. 'What?'

'There is a lot of reflections in this film. And I haven't seen the boom in any, what a miracle!'

David studied me. 'You haven't been *intentionally* putting lots of reflections in, have you?'

I shook my head.

'The scene in the lads' bogs,' David said, listing with his fingers, 'the windows outside the art room, the shiny lockers... Luka's right, they're everywhere. Almost like—'

'Like a visual theme.'

The three of us took it in.

'Right!' I jumped down. 'Any time we get the chance, get a reflective surface into the shot. These characters who can't stop worrying about how they're seen, we're going to make them keep seeing *themselves.*'

Luka said, 'But no reflected booms.'

He made this comment for the benefit of Ollie, who was passing by on his way outside for yet another rolled-up cigarette. 'I'll *smack* you with the boom if you get it in shot,' our sound man laughed.

We hit a snag in the scene where Barry is helping Nigel and Vicky break into the cabinet where the canteen money is kept. The idea had been for Barry to force the cabinet open, and in doing so unwittingly break through the spiritual barrier that was keeping the school's suppressed demons at bay. All the years of negative vibes that the place has absorbed: the bullying, the pettiness, the humiliations.

But there was a problem. *We* can't very well break into a locked cabinet. I mean, *actually* do it.

I couldn't come up with a way to shoot around it. Everyone was standing about waiting for me to make a decision.

I realised that I couldn't figure it out on my own.

I said, 'Okay, group meeting. Let's take a break, smoke a fag or have a cup of tea, then meet in the assembly hall in ten minutes.'

Those of us who had been working on the scene joined the actors who were already in the hall chilling out while they weren't needed, and we all brainstormed how to get what we needed from the scene.

It was Ruth who got the ball rolling. 'Hold on, can't Barry go to kick the cabinet but you cut away before he connects?'

Luka said, 'Yes, we could maybe do it from an angle that makes it look like he touches it, but really he is missing.'

Ollie said, 'Then we can record just the sound of him kicking the door and dub it into the mix later.'

I stroked my chin. 'It's worth a shot.'

'There must be some unlocked cabinets in this school,' David said. 'We find one and shoot a close-up of it swinging open. It should match if it's the same kind of cabinet.'

Peter and Kevin scampered off and soon came back having found just the ticket in a Geography classroom.

So, we had enough elements to shoot the scene, but I still can't be sure whether it'll work until I try editing it all together.

As we got up to head off and give it a try, David said, 'Can always splice in some cutaways as well, like reaction shots or exteriors. Paper over the cracks.'

I said, 'Fix it in post, you mean.'

If there's one thing all the film books agree on, it's to not rely on the editing process to somehow magically produce essential elements that you need for the scene but never actually got on the day.

But sometimes, all you can do is grab as much footage as you can and just move on.

Thursday 30th May

Night shoots from now on until the end of production, with 8 p.m. starts and dawn finishes.

First I got my night-time establishing shots of the school by scurrying up the telephone pole again, with David holding the ladder below. Then we met Luka inside, who suggested that we re-order the shooting schedule so that he can put the electric lights away for some scenes and make best use of the natural light coming through the windows at sunrise, the so-called *magic hour* that brings with it a brilliant orange glow. If you've ever seen a Tony Scott movie, especially *Top Gun* or *Days of Thunder*, you'll know what I mean.

Luka said, 'I hope you don't mind the inconvenience.'

'No, course not! Great thinking, mate.'

My trusty cinematographer has been full of these ace ideas. He'll suggest them to me on the sly, so the others don't have to know that they are coming from him and not my own brilliant mind.

Total legend.

I *can* claim some brainwaves as my own. I told David to remain unshaven for the shoot's duration, so as we move through the hours of the gang's night in the haunted school, the stress of it is reflected in David developing several days' worth of growth. (Okay, it's not entirely my own idea: I read that George Lucas did something similar in *American Graffiti*, filming it in sequence to show the characters getting fatigued over one long night.) In addition, Stella's been adding bags under David's eyes, and now that the evil within the school has been unleashed, Luka has made the lighting gloomier and more ominous, with plenty of purple filters that get more intense the closer we are to The Purple Room, which holds the money cabinet that was concealing not just a pile of crumpled cash but the door to hell itself.

When Kevin and Peter had finished decorating the school corridor with acrylic paints, we filmed some of the messed-up group hallucination sequences that come when the school really starts screwing with the characters' minds. Kevin and Peter also play zombified visions of the characters' paranoia about what people think of them. Again, Stella's make-up looks wicked.

We've now completed all the scenes Nigel is in, but he's happy to stay on for the rest of the shoot and help out where needed. His character is the first to die, when his spell book becomes possessed and attacks him. I gave up trying to figure out a way to make being strangled by a sentient book look realistic and went for the less-is-more approach. We simply pan away, cut to the book flying through the air and then hear Nigel choking off-screen.

Elsewhere, I made some progress with Barry. I told him to stop acting.

He said, '*Don't* act?'

'Yeah.' We were prepping his big scene in the woodwork classroom and I had taken him aside. 'Barry, in real life you're always acting, putting on a show. Every day for you is a performance. Here, I just want you natural. You created this guy and I know that there's a lot of you in him.'

'So, your advice is... be myself?'

We both laughed at such a cliché.

'Just try it out for size.'

Try it he did and the effect was instant. Barry was finally just Barry, and yet he was his character at the same time. It's hard to explain, but he managed to use something real from inside himself to do something that wasn't real, and through that made it feel *really* real. We ended up getting through his scenes ahead of schedule.

Food tonight came courtesy of Ruth, who brought in some pasta bake for us to heat up.

Everyone wolfed it down except Stella. I said, 'Not having any?' My own mouth was overflowing.

She said, 'No.' Then she gave Ruth this look.

Our first night shoot wrapped at 6 a.m. David and I were yawning as we locked up the school gates. Having clicked the padlock home and given the chain a satisfying jangle, we were just turning to leave when a fast-moving beige blur entered our peripheral vision.

A voice said, 'Hello there, excuse me?'

David and I were confronted by an elderly man marching across the road in his tatty dressing gown and slippers.

'I say, excuse me?'

David whispered, '*I say?*'

'Oh God, this isn't going to be good.'

This bloke demanded to know 'just what the devil' we had been up to in the school 'all blasted night'. This sad-case was quoting times that we were in each building, like he had a copy of our fucking shot list.

I said, 'We're making an educational video on the importance of extra-curricular study.' I lifted the camera for him to see.

He frowned. 'And for how long?'

David said, 'We'll have the subject covered by the end of the week.'

The nosy-neighbour narrowed his eyes. 'I want to see a permit.'

'Of course. We'll bring it next time and pop it through your letterbox.'

'Make sure that you do.'

What a nutter. We just wanted to get the fuck home to bed.

David and I were still laughing about the guy when we got to David's house.

'You know,' he said at his front garden, 'you can stay over at mine for the rest of the shoot. Closer to the school and it will give us more time for prep and to review footage.'

'Nah, that's okay. It's good to have time on my own to digest the day, think about tomorrow, write my diary.'

He looked disappointed and turned to open his front gate.

I said, 'But, I mean, thank you for the—'

'All right, look.' David took his hand off the gate.

He looked at me. My heart stopped.

'About what happened back in the day.'

'No, David, don't—'

'No, let me talk.'

He waited for me.

'All right. What d'you want to say?'

'I want to say that we were only kids.'

'I know we were—'

'And you need to know that it didn't mean anything. We didn't *do* anything. And what we did do, it doesn't mean that you're—'

'Because I'm not—'

'Right, you're not. I'm not either. Not that it would matter if either of us were.'

'No, of course it wouldn't matter.'

It was my turn to wait for him.

'But if it didn't matter—'

'Then why did we fall out?'

He nodded.

Man, this was hard.

'I guess I freaked out. Because life is hard enough, you know? If I turned out to be gay, then I didn't want to have to deal with people's reactions to *that* on top of all the other bullshit.'

'I understand. I do. But... so much time.'

'Wasted.'

'Yeah.'

'Two years.'

He nodded.

'So, you're sure you don't want to come in.'

I hesitated. 'Better not.' Then I smiled. 'But I'll see you on set tomorrow.'

He smiled back. 'See you there, boss.'

He opened the gate and I watched him walk all the way up the garden path.

Friday 31st May

Toughest day yet.

We were all prepped to film Ruth's death in the girls' toilets: lights, make-up, sound, actors on their marks.

David said, 'Roll sound.'

Ollie said, 'Speed.'

David said, 'Roll camera.'

Luka said, 'Rolling.'

David said, 'Mark it.'

Kevin leaned in front of the camera and snapped the clapperboard shut.

And I said... nothing.

'Hold on a sec.'

They all waited: Ruth, standing there in front of the mirror, Ollie with his sound boom held aloft, Gavin with his scriptment covered with notes on continuity and usable takes, Luka holding the camera, Nigel standing next to me ready to help if needed.

'This can be better.'

Ruth said, 'What do you mean? She gets strangled by her Tiffany necklace. It's her vanity turning on her. It's perfect for the character.'

I said, 'It's not perfect.' I wasn't looking at her or anyone else. I was focused, my hand running back and forth over my scalp.

Nigel said, 'We did just have me die by something getting my neck. Do you think it's too similar?'

Finally, I said, 'I think that it *is* that, but it's not *just* that. There's more we can get from this scene.' Then I smiled. 'And it's staring right at us.'

So we changed Ruth's death. Now she gets stabbed by shards of a shattered mirror, an even more ironic comment on her vanity that also supports the film's visual theme of reflection. Luckily for us, one of the toilet mirrors was already missing so we used some of Clive's dad's sugar glass in its place. We filmed most of Ruth's death as an extreme close-up of her terrified eyes, just like in Dreyer's *The Passion of Joan of Arc*.

When she watched the footage back, my lead actress was thrilled and hugged me. 'It looks brilliant! Take one is perfect, we nailed it first try!'

I let her hold me for a little too long and then pulled away sharply. Stella was thankfully nowhere to be seen.

What Ruth didn't realise was that I'd been so focused on improving the scene that I'd actually forgotten to press *record* for her first take. Luckily takes two and three were also usable.

I was annoyed with myself about that gaffe but it wasn't terminal, and I would have forgotten all about it if it wasn't for all my other cock-ups today.

We'd finished the scene where the remaining teenagers (David, Vicky and Barry) argue about why the other two have been brutally killed. As everyone was setting up for the scene after, I rewound the tape to review the footage of the argument scene. After a few seconds, I knew it was good and so stopped and went to press fast-forward to get to the end of the takes and so be safely on blank tape again.

But I made a mistake. I wasn't looking and I hit rewind again instead of fast-forward. We started filming the next scene, and it wasn't until we were halfway through that I glanced at the timecode and realised my mistake. I'd ended up recording over the best take of the previous scene. I had got other takes, and they were okay, but something from each was wrong: a performance, a camera wobble, a missed mark.

So I told everyone that we needed to go back and reshoot the whole scene, including spending another hour setting it up again.

Vicky said, 'Oh, come on, you said we got a great take.' Stella had already started doing her make-up for what was next on the schedule: Vicky's big death scene.

'I know Vicky, but there's been a cock-up. *I* cocked something up.'

She groaned.

And so the atmosphere when we did get the argument scene in the bag and could finally move on to Vicky's death scene was less than harmonious. And it just so happened that her demise was the hardest thing we've had to shoot so far.

Vicky is supposed to get choked to death by the money she was so desperate to steal. I'd never been happy with the paper mache fake cash we'd planned to use, and Vicky refused to have her mouth filled with it anyway.

She said, 'Can't we just film my eyes the whole time, like you did with Ruth?'

I said, 'Vicky, we need a shot of the money in your mouth, otherwise the poetic justice will be lost.'

'So that was all right for Ruth's big scene but not for mine?'

'That was different.'

'Why, because you fancy her?'

I had to gloss over the awkward moment. I had to resist looking at Stella. Luckily, Ruth herself was over in the assembly hall chilling out.

I called lunch.

I ate outside alone with David. It was the first time the entire cast and crew haven't all sat together in the canteen.

David said, 'It's just been a hard day. We're near the finish line, but because we're all tired it still seems far away. The creative energy is down, but things will pick up again.'

'I guess.'

He patted me on the back.

'On your feet soldier, on your feet.'

I ended up with more takes and camera set-ups for Vicky's death than on any other scene, using eight or nine different angles. Lots of coverage. Among that lot should be enough usable footage for me to cobble it together somehow. Yes, I'm going to have to rely on fixing it in post. Not the most secure feeling.

When we were finally done, I sought out Stella while Luka set up for the next sequence.

I found her at the canteen's Coke machine.

I said, 'Hey.'

She said, 'Mmm.'

'Um, look, I don't know what Vicky was talking about back there.'

'When?' She was very carefully considering which drink to choose.

'About... you know.'

She seemed to have got it down to either Apple Tango or Diet Fanta.

'What Vicky said. About Ruth.'

'Why would it matter to me? We're just friends. I thought that was clear.'

She grabbed her can of Tango and walked away.

To top off this day of days, during the final set-up I let the fucking battery run out and then realised that I had forgotten to charge the two spares.

Ollie said, 'You've got to be kidding me.'

Barry said, 'That's like an *old Steve* move.'

Even Luka was unimpressed, but had the good grace to hide it.

In the end, I had to film the scene of Barry and David grappling over the caretaker's keys with the camera plugged into the wall, which completely fucked up the shot list and forced me into a hit-and-hope style that was most definitely like the old Steve.

I'm glad Mr Beige Dressing Gown didn't come out again when we finally wrapped, as I would have told him to piss right off. The day was so stressful that I ended up regularly going outside to smoke rollies with Ollie.

Gonna need something special to turn things around tomorrow.

June 1996

Saturday 1st June

In the end, I tried two things. One worked wonders. The other... less so.

The first thing I did was address the low morale. I had bought personalised baseball caps for everyone, with the movie's title on the front along with the person's name and their role on the project. I was going to save them for the last day of shooting, but decided to give them out while we were preparing today's first set-up.

Vicky said, 'Wow, thanks.' She looked almost humbled.

Gavin studied his. 'So this is what the film's called?'

'Yep. I just wanted to give these out as a token of my appreciation.'

I could feel the black cloud from yesterday evaporating.

'*Dawn Never Comes*,' Nigel read from his cap.

David said, 'You finally decided on a title.'

'Yep.'

Luka said, 'I like it.'

Buzzing now, I announced my second idea to David, Luka and Ollie while we were having our mid-morning snack.

'We're gonna shoot the sequence of David chasing Barry through the school from behind, entirely handheld. One shot, one continuous take.'

The three of them looked at each other.

David said, 'Why?'

'Because it will look amazing. Like the opening of *Halloween* or that bit through the nightclub kitchen in *Goodfellas*.'

'But how will it benefit the film?'

'I just told you how, it will look fucking awesome.'

Luka said, 'But this will be very complicated to plan, both with the actors and the lighting, not to mention keeping the sound so everyone can be heard...'

We all looked at Ollie.

'I need a fag,' he said, green Rizla already in hand.

We decided to give it a go.

But it didn't work. Logistically it was just too complicated. We couldn't keep the lighting consistent when we were moving in and out of different buildings, the actors found it impossible to maintain pace with the camera that was following them, and Ollie couldn't stop the boom from bobbing into shot as he raced to keep up.

David's simple *why* question was ringing in my ears when we finally gave up, more than two hours later. I didn't have an answer. But I wouldn't let it go.

I said, 'We'll try this again tomorrow.' I didn't see confidence on their faces. 'Look, I know we can pull it off.'

The next sequence was more straightforward: David's death scene.

We decided to go heavy on the gore for this one, no holding back or cutting away. Since this will be the only time we lay it on thick, it'll have more impact. And we need it to be impactful: we're shocking the audience by killing off the protagonist (probably the only thing I like about the original *Psycho*.)

What happens is that the school possesses David's Aviator sunglasses and hurtles them through the air to stab him in both eyes.

While we were setting up, Vicky said, 'It's phallic symbolism.' Stella and Ruth nodded.

We used more leftover Clive effects and it ended up looking wicked.

So, with David a goner, late-to-the-party Barry ends up as the new lead and sole survivor. He's gone from a stoic tough guy to being deeply affected by the unexplainable murders of his peers over this long night, events that only add to his existing trauma. He breaks down, fleeing through the school without aim or destination, getting lost in corridors that he should know but which seem to be changing in front of his very eyes. We used lots of wonky camera angles and uneven framing to enhance this effect. Barry ends up on B Block roof. He's distraught, strung-out... the sun is starting to rise... and something evil is telling him to step forward, just do it, jump and put an end to it all...

But he fights the urge, and what he sees below snaps him fully back. The purple glow of the school's repressed evil is starting to seep out and leave the premises.

In a bravura solo performance, Barry struggles through his conflicting emotions, pulls himself together and decides that he just can't let the horrors of tonight affect any more innocent people. He rushes back to the stairs that took him up to the roof.

When we finally cut, the roof was silent. We were out in the open at 5 a.m., so we held our peace as we filed back down the roof stairs.

Then the moment Peter closed the fire escape door behind us, we erupted into applause and smothered Barry.

Sunday 2nd June

No one wanted to retry my single-take sequence, which has been dubbed The Hollywood Shot. I couldn't come up with any reason for it. It was the last day (night) of shooting. We were all strung out, exhausted.

So I scrapped it and we went back to doing the scene the way we originally discussed.

Once we had it in the can, to coin a phrase, David sought me out as I returned from a walk around the school field on my own in the dark. I needed some space to get over losing the opportunity to show off that I'd been craving so badly.

David said, 'It was for the best.'

'I know.' I sighed. 'I just wanted to have that one impressive, standout sequence, you know? I had started to feel confident enough to pull it off.'

'We *do* have an impressive, standout sequence. We just don't know which one it is yet. The audience will decide when they watch the film, we don't choose it for them while we're shooting.'

He was right, as always.

Other than that it was a straightforward final day, with only one actor left and the end in sight.

In the final scene, Barry breaks out of the school, which had been imprisoning him both mentally and physically and driving him to contemplate suicide. He opens a first-floor window, shimmies onto the drainpipe, and jumps over the school's outer fence onto an off-screen crash mat.

We close the movie on him racing east towards the sunrise, exiting the frame under a street sign that reads 'Bromley town centre: 2 miles'.

'Nailed it,' I whispered to David.

He squeezed my shoulder.

At 6:09 a.m., the cast and crew of *Dawn Never Comes* walked out the school gates together. Each of us felt a sense of accomplishment, of being more than we were a week ago.

Nigel summed it up best.

'We deserve an *epic* wrap party.'

I laughed. 'We'll have one. We've earned it. But let me edit this thing first.'

Luka said, 'That is where the real work starts.'

Yes. Editing will be mammoth. And what's more, I'm going to do it properly this time.

SUMMER

Monday 3rd June

No rest for the wicked. Back to the unwanted distraction of school today. No arsing off for an extended summer holiday either, unlike last year when we did our GCSEs, or the Upper Sixth who have just now done their proper A Level exams. Although once the school get my grades from the mocks, I doubt they're actually going to want me to stay on to next year. I'd been on an upward curve recently with my coursework, sure, but pre-production on the movie meant that I wasn't exactly giving those exams my all.

And my priorities haven't changed. Being in the educational prison is annoying at the best of times, but right now I have to edit a whole fucking feature film, too. I've used what little budget I had left to buy some top-of-the-range post-production software, so that I can hook the camcorder up to a PC to edit (like we do at school) instead of relying on the old-fashioned and poor-quality method of connecting two VCRs (like I did for my shorts). So I need a lot of time on the family computer, which means finding a window when Mum's not playing *Solitaire* or Dad's not working on his spreadsheets while listening to his mind-numbing classical music. Luckily, I've managed to persuade them to let me temporarily move the PC into my bedroom. For my coursework, of course.

And I have not got at all long. The Kent Film Festival itself isn't 'til 17th August, but the deadline for entries is 29th July.

Despite us all scrubbing away at the end of the shoot, there is still some acrylic paint visible around the school, especially just outside the canteen where we filmed the most intense footage of Bazza losing his marbles. Hopefully no one will notice.

Had none of the expected pushback today about my shaved head. I'm glad, as I really don't want the teachers thinking it's part of some lame rebellion.

Tuesday 4th June

Oh man. We have *a lot* of footage: five one hundred and twenty-minute hi-8 tapes' worth, giving me ten hours to trawl through. The mixed curse and blessing of shooting as much as possible.

Hard to tell how I feel from first impression. Certain bits look good, but how does it fit together as a whole? Well, I've got what I've got and will just have to make the most of it.

Wednesday 5th June

Someone noticed the paint.

Some anonymous jobsworth, some *schools*worth, reported me to Mrs Rebus, our trusted Head of Sixth Form and Kent's (or southeast London's) number one Margaret Thatcher lookalike.

So I step into old Thatch's office, expecting the usual bollocking. Instead I find her there with Vicky, and instead of her usual caterpillars-meeting frown, Rebus has this big, warm smile on her face. Vicky, meanwhile, is fixing me with this smug look.

Rebus goes to me, 'Ah, Mr Ricketts.'

I go, 'Mrs Rebus.'

'I hear you've been defacing school property in the name of art.'

'I don't know what you mean.'

She brushes aside the whole accuse/deny process with a dismissive wave.

'Stephen,' she goes, 'Victoria has been keeping me informed about your little film project. Closely informed.'

I look at Vicky. Standing next to Mrs R, she seems very much on that side of the desk. Part of the establishment. I'm trying to figure out just what the bloody hell is going on.

'I've been very impressed,' Rebus continues.

I just grunt.

'Stephen, I'm sure an entrepreneur like yourself is aware of the importance of funding. Do you, by any chance, know how schools are funded?'

'By the government?'

She gives me a patronising little smile. Worse, so does Vicky.

'Of course. But things are more complicated with a Sixth Form. It may be just another school year to you, but you're now in non-voluntary education.'

Vicky goes, 'You don't actually have to take any A Levels, by law.'

'Yes, *Victoria*, I understand.'

Rebus gives her a short look then starts up again.

'Funding for our connected Sixth Form College relies on many factors. Exam results, attendance, and so on. One way of receiving more funding is if we specialise. Our intention is to soon become a Media Studies college, but Bromley Council won't grant us this status unless we can prove that we deserve it. Our grade average is fine, but what if there was something more, something special. Something like one of our students making a feature film? About which we can get press coverage and which may be shown at a film festival? It wouldn't even have to be a *good* film, so long as it was finished. And so, when Ms Harper told me about your project, I decided to do everything in my power to help.'

'The thing with the coursework...'

'And allowing you to film at the school during the holidays, and instructing your teachers to be lenient at parents' evening, and turning a blind eye to stunts like that horrendous *buzz-cut* you have on top of your head. But obviously I needed someone... on the inside, as they say in the spy movies of which you are no doubt fond.'

She nods at Vicky, somewhat unnecessarily.

Then she frowns. 'Your parents don't know about our little Media Studies coursework arrangement, do they? Despite me having a form signed by them in my drawer?'

'You can't prove that.'

'I could always ask them.'

She's got me there.

Mrs Rebus goes back to smiling again. Vicky copies her, like she's... whoever Margaret Thatcher's second-in-command was.

They're waiting for me to say something.

'There's just one thing I'm still not clear about.'

'Yes?'

'Does this mean I'm *not* in trouble for the paint?'

Rebus laughs.

'Stephen Ricketts, I do sincerely believe that I shall miss you once you've passed through my school and out the other end.'

In the corridor Vicky tries to give me the slip but I corner her by the Coke machine.

'What the fuck, Vick?'

'Come on, Steve. You can't honestly have believed I was helping you out of the goodness of my heart?'

'I thought that... you said want to be an actress...'

'What I want is to get into the Oxford School of Drama. But my grades have been slipping, and my *focus has been shifting*, as my parents put it. You'd think they'd understand, they were young once. Apparently. There's so much pressure to fit in, to go to the right parties, to be seen out with the right people...'

'Harris—'

'Don't mention that name to me!'

I keep my trap shut and wait for her to speak again.

Vicky sighs. 'A letter of recommendation from the Head of Sixth Form would make up for my grades. But Rebus said she would only give me one if I made sure you finished your movie. And you don't make it very easy for yourself, do you? Like with your antics during the play before Christmas, or that God-awful first attempt round Adrian's house. Rebus nearly called the whole thing off, except she remembered being impressed by some kitten video you made for your General Studies teacher and decided that maybe you could pull it off after all.'

'So, you used me. And you lied to me: the warehouse was never set up as a filming location, was it?'

'Like I say, I had to keep you going. You're not the only one who can make things up on the spot. Wake up, Steve: no one does anything for nothing, everyone has their own angle.'

I just stand there in A Block corridor, utterly stunned.

'Look...' She seems genuinely conflicted. 'It *was* fun. And I *do* think you'll end up with something good. So how's editing going, anyway?'

Thursday 6th June

Popped into Video Nation after school, for maybe the last time ever.

Eamon said, 'How was the shoot?' He'd just finished selling someone a copy of *The Lost Boys*: everything is to-buy now, no more rentals.

By way of reply I gave Eamon a wide-eyed, puffed-cheek face. He laughed.

'Got a buyer for the shop.'

'Oh.' I turned and had a proper look at the place. Noticed for the first time that it's maybe a little shabby, maybe a little faded.

Eamon said, 'Come on, I'll buy you a pint. No missus to get back to, we single men can do what we want.' When he saw my face drop, he cleared his throat. 'Eh, I'll just stick to the Guinness this time. Laying off the Jameson's, so I am.'

We sat down in the pub. I said, 'So is it still going to be a video shop?'

Eamon wiped off his foam moustache. 'Can't say. But I wouldn't bank on it.'

'Really?'

'Stephen, this is a blessing in disguise, you know. I'm not saying I wanted your aunt to leave me, or that I have much chance of another career at my age. But video shops, they're on the way out.'

'They are?' A cold terror ran through my veins.

'Yeah, to be sure. Distributors are nervous, other shops are nervous. Have you heard about digital versatile discs, DVDs?'

'Like CDs?'

'Yeah, they're movies on a CD. That's the next thing. Not Laserdisc, rather a more affordable, mainstream way to get better picture and sounds. Word is the viewer will become the director, choosing which shot in a film to watch, basically editing their own movie.'

That sounded ominous for the likes of me.

'No one's gonna want VHS tapes soon. Old tech. So I'd have had to get a whole new stock in. That's okay for Blockbusters, but a major hit for the wee man.'

We both drank, contemplating a brave new world.

'Keep an eye on the tech, young Stephen. But never let it be your master, make sure *you* master *it*.'

Friday 7th June

Most people are taking advantage of the long days and are passing their evenings sitting outside in pub gardens with a drink. I, however, am spending all my free time alone in my bedroom with the curtains drawn.

Editing is a process that is equally invigorating and tedious. Basically, it's a matter of watching all the takes of one scene, choosing which one came out the best, and then moving that onto the master cut. You just have to make decisions. It was like that on set too, there was a multitude of things that could either be done one way or another, and ultimately the buck stopped with me.

Whether or not I make the *right* decisions is another matter entirely.

Saturday 8th June

David came round to see how I'm doing. He watched a bit of what I've edited so far and was positive on the whole, although he added that it was really too early to tell.

We spent some time working on the application to the Kent Summer Film Festival. I immediately doubted our chances. They want all this justification for every step, our motivations... my whole life seems to revolve around filling in applications!

I said, 'How do you reckon we can spin this so that we're saying what they want to hear?'

David said, 'You could just put down the truth.'

It's like a whole new kind of blag. Could just be crazy enough to work.

Sunday 9th June

On Friday we got our mock A Level results, but I only had the guts to open the envelope today. They give you your exam result and coursework mark for each subject, and then they combine those for your predicted final A Level grades. Those are what we'll slap on the uni applications that we'll be doing when we come back after the summer hols.

I am predicted C, C, D, E.

Well, I was pleasantly surprised that it wasn't an F for General Studies.

So Mrs Rebus's powers aren't limitless: they don't extend as far as the bods who mark our stuff over at the exam board.

Tuesday 11th June

Have been losing myself in the editing, which is doing a good job of distracting me from the consequences of my slipping school performance. Although now I'm starting to wish I had something to distract me from the editing, too. God, it's taking forever.

It may be a laborious process, but it does throw out the occasional ray of light. Today I found something that didn't work for the scene it was filmed for but that I can use elsewhere. When Nigel surprises Vicky by throwing her the keys, her genuine look of surprise is a bit over the top for that scene. But it fits perfectly into her death sequence, which is missing a good reaction shot with the footage we did shoot for it. You can't tell that it's a mishmash of shots from different scenes and it really makes her demise work.

For some unknown reason, I quite enjoyed re-watching Victoria

Motson being killed.

Wednesday 12th June

Could put off showing my parents my predicted A Level grades no longer.

I tried to explain how stressed I've been this year and how I'd suffered from depression. Not entirely untrue. It might have worked, but then I made the mistake of aligning said depression with the failed *Murder House* shoot.

My dad said, 'Well, there's an easy solution to this.'

So now there is a password on the PC and I'm only allowed to use it for schoolwork, and they say that they'll be checking up on me every fifteen minutes.

This has my disrupted my editing schedule somewhat.

And yet I feel the calmness of the criminal who gets busted but knows he has the best lawyer in town.

Thursday 13th June

Defence Attorney Margaret Rebus was off today, so I couldn't call on her to litigate me out of this parent-shaped hole. Still, a couple of days' break from the editing screen could actually do me some good.

Asked David when he was picking up Freddy whether he wanted to grab the editing reins while I deal with this temporary inconvenience.

He said, 'Sorry mate. I wouldn't know one end of an editing program from the other.'

Hasn't stopped me.

But it's probably for the best. If a director trusted someone else to edit their film, who knows in what sort of state it would turn out.

Friday 14th June

'Don't worry, I'll take care of it,' Mrs R said when I told her about my parents' unreasonableness. 'You'll have a letter by the end of the day delivered via your form tutor.'

The letter encouraged my parents to 'not stifle Stephen's creative development' and went on about how my extra-curricular activities are just as important as my schoolwork and that allowances must be made. It then invited my mum and dad to a meeting tomorrow morning, after Rebus has finished presiding over a Saturday detention.

Wow. Untouchable, like Elliot Ness.

Saturday 15th June

The meeting turned out to be nothing but a sheer love-in from Mrs Iron-Knickers towards your humble narrator, to a near-uncomfortable degree. My parents didn't suspect foul play, blinded as they were by their host's non-stop compliments about how well they've brought me up. This about a student who she once described as 'insolent and cocksure to the point of exasperation'.

The long and the short of the meeting is that I will be allowed to re-submit my coursework during the summer holidays.

Rebus concluded the chat with, 'You should be glad that Stephen is channelling his energies into something creative, not hanging out on some street corner pursuing fornication and debauchery.'

Blimey, I thought as we all stood up and shook hands. I wouldn't mind a bit of the old fornication and debauchery, if you'd be kind enough to point me in the right direction, Missus.

So the PC is mine once again. What's more, Mum and Dad are now keen for me to do film at uni after all. I also took this opportunity to mention that I've 'resigned' from my part-time job at Asda to concentrate on my studies.

This doesn't mean that I'm completely stress-free, you understand. I'd better make sure I get *Dawn Never Comes* accepted into that festival, thus getting into a film uni and giving the school's Media Studies college pitch a boost. Now I've seen how lethal Mrs R is at dealing with anything that stands in her way, I'd hate to *become* one of those things. Although she's covered it up so far, she can expel me any time she wants for my permission form forgery.

Was thinking about Ms Harper while lying in bed (no, not like that). Did she know about Rebus using me for this Media Studies college application?

Sunday 16th June

Have started to edit with my tunes on in the background. It's helping me to shape the film's rhythm and pacing and I'm applying what I'm learning about musical structure to how I put scenes together.

My playlist is basically a journey into the origins and development of dance music, a combination of stuff borrowed from Ollie and Martin and some places I've found on the Internet, where you can order songs that haven't even been released yet straight from the record label.

Weirdly, I'm finding that I actually prefer the original Simple Minds song 'New Gold Dream' to 'Open Your Mind', the dance track that samples it. Overall, though, the newest stuff is still the best: 'Café del Mar' is rarely away from my hi-fi.

Tuesday 18th June

Ms Harper *did* know about Rebus's plan for my film! I confronted her after class today. She said that she didn't tell me because she didn't want to put extra pressure on me.

Well that really worked out, didn't it? Not like I don't *now* have a shit-ton of pressure on me or anything.

Especially after today. I *had* started to feel quite positive about the editing, especially the last thing I did yesterday. The scene of Barry and David fighting over Nigel's keys that my incompetence forced me to shoot with the camera plugged into the wall actually came out really well. You'd never suspect that we didn't plan to do it that way.

Enthused by this, I decided to watch back everything I've edited up to now, a rough cut of the film so far.

Oh dear.

It's terrible. I can't put my finger on why, but something is definitely up. And there was me thinking I was ahead of schedule.

One big concern is that the camera shakes about too much. It's going to make people feel giddy, like motion sickness. But it's a horror film, so that's a good thing. Right?

Wednesday 19th June

Shit. Shit. Shit.

What was I thinking? Just point the camera and shoot? Improvised script? Bromleigh 96? I must have been out of my mind.

You would not believe the paranoid thoughts I've been having. Like, maybe David wormed his way back into my life just to sabotage the shoot. He could have been in league with Vicky the whole time, raising the stakes so I could fall from a greater height.

Calm down, calm down.

Went for a walk and came back feeling better.

The David stuff is bullshit. It *has* to be. I'm just letting the old wound reopen and cloud my judgement.

I think the major problem is that I can't see the woods for the trees. I'm watching the footage in front of me, but in my mind I'm seeing what took place in order to *get* that footage, not what's actually on the screen. I'm seeing Barry nearly giving Nigel a black eye from demonstrating how to throw a fake punch, I'm seeing the chase scene where I dropped the camera after noticing Stella leaning forward in a low-cut top, I'm seeing Ruth and Vicky having a heated argument about whose fault it was that their scene turned into a fit of giggles. I'm seeing everything that happens before *action* and after *cut*. The shoot, not the shots.

Saturday 22nd June

At 11:45 p.m. I took a breather from editing, which I had been doing non-stop since I got home from school, and collapsed on my bed. I looked up and stared at my video collection and for some reason my eyes settled on my copy of *Dead Ringers*.

I pulled the tape from the shelf, turned it over, and scanned the credits.

Long ago, I noticed how David Cronenberg uses many of the same crew on all his films. Music by Howard Shore. Cinematography by Peter Suschitzky (Mark Irwin on earlier films). Production design by Carol Spier. Costume design by Denise Cronenberg, his sister.

And edited by Roland Sanders.

Shit. *Of course* proper directors don't edit their own material. Cronenberg always uses this guy Sanders.

I need to find an editor for this film or it's doomed.

Sunday 23rd June

Okay, need to chill out again.

First of all, there is no other chump around who is going to edit this film for me. No one from the cast or crew anyway. Maybe I could take an ad out in *Film Fanatic* or one of the other magazines or see if Luka and Ollie know anyone, but I'm hardly blessed with time here.

Secondly, I rang Eamon up and asked him if he knew of any directors who have edited their own films. He reeled off Robert Rodriguez, George A. Romero, Michelangelo Antonioni, Akira Kurosawa and the Coen brothers. John Woo on *Bullet in the Head*, as well. Eamon also pointed out that directors usually *have* to edit their early features, much like they often have to be their own DPs, or first ADs, or production assistants, or whatever else. And that when they do start to get their films edited by someone else, they're still heavily involved, it's a very collaborative process.

So yes, I am calmer. But that doesn't change the fact that what I've edited so far is awful. You don't feel like you're watching something that's a whole, it's more like a series of vaguely connected scenes strung together. You don't feel involved in the action.

With my shorts, all I did was slap all my one-take scenes together, maybe trimming a few seconds from the start or end, and adding slow-mo here and there. Now, I have several usable takes to choose from but I don't know how to pick the right ones.

Tuesday 25th June

Today David came over to try and help.

He said, 'You edited your shorts, right?'

'Sort of.'

'So, I thought you knew what you were doing?'

'So did I.'

David helped me choose some different combinations of takes on a couple of scenes and some did work out better, but since I don't even know what I'm doing wrong, fixing it is hit and miss. Even if I could go back and re-shoot everything, I still wouldn't know what to do with the footage when I got to this stage.

I called up Eamon for some more advice and we're going to meet up with him in person the day after tomorrow.

Meanwhile, I took some time away from my post-production hell to pop to The Glades in Bromley. Did a bit of window shopping at clothes and then went to Nigel's house to play *Magic: The Gathering*. Clive was there and he was pleasant enough, but I don't think we'll ever really see eye to eye again. No blowout, no confrontation, just this kind of drifting apart. The weird thing is, I think we're both okay with it. I suppose we just want different things from life right now, or something like that. Just one of those things.

Thursday 27th June

David and I met up with Eamon for dinner in the beer garden of The Pickhurst.

'Let me ask you something,' my uncle said, chewing on his burger. 'What are you editing *for?*'

I glanced at David. 'Not sure I understand.'

'Are you editing for the story, or are you just placing the shots that look coolest one after the next?'

'Well, story, I guess...'

'You can't guess, Stephen. You have to know. Always have the story in your mind, always be thinking about where you are in it, what's just happened, and what's happening next. You have a theme for your film, am I right?'

'The fear of what people think about you. Visually, it's reflection.'

'Good. Always defer to those. And always leave a scene on a shot that communicates the whole purpose of the scene, the thing that you want people to remember. And if you can't figure out the scene's purpose...?'

'Cut it?'

'Cut it. And also make sure a scene ends on something that links smoothly onto the start of the following scene.'

I was nodding away. This was great stuff.

'It would also be useful,' Eamon mused, 'if you had some pick-ups. Tiny wee shots from your location that you can use to tie a scene together. Just a few seconds here and there can work wonders.'

'Yeah, I do wish I had more footage. We shot loads of coverage, like you said, but what I wouldn't give for even more options.'

David said, 'What about the CCTV?'

I gasped. 'I forgot all about that!'

Eamon raised his eyebrows. 'Think you can get it?'

I leaned back in my chair. 'No problem.'

Friday 28th June

So I bowl round to the security office today and ask to see whoever is in charge of the CCTV. The office is in this weird little grey caravan thing round the back of the tennis courts. It's always been sitting there but I've never thought anything of it until now.

I knock on the front door and this burly bloke in a red Yves Saint-Laurent polo shirt emerges.

'Yeah?' He stands there blocking the entrance, taking up the whole frame so I can't even see beyond him, let alone go in any further.

'Hi, I'm one of the Sixth Formers here.'

'So?'

'I was making a film in the school during the holidays and—'

'Making a film? Like a porno?'

Guffaws from his colleagues further back.

'Mrs Rebus, Head of Sixth Form, was fully involved.'

'Yeah, I bet she was!'

More laughter.

I keep my composure. 'I need to see the CCTV footage from when we were in the school.'

'Why, something stolen?'

'No, nothing like that. I want to use the footage for our film.'

'Did you forget to bring your camcorder?'

I ignored this question and waited for the giggling to die down.

'If you have the security footage on tape then that would be best, as long as they're labelled with the times. In fact, I can give you a list of the exact hours that we—'

'Not going to happen, mate. Can only release that stuff for a police matter.'

'Look, I can get Mrs Rebus in here and she'll explain how important this film is to the school.'

'Unless she's a member of the Metropolitan Police Force or suspects that a crime has been committed, I couldn't give a monkey's. Now, haven't you got a class to get to?'

I thought that it would just be a matter of coming back again later with Mrs R in tow.

'Sorry Stephen,' she said when I'd caught up with her as she was leaving her office, 'but security is outsourced by the council. I've got no authority over them.'

'But Miss, I can't finish editing this film without that footage.'

'Industrious boy like you, I'm sure you'll find a way.'

At least the footage I *have* got is starting to look in better shape. I've stuck post-it notes on my PC monitor saying 'story first' and 'fear of what others think' and 'reflection'.

But I'm determined to get those bloody CCTV tapes.

Sunday 30th June

A *Sneakers/Hackers*-style computer infiltration is beyond my means. Contemplated reporting a crime to the police, but that would only mean they get the footage and I doubt they would share it with me.

Am still editing away, but with those security tapes always at the back of my mind...

July 1996

Monday 1st July

Gavin and Barry were asking me in the common room today about the wrap party. I said that things are pretty hectic at the moment with editing, but we'll definitely have a booze-up on the night of the festival. And if we don't get in, we'll have one anyway.

Then Nigel told me that him and 'the boys' are planning a holiday down to Newquay in Cornwall at the end of the month and that I'm welcome to come. They go a couple of days before the deadline for the festival. I'm so keen to re-join society that I said yes right away, without even asking about how much it will cost, or worrying about spending a week in a caravan with Clive.

So the festival wants entries in by Monday 29th July and Newquay is on Saturday 27th. Looks like my deadline has just got tighter.

Tuesday 2nd July

Was called out of Psychology to Mrs Rebus's office this morning. When I got there, she was sporting her bulldog-stung-by-a-wasp facial expression. Not a good sign.

Standing next to her was the neighbour bloke who had asked to see our filming permit.

'Mr Hawthorne is a concerned local resident,' Rebus explained. 'He said you promised to deliver to him proof that you were allowed to film on council property.'

'Eh?'

'The school, Stephen.'

'Oh yes, that's right. Yes, of course we had permission.' I felt the familiar cold sweat of the blagger out of his depth.

This Hawthorne said, 'Permission from the *council?*' He stared over his thick paedophile glasses and wiped his comb-over off his forehead.

'Yes.' I glanced at Rebus. Shouldn't she have covered something like this coming up when she was plotting her master plan?

'Please provide Mr Hawthorne with some proof.'

'Okay, so here's the thing. I lost it.'

Hawthorne said, 'You can easily phone Bromley Council and request another copy.'

Christ, don't these morons have anything better to do with their lives than hassle sixteen-year-olds?

I said, 'Sure, but it took us about a month to get this one sent out. Red tape, you know?'

The paedo just shuffled around on the spot all agitated.

'Mr Hawthorne is convinced that you sneaked in to behave inappropriately, that a crime or crimes may have been committed. I assured him that—'

'Look,' Hawthorne interrupted, 'I would be satisfied if there was something that officially verified that you were actually doing what you claim.'

'Stephen can provide you with his video camera tapes.' Despite her level tone, I knew that Rebus would be seething from the man's interruption.

'No, Mrs Rebus, I said *official* verification. He could have done anything to his own tapes to try and fool me.'

Lightbulb moment.

I said, 'In that case, would it be all right if I escorted Mr Hawthorne to our Head of Security's office at a time of his convenience?'

Thursday 4th July

Our knuckle-dragging security supremo left me and this Hawthorne idiot alone to view the CCTV footage while he went to buy a copy of *The Sun* or something.

The nosy-neighbour was satisfied after a few minutes and scuttled off back to under his rock. Just wanted some attention all along, no doubt.

Meanwhile, I was left alone. The security room looked just like in the movies: dark, isolated, a bank of monitors with dials and buttons and video recorders. For the first couple of minutes, I was fascinated just watching the live feed: students coming in and out of entrances, Harris and his gang smoking behind B Block, the queue for the canteen snaking its way onto three different cameras. But I shook myself out of it: I had a job to do and not much time to do it.

I rummaged through a cupboard of tapes and found the ones I needed. There was a TV/VCR combo in the corner that I used for watching the footage, prioritising the tapes that showed the school's main corridors. I had brought my camcorder along and whipped it out, putting the CCTV footage on super fast-forward while I recorded it, grabbing as much as I could and figuring that I'll slow my own tape back down later when I come to use it.

I managed to get a good chunk before I had to stuff the video camera back into my bag when I heard the Head of Security coming back in.

He said, 'Where's that bloke gone?'

I said, 'Apparently he'd seen enough. Something about the hospitality here being too much for him.'

The Neanderthal grunted and I left his hovel.

Friday 5th July

Chatted to Nige in the canteen queue at lunchtime about Newquay.

He said, 'I for one need a holiday. Just split up with my missus.'

'Ah, sorry to hear that.'

'Nah, don't worry about it. We're going to the best place for getting over a breakup.'

'Cornwall?'

'My brother used to go to Newquay every year with his mates. The place is teeming with birds.'

'Really? More than places like Magaluf or Ibiza?'

'And you can afford somewhere like that?'

He had a point. I'm not even sure how I'm going to pay for *this* holiday. Have just about enough cash left for the train tickets and my share of the caravan hire, but as far as spending money goes, I'm skint. My only source of income currently is the dog-walking. I haven't done Sherry-lady's ironing since Vicky made me feel guilty about exploiting her, and no one else has ever responded to my Eazy Ironing ads.

'Trust me,' Nigel continued. 'I'm talking about girls on holiday without their parents who are celebrating finishing their GCSEs or even

A Levels. All those months of revising and exams and stress, finally it's all over and now they need a release. They need blokes.'

Intriguing. Am going to redouble my editing efforts to get finished in time.

Thankfully, the CCTV footage has re-energised the project. It adds a sense of danger, of being watched, and will plug some of the gaps where things are a bit disjointed. Having to slow the footage back down after filming it in fast-forward has had the unexpected bonus of giving it this eerie, wavy quality, like we filmed it through water. Perfect for an evil spirit's point of view.

Sunday 7th July

I now realise that if I'd have managed Gavin better during the shoot, I wouldn't be having so many problems with the editing.

Gav was supposed to be checking the continuity and I don't think he took his job very seriously. We've got clothing coming off and on again in successive shots, injuries that change position and severity, wild fluctuations in actors' performances. And that's just in one scene.

After the initial hassles with him on set, Gav was a good laugh and helped morale, but no one watching this shit-show is going to care about that. I think what happened was that after I'd picked him up on his attitude and diffused the situation early on, I was so pleased with myself for taking action that I didn't pay attention to whether that action had actually been effective. I told Gavin when we had our little chat outside that he was basically doing a good job. But was he, or was I just sugaring the pill? The truth was, I hadn't been paying attention to whether he'd been doing a good job or not. I'd assumed that what he'd been writing all over his scriptment were continuity notes, but now I see that they were mostly just doodles.

I remember something David said to me a couple of months ago: trust is the most important thing. Gavin has broken my trust.

Lesson learned, all well and good, but I still have some major continuity problems to solve here and now.

Back before we shot *Dawn*, David said that it sounded like *The Shining* meets *The Breakfast Club*. With *The Shining*, Stanley Kubrick famously messed with the geography of the Overlook Hotel to put the audience ill at ease. Maybe I can try something like that, use the inconsistency to my advantage, create some atmosphere?

Monday 8th July

No. *The Shining*'s trick doesn't work in story terms. It might have done if the people in our film were meant to be nuts from the very start, but I need everything in the first half of the story to look normal.

Thought about ringing Gav up to have it out with him, and had my hand on the phone, but then I thought back to the shoot. Was it his fault that I never checked up on his work to see how the continuity was looking?

No. I was complacent, too busy spinning all the other plates I had in the air. Plus I now realise that I only got Gav to do continuity because I wanted him to feel important and I hoped that would make me feel less guilty about how I'd behaved recently. Whether or not he would actually do a good job never came into the picture.

Well, I am where I am. Worse films have been saved in the edit.

I mean, surely?

Tuesday 9th July

Ollie came over today and brought two CDs with him. One with some of the sounds he recorded on the set (minus visuals) and another that was full of stock noises.

He said, 'Options, mate. Sound has saved many a film.'

He also had with him this PowerPoint presentation, printed out from one of the lectures he had back when he was at uni with Luka. I flicked through and read some of it aloud.

'*Sound is the subliminal way in which you create a place for the audience to totally lose themselves and really experience your film. It's the only element that runs all through your film uninterrupted and, therefore, is both the film's spine and its foundation.*'

I looked up at Ollie, who was nodding along. I wondered if he had this committed to memory.

I continued. '*Sound allows an audience to feel what you want them to feel. Your audience will experience things happening that actually are not. On a more basic level, it can glue together otherwise incompatible shots, or draw attention away from imperfect elements, such as in performance, continuity or narrative.*'

I was sceptical, until I saw the results.

A big impact was made by Ollie's eerie music, which rises and dips in intensity to match the action. But beyond that, he enhanced so many moments by adding noises: echoes on footsteps, the creak of a door opening, fight noises like grunts and bodies slamming against walls.

For the times where the sound effects he'd brought along didn't cut it, Ollie introduced me to the concept of foley sound. You record some real-life noises to meet the requirements of your scene.

Ollie said, 'For instance, we need to get the sound of all that money flapping about when Vicky drops it.'

'Okay, but I don't exactly have a pile of ten-pound notes lying around.'

Ollie gave me a dismissive wave. 'Got a deck of cards?'

I found one in the sideboard, and spent some time throwing the cards around in my bedroom while Ollie pointed his mic at them.

'Fucking hell, that sounds just right,' I marvelled when we'd mixed the sound into the scene.

We did the same thing in loads of other places: swiping a stick in the garden to get the *woosh* of the spell book flying through the air to attack Nigel, snapping some celery for when zombie Kevin's neck breaks under Barry's boot, rubbing a stone across a paving slab for when the door to The Purple Room slowly opens.

And we created a wicked supernatural hum by turning on a hot tap, capturing the noise of the boiler heating up, and then slowing the recording down and adding some reverb in the mix. Simply putting this hum over a scene creates a fantastically ominous mood.

'What did I tell you?' Ollie said proudly when it was dark and we were finally done for the day. 'Now, coming outside for another fag, or what?'

Wednesday 10th July

Got a letter telling me that my short film *Fatal Diagnosis* has been accepted to be shown at the Eastbourne Annual Horror Festival this coming October.

The what? Eh?

I quizzed my mum while she was watering the flowers.

She said, 'Well, while you were looking so down during the Easter holidays, I decided to watch your films.'

'You came into my room?!'

'Who do you think changes your bin, the litter fairy? All those tissues you get through.'

That was unnecessary.

'I have to say, I don't know where you get all these violent ideas, and some of the gruesome effects... no, wait,' (I was rolling my eyes and turning away) 'but some of the films I really enjoyed. Especially the *Frankenstein*-inspired one about the doctor who works on corpses.'

'That's actually a rip-off of *Re-Animator*.'

'Well, anyway, then I started leafing through one of your film magazines and saw invitations for this horror festival. So, I take it you got in?'

'Yeah, I can't believe it!'

'That's great! There you go. Don't give up, sweetheart.'

'I don't know what to say, Mum.'

'That's a first.'

'Thank you.'

'You're welcome. And there's something else. I've been thinking about this long one you're editing now... what's it called?'

'*Dawn Never Comes*.'

She put down the watering can and turned to me full-on.

'Do you want me to design a poster? You could make copies and advertise where it's going to be shown.'

'Mum, just because I got into that Eastbourne film festival, it doesn't mean that the Kent one will accept me too.'

'Stephen, you're far too hard on yourself. You don't give yourself nearly enough credit.'

And she gave me a kiss on the cheek.

I returned to editing feeling pretty good.

Saturday 13th July

I'm sitting at the PC, thinking how much the film has improved, and at the same time, how it would be even better if I could do as Eamon suggested and get some pick-ups. If I could go back and film little inserts, things to help tie certain scenes together.

Then I thought, why not?

I can do it by myself. I don't need anyone else in order to get a close-up of this or a long shot of that. The lighting may not be perfect but I can tinker with the contrast so that it will match well enough. I can film my own hands doing little things like picking up or putting down props.

Of course, I won't be able to get these shots now that it's term time. Not during school hours, anyway.

Monday 15th July

Rather than risk Mrs Rebus vetoing my plan for health and safety or whatever bullshit reason, I went rogue.

I hung around the common room at the end of the day, working on coursework until I was alone. I scanned the TV channels, read my *Film Fanatic*, and then, making sure the coast was clear, I made my way to the sports hall, having already pinched the spare set of keys from the caretaker's room at break time when he was off on some errand.

I unlocked the sports hall, slipped in, and re-locked it from inside. There were Pepsi and chocolate vending machines in there, so I was all right for dinner. Then I settled down on some crash mats with my jacket over me for a bit of a nap.

I woke up after nine o'clock. It was starting to get dark and I was alone, the car park was empty.

So, I wandered over to A Block, let myself in, and spent a good while getting lots of little shots. I had with me a list of scenes that I thought could do with some extra filling, so started with the ones of those that took place in A Block. A shot of my hand opening every door that the characters used, a few long shots each way down the corridor, point-of-view shots of people turning in surprise, a few ominous, shaky POV shots to represent the school's evilness closing in... then I repeated the process in every other building that we filmed in. I wasn't worried about being caught, I knew from that security twat that they won't watch the CCTV unless I stole a computer or something.

I considered going home when I was done, but I'd already told my mum I was staying round David's and would have had to walk back since the buses had stopped. So, I thought, screw it, and went back to my makeshift bed in the sports hall.

Tuesday 16th July

Woke up at about 6:30 a.m. Had myself a hot shower (nice and roomy without having to share with thirty other blokes), got dressed into yesterday's clothes, and watched back my footage on the viewfinder until it was a reasonable time to emerge.

I locked up the sports hall, returned the keys, and went to sit in the common room, alone again until my fellow Sixth Formers came pouring in.

Thursday 18th July

These pick-ups are really getting me out of some holes. They've given me extra options, which frees me to be more ruthless with getting rid of things that don't work.

For instance. We spent ages on the kicking-the-money-cabinet scene, but I've had to face the fact that it just doesn't edit together, not with good sound design, not with CCTV, not with pick-ups, nothing. I had to just cut to a close-up of Vicky with her bundle of cash, the couple of genuine ten-pound notes that we did have poking out through her fingers.

When I think of all the time we spent trying to nail that scene I get a sinking feeling. But we still see that Vicky has got her money and that's what was essential story-wise. We then quickly cut to Kevin and Peter as zombies trying to break in from outside, putting the audience straight into a tense sequence before they've had a chance to gather their thoughts.

So I don't *think* the film will suffer from losing the scene.

Friday 19th July

Last day of school. Not many people left, what with Years 11 and 13 having buggered off on their endless summers. As the eldest left in the school, it fell to me and my fellow Year 12s to administer the standard school's-out pranks to all the years below us.

Now, let's get something straight. I hate all that pranking stuff, which is usually played for such laughs in high school films like *Dazed and Confused*. Yeah, I've been on the receiving end, but it's not that I'm bitter. I just think the whole thing is cruel and stupid. Now that I'm one of the older ones and the tables have turned, I have no desire to take petty revenge on the next generation.

Of course, the likes of Harris and Adrian were ringleaders, rounding up the poor little Year 7 to 10s and pelting them with eggs and flour. As I was about to leave at the end of the day, I found three boys cowering behind my locker, squeezed into the tiny crawl space.

One said, 'Please...' He was trembling.

Harris, Adrian, Sean Birrell and the rest came running down the corridor swinging cans of black paint.

'Steve, mate,' Adrian called out, all pally with me. 'Have you seen any—'

'They went round to C Block,' I said without turning around.

Harris said, 'Cheers, Spielberg.' As they passed they left drops of black behind them, like a car with a punctured oil tank.

I had made it to the gates when someone called out my name. I turned around to see two female figures, one broad with dark features, the other short and terrier-like.

'Oh, come on, I'm mere steps from freedom.'

Ms Harper said, 'Just one more moment of your time.'

As they approached me, Mrs Rebus handed me something. 'That's my card, and here,' she scrawled on it, 'that's my home number.'

Ms Harper said, 'And this is mine.'

I said, 'What's all this?' I glanced around, feeling that old self-consciousness for the first time in ages.

Mrs Rebus said, 'Please keep us informed about the festival.'

'Yeah, okay.'

'And if... *when* you get in, we want to attend. And we're not the only ones.'

So there you have it. I've managed to get more phone numbers from teachers this year than I have from girls.

Saturday 20th July

Luka came over and watched the edit-in-progress with me.

He rubbed his little chin-beard and said, 'Hmm.'

I said, 'What do you think?'

He said, 'I like it.'

'Really?'

'Yes. It is a *little* bit shit, but I like it.'

'Shit? Wait… what?'

He smiled at me. Probably some kind of joke that gets lost in translation.

He did give me one important bit of advice: stabilising.

'What, to stop some of the shots being so shaky?'

'Yes. I'm sorry for it, but I did say we should purchase a rig, but you didn't have the budget and you didn't want to use a tripod.'

(That's because I broke the tripod for my camcorder years ago during a stunt on the original *Slaughter*.)

'This way you can choose when the viewer is sick,' Luka went on, 'and when they are not. They can't be sick *all* of the time.'

Stabilising. Didn't realise you can do that.

Should really have read the manual for the editing software, I guess.

Sunday 21st July

Eamon took me to the National Film Theatre on the Southbank today, where they were showing a double bill from this old-time director, Howard Hawks: *Rio Bravo*, John Carpenter and Quentin Tarantino's favourite western, and *The Big Sleep*, this Humphrey Bogart film noir.

I enjoyed *Rio Bravo*, although it was a bit slow in places. *The Big Sleep* was good, despite the fact that after about an hour I didn't have a clue what was going on.

'Don't worry,' Eamon said as we were getting a beer in the NFT bar afterwards, 'neither did the screenwriters or the fella who'd written the novel.'

I was glancing through the programme we'd got and read something shocking.

'Wait, so this Hawks bloke is the same director who did those annoying screwball comedies?'

'*Bringing Up Baby* and *His Girl Friday*.'

'We watched clips of those in Media Studies. We had to show examples of couples getting together. I used *True Romance* and those early bits from *The Fog*, with Jamie Lee Curtis and the guy from *Halloween III: Season of the Witch*.'

'Right. Yeah, your man Hawks had quite the career.'

I'll say. Doing some really macho films and also those Vicky Motson relationship-banter ones.

Eamon said, 'So, then.' His Guinness moustache crept into a mischievous line. 'Fancy coming to the Bergman season in September?'

'*The Seventh Seal*, right? Playing chess with Death?'

'Sure, but wait 'til you see *Wild Strawberries* and *Persona*.'

During the walk back to Waterloo station beside the Thames, Eamon handed me a card in an envelope.

'Oh, but my birthday's not 'til next month.'

'Open it, lad.'

There was a cheque inside.

I gasped.

'Eamon, this is a lot of money!'

'Just your share of the shop sale. Rentals shot way up as soon as you started coming in and chatting up the customers. Treat yourself and enjoy your wee Cornwall holiday. You deserve it, lad.'

'Thanks, Eamon.'

We walked a little further, the low sun glistening off the water.

Eamon said, 'How you feeling about the video shop going?'

I said, 'Definitely the end of an era.'

'It's going to change things for both of us. You won't have any movie you want on tap anymore, grabbing dozens of them for free then watching them for hours on your own in your room.'

I thought about that.

I said, 'Might not be such a bad thing.'

Monday 22nd July

I have to send *Dawn Never Comes* off to the Kent Summer 1996 Film Festival by the end of this week.

Am still editing while listening to music and have been getting into these trip-hop people, Tricky and DJ Shadow and Portishead. I got this idea to take samples from their songs and splice them into the film to enhance certain moments: a few seconds here and there, sometimes drawn out, sometimes sped up. It was fun. No wonder John Carpenter scores his own flicks.

Wednesday 24th July

Have got to the end of the edit!

But it's clocking in at a hundred and fourteen minutes, far too long for a horror film. I'm going to have to do that thing they drummed into us in GCSE English and murder my darlings.

Thursday 25th July

Can only get it down to one hundred and two mins, which is still too long. Needs to be around the ninety mark to be an effective horror film. Short and sharp, keep the interest up, no sag, no fat.

I invited David, Luka, Gavin and Barry over to watch the current cut. I had the timecode on at the bottom of the screen and asked them to tell me when they thought something could be trimmed, and then I made a note of the time.

In general, they were pretty positive. They especially liked the new music cues that I put in yesterday.

David said, 'Where did you get that stuff from?'

I shrugged. 'Just cobbled it together.'

Friday 26th July

Down to ninety-three minutes. That will do, but I still need more outside perspectives. I'm risking running out of time for making the Newquay trip, but damn it, I'm like a man possessed. If I end up needing the weekend to finish up and missing my train to Cornwall tomorrow, then I'll just have to live with it. There will be other caravan sites full of girls, but there will only be one first Bromleigh 96 production

I asked Martin if he and his raving pals would mind coming over to watch the film before they went out up London tonight.

My brother said, 'You don't mind if we get lagered up?' He cracked open a can of Heineken. 'Lot of people get pissed in front of a horror film, don't they?'

My first impartial audience seemed to enjoy themselves: wincing, laughing, squirming and clapping. I found it pretty exhilarating overall, and although their reactions weren't necessarily in tune with where I expected them to come (there was some laughing at serious bits and some silence at bits that were supposed to be funny), it was probably just down to all the booze.

When it was over, one of Martin's mates, the girl with the pink hair who David shagged round Martin's flat, turned to me.

She said, 'Portishead was in there, right? And DJ Shadow?'

I said, 'Yeah.'

Martin said, 'My CDs.'

Then this one bloke said, 'Have you got permission to use their music?'

'Eh?'

'Oh yeah,' the pink-haired girl said. 'I did a unit on copyright law. If you plan on anyone outside of friends and family seeing this, you could get in serious trouble.'

Shit. Arse. Bollocks.

Martin said, 'Coming out, Stevie boy?'

I ejected the tape in a hurry. 'Sorry mate, next time. Pulling an all-nighter.'

'Ha, us too, mate.'

Saturday 27ᵗʰ July

I'll bet Martin and his gang had a better time on their all-nighter than I did on mine.

Managed to remove all the copyrighted music. I had to re-edit some of the sequences, but I got it done, and even slept for a couple of hours. I know I'll never be totally happy with the film, but it *is* finished.

Alarm went off at 8 a.m. and I grabbed my holiday bag and was straight out the door. While waiting at the bus stop for the 138 I rang David from the phone box.

I said, 'It's done.'

'Good job.'

'Well, you haven't seen it...'

'Have a great time in Newquay. Don't do anything I wouldn't do.'

Who the fuck knows what David Nolan would or wouldn't do?

I was the first in the Bromley post office when it opened and I mailed my package to the festival, special recorded delivery. Then I hauled arse down to Bromley South station and met the Newquay gang outside: Nigel, Gavin (who has had his hair cut like mine and now looks a bit like Ewan McGregor with a ginger skinhead in *Trainspotting*), Barry, Kevin and Peter... and Clive.

Barry had a bottle of vodka on him, chilled after a night in the freezer, and we passed it around on the train up to London Victoria. I felt exhilarated: movie done and sent off and *en route* to my first lads' holiday, with the sun shining outside.

Clive was sat opposite me. I gave him a nod and he returned the gesture. I don't think you can exactly call us friends anymore, but we're not enemies or anything. Acquaintances, that'll do.

'You just wait 'til you see the birds, boys,' Nigel was saying, winking away like he had something in his eye. 'On holiday, they've got *no* standards.'

Gavin said, 'Yeah, even you could pull, Steve.'

'Didn't I tell you, Gav, I'm saving myself for your mum?'

Barry said, 'Hate to tell you, Steve, but the rest of us have already been there.'

This must be that famous laddish banter that I'm always hearing about.

From Victoria station it was a tube round to Paddington, and then a five-hour train ride to Newquay. We had picked up cans of M&S own-brand lager, so by the time we got to the coast I was already well pissed.

Newquay turns out to be your classic British seaside town. When we got off the train it was bathed in brilliant sunshine and smelling that fish and chips and sea air filled us all with excitement. Not to mention the sight of dozens of girls wearing denim shorts and vest tops and miniskirts and boob tubes.

'Oi-oi, saveloy!' Nige called out as we carted our bags out of the station. When the girls ignored him, he turned to me. 'The frigid ones hang about in the town. The caravan site's where it's really at.'

We jumped in cabs. After driving across this cliff next to the sea, then along some country lanes and down a long path, we finally arrived at Sunnyside caravan site.

The place was buzzing with people either signing in or leaving. I swear no one here is older than twenty-one, including the staff.

Can't describe the thrill of unlocking the caravan and stepping into our home for the next week. No one bothered to unpack, we just tore into the forty-eight-can crate of Carlsberg we had picked up from the onsite shop. Every caravan had the doors and windows wide open and all around were other groups of blokes and girls arriving, meeting neighbours, blasting out the summer tunes (Peter Andre's 'Mysterious Girl' is everywhere, as is 'Oh Yeah' by Ash and The Spice Girls' 'Wannabe') while getting hammered in the middle of the afternoon.

Unpacking in the caravan next to ours was a group of girls and I even made eye contact with one and she smiled right at me.

Before long it was time to get ready for our first night out. We took it in turns to shower, taking our beers in with us, and then it was change of clothes (for me: checked Ben Sherman shirt, navy Kickers jumper, boot-cut Wrangler jeans and white Reebok classics) and out the door. We grabbed hot dogs at a stall and bought a couple of rounds in one of the pubs and then explored the onsite club, Oblivion, which was heaving, and had no dress code. They played loads of what Martin calls *cheese dance*, like 2Unlimited ('No Limit'), Culture Beat ('Mr Vain') and The Real McCoy ('Another Night'). We loved it and no one got asked for ID. The bouncers seem to be only for show or maybe to break up fights, not that I can imagine anyone kicking off around here in an atmosphere this laidback.

We got back to the caravan at who knows what time and carried on drinking, then at some point I crashed onto a narrow bed next to my roommate, Barry. This is the life!

Sunday 28th July

Have no idea how much I drank yesterday, but such is the up-for-it atmosphere around here I barely felt my hangover this morning. Peter and Kevin had run to the shop first thing and were frying up eggs and bacon, folding pieces of white bread around them. Breakfast of champions. They'd also replenished our stock of lager and I cracked open a can of Carlsberg, the foam splashing all over my plate.

Got a bit more of a look around the caravan this morning, after the whirlwind of yesterday. You walk into this main living room area, with a 14-inch TV, breakfast table and a bunch of cupboards and shelves, which we've already started to put our empty beer cans on. The two sofas are also pull-out beds. Peter and Kevin have this room, and there are two more bedrooms with single beds (extremely narrow and with mattresses that are so thin as to barely be there), one room for me and Barry and another for Clive and Gavin. There's one more bedroom, a double, which Nigel claimed since he organised the trip. The bathroom is just this walk-in shower only a couple of feet away from the sink and the bog, and there's a basic kitchen as well. Everything a group of young lads away on holiday on their own for the first time might need.

Today we ventured into town and onto Tolcarne Beach. It wasn't quite as sunny as yesterday but we managed to have a laugh, playing beach tennis and burying Barry in the sand. We rented these small surf boards called boogie boards. You take them a little bit out into the water, turn around, and at exactly the right moment you lie on your stomach and let the wave take you back to shore. Not exactly *Point Break*, but if you get the timing right, it's quite exhilarating.

Had to stop looking at the girls in bikinis as it was driving me insane. Was surprised to find that I didn't feel self-conscious about my milk-bottle legs and hairless chest.

When we got back to the caravan site, we bumped into three of the birds who are staying next door to us. It was like diversity in action: one was blonde, one was a brunette and the other was a ginger. I would go with any of them, although everyone takes the piss out of you if you pull a ginge.

The brunette said, 'Been to the beach?' She was a bit on the skinny side but quite pretty.

Barry said, 'Yeah, just catching some waves.'

The blonde said, 'Oh, you lot are surfers?' She's the one I made eye-contact with yesterday.

Her note of sarcasm pointed me towards caution, but Gavin, thinking with an organ other than his brain, blurted, 'Oh yeah, we surf all the time.'

'Maybe you should take us to the beach,' the brunette said. 'Show us some moves.'

'Yeah, definitely.' Gav was salivating by now.

''Bye, boys.' The girls entered their caravan and once they were inside, they pointed us out to their other friends and they all waved.

Well, we may have come across as desperate and they may now be expecting a mix of Keanu Reeves and someone from *Neighbours*, but first contact has been made.

In the evening we had our first night out in Newquay town. And guess who pulled!

We started off in Sailors pub. After banging through some tequila shots and countless bottles of Hooch and Two Dogs and Smirnoff Mule, we stumbled into the attached Sailors club. I didn't even think about ID, and by the look of the bored bouncers, neither did they.

The club was brilliant. The music was a crowd-pleasing mix of cheese and house, with a big dance floor flanked by stairs, meaning you could look over the railing, see a group of birds you liked, and then head on down and approach them.

We did just that, and after attempting to get noticed by a couple of girls, I just forgot about pulling and enjoyed the music. I even joined in with the dreaded 'Macarena'. This brunette in a crop top next to me noticed that I didn't really know the moves and she showed me. When the song changed, I carried on dancing with her and at some point, during either 'Show Me Love' or 'The Key, The Secret', she stuck her tongue down my throat.

I tried to ask her name, but she shouted that she had to go to the loo. The others mobbed me and Nigel went and bought another round of tequilas. I never saw the girl again and I didn't even care.

This place is the absolute best!

Monday 29th July

Went into Newquay town during the day. We stumbled across some mini golf. I was terrible, but it was just a laugh. Then we ended up having an impromptu pub crawl, our version of exploring the local sights.

Am discovering something new: you can drink solidly all day with no problems, so long as you eat something absorbent (burgers, chips, pizza) from time to time.

I did start to get a little fatigued, but a hot shower back at the caravan in the late afternoon soon sorted that out.

Someone knocked on the door while I was washing my face and handed me a can of Carlsberg.

'You forgot something, mate,' came Nigel's voice.

'Cheers, mate.'

Barry called from the living room, 'Hey, Steve, how many bottles you take into the shower?'

I shouted back, 'Zero, I take a can, you cunt!'

Bit of a holiday running joke, taking the piss out of those Head & Shoulders shampoo ads.

We had another onsite evening, starting with karaoke in the pub. Groups shrieked their way through the likes of 'Love Shack' and 'Total Eclipse of the Heart'. We didn't go up to sing ourselves, but instead got chatting to this group of lads from Manchester and carried on with them into Oblivion, where we all shouted along to 'Don't Look Back in Anger'. Then 'Football's Coming Home' came on, and despite the fact that we ended up losing to the Germans and even though I hate football I belted my heart out with everyone else.

At one point one of the Manc lads said, 'So, you boys are proper Cockneys?'

Gavin said, 'Yeah, Bromley. Southeast London.'

Good old Bromley. If the news is reporting a crime, it's southeast London. If there's a Women's Institute bake sale, it's Kent.

Oblivion is little more than a room with a stage and a bar, but has enough loud music, lights, cheap drinks and up-for-it atmosphere to rival any of the other clubs I've been to. After a bit we left and did a tour of the caravans, popping in and out. At nights this place is like one giant house party and individual caravans are like the different rooms. They're all arranged in rows and only seem to be occupied by young piss-heads, no families or anything like that. I met loads of random people and had loads of great conversations, most of which I've already forgotten. One girl complimented me on my clothes. Well, I was wearing my maroon Fred Perry polo with cream tips, stonewashed Levi's 517 orange-tab jeans, an olive-green Lambretta Harrington jacket, and my royal blue suede Ellesse trainers. I thought about trying to pull the girl, but we got split up before I could make a move, and by then it didn't seem to matter anymore.

Had been hoping we'd bump into the birds from our neighbouring caravan, but we didn't see them all night.

Tuesday 30th July

'Look, lads,' Barry said.

We were devouring yet another bacon, egg and lager breakfast, listening to one of my dance mix tapes on maximum volume while staring at daytime TV on mute. Bazza was looking out through the window and when he spoke up, we all followed his gaze. He was watching the girls next door who were leaving their caravan.

I said, 'Come on, let's get our skates on. If they're getting the bus to town, we can go with them.'

Nigel said, 'What's the rush?' He sucked on a Marlboro Light. I've smoked a few myself. Just the holiday vibe.

Peter said, 'I thought you were on the rebound, Nige?'

'Yeah, but I don't like any of those girls.'

Gavin rolled his eyes and then me, him and Barry went outside.

Ten minutes later we were all sitting with the girls on the open-top bus that runs from the caravan site to town and back all day. People drink and smoke on the top deck and no one gives a monkey's.

We all went to Fistral Beach. It was much bigger and busier than Tolcarne and full of surfers. Long hair, washboard abs. The girls we were with have got some bodies on them, too. They're from Bristol, and despite being in the same year at school as us they look about twenty.

There are six of them in all. If I could pull one, it would be the blonde or the brunette that we met first time, Emily or Lydia. But I'm hardly picky. Hanging out on the beach with them was brilliant. We sat around on towels and ran into the surf to splash about. But they still flirted with every surfer dude who walked past and even went to watch some of them tackle the waves.

If I'd've grown up next to the sea instead of next to Croydon, I'm sure *I'd* be a fit, tanned surfing pro by now as well.

We got the bus back with the girls and they told us that tonight they were going out to Berties, another club in town. By coincidence, or so we told them, that was our plan, too.

Berties was okay, not a patch on Sailors. But it did have a lot of raised areas and if you stood up on one to dance, they were so packed that you were often pushed right up against a girl.

Unfortunately, binge-drinking bottles of WKD and Smirnoff Ice with shots of Tequila or Sambuca between each round took its toll and I had to pop to the alley outside to throw up.

Nigel followed me. 'Tactical chunder.' He nodded approvingly.

'Yeah,' I said, wiping my mouth.

'Have some water, you'll be fine.'

He led me inside and ordered me a pint of tap. After I downed that I was fine and carried on where I'd left off, ordering Nigel and me two pints of Carling. But I was still worried that I smelled of sick, even after chewing two sticks of Wrigley's Double Mint and tipping the guy in the bogs a pound to drench me in Versace Blue Jeans aftershave. Meanwhile, Barry got off with some random bird and Gavin pulled Lydia from the caravan girls.

Nigel confided to me, while we sat at a table watching our mates mid-pull on the dance floor, that he's still hung up on his ex and that's why he hasn't been trying it on with any girls on this holiday. Well, all the more for us chaps.

I walked next to Clive after we all left the club and were wandering around trying to find a cab. He asked me how the feature shoot went. I said it was fine, and explained how for this one we made it more like the original *Halloween*: mainly suspense and not much on-screen violence.

Clive looked bemused.

He said, 'Well, you know, if the next one *does* need more effects, let me know.'

I smiled. 'Cheers, mate. I'm gonna still give you a *practical effects by* credit on *Dawn Never Comes*.'

'Appreciate that, mate. But I still don't understand.'

'Understand what?'

'Why you didn't use your feature as a chance to pack in even more gore than ever.'

'Like I said, it wasn't that kind of film,'

'But it was a horror.'

'Yeah, but instead of throwing blood and guts around, we developed a theme and made it character-based and—'

I saw that I was losing him.

'Never mind. Look, there's a taxi rank up there.'

Wednesday 31st July

Rained all day so we just entertained ourselves onsite. There's plenty to do, if you wander about enough: arcade games, pool tables, pub, woodfire-cooked pizza for lunch. The vibe during the day is just as friendly as at night: you walk around and say 'all right, mate?' to other blokes and, if feeling confident, 'all right, love?' to the girls. The place has like a friendly village atmosphere. Plenty of people were getting on the piss in the middle of the day, so I guess you can say it's got a friendly drunken village atmosphere. We noticed that there is actually a field of tents, so some people have come here to camp (fuck *that*) and there is an outdoor swimming pool, but I don't really see the need when the beach is just a shuttle bus away.

When we were bored of touring the site, we went back to the caravan for some TV, music and *Magic: The Gathering*. Didn't see the Bristol girls all day, they must have been out somewhere.

The weather had cleared up by the evening, but none of us fancied a big one again. So we ate at a pub garden BBQ and played pool with the Manc lads and some other randoms, and then we went for a walk off site. We wandered up a few country lanes and ended up at this pub off the side of the road for a couple more quiet pints.

We sat on a bench outside, enjoying the warm early evening. After talking about the girls we've seen and met since we've been down here, the conversation turned to actual shagging. Nigel is the only non-virgin among us.

I said, 'So, come on. What's it *actually* like?'

He laughed. 'Didn't you cover sex education in Biology?'

I rolled my eyes. 'Come off it. Give us the lowdown.'

He thought for a moment.

Gavin said, 'Is it so much better than having a wank?'

Nigel laughed again. 'Maybe not, if you don't like the girl much. But with my missus, it was ten times better. But then you get the emotional fall-out when it ends.'

Nigel's morose face as he took a drag on his cigarette made me actually feel a bit sorry for him, even though he's lucky enough to have popped his cherry.

Then I thought, nah! He got to shag this girl who loved him to bits. For that I'd take a bit of moping around when it all goes tits up.

We all turned in early. My roommate Barry was in a chatty mood.

He said, 'Making the film was proper quality.'

'We'll see how it turns out. I just hope it impresses these festival bods.'

'Ah, bollocks to them. Who cares what they think?'

He shifted in his bed to face me.

'So I've decided. I'm gonna go for it.'

'Go for what?'

'Acting. Properly. Get lessons and all that, join a club or whatever.'

I propped myself up. 'You should, mate. You're a natural.'

'I never thought about it seriously before.'

'I reckon it's a wicked idea.'

'Plus, think of all the birds.'

'Oh, absolutely.'

August 1996

Thursday 1st August

Nicer weather today. So after seeing that the Bristol girls weren't in their caravan again, we went down to the beach on our own.

Then when we got back in the afternoon, Emily and Lydia came up to us all cross.

Emily said, 'Why have you been ignoring us?'

I said, 'Eh?'

'Didn't you think *we* might have wanted to go to the beach today?'

Gavin said, 'But you weren't—'

Lydia said, 'Typical boys.' And with that they went back into their caravan and slammed the door.

We didn't know what the fuck that was all about, so did the only sensible thing: entered our own caravan and cracked open a fresh crate of Carlsberg.

So we figured that we'd ruined our chances with the Bristol girls. But when we bumped into them in Sailors club tonight, they were all hugs and cheek-kisses and they invited us to sit with them. They even left a group of surfer dudes behind for us. Must have been after some more intellectually stimulating company.

As soon as we got back to the caravan site, we all bundled into Oblivion, and I pulled Emily! And Gavin pulled Lydia again.

The four of us ended up back at the girls' caravan. It's exactly the same as ours, except without all the empty beer cans and paper plates of half-finished food with fag butts sticking out.

We cracked on the TV and *Castaway* was showing, that film with Oliver Reed and Amanda Donahue on a desert island where she's naked the whole time.

Lydia said, 'Do you think she's pretty?'

Gavin and I exchanged a glance.

Gav said, 'She's okay.'

Emily said, 'I wish I had tits like that.'

Lydia said, 'You've got lovely tits. Don't you agree, boys?'

I said, 'Um, they're great.'

I thought for a moment she was going to whip them out right there and then.

Lydia said, 'Hey, what about mine?'

Luckily, I didn't have to answer as Gavin pulled Lydia up and said, 'Come on, why don't you show me your room?' like John Connor to Miles Dyson's kid in *Terminator 2*, and there was indeed something so charmingly innocent-sounding about the question that Lydia laughed and led him away.

So Emily and I were left sitting there. After a couple of minutes, we heard banging noises coming through the paper-thin wall.

Emily said, 'That's some really cool dance music you lot have been playing.'

'Thanks, they're my mix tapes.' Not knowing what else to say, I started rambling. 'They're a combination of classics together with some newer cuts. This one track, "Café del Mar", it's not even out yet, but I think I've listened to it more than—'

She cut me off by leaning in and snogging me.

My hand was straight up her top. Her tits were smaller than I anticipated (Wonderbra?), certainly smaller than Stella's and with no piercings. But they felt amazing, and when she took off her top and her bra, I started going at them with both hands and my mouth. She was moaning and gripping hold of me, so I must have been doing something right. I took one hand away and moved it down toward her jeans, and she started unzipping them for me and wriggled out of them. She was wearing these sexy light-blue frilly knickers and I thought I would explode. But I somehow managed to keep it together.

Emily guided my hand further downwards.

I was dimly aware that someone might burst in at any second but I wasn't exactly going to stop.

'Come on,' she breathed.

I felt some hair, but there wasn't as much as I'd expected, and I wondered vaguely if she'd trimmed it or if just not much grows down there and how much was a lot anyway and...

She gripped my fingers and started moving them around. There was more moaning, so I took that as an invitation to speed up.

'Ow!' She squirmed away.

'Sorry.'

'There.' She moved me a bit higher up then started guiding me again, rubbing my fingers against her in this slow circular motion. 'Like that,' she whispered, her breath in my ear.

I figured she knew what she was doing, so I let her lead me while I kissed her and played with her breasts with my other hand.

After a while she let out this little yelp. She wriggled away and her face was all flushed.

Then she uttered the greatest sentence I have heard in my life.

'Now sit back and let me return the favour.'

She pulled my jeans and boxers down.

'Nice Calvin Kleins.'

'Thank you.'

Then she started to do her impression of shaking a can of spray paint.

None of the other boys were back from the club yet when I returned to our caravan. Someone had left an opened pack of ten Marlboro Lights on the table and I sparked up for a solitary smoke.

Then I turned on the TV and watched *Castaway* until they got back.

Friday 2nd August

Gavin lost his virginity to Lydia! We were so proud of him when he told us this morning that we drenched him with our breakfast beers. I wondered to myself whether girls make fun of each other for going with a ginge, or if that's just a bloke thing.

On our way out after breakfast, we bumped into Lydia and Emily and the others.

I said, 'All right, Emily?'

'Yeah, you all right?' She didn't break stride.

And that was it.

Huh. I'd assumed that she'd want to talk about last night.

We lads went to town to all the cheesy souvenir shops and picked up the tackiest crap we could find. Sticks of rock, *I love Newquay* T-shirts. Bazza even bought this thong from one of those plastic egg vending machines and wore it for the rest of the day. He kept it on when we went out clubbing and was cheekily showing it to all and sundry, which actually made one girl laugh so much she pulled him.

We ended up in a club called Tall Trees where they were having a foam party. It was utterly bonkers. Halfway through 'Rhythm Is a Dancer' these massive cannons started shooting white stuff everywhere and before we knew it the dance floor resembled the ending of *Ghostbusters*. It just kept coming and coming and I swear it was up to our waists before they turned it off. People were slipping around over each other and throwing it about and wiping it from their eyes.

Somewhere in all that I bumped into Emily and got off with her again.

Our two groups merged and we carried on dancing and drinking. Lads' hair was all messed up, girls had make-up smeared down their faces, and everyone's clothes were soaked. It was brilliant.

The end of our final night was spent in and out of caravans, swapping phone numbers and email addresses, making promises to stay in touch.

Emily and I got separated and I thought I'd never get the chance to have a chat with her. Eventually we found ourselves sitting together in some random caravan. But when I leaned in, tongue poised, she pulled away.

'I've got a boyfriend.'

'Oh, right.'

So that was that.

Later, lying next to a snoring Barry, I thought about my whirlwind holiday romance that was over before it had started. Some girl cheated on her boyfriend with me. I was deemed worthy of infidelity.

This is the happiest day of my life!

Saturday 3rd August

We had to clear up, pack and be out of our caravan by noon. Must have filled a dozen bin liners with rubbish.

Then we said our goodbyes to the Manc lads and the Bristol girls.

'Remember to mention me in your Oscar speech,' Emily said and she gave me a kiss on the cheek.

We joined the queue for cabs to the train station. Bruised, battered, hungover, and victorious.

Sunday 4th August

Barry, Gavin, Nigel and I fought the post-holiday blues to meet up with David for a movie.

Over pints beforehand, David said, 'And so how was Newquay?'

I said. 'Oh... mate...'

We recapped some of the incidents and banter. David just smiled wryly and said, 'I'll have to tag along next time.'

We saw *Mission: Impossible*. I really appreciated the tight plotting and Brian de Palma's control of the suspense set-pieces.

'Could have done with a few proper shoot-outs,' was Gavin's assessment. 'Loads of blood splattered about and all that.'

'Hmm... yeah, sure,' I responded.

Monday 5th August

This morning the postman delivered a brown envelope with a logo depicting a movie camera on it.

I delayed opening it all day, until Dad came in from work and snatched it from the pile and ripped it open.

'Hey!'

He looked down. 'Oh sorry.' He pretended to read the front. 'I thought it was for me. Hmm, what have we here?' He took out the letter and made a show of reading it, keeping me at arm's length so I couldn't grab it, while Mum watched on in amusement.

'Come on, Dad, if it's a rejection then just put it in the—'

'Read it.' He finally gave me the letter.

I scanned the page. All the words were a blur except for one that jumped out: 'accepted'.

First I rang David. 'Naturally,' was his response to the news. He told me to send an email out informing the cast and crew.

Then I dutifully rang my teachers like the good student I now apparently am.

Mrs Rebus said that she would update the Media Studies college application. I didn't get so much as a *well done*.

Ms Harper, however, congratulated me over and over again. She asked if I was nervous. I said that before I can start worrying about the day itself, I've got pages of their getting-to-know-you questions to plough through. She offered to help.

I rang Martin and he told me that I need a press pack.

'What's that, then?'

'For promotion. Send it to the local rags, stuff like what your film is about, background on you and the rest of your lot that made it, basically why they should give a shit about *Dawn Never Comes* and then shout about it to the good people of the London Borough of Bromley. You should use that poster Mum's done on the cover. Don't worry, I'll help.'

'Sounds horrendous. This has got David written all over it. I'll get him to give you a call.'

'Fair enough.'

The festival is a week on Saturday and there is so much still to do.

Tuesday 6th August

Turns out Eamon has been busy since the last time I saw him.

David and I met up with him in The Pickhurst's beer garden again to discuss the festival and he brought along these two Hell's Angels-looking blokes, all beards and bandanas and bellies. It turns out that Eamon has renewed his membership to the Freelance Filmmakers Society, and the pair are a couple of his old pals.

Eamon said, 'I just thought, well, I've got a bit of time on my hands, so I have.'

'Eamon's helping us with some projects,' one of these geezers said. 'It's going to be *him* doing the festivals soon.'

'Ah, be off with you.' Eamon waved dismissively, but he was beaming.

I gave my uncle a shocked-and-delighted look in response to these recent developments. He came back with a nod and a wink.

These two blokes have apparently got a lot of festival experience and so they gave David and me some advice.

'Generate plenty of interest,' one told us. 'Speak to the local press, canvass posters, invite everyone and anyone to the festival. Then on the night, network as much as possible. Take everyone's business card, bring your *own* cards.'

'Got it.'

'So, your debut's a horror, eh?'

'Yeah. Just kind of happened that way.'

'Worked on a few myself in my time.' The biker bloke reeled off a few independent British horror titles, some of which I've actually seen.

The other guy said, 'You know why people *really* enjoy horror films, Stephen?'

'Not really.' I'd never thought much about it.

'Horrors takes us back to childhood, when things really scared us,' he explained. 'They give us the thrill we had before we grew up and got desensitised to everything, before we got distracted by the banality of life as a responsible grown-up. They allow us to return to a time before adult worries.'

Worries like being concerned about what people think about you...

We took Mum's film poster to the library to make colour photocopies. It's an isolated school that's glowing purple as if struggling to contain all the evil that wants to burst out of it. *Dawn Never Comes* lurks above it in creepy letters, with *A Stephen Ricketts film* above that. Then Dad and Martin joined us in putting the posters in local shop windows and on telephone poles. When we were done, Dad picked up kebabs for dinner.

Wednesday 7th August

Got a call from this journalist from the *News Shopper*, some bloke named Wayne, who was responding to the press pack Martin and David made and sent out a couple of days ago.

'So Stephen, tell me,' this Wayne said down the phone. 'How were you able to continue your studies while making a feature film?'

'School is the easy part. I've been turning up there since I was five. But I only started making films when I was around ten.'

Then he asked me whether I think we'll win a prize at the Kent festival.

'Eh?'

'You're up for best film and best newcomer.'

I'd read in the letter that we were nominated, but figured that they just do that to make sure you turn up.

Win something? The last thing I won was a toy car that changed colour when you got it wet, and that was for pinning the tail on the donkey at Dean Harris's eighth birthday party.

Do I have to rent a tuxedo?

Friday 9th August

Hectic couple of days. Roped David and Nigel into putting up our remaining posters further afield: Beckenham, Petts Wood, Keston.

Went round Ms Harper's flat in Elmers End yesterday. It was weird going to a teacher's place but she was really chilled. After she'd made a pot of tea and we started chatting, I soon relaxed.

I pointed to a pile of papers. 'What's that?'

'Marking. Planning. Syllabuses.'

'Wow, I didn't realise that you taught so many classes.'

'That's just for one class.'

'What!'

She shrugged. 'I just tell myself that increased standardisation is an inevitable consequence of overpopulation.'

I didn't really understand what she was going on about, but said, 'And does that help?'

'Not one bloody bit.'

And all this paperwork during her so-called holiday! It almost made me feel bad for all the times I've acted up in my classes over the years.

Ms Harper then started talking to me about my *profile*, which is something that I am supposedly building through answering all these festival questions and getting media attention. She encouraged me to not exaggerate and 'just tell my story'.

First David wants me to be truthful and now Ms Harper. This is becoming a habit.

When I was getting ready to leave her flat, I gave her one of the personalised *Dawn Never Comes* baseball caps. I've put her on it, and in the end credits, as *technical advisor*.

'You know,' she said as she was opening her front door, '*Psycho II* was on Channel 4 the other night. I'd never actually seen it.'

I grinned. 'And?'

She broke out into a smile. 'It's not bad, you know. Maybe I should watch parts three and four now.'

'Nah, don't bother. They're terrible.'

Then not long after I got home, some guy from the festival rang and invited me to visit the venue tomorrow.

Saturday 10th August

After a morning of trawling through all the Internet film chatrooms trying to spread the word about the festival, David, Nigel and I headed to the venue.

Orpington Town Hall is not exactly Mann's Chinese Theatre on Hollywood Boulevard. For our feature film's premiere, we get a few rows of plastic seats in front of a medium-large TV, inside a hall that's about half the size of the one where we have our assemblies at school, and which has paint peeling off the walls, yellowed posters for events that took place years ago and this weird, musky smell. It's the kind of place that you might have gone to a birthday party when you were seven, and even at that age you would have realised that the kid's parents either didn't have much money or couldn't be arsed to put much effort in.

David said, 'Not much in terms of acoustics,' looking at the ceiling.

'Nigel said, 'Are there gonna be any more blinds?' He'd noticed that only half of the windows have them. 'Could be hard to see the screen.'

The festival bod turned out to be this skinny weirdo in his forties, dressed in a cheap suit that I wouldn't be seen dead in, his shirt buttoned all the way up with no tie like he thought he was David Lynch.

He said, 'Good thing you made your movie on video. We've had to turn down some entries on film as we don't have the means to project them.'

I shared a dubious glance with the others.

Still, humble beginnings and all that.

Turns out *Dawn Never Comes* will be on last, so I'll have to sit in clammy anticipation for hours before I can experience it on the (somewhat) big screen with an audience.

Monday 12th August

Preparing for this fucking festival is more graft than making the actual film was.

That organiser bloke rang me again yesterday to say that they need some production photos for their brochure. Well, I don't have any, so I had to play the film, pause it at some good bits, then take a photo of the screen with a Boots disposable camera.

You could say that I was somewhat unprepared for this stage of the filmmaking process.

Tuesday 13th August

Today it was my old pal Mrs Rebus who was ringing me up and hassling me.

After some preamble about how the Media Studies college status is in the bag and how grateful the school is to me (whoop-de-do), she got straight to the point.

'I've got a proposition for you, Stephen.'

I should have known she'd be after something.

She wanted to know if I'd be willing to mentor some of the new GCSE Media Studies students, including her own son.

'I should think,' she said in an *and-this-is-the-clincher* voice, 'that after all the school has done for you, you would be keen to give something back.'

Give something back? I've already given that place the best years of my life, most recently helping them fleece however many extra millions from the government for new filmmaking kit and whatever else. Stuff that, I might add, I probably won't even get to use before I bugger off forever.

But I said, 'Of course, I'd be delighted to.'

Babysitting some twerps who have just seen their first 18-certificate and now think they can be directors. Great.

Wednesday 14th August

Now someone else is demanding photos: Wayne, the *News Shopper's* ace junior reporter, needs snaps to accompany his story. I tried to palm him off with my faux-production stills, but he said he needs originals, and that he wants to meet us where we shot *Dawn*.

All I want to do is make films. Why do I have to deal with all this other bollocks?

David came along for the photoshoot. Not only is he the other member of Bromleigh 96, but as a wannabe actor he's a lot more comfortable in the limelight.

Wayne was already there, waiting for us with this bloke who, judging by all the kit he was lugging around, was evidently the newspaper's Jimmy Olsen. Wayne is, sadly, no Lois Lane/Margo Kidder from the old *Superman* movies. He's more like one of those spotty, squeaky-voiced teens from *The Simpsons*, but with this really pushy, kind of entitled air. With his breathless, non-stop questions, he reminds me of one of those little chihuahuas I see on my dog-walking rounds that chew on a rubber bone and never let go, all the while making annoying whining noises.

Wayne had brought some props along, so he could have us doing things like studying fake script pages outside the school gates, or posing with video cameras like they were guns. Cringe City.

Towards the end, Wayne asked us how long we'd been making films together.

'We started when we were really young,' I explained, 'but then we didn't work together for the last couple of years, until this project.'

'So what happened? Why the gap?'

I forced myself to stay calm.

'There must have been a reason.'

'Creative differences,' David said with a smile.

'Oh, I see.' Wayne scribbled more weird dashes and shapes on his little notepad.

I'm looking forward to all this being over so I can go back to being anonymous. Well successful, obviously, but successful and anonymous.

Thursday 15th August

With friends, family, cast, crew and their significant others, we should have nearly thirty people coming to the premier of *Dawn Never Comes*, as well as my fellow filmmakers and whoever has come along to see their films.

The festival's not free entry either, which makes it a nice little earner for the Kent Film Society. And we starving artists won't see a penny. Doesn't seem fair. How hard can it be to organise a film festival?

Saturday 17th August

Day of the screening. We didn't win anything.

Best newcomer was some arty bollocks. Soft-focus shots of fields of wheat and clouds moving by, all of that crap, set to some grating classical music. God, do I hate classical music.

Best film went to this documentary. A documentary! It was on that mad cow's disease, BSE, that was a huge deal earlier this year. All about the cows and how loads of them had to be killed off. At the end it had all this rolling text listing facts and statistics that I thought would never end.

By the time *Dawn* came on, everyone was there: David, Gavin, Barry (who snuck in some cans of beer), Nigel, Luka, Ruth and a couple of her friends, Vicky, Peter, Kevin, Ollie, Clive, my parents and my brother. Everyone who worked on the film came wearing their personalised baseball cap. Ms Harper was also there with Mr Bryant (apparently, they are an item!) as were Mr Irving and Mrs Rebus (who dragged her mentor-ready kid along and wouldn't you know it, he's one of the boys who I saved from Harris and Adrian's paint attack on the last day of school). Eamon and his film pals were there as well, and Stella, who looked rather lovely in a classy little black dress and down-played Goth make-up. I hadn't been sure if she'd come. I've been so busy that although we've spoken plenty of times on the phone, it was the first time I'd seen her in person since before Newquay.

I found it impossible to assess the finished film's quality, since just like when I was editing it, I was thinking about the context around each scene. My shot choices, the things that had gone wrong in so many ways: technical, performance, continuity, framing, pacing.

I didn't see anyone yawn and no one walked out, so I was starting to feel quite optimistic.

Then it all started to fall apart. People began laughing, which would have been fine, as there *are* elements of black comedy in the film. The problem was they were laughing at the wrong parts, including when they were supposed to be scared. It's the same thing that happened when I showed the film to Martin and his raving gang and I'd chosen to ignore their reactions. Disastrously, it turns out.

I cursed under my breath and stormed out in the direction of the toilets.

Stella was waiting for me when I finally came out of the gents.

She whispered, 'You okay?'

I was distraught. 'They're *still* laughing at me. I put everything in, all of myself, and still it's just one big joke to them.'

She was shaking her head. 'No, you've got it wrong. Listen to the *way* they're laughing, Steve.'

'What d'you mean?'

'They're not mocking. It's nervous laughter.'

'Eh?'

'Like laughing after you get a fright. Comedy and tragedy are two sides of the same coin: ramp up the peril enough and it gets funny. It doesn't stop it being scary, it's a *consequence* of it being scary. It's proof that it *is* scary.'

Stella led me back to my seat and we watched the rest of the film holding hands.

The end credits rolled up over a freeze frame of Barry, the sunrise and the 'Bromley: 2 miles' sign. Everyone stood up and clapped and I guess I should have been feeling proud, but actually I found myself embarrassed by all the attention.

I went around swapping business cards with my filmmaker peers. I'd got my own cards printed at this machine in WH Smith's:

```
          Bromleigh 96 Productions
    Stephen P Ricketts, filmmaker, co-founder
            Telephone: 0181-555-2368
         Email: moviemadlad79@snailmail.co.uk
```

One guy, this fifty-ish bloke called Jim, took my card but didn't have his own and said, 'I have a paid job you might be interested in. I'll be in touch.'

When the festival was over, everyone headed back to my house for the belated wrap party. I enjoyed it much more than the festival itself.

The party was a weird mix of people. I'm still not used to seeing teachers off the clock. I think from a young age you just kind of picture them living at the school, sleeping in stationary cupboards.

Bryant was being all chummy, opening a bottle of beer for me in the kitchen and patting me on the arm.

'Ricketts,' he said with a grin, 'if you're the future of motion pictures, then God help us all.'

His ladyfriend Ms Harper was smiling too. I told her how disappointed I was that Miss Yates didn't come, as I'd wanted to apologise for being such a little shit all year in General Studies.

'Amanda? No, she was only doing her NQT year. She's gone now.'

Ollie was DJing, having brought his decks over and set them up on the patio.

At one point, he played some *really* old-school dance music.

'Kraftwerk,' he told me, one hand on his headphone-clad ear and the other changing the record on one of the turntables. 'Now, I know you're gonna recognise this next one.'

He mixed into the opening of 'Café del Mar'.

I nodded my approval.

'I bet you didn't know,' Ollie continued, 'that this brand-new track that you've been banging on about to anyone who'll listen is actually based on a classical piece?'

'It *is?*'

'"Struggle for Pleasure" by Wim Mertens, a Belgian composer.'

'Really?'

'Yeah, it's great. Just him on the piano with some violins and a choir. You should check it out.'

'How do you even know that?'

He shrugged. 'Studied classical at uni, Renaissance all the way up to Modern.'

I walked away a little dazed. Feels like no matter how far I've come this year, there's still so much more for me to learn.

Vicky was uncharacteristically sheepish when we found ourselves alone together at the drinks table.

She said, 'You did well, Ricketts.'

'*We* did well. You helped loads.'

'Yeah, and you know why.'

'Vicky...' This was hard. 'Your determination... it's kind of inspiring. You did what you had to do. You were right, people don't do anything for free.'

'Human nature.'

'Right.' I hesitated. 'Look, there's something I've got to know...'

'What?'

'Why Harris? What was the appeal?'

'I could ask you the same question.'

Touché.

'Look, nothing actually happened in Berlin, you know. All we did was snog for about five seconds. He tried to come in for more and I told him to piss off.'

'But why did you get off with him at all?'

'It was just... I was just getting drunk with the wrong people trying to prove... something. You wouldn't understand.'

'Vicky, you may get straight-As and be Head Girl, but you don't know everything.'

And then she actually smiled at me, and I smiled back.

She said, 'You know, you really seemed to know what you were doing during the shoot... and I appreciate how you put up with me being such a diva.'

'Don't worry about it. Six years of you at school, I'm used to it! But seriously, I was impressed too, you did a really great job.'

She smiled again, perhaps almost blushed, then quickly said, 'All right, enough of this love-in. Are you gonna fix me a drink or what?'

Everywhere I turned, people at the party wanted to congratulate me, or ask me about why I make films, or how I got the high-up establishing shots, or whether an on-set story they just heard was true. The weird thing is, now that it's finished and people have watched it, I'm really not interested in *Dawn Never Comes* anymore. I put all of this energy into it and I got it over the line and it's been screened, but now it's done for me and I just want to move on to the next thing.

So once I'd found David, I asked him to deal with all the questions and I retreated to the kitchen for a breather.

It didn't last long. After less than a minute I felt a tap on my shoulder.

It was Wayne. I don't remember anyone inviting him back to the party.

'My review will be in the paper's next edition,' he said.

I said, 'This is all so surreal.'

'I'll bet.'

'I mean, I wasn't even sure that we'd get into the festival.'

'Oh, you were always going to get in.'

'What d'you mean?'

'Because of your story.'

'The plot?'

'No, Stephen, *your* story. It doesn't matter how good or bad your film is, you make great copy.'

'Because of my age.'

'That's right. Look, I'm not saying that they didn't like it as well, but the point is it's all political. The cow documentary was your classic hot-topic bandwagon-jumping, and the best newcomer knows half the judging panel.'

A bit unsettled by my chat with Wayne, I sought out a very drunk Martin in the garden. He was staggering around with a bottle of white wine in his hand and someone's *Dawn Never Comes* cap on his head.

'There he is! Our shaven-headed prodigy!'

'Yeah, yeah.'

'Course, you couldn't have done it without me.'

'What d'you mean? What did *you* do?'

He swayed on the spot as he pondered this. 'All those positive vibes I was giving out, mate.'

I rolled my eyes. 'Martin, be honest. The film, is it any cop?'

He thought about it. Saw how eagerly I was awaiting his answer and forced some sobriety into himself.

'I mean... it's definitely a little rough around the edges. But it's a hell of an achievement, mate.'

'But is it any *good?*'

'You might have to wait a bit longer for the Academy Award. But it's one hundred percent the kind of thing that some mates would have a good laugh with over a few beers and a pizza.'

You know what? That's bloody well good enough for me.

I left Martin to stumble away and went off in search of Stella.

Sunday 18th August

Now that things with the film have died down a bit, I had The Chat with Stella over the phone today. The result: we are now officially boyfriend and girlfriend.

When I found her at the party, she told me how much she'd missed me these past few weeks. After that, we got off with each other for the rest of the evening. People at the party naturally assumed that we were going out, and now it's actually true.

During our phone call, she said, 'Do you *want* to go out with me?'

I said that I did.

This is the way I figure it: I no longer feel so embarrassed about her Goth-ness when people see us together, so my feelings must at least be stronger than they were.

I decided to come clean to her about my antics with Emily in Newquay and she said she found them 'amusingly debauched'. Well, it wasn't like we were together at the time or anything.

As we were wrapping up our conversation, she went quiet for a bit and then said, all intensely, 'Just don't hurt me, okay?'

I said, 'Of course I won't.'

Sounds like a lot of responsibility to me.

I spent the rest of the afternoon ploughing through my coursework resubmissions. Wasn't like I got special allowances for my other subjects like I did for Media Studies. And since now I've put the feature behind me and I have all this spare creative energy, I decided to try something new: I channelled that creativity into my schoolwork. Maybe Mrs Rebus is right and I do owe them. So here you go school, here's a glimpse of what I've been holding back, just to show you what you've been missing. Not that I'm going to keep this up come September, you understand. There'll be new films to make by then.

Independence Day is out. My mates have seen it already, so I thought I'd have to go on my own. But then I remembered Stella, and rang her back to see if she was up for a cinema trip.

Film was an absolute, total, complete and utter blast.

Tuesday 20th August

There are two articles about *Dawn Never Comes* in this week's *News Shopper*.

First is the interview with me and David. Thought that Wayne gave it a bit too much of a 'he's anti-education' spin. Makes me sound like this arrogant arsehole who thinks he's better than everyone else. No one appreciates how hard it is to put in so little effort but get away with it.

Then there was Wayne's review of the film itself. It was just a couple of lines in a wider roundup of the festival:

Next came this inconsistent but impactful debut from the 16-year-old (yes, sixteen!) first-timer Steven Rickets. The young director is clearly influenced by the German Expressionism movement, and has studied Polanski's Repulsion *for how to ramp up anxiety in trapped characters. He definitely has something to say about how being confined brings out our most animalistic tendencies. Three out of five stars.*

German Expressionism? What's that? And *Repulsion*? Never seen it. 'Animalistic tendencies'? What the hell is this bloke on about?

Wednesday 21ˢᵗ August

Mr Pulitzer himself called me up and asked what I thought about the articles.

'Well,' I started, 'I have to say, I—'

'How would you like some more coverage?'

I wanted to joke about how I could have done with some extra coverage when I shot *Dawn*, but figured it would go over his head.

Instead, I asked him what the hell he was talking about.

'It's a good story, Steve, someone as young as you achieving what you have. We could run and run with this, follow what you work on next. You've done really well with your marketing so far...'

'I have?'

'Sure, with the posters and your press pack and how well you interview. Not to mention the brilliant painting you used on the poster and for the cover of your press pack, which encouraged me to even open it in the first place.'

'I'd rather just get back to making films, thanks.'

'You have to self-promote, Steve, or you won't have much of a career. So tell me, what *are* you planning next?'

I do have a couple of ideas, but decided to keep it vague and told him that I'm still weighing up my options.

'Might I suggest you tone down the intensity next time, try to appeal to a more mainstream audience?'

'I'll think about it.'

'What if I was to come along on your next shoot, document the artistic process?'

'Suppose.'

Who knows, it might get the national newspapers interested. I could end up dating a Page 3 model. I'm sure Stella and I could come to some sort of arrangement.

Thursday 22nd August

My girlfriend (can't believe I can say that) came over to my place and we had a nice evening just watching TV and chilling out.

I tried to move things upstairs when my parents got home, but she preferred to sit in the living room with them! For some reason, she wants to *get to know them*. Naturally they dug out their most humiliating anecdotes about my childhood.

But after the initial shock, it was okay. Stella stayed for a curry and I let her share my keema naan, which I'm normally very territorial about. Ultimately I wasn't embarrassed, rather I felt this kind of glowing pride.

Must be going soft. I'll be making romantic comedies next, though hardly think I'm ready for that kind of Howard Hawksian diversity just yet.

On her way out, Stella gave me a posh notepad and pen for my birthday.

'For all those big ideas in that beautiful head of yours.'

And she kissed me on the forehead.

Like I said, glowing.

Friday 23rd August

Made good on my promise to help Mum out with her day care kids.

We went swimming at Water Palace in Purley. Two boys and two girls, David's Freddy not among them. At first I was apprehensive, but I ended up having fun. Holding them on my shoulders in the water, going down the slides, general splashing and horseplay.

I noticed how my mum manages the kids. She treats them equally while subtly playing to their strengths. The eldest girl was getting sulky and saying Water Palace is for babies (she's mental, it's brilliant). Instead of arguing with her, Mum told her that, as the eldest, she has a lot of responsibility and is next in charge after the grown-ups. The girl liked being seen in this light. Then there was the littlest boy, who was lacking in confidence. Mum gave him a lot of praise but made sure to not unfairly favour him.

Have to say, I was impressed with the old girl's work and am seeing her in a whole new light.

In the evening, I went out with my mates for my birthday piss-up. I'd brought a new red, blue and brown Ben Sherman and white Lee jeans especially for the occasion. I decided on a Bromley pub that's far from trendy: The Firkin. The music was cheesy, crowd-pleasing stuff, like Bryan Adams' *Summer of 69* and *Livin' on a Prayer* from Bon Jovi. I'd have preferred to be throwing shapes in Turnmills or Fabric, but figured that this would keep the majority happy.

Got into the pub with no problems. I've noticed that since I started getting serious about my films, I've not been ID'd once.

Now that the dust has settled following the festival, people have been looking to the future. Luka, for instance. During doubles pool with me against Barry and Ollie (yes, playing pool on my birthday again, except this was totally different to the smelly old man's club for my sixteenth), Luka humbly asked if he can be the DP on our next film.

I said, 'Of course, mate! *Dawn* would have looked rubbish without you.'

He beamed. 'There is so much more we can do. Maybe try 16mm? There are different lenses, shutter speeds, screen aspect ratios. Shooting at different frames-per-second. Image over- or under-exposed. And grading, to tweak the film's colour in post.'

He may as well have been speaking Dutch. As I've been realising, there's still so much more for me to learn.

Then Luka said, 'Next time we should do ADR. We can rerecord the actors afterwards to improve the sound mix.'

He then realised that his mate Ollie was standing right next to him. Our audio guru just laughed.

He said, 'I'll get some radio mics next time, much better than relying on booms alone.'

Later, I bumped into a sozzled Nigel on my way to the gents. He stopped me in my tracks, raised one finger, and said, '*Meet with triumph and disaster and treat those two imposters just the same.*'

'Eh? What's that, a Phil Collins lyric?'

'It's all about the work, Steve. The work is the only thing that matters.'

He gave me this knowing look and then staggered back to the dance floor. The next time I saw him he was getting off with Vicky in a corner.

Later on, I was at the bar with David, Stella and Ruth.

Ruth said, 'I can't believe we made a movie! An actual movie! We did it!'

Yes, she was pissed too.

'I'm not surprised, you know,' she continued. 'You've always been so confident.'

'*Me?*'

She turned to David and Stella. 'He's always just done his own thing, not worried what other people think.' The other two raised their eyebrows slightly and nodded slowly.

Then Ruth leaned in really closely and whispered to them, 'Although, I *did* think he was probably gay.'

This sent all of David and Stella's four eyebrows right the way up.

'Surprised at you being seen in a place like this, Ruth,' I said in a desperate attempt to change the subject.

'Eh? What you mean?'

'It's not a *cool pub*. Not one people show off about in the common room.'

She gave me this funny look. 'You what? What are you talking about? Come on Stella, let's leave these boys alone together, the way they *really* want it.'

The two girls took their drinks back to our table, Stella's eyebrows remaining up as she watched me over her shoulder.

David concentrated on getting the bar staff's attention, while I drew out the process of lighting a cigarette.

'You know, Steve,' he said eventually, 'there's something I've learned. People are so busy worrying about what others think about them, they don't have any time left to judge other people.'

Well, I thought as David ordered us two pints of Kronenbourg, I can hardly argue with that.

We re-joined the girls on the dance floor and within minutes David was snogging Ruth's face off.

On seeing this, I immediately grabbed Stella and gave her the same treatment.

Saturday 24th August

That bloke Jim I met at the festival who said he had a job for me rang yesterday. I'd forgotten all about him. Turns out he's the manager of Dixons on Bromley High Street and he sees me as the ideal fit for their part-time sales assistant vacancy. So he invited me to come in for an interview tomorrow, as in today, as in this morning. After staying up well beyond closing time drinking.

Now, I may have somewhat exaggerated my knowledge of audio and visual equipment when I was chatting to old Jim after the *Dawn Never Comes* screening. But this morning I figured I had nothing to lose, so took my hangover and my least scruffy suit (planning to get all new clobber for school before it starts week after next) and turned up for the interview at 9 a.m. on the dot.

It was a formality in the end. Despite his outer appearance as just another grey-haired, grey-stubbled, boring wage slave, poor Jim's excessive interest in my film makes him reek of a failed artist as much as I reeked of last night's booze. All he asked me about was how I made *Dawn*, going into so much detail that I had to start making things up just to keep him happy. He had this woman 'from HR' with him who had to keep steering the interview back onto the conventional stuff, like do I like dealing with the public, what hours can I work, et cetera.

I start next week.

As well as the obvious cash injection, this Dixons gig could be another source of equipment to pilfer, so I don't have to rely solely on the school's gear.

Let's just hope they don't ask Asda for a reference.

Sunday 25th August

What better way to spend my Sunday afternoon than round a teacher's house?

Was invited by Mrs Rebus to have a *get-to-know-you* chat with her son ahead of mentoring him for GCSE Media Studies.

She left this Zack and me alone in their kitchen. Neither of us mentioned the incident around the back of the lockers on end-of-term prank day, even though it was clear when we met at the festival that we recognised each other.

Zack had these sheets of paper laid out in front of him on the table.

I said, 'What's all this?'

He cringed. 'My English coursework from last year. My mum thinks you should look at it to see my, what was it...'

'Your potential?'

'Something like that.'

I had a glance through. *Of Mice and Men*, *Lord of the Flies*, *Romeo and Juliet*... Jesus, some old dead authors' families just get richer and richer year after year.

'Look, I'm not going to read any of this, mate.'

Young Zack looked relieved.

'Just tell me one thing. Do you like films?'

'Yeah, love them. Making my own, I mean, that would be wicked.'

'So, what's stopping you?'

He shrugged.

'Well, what kind of stuff do you like?' I'm sat there expecting bloody *Mighty Morphin Power Rangers*.

'I'm into the classics, like *Commando, Running Man, Predator*...'

I nodded approvingly. 'Does your mum know you watch that sort of thing?'

'Nah, I put them on in my room when she thinks I'm doing homework. Pick the videos up from boot sales, mostly.'

Done the same thing myself plenty of times.

'So, big Arnie fan, eh?'

'*Eraser's* just come out, but I'll never get into a 15.'

'Well, maybe I should take you on a field trip.'

He perked up at that.

'If you put it that way to my mum, she'll pay for us.'

'Oh yeah?'

'Probably throw in for popcorn, too. Call it *educational* and she lets you do anything.'

Ha! This kid is all right.

Monday 26th August

Another day with Stella, just chilling round her house. Her parents were both at work so I didn't have to meet them, thank God.

We watched a couple of romantic movies. Not what I would have chosen, of course, but I picked ones that I can handle: *An Officer and a Gentleman*, with Richard Gere's amusingly bad acting, and *Top Gun*, where the real love story is clearly not between Tom Cruise and Kelly McGillis, but his character is too dumb to realise it. I would have been okay with the Tim Burton movies she told me she liked when we first met, *Beetlejuice* and *Batman*, those kinds of things, but she says that she's not really into that stuff anymore.

Instead, she promised that next time she's going to 'put on something *really* girly'.

Have to be in with a shag here soon, surely.

Tuesday 27th August

Met up with David in Bromley for a Burger King lunch.

David chewed on his Whopper. 'So, what's next for Bromleigh 96?'

'We shouldn't throw ourselves into another feature just yet,' I said. 'Think there's still some mileage in shorts.'

'Thought you said you were done with short films?'

'Artistically, I'm a bit bored with them, but on a practical level, we should keep things short for the time being. There's a quicker turnaround, for one thing. Can get more entries into festivals and competitions. More chances to experiment as well, to keep learning. Oh, did I tell you: I'm going to meet up with Nigel and have a brainstorming session.'

'Really? So you're going to write something together?'

I shrugged. 'We'll just see what comes out. Also, don't forget I've still got a chunk of the money left from my uncle selling the video shop. So we've got a head start on the budget for the next project.'

David nodded. 'Maybe we need to look into other ways of funding a film, beyond dog-walking and ironing. No offence. What did the Coen brothers and Sam Raimi and all those guys do?'

'Not sure. I'll look into it.'

We both munched on our food for a bit.

'The horror fest down in Eastbourne is only a couple of months away,' David said with a slurp of his vanilla milkshake. He grinned. 'Should maybe make your mum a co-producer, after she got us into it and everything.'

I gave him a look.

'Seriously, though,' he went on, 'she should definitely keep designing us cool poster images.'

'That much I can agree with. So, got any marketing ideas ahead of the festival?'

'One or two.'

'Good. Happy for you to take the lead on all the promotional stuff.'

Then David was all thoughtful.

'What?' I said.

'That Kent festival was a bit of a joke, wasn't it?'

I shrugged again. 'Only our first.'

'Didn't you think though—'

'That we could put on something like that ourselves?'

He broke out into a grin.

Got to say, he's a handsome bastard when he smiles.

Then David did something that was both really weird and totally ordinary at the same time.

He reached out and shook my hand.

We finished our meal without another word.

Wednesday 28th August

Eamon took me and David as his guests to a Freelance Filmmakers Society meeting, in this hall round the back of a church.

It was pretty laidback, just people taking it in turns to stand up and talk about what they'd been up to over the past month, in some cases asking if anyone could help out with this problem or that. A lot of it was about raising money, but there were people with skills gaps on their projects as well or those who were just after some advice. David and I didn't want them to think that we see ourselves as big shots because we've screened at one film festival, so we just sat in the back and listened. We were the youngest there by about thirty years but could still relate to a lot of their experiences and anecdotes.

After the meeting, when everyone was chatting over teas and coffees, I mentioned to this producer woman that I was disappointed that no one who's watched it seems to get what *Dawn Never Comes* is really about: the horror of worrying about what other people think and what this reflects back about you. I'd thought that it was pretty obvious.

'Better than viewers complaining that you've shoved your message down their throats,' the woman told me. 'If the film works, and Eamon tells me that it does, then you've done it well. If people like your film for reasons that are different to your intentions when you made it, who cares?'

While I was still pondering this, she gave me her own interpretation. 'I like the double meaning of the title, by the way.'

'Double meaning?'

'*Dawn Never Comes*, with "dawn" as in the start of the day, but also the way that something can dawn *on* you, as in you realise it. So I took the title to mean that the characters never really learn their lessons. It's got a nice nihilism to it.'

I had never considered the double meaning of 'dawn' (and will need to crack open the dictionary about 'nihilism'.) Might have to trot the producer woman's interpretation out and claim it as my own, if I ever want to sound extra clever.

A lot of people offered to help out with our next project, and we've promised to come to next month's meeting and screen *Dawn*.

Eamon was all serious when he gave us a lift home.

'This is a key time for you boys. You have to decide whether you're just messing around for the craic, or whether you want to put everything you have and everything you are into this racket.'

Sitting in the passenger seat, I made eye contact with David in the rear-view mirror.

Then I patted Eamon on the arm.

'We're up for it if you are, Uncle.'

Thursday 29th August

My first shift as part of Dixons' *service crew*.

There's a lot more customer interaction than at Asda. There, it was just people trying to locate the dairy aisle or whatever. Here, people were asking me things like what is the best sound system for their living room or can I recommend a portable CD player for jogging.

It's all basic stuff that any moron could figure out for themselves, but wearing these polo shirts with name tags somehow makes us experts. My training has consisted of being told which products to push and learning some buzz phrases to throw about: 'crystal-sharp picture', 'reverberating sound channels', that sort of bollocks.

Old Jim kept coming up to me when I was with customers and declaring, 'This is our very own Steven Spielberg!' I just smiled and nodded along each time. He's harmless enough and he means it as a compliment.

'You know, Steve,' he said at the end of my shift, 'you could be a real asset here. Bring some legitimacy. Get a bit smoother with the customers and I'll put you on commission.'

Big-budget self-funded blockbusters here I come!

Took young Zack to see *Eraser* in the evening. Not top-drawer Arnie, but enjoyable nonsense nonetheless.

Walking through the foyer afterwards, I pointed out to the kid that it was obvious James Caan would turn out to be the film's bad guy.

He said, 'How come?'

'If a big star is introduced in a supposedly minor role,' I explained, 'and by about half way through the film no main villain has been established, said star is going to be revealed to be evil in a dramatic so-called twist.'

'Huh.'

See, he's learning already.

Friday 30th August

In the morning, I helped Mum out with her day care kids on a trip to Kelsey Park. Then I spent the rest of the day tweaking my re-done coursework, ready to hand in when school starts on Monday. Fortunately, I don't have to re-sit my mock exams. Mrs Rebus has wrangled me out of that particular indignity. But I'm going have to really come through with this coursework.

Talking of Rebus, had an email from her, saying that Zack loved his trip to the cinema and how thrilled she was that I was 'helping him broaden his cinematic palate'. Lord knows what the kid told her we went to see.

Rebus wants me to say few words in Mr Irving's Year 10 GCSE Media Studies class on Wednesday. Find myself oddly looking forward to it.

Saturday 31st August

Can't believe it's back to prison on Monday after six short weeks.

And I've gone and landed myself all this extra responsibility. However many kids I'm supposed to be mentoring, with whatever that ends up involving, my reputation as a proper filmmaker to live up to, this journalist Wayne sniffing around me like a dog in a butcher's. Not to mention I'm going to have to actually apply some effort to my A Levels, if I want to get into a half-decent place to study film: we start working on our uni applications next month. Guess I'll be finding out if *Dawn Never Comes* floats these admissions people's boats soon enough.

But all in all, life's not too bad. Martin's taking me clubbing at Ministry of Sound in Elephant and Castle next weekend, and this time all my mates are coming. David, of course, along with Luka, Nigel and Vicky (they're a couple now) and Barry. We're going to catch Ollie DJing in a nearby bar first. And we're going to see David in a local play the week after next, in which Barry has snagged a non-speaking background role, his stage debut. Ingmar Bergman season at the National Film Theatre is underway, so I'm going to catch a couple of those with Eamon next weekend, plus there's a Schwarzenegger all-nighter coming up at The Prince Charles Cinema, so might see if young Zack can get away with attending that.

I'm still a virgin, but seventeen is the British average so I've got nearly a whole year to go if I want to avoid being sub-average. Now I've got a girlfriend my chances are better than ever. We still haven't taken things very far, but next time I see her I'm going to find out when we're gonna pick up the pace.

And things are good with David, so who knows, we might be the first world-famous filmmaking partnership to come out of Bromley, Kent. I mean, southeast London.

Right then, think I'll go stick a film on.

Printed in Great Britain
by Amazon